To You,
From Me

 FriesenPress

Suite 300 - 990 Fort St
Victoria, BC, V8V 3K2
Canada

www.friesenpress.com

ISBN
978-1-5255-2775-3 (Hardcover)
978-1-5255-2776-0 (Paperback)
978-1-5255-2777-7 (eBook)

1. FICTION, ROMANCE, EROTICA

Distributed to the trade by The Ingram Book Company

Dear
Best wishes always!
TJ Corman

TO YOU, FROM ME

A story of seduction, love, and lust

T.J. CORMAN

For Shirley, Lisa, Deb and Sue

"In sickness and in health. 'Til death do us part. That's how much he moved me. That I could say that to him and mean it. That everything would feel right about it when I did."

—Anonymous

Table of Contents

Acknowledgements

This project has been a labour of love right from the beginning. Imagine having a group of friends who like one another so much and feel so confident in their friendship that they think they can write a novel together. That's the kind of friends I have, and it is this group of women I thank for the inspiration behind this novel. These friends are the ladies of the book club to which I belong.

We were discussing the merits of a popular erotic bestseller one cold winter night when Shirley suggested we write a romance novel together. We ruminated over suggestions and enjoyed mischievous giggles while reading erotic stories aloud from the internet. We left that meeting with a plan and homework. We were to generate an idea that we would revisit upon our next meeting. I was the only one who completed the homework. I had finished Chapter One and launched my adventure with Ginny, Jessie and Paul.

As a first time novelist, I discovered an intimate relationship with the characters in my book. I was very disciplined about my writing, and each night I could hardly wait to see what was going to happen next as the story unfolded. Imagine my joy and fear when I finished my novel. It was time to let someone read it.

I could hardly wait to pass my raw, unedited manuscript to my friends to see what they thought. Again, imagine having friends you feel safe enough with, to hand your work over to them and face their scrutiny. I was elated when they read it and came back to me with accolades. Not only did my friends like my novel, but their husbands did too! The first person to read my book was my friend Rhonda. She asked me, "How did you get all those ideas?" She admired my accomplishment, and I felt proud.

My manuscript sat at the bottom of a drawer for the longest time before I decided to publish it. Enter my friendship group once again. I had my editor at FriesenPress to help me, but I relied heavily on my reading and editing team's feedback, otherwise known as my friends. My friends gave me constructive feedback that helped me to understand how a narrative reads. They also helped with proofing. I thank them for their suggestions, time and help. I discovered the difference between writing a story (the intention), reading an account (the interpretation) and editing a novel (what the author meant to convey, written correctly). These are different skills, and I learned that when you publish a text, you peel back its layers one by one until you reach its core. Remedy one layer and another layer exposes itself. Editing takes time, patience and perseverance.

My most heartfelt thanks to my friend Lisa who volunteered many hours of her time helping me hone my craft. Her encouragement and enthusiasm about my writing means a lot to me and helped me to have faith in my work. I appreciate her eagle-eye and sharp intellect, passion for the written word and the power of a story. Her dedication to my project and her ideas and suggestions helped me develop and fine-tune my work. I couldn't have finished my clean manuscript without her kind patience and support.

My sincere appreciation goes to FriesenPress for providing the platform for making this story into a published book. Special thanks to Ari Miller and Hayley Copperthwaite for their support, guidance and patience regarding this novel's publishing. Thank you to the entire team at FriesenPress. This learning experience has been an incredible journey.

I remind readers this novel is a complete work of fiction. Although it takes place in the town of Whistler and the city of Vancouver, British

Columbia, Canada, many things in the story don't exist, including people (living or dead), places, events, businesses, buildings, clubs, associations and institutions.

Lastly, thank you to my husband, who is *still* my husband, after many months of being mostly ignored by me while I worked on my book. Like I said when we got married, he is good to me every day of my life and, for that, I am eternally thankful. I appreciate the love and devotion he shows me and the faith he has in me. This loyalty and steadfastness make home the most wonderful place to be.

Chapter 1
Get Ready, Get Set, Go!

What am I going to do? I feel so nervous. I haven't considered a serious date in—what—thirty some odd years? Not since Tony first asked me out. He was my one and only. He picked me up from my last exam at the end of my second year of university, and we went out on the town. What a fun night that was. We had steak and drinks and danced the night away. Our first kiss on the dance floor sent magic through my bones. I was tingling right down to my toes. Oh, he knew how to please me. I have never been able to imagine being with anyone other than him.

After he died, I was so busy looking after our daughters and making ends meet I couldn't face being with a different man. I loved Tony very much. I've felt that if I were with another man, it would be like cheating on my husband. He was my first love, my only love, and I still miss him. Then why am I going on a date tonight?

Because it's time—that's why. I'm a grandmother for goodness' sake. For the first time in an uncommonly long time, I've met someone who interests me. I could have fun with Mike. I like his look and the curve of his thigh in those grey linen pants he wears—there is hard muscle hidden under there. Best of all, he stirs that old familiar (or not so famil-iar) feeling deep inside my body.

It's been a long time since I've gone there. Had intercourse, I mean—get sexual with someone other than myself. I guess you could say I'm celibate. I'm getting old and dry. Menopause is hard on a woman. Your body spends a lifetime producing estrogen, then it seems just when you've gotten used to it, it leaves, and you become a cranky, sweaty, dried up prune. It's just not right. My eyes are dry, my mouth is dry, my skin is dry, and my vagina is dry—sometimes it aches, and not in a good way or for the right reasons. Paul tells me there is a pill for that, and he should know—he's been a doctor for almost thirty years.

There seems to be a pill for everything. Paul says it's an estrogen pill that you put *up there,* and it rebuilds tissue. Imagine needing to rebuild tissue inside your vagina—whoever heard of such a thing? Can a body part like that wear out? The things old ladies never tell you when you are young, so you don't know to expect them as you age. The pain of childbirth—*sure*—they go on and on about that and scare the living bejeezus out of us, but they don't tell us anything important that we need to know about our health as women! That's the way it was in my experience anyway.

Oh, how Tony could make me ache down there. He'd get me so wound up I thought I might lose my mind before he satisfied me. I had the confidence to be "naughty Ginny" with him. I wonder if I will ever have that again. The thought scares me. I'm not sure if I can get naked in front of another man.

Here I go—putting the cart before the horse—overthinking everything. It's probably my worst trait. Mike and I haven't even had our first serious date yet, but I know that if I'm thinking about getting naked, he will be too. Men always have sex on their minds. It doesn't matter how old they are. But then, of course, so do I! Listen to me going on and on.

I wonder what I should wear? It's not like I haven't been planning what to wear for a couple of weeks now. I know exactly what I will wear. I'm going to wear what I always wear to the yearly fundraising gala. My little black dress, of course. It's a classic and possibly considered vintage by now. A woman can never go wrong with her plain black dress, a double string of pearls and her timeless black leather pumps. My black cashmere sweater will finish off my outfit perfectly. It's an effortless and uncomplicated look.

But, I want to shake things up this year. It's not that I care that it's the same outfit I wear year after year—it's that I am restless, bored even. I dropped by a lingerie store in West Vancouver the other day when I was in the city to see what I could find. I bought myself a deep, royal purple bra and matching lace panties—in silk no less. I spent a small fortune on the set, and as I was handing the cashier my credit card, I couldn't believe it myself that I was purchasing such items. Aphrodite was peeking over my shoulder, shaking her dopey head and rubbing the sleep out of her surprised eyes.

My daughters try to coax me into buying new clothes. "You've had that old top for a million years, Mom!" "You wore that in the eighties, Mom!" I can just hear them. The two of them, trying to persuade me to spend my hard-earned money on things I don't need. I think a woman can't go wrong with the classics, and if you spend some money on good quality to start with, it will last you a lifetime. "A lifetime isn't thirty years, Mom. *Six months* is a lifetime when it comes to fashion!" I can hear them chime in unison. I just shake my head when they do that.

As I walked out of the store that day with my purple lingerie tucked under my arm, in a discrete nameless bag, there was no one more surprised than I was. The girls probably don't have intimates in mind when they are teasing me about my clothes. Imagine, panties costing a hundred dollars! That was just the panties. The bra was another hundred and eighty dollars on top of that. What's gotten into me? "Him, I hope!" squeals Aphrodite, who is now sitting comfortably on my shoulder like a pixie. I tell her to shush.

My new bra and panties are currently laid out on my bed, along with my dress and sweater. I have decided to put my hair in an up-down style. I don't want to wear my usual chignon. I want something sexier. I practiced my hairdo a couple of weekends ago with my daughter Catherine when she was home. She showed me how to loosen it up and pull some

17

strands free to frame my face. My hair is a bit curly and has some bounce to it. They've come up with twisted bobby pins that are long and stick into your hair like corkscrews—fantastic technology. Hair products and accessories have certainly improved in the last few years. I do my usual light makeup and finish it off with a touch of pink lip gloss.

Slipping out of my bathrobe, I assess my body in the mirror. It's not bad after all these years. My breasts still have some bounce to them. They are full, but somewhat droopy after two kids and forty years of gravity. It's nothing the right bra won't fix. I somehow got lucky in the nipple department. Some women have huge nipples that never return to normal after they give birth to a child. Miraculously, somehow mine did. They are kind of perky and haven't darkened much. I won't complain. I put on my new bra, lean forward to adjust my breasts and step back to have another look. It's a beautiful bra. There is just enough lace to tantalize, but not so much to be overdone.

I step into my lovely, new panties. I didn't know panties could be this nice. Well, I did know, but I haven't had a new pair of French-made, silk panties since Tony and I went on our honeymoon to Paris. We went into a shop somewhere near the Champs-Élysées, and both giggled with delight at the pretty undergarments they had for women. We were young and naïve. We felt brazen in there, and even though we couldn't afford them, we bought a pair of French lace panties in rose petal pink. We had fun with those panties. They were part of my wardrobe for years. I still have them in my bottom drawer. They are faded now, and the lace is worn on the edges.

I got pregnant with Christie because of those panties. I remember jumping out of the bed when we finished making love and calling out in a big voice, "Oh my goodness! I'm pregnant!" I just knew it. I felt different right away. Tony just laughed and grabbed me around the waist, hauling me back into bed, kissing my tummy and burying his head between my breasts, saying, "Good. One more best girl to love!" How did he know she was a girl? I guess the same way I knew I was pregnant. Some things you just know.

Christie was a gorgeous baby—dark with curly hair like her father. Big blue eyes shining up at me that I knew would stay blue. She had the most perfect, pink rosebud mouth. She was my first baby girl, and she was born headstrong. I remember telling her not to do something, but she would look at me with a smirk and do it again. I couldn't believe it. I had no idea what I was in for at that point.

Taking a sideways look at my profile, I'm pleased by what I see. The panties are cut high on my thigh and make it look like I have a bit more leg. They hug my hips, and there is no visible panty line. They are perfect. The colour is exquisite—not quite black, but a sultry, sexy shade of purple—aubergine, I think they call it now. It suits my skin tone beautifully.

My legs have had a good clean shave—there are no nicks or stubble. I like my legs. I got lucky with that physical attribute too. They are muscular, and I don't have a real problem with cellulite like some ladies do. Sliding into my pantyhose, I continue to assess myself in the mirror. Yuck. What a way to destroy a beautiful pair of silk panties. I simply can't smother them in control top, reinforced toe nylons. I think only an old lady would do that. The image staring back at me is like a nerd with his pants pulled too high. I just can't do it. I take the pantyhose off and throw them in a ball on the floor in disgust.

Somewhere in my lingerie drawer, I have a pair of stay-up stockings that will do the trick. I don't know why I didn't think of them first. There are the old garter belt and matching demi bra I used to wear. Why do I still have this stuff? What else am I supposed to do with it? It's just as good in my drawer as in the landfill. I can donate them to a museum one day! Oh, and there's Bob—I haven't used him in a couple of weeks— perhaps I should dust him off and give him a go sometime soon. My poor thin-skinned vaginal walls might not be able to take it. More importantly, I may not need Bob anymore if all goes well.

Spying my hosiery bag, I carefully fish out what I'm looking for. I'm relieved I found them. They are much cooler to wear than pantyhose. I'm going to be sweating enough tonight. They are almost as sexy as stockings and still accomplish that polished look. Stockings and a garter belt are over the top for tonight. I'm not sure I could handle it. Being careful not to snag the soft fabric with my nails, I gently pull each one over my calves and thighs. They are sensual, and I can feel the soft silk of the panties between my legs. Nice. I check how I look in the mirror, and everything meets my approval. I'm all tucked in, shaved, powdered and as perky as I can be.

I'm careful not to catch my hair as I shimmy into my dress. I sneak a pair of Catherine's shoes from her room. She has red slingback heels that are just festive enough for tonight and a step away from my usual look. Picking my sweater up from the bed and throwing it over my shoulders, I make my way downstairs. I'm almost ready to go. When I'm at the front door, I carefully dig out my black velvet swing coat from the back of the closet, that—yes—I did purchase in the eighties, but it is truly timeless. I put my black suede gloves into the pocket of my coat, and I'm ready. Deciding to forego my usual pink lip gloss, I dash back upstairs and rummage through Cath's drawer in the bathroom because I know she has red lipstick. I find it and apply a thin layer. Blotting it carefully, I step back to examine myself in the mirror. Perfect—the lipstick matches the shoes.

I'm glad I left my store, Pangaea, early today. I've made it a practice not to close up shop before quitting time, but tonight seemed an exception. It's all in the name of fundraising, after all. I wanted to have time to take a leisurely bath, wash my hair, and shave my legs. I like to let my hair air-dry a little before I blow it dry. It gets fluffy when I do that, and I wanted some of those curly tendrils to work with my hairstyle. This kind of preparation all takes time. Thank goodness I still have fifteen minutes before he gets here. I did not want to feel flustered or panicked when Mike arrives, knowing that he would be here at seven-thirty sharp. He's the kind of guy who is prompt, so I didn't want to be running late.

I get the wine glasses out—plain and simple, elegant stemware—my favourite. Tony and I received them as a wedding gift. I've had them for such a long time. I also get the old-fashioned glasses out, (I'm not sure I like that name), in case he would prefer a scotch or a highball. I invited him to pick me up early so we can have a cocktail before leaving for the gala, but suddenly I'm overwhelmingly nervous about being alone with him at my house. He asked me for this date a few weeks ago, when he was last in town, and I haven't seen him since then. He phones me to stay in touch, but he's not in town very often or for very long. I haven't prepared any food. I hope that's okay and not bad manners. There are copious amounts of food at the gala, so I didn't want to overdo it here. I have a bowl of olives to put out in case he would like a martini. That's food covered.

I'm not a chef. I've never been into food and spices and baking and all that. I'm a practical cook who prepares food because I have to, and I eat because I'm hungry, not for the pleasure of it. I don't get too excited about making big meals with appetizers and desserts. That is, of course, unless it's Christmastime.

Christmas is different. Christmas is like childhood—it's loads of fun and over before you know it—so you may as well enjoy it for as long as possible. People tease me because I decorate my house and store early in the season. I pride myself on being respectful—I wait until Remembrance Day is over. To me, that's the beginning of the Christmas season. I start by putting lights on my house, and I don't go overboard—I keep things in perspective. I have a two-storey, cottage style home that lights up like a gingerbread house—it's just perfect when winter comes, and the fairy lights twinkle through the powdery snow.

I decorate the inside of my house before the end of November, in time for the annual gala, which is the first Saturday of December. The second Saturday of December is the day we set aside for decorating the Christmas tree. Tony and I decided long ago that if we decorated the tree too early, it would be too long for the girls to wait until Santa arrived. To this day, my girls make sure to be home for the event, and they bring friends. We drink homemade eggnog (a specialty of mine) and eat Scottish shortbread (my best friend Jessie makes those—her great-grandmother's recipe). Christmas music plays in the background until we finish decorating. Then we crank up the volume on the playlist and dance the night away. We have such a good time. By the time the party is over, I am in full tilt Christmas mode.

On the other hand, Jessie is a fabulous cook. Some people just seem to have a knack for it. Her years of working in the hotel business and her adventurous nature and creative mind, have influenced her cooking. She probably picked up some tips from her mom along the way too. Mrs. McPherson was constantly feeding a household full of kids. Jessie was a pretty basic cook at university, but her culinary skills have grown tenfold over mine. She can take canned food and somehow make it come out gourmet. I'm not sure how she does that.

Jessie has the best figure of anyone I know in real life. We wear the same size, but I have more of an up and down boy type of body shape, where she is all curves and muscle. She has been a runner as far back as I can remember, which explains the legs that never end and her flat stomach.

For as long as I've known her, she's been stacked. I swear she used to drive the boys crazy with those boobs. Mine were slow growers— not exactly attention grabbers—I never had much of a bust as a young woman. My breasts were like the proverbial tortoise—slow and steady in their growth. I used to lament over them, and I felt shy about them for the longest time. I grew a whole cup size the year Tony died, and I thought maybe I was pregnant again.

But, Jessie has always had an ample bust. She was one of those girls who grew into a D cup at age thirteen. By the time we were twenty, her thirty-four double D's regularly caught the boys' eyes on campus. I thought their behaviour was disgusting, even though I was a bit envious of the overt attention boys would lavish upon her. However, I was also relieved that I didn't have to deal with the same sexual pressure she had. I knew all they wanted to do was "eff" her.

I can't say f-u-c-k. I can only say the first letter of that word. It's only in a specific, very trusted company that I will say that. To me, it's like the "c" word. It's impossible on my tongue. I said f-u-c-k once when Tony and I were doing it. I yelled out, "Fuck me!" It was erotic at the time, but I was as embarrassed as could be afterward. It's just not ladylike. It's not that I'm such a lady, nor am I a prude; it just doesn't suit me to speak that way.

Jessie still has a knock-out figure. And, she knows it. She has used it to her advantage more than once. She's had a lot of fun with it, but it's also brought her a fair share of heartache. She's slept with a lot of men. I don't know if she's counted how many, but I know it's quite a few. Her strawberry blonde hair is a halo of loose curls around her head. She keeps it cut in a short, layered bob, and it's gorgeous on her. Her hair doesn't seem to get grey. It just gets lighter. Her green eyes twinkle, and she truly is the belle of the ball when she puts on her charm. She'll be in full form tonight. She said she is going to wear her green dress, so she'll be knocking them dead all around her. Men are just old boys who still really only want to "eff" her. I wish she could see through that. She only wants to be loved, just like the rest of us.

I remember the first time I met Paul. Jessie and I were headed into the main library to do some studying, and Paul happened to be going in at the same time. Jessie knew Paul already. She had met him somewhere or other. I hadn't paid that much attention when she was telling me about him. She just kept going on about this guy she had met and how gorgeous he was. She had that excited tone to her voice that young women get when they are all hot and bothered by a guy. You'd think she'd been on umpteen dates with him and was going to marry him.

So that day, when she saw him coming our way, she just about peed herself with glee. She whacked me on the arm and whispered sharply from the side of her mouth, "There he is! The guy I told you about! Paul! Act normal!" As if there was any other way to act. At first glance, I didn't think much about him. But, when we got up close and "bumped" into one another at the door, Jessie—all breathless and sweaty—sickening really—I got a closer look.

He was a typical twenty-something guy, tall—I guessed about six-foot-three or maybe four—and gangly. Later, I learned that Tony's nickname for him was Stretch because he was all arms and legs. He had dark brown hair and an impressively chiselled jawline. He was wearing jeans and a chocolate brown, hand-knitted wool sweater that matched his eyes. He had broad shoulders. But, his most beautiful feature was his eyes. I'll never forget looking into them that first time.

Paul is the kind of person who looks at you intently. It's probably one of the qualities that people like about him as a doctor. His eyes are dark brown, almost black, and hooded by black eyebrows. They are big and wide-open and full of life, with a look like he knows something about you that you don't even know yourself. It's a look like he knows something about women that you wished you knew even though you are one. They are the kind of eyes you can get lost in. They have a liquid quality I found myself drowning in upon first glance. I extended my hand in greeting as I tore my eyes away, and I caught a glimpse at Jessie and felt embarrassed for her. She was pink in the cheeks—not unusual with her complexion—and was gushing her hello to him while making introductions.

Later, when I learned that he was planning to be a doctor, I just shook my head. I couldn't imagine going to see a guy like that as my doctor. I thought about getting my breasts examined or getting an internal examination. Ugh. How awful. He's the kind of doctor women hope for but never get—a soap opera doctor. The type of doctor you might fake an illness for just to go in and have him examine you, but in reality, it's you performing the examination.

The doorbell rings, and my heart jumps into my throat. That's Mike. Oh my goodness—what am I going to do? Breathe. Focus. *You can do this,* I tell myself. I wipe my hands on a kitchen towel, pat my hair, check my lipstick in the foyer mirror and walk purposefully to the door.

"Hello! Come in. You're right on time," I say automatically and a pitch too high. I should have invited Jessie and Paul—just to help break the ice. But intimacy is what this date is all about. That's why I didn't ask them. Besides, Paul is out of town, and Jessie alone is too much. I didn't want to deal with her flirting.

"I aim to please," Mike replies as a lazy smile sneaks across his face. Damn, he's sexy.

"Let me take your coat," I comment stiffly. My fingers brush Mike's arm as I reach around his back. His arm is hard and warm. His shirt is high-quality, sharply pressed, crisp cotton with a starched collar. An involuntary squeeze between my legs shocks me, and I wiggle in my spot. I can't believe the effect he has on me. Oh my, but he smells nice.

"Thanks," he says casually.

"Come in, come in," I say, motioning toward the living room. "What would you like for a drink? I've got wine, scotch, gin—anything you like. Thanks for coming early. It'll be nice to have a quiet drink out of the crowd."

"Yes. It's my pleasure. Thanks for asking me. I've been looking forward to it." His smile gives nothing away. "I brought you something," he says, handing me a small box.

"Oh my—it's lovely," I say, opening the box to find a simple red rose corsage. I'm delighted with my choice to wear red shoes and matching lipstick. I like things that match. "Thank you. It's been years since someone has bought me a corsage."

"You're welcome. Again, it's my pleasure. Here—allow me." He takes the corsage from my fumbling fingers and adeptly pins it to my left shoulder. His fingers scorch my skin, and I'm afraid I'm going to squeak if he doesn't let me go. Is it my imagination, or are his fingers lingering? Is he taking his time? Breathe. Focus. Oh no—don't start to sweat!

"Cocktail? Highball? What can I offer you?" I ask, trying to gather my composure.

His eyes gleam as he tells me he'd like a martini. Thank goodness I put out the olives. I make a gin martini because it's my favourite. I didn't think to ask him if he prefers vodka. I really am sweating now—I hope he doesn't notice. I keep my back turned to him while I discretely pat my brow with a bar napkin. Martinis in hand, I pass him his drink. He has made himself comfortable on my overstuffed couch. Oh my, he looks good in those slacks. I swallow dryly and try to find my voice.

"Did you have a good day? How was the ski hill?" I ask.

He had mentioned to me earlier that he was going skiing today. His face appears to have windburn. He's not in town all that often, and

I know he doesn't have much time in his busy schedule to hit the hill, so I'm hoping the conditions were favourable. I know he makes time to go to the gym regularly. The kind of muscle he has doesn't just happen. Skiing is such a pleasure and a different sort of workout. I call it authentic exercise.

"Terrific! It wasn't too busy. The runs were well-groomed. It was good to be out in the sunshine." He smiles and assesses me with a long lingering look. "You look lovely."

"Thank you," I reply with a shy reserve. I bow my head toward the floor and try to mask my blushing face. I like that he uses the word "lovely." I use that word all the time. It's familiar to me, and hearing it helps me to breathe.

"Don't put your head down. You're a beautiful woman. Hold your head up and let me see your eyes. I want to look at you."

I look at him sheepishly. "It's been a long time since I've been complimented on the way I look. I'm not used to it," I say softly, feeling bashful.

"You're lovely," he says again.

His look moves deliberately down my body, surveying what is in front of him, blatantly taking me in with appreciative eyes. There's nothing timid about that look. His eyes move slowly back up to my face and rest on my lips. I'm sure he's looking at my lips. I squirm. The times we've met for coffee, he never looks at me with such sexual hunger. He keeps a respectful distance. His intense gaze rattles me.

"Thank you," I reply quietly, turning slightly and taking a sip of my martini. Thank goodness for alcohol. I take another, somewhat bigger sip. I wish I had some food to offer to distract him.

"How was your day?" he asks me.

"Good. It was good," I answer too quickly in a voice that doesn't sound like mine. "I closed up the shop early, so I didn't have to rush. So I'd have time ..." I catch myself. I was about to tell him about giving myself enough time to get ready. I'm horrified at my faux pas. I blush and turn away slightly once again. His eyes are snapping with mischief as he catches me sneaking a peek at him from the corner of my eye.

"You don't have to be nervous," he replies with that slow lazy grin. "I'm not going to bite you."

I noticeably squirm at the suggestion of his lips on me, biting me somewhere. He takes my hand and turns my body toward him. He is much more sophisticated than I am. I am agonizingly out of practice, not that I was ever very good at this.

"What do you say we drink up and get over to the hall? We'll get a good table, and we'll get the best of the hors d'oeuvres. We can watch the crowd as everyone arrives." His eyes are kind. He is giving me an out, and I'm relieved.

"Sure. That sounds like a good idea," I reply lamely. It's so quiet I can hear myself breathing. I forgot to put on background music. I am excited to go, yet disappointed at the same time. "I'll get our coats," I say as I tip back my glass and quickly finish my martini.

He's incredibly self-composed and much better at this than I am. He's a good sport for suggesting that we make our way to the gala. Thank goodness I'm ready to go. He holds my coat for me and expertly pulls it over my shoulders as I put my arms through the sleeves. I grab my clutch and slip on my gloves. We step out into the cold and quickly slide into his sedan. Mercifully, we arrive at the venue without further awkwardness and make our way into the party.

I've lived in Whistler for so long that I know all the locals. Being a shop owner gives me somewhat of a high profile in the community. It's not that I'm a high roller or anything like that, because I'm not, but I know a lot of people. Mike and I find a seat in a whirlwind of greetings and smiles. Mike orders us two more martinis, and before I know it the night is in full swing. The music starts and Mike asks me to dance. He takes my hand before I have time to answer one way or another and leads me onto the dance floor.

Tony was such a good dancer. He had rhythm, and together we tore up the dance floor. We even knew how to do the two-step, which is quite an accomplishment for a couple of West Coast kids. We would have a couple of beers and some snacks, then dance the night away alone in our living room. We had so much fun together.

Mike places his hand on my waist, just above my backside, and expertly swings me across the floor in time to the music. It feels good to be this close to him, and he smells fantastic. He moves smoothly and confidently and does not have two left feet. "Rhythm on the dance floor, rhythm in the bedroom," Aphrodite whispers in my ear. Oh my! "Shush!" I tell her in a moment of panic. We are in the middle of a jive move when I notice Paul standing in the doorway, talking to someone. He looks up and meets my eye. I flash him a smile and wave to where our table is. He nods that he understands my message and returns his attention to the person he is conversing with. When Mike and I return to the table, he is there, talking into Jessie's ear.

"Hi!" I say, giving him a warm embrace. "What are you doing here? When did you get back?"

He returns my hug and kisses me on the lips in his usual matter-of-fact way. It's just the way we greet each other. We've done so for years. He looks over my shoulder and openly scrutinizes Mike, reaching a hand out to him in greeting. The two of them met briefly once when Paul bumped into us at the coffee shop we frequent.

"Good to see you. How are you this evening?" Paul asks Mike in a friendly voice.

"I couldn't be better. Thanks for asking. Can I get you a drink?" Mike offers.

"Sure, I'll have a beer." Mike moves toward the bar, and Paul watches him as he goes. Turning back to me, he asks, "Having a good time?"

"I'm having a very good time!" I giggle my response. "We've danced the night away. I'm happy you made it! You didn't answer me. Why are you home early?"

"The symposium wrapped up, so I thought rather than stay another night and miss the gala, I'd fly home early."

"I'm glad!" I pat his hand as I look at his handsome face.

He had been attending a medical conference in Seattle. He is a general practitioner with a specialty in sports medicine. It's a perfect combination of skills in a ski town. Paul is genuinely dedicated to the community here. He is the reason we have a gala in the first place. He was instrumental in organizing the first one, and the tradition carried on for the next fifteen years until he finally passed the torch to an organizing committee. The event has grown in popularity and was getting to be too much for him to plan. Understandably, he would never want to miss it. It's good to see him. I'm happy that he is here.

I remember when Tony and I first moved up here to Whistler. My dad thought we were insane. Tony and Paul had both recently finished their residencies and had become full-fledged doctors. Paul is an enthusiastic outdoorsman. He is quite an accomplished athlete, but he would never admit to it because of his humble nature. At one time, he was scouted to play professional baseball. Professional sports hadn't worked out for him, but his true passion was medicine, and he pursued that with an intense drive and determination. He has spent loads of time hiking and back-country skiing in the wilds of Garibaldi, along with kayaking and diving at Porteau Cove in Howe Sound. He suggested to Tony that we should all move to Whistler and that they should open a practice together and become business partners.

Tony and Paul were like two peas in a pod. They had just spent the better part of ten years of their lives together, slaving at the hospital. They knew everything about one another and had spent as much spare time together as humanly possible. It was expensive to buy a house in Vancouver back then and just as costly to buy or rent a commercial property. The town of Whistler was nothing at the time—just a tiny community that no one except a few old-timers and mountain folk knew about—hardcore ski bums and homesteaders. The development of the whole area was in its infancy.

Property here was cheap back then, comparatively speaking. It was less expensive than Vancouver anyway, and we thought that between the three of us, we could make a go of it up here. Tony and I had been saving for a down payment on a house. We had been married for about three years and didn't have any kids yet, which made it an excellent time to move. Our timing couldn't have been luckier because, in just a few short years, the Whistler townsite grew and grew. Look at what it's become— one of the most exclusive resort towns on the world stage. If we had waited, we would never have been able to afford to live and work here. Now I own the building where Pangaea is, half of the medical office and my home. It's strange how life turns out.

"You must be tired," I comment congenially, searching his face.

"Not bad. It was an easy flight, and the road was in good shape."

I involuntarily shudder at the mention of the Sea-to-Sky Highway. That's the road that took my Tony. It's the road that killed my love. We never knew for sure what happened. The police report said there was no excessive speed or alcohol involved. Maybe a deer or a bear stepped onto the roadway. Perhaps he fell asleep, although I've thought that was not likely as he was used to staying awake an ungodly number of hours working at the hospital. It was a single-vehicle accident on a dark, rainy stretch of winding highway. A highway he had driven innumerable times.

"There you go, Paul. Cheers!" Mike smiles as he hands Paul his beer and bumps glasses. Mike has changed his drink to beer—it's easier to make it through the night on, he says. I think it's all about pacing yourself.

"Come to the bathroom with me!" Jessie leans across the table and calls loudly into my ear. Leaving the men to their own devices, I grab my purse and follow her sashaying ass through the crowd. She looks marvellous in the dress she is wearing. It's a great view even from the back. She looks good, coming or going. If I didn't love her much as I do, I'd have to hate her for being so gorgeous.

"Phew! I'm hot!" she exclaims, shaking her glorious head once we step into the ladies' room. She sits down at the vanity and reaches into her bag to retrieve her compact and lipstick. Squinting into the mirror— she needs glasses, but won't admit it—she checks her eye makeup for smudges, quickly powders her nose and touches up her lipstick. She wears peach coloured lipstick—winter or summer—and it looks perfect on her.

"Tell me! Are you going to 'eff' him tonight?" She grins at me with a suggestive tone. Her green eyes are laughing as she teases me, and she rubs her pointer fingers together as if to say "shame, shame" the way we did when we were kids.

"Shut up!" I bark at her, whacking her on the upper arm while frantically looking under the toilet stall doors to see if there is anyone behind them. When I discover there is not, I flop onto the chaise in the lounge area with utter relief and start to giggle.

"He's a dreamboat," I manage to utter. "There's part of me that can hardly wait to sleep with him!"

"Well, why are you waiting? Make it happen. Do it tonight. The suspense is too much. He's hunky. If you don't lay him, I will. Waste not—want not. You know, 'a bird in the hand' and all that bullshit. Go for it, Ginny! You don't have anything to lose. What are you waiting for— Christmas?" She winks at me. "It's just a few more shopping days away!"

"I'm just so nervous about it. What if I disappoint him? What if he doesn't like me naked? Ugh—I can barely stand the thought of it!"

"I never took you for a brainless person. That is the silliest thing I've ever heard you say. What man ever saw a naked woman he didn't like? Disappoint him? Pardon me? Do you *have* a mirror at home? I can't believe what I am hearing. You are stunning, and he is hot for you and lucky to have you. Don't be stupid—it's just like riding a bicycle—you never forget. Lay him—tonight!" It was an order. I shake my head and don't comment as we finish in the bathroom and make our way back to the party.

The rest of the evening was perfect, and it appeared that we all had a splendid time. An uneventful drive home landed me in my doorway with a well-muscled, well-dressed, ready, willing and able (I hope!) man. I bite the bullet and ask him in for a nightcap. He agrees and lets that slow smile slide across his lips as he steps aside to allow me through the door ahead of him.

Chapter 2
False Start

My phone rings bright and early Sunday morning. I don't have call display because I have old phones. Like many things in my life, they are leftovers from the past. But I don't care. I don't see a reason to get new ones. I don't need to see who is calling—my number is unlisted—if they've got my number, it's probably someone I know and like. Besides, I enjoy the thrill of wondering who is calling. I don't screen calls either because I don't have an answering machine. If I don't want to answer, I just don't. Whoever it is will call back. This time I know who it is. It's Jessie, calling for the full news report. She's an early bird, regardless of how late she stays up or how much she has had to drink. It's still dark out. I don't pick up.

My doorbell rings. I open a bleary eye and squint. At least it's not entirely dark now. The sun is just starting to peep over the mountains. I grab my robe and slide into my slippers. They are the best because my orthotics fit into them. I have to wear shoes most of the time these days because my feet get sore if I don't. My feet are killing me this morning after a night in high heels. I wince as I take my first few steps. My robe feels snuggly and warm as I pull it up around my neck. My house is cold this morning.

"Give me the play-by-play! Is he here?" Jessie asks as she pushes through the doorway. "Brr—it's cold out." She passes me the two extra-large coffees she's brought so she can shake out of her winter coat. She drops it in the foyer as she sits on the floor to take off her boots. "You are going to have to get some fancy-ass seat for this foyer. I don't know how many more years of sitting on the floor I can do to get my boots off. Help me up."

I extend my hand and brace my shoulder, protecting a tennis injury I earned a couple of summers ago. I won the tourney, but have suffered for it ever since. I'm going to have to learn to become a lefty.

"You weigh more this morning," I say to her.

"Fuck you," she replies with a grin on her face, ever eloquent in her choice of words. She knows I'm joking as I know she is.

I smile back at her and say while laughing, "If he was here, do you think you should be? I could be up in my room effing!"

"Well, he can't possibly be here, or you wouldn't be talking with such a potty mouth. I figured if he was here, he might as well get used to me sooner than later, and if he wasn't here, you might need my shoulder to cry on. How's your virtue this morning?"

"My virtue is just fine. Thank you. Let's nuke this coffee and get it into decent cups."

We move into the kitchen and settle down at my antique table. I put up a leaf, and we nestle in.

"Use a coaster," I say as I push one toward her. She is mindless about where she puts her beverage container. She'll put a sweating highball glass onto my oak sideboard and leave it there while she works the crowd. I'm forever going around behind her, putting coasters or bar napkins under her drink. She drives me to distraction some days.

"Put a plastic tablecloth down and get over it," she comments.

I shudder at the thought. As if she would do that in her house.

"So? Hurry up and spill it—I don't have all day—I'm going for a run soon. What happened?" she asks.

"You know I don't kiss and tell," I reply.

"Oh—don't try to be coy with me. Get on with it. What happened? The last I noticed, you were heading out the door with a big smile on your face. I take it he either didn't stay over or is cowering in fear in your bedroom at the thought of coming down here and facing me!"

"Well, that's probably just what he's doing! You have no shame!" I retort.

"I've got to go up and catch him in his underpants!" she says as she makes a move from the table, pretending to run up to my bedroom.

Giggling and reaching out to catch her, I reply as if she didn't already know, "He's not there. Don't be silly."

"I know, I know. Well—what happened? Are you alright?" she queries.

"I'm fine," I say, with a soft smile on my face. "I had a great time and a lovely end to a wonderful evening."

"Oh, come on! Everything is *lovely* to you. Give me a better adjective. I didn't ask you the size of his erection. I only want to know what happened!"

"He kissed me," I reply, without divulging further. My mind flashes back to his lips on mine. I remember his tongue gently probing my mouth, searching for more—the feeling in my chest as my body responded—the longing I felt in my heart.

"Ooh, he kissed you! Was it a peck on the cheek at the door or a full-on necking session? Come on. This conversation is getting tedious. Don't tease me anymore," she pouts.

"Okay, I'm sorry. It was a full-on necking session. Oh my goodness, it was amazing. I haven't been kissed like that in forever," I say, hugging myself and blushing at the memory of it.

"You're blushing! You did it! Tell me everything!"

"We didn't do it. We got pretty hot and bothered, but when it came down to it, I just couldn't. I don't think I know him well enough." I remember his hands tenderly holding me in a sweet embrace. He had one hand firmly planted on my back, and the other was just above my waist, his thumb rubbing the side of my breast, my nipples responding with aching tightness as they craved a full touch. He drove me wild.

34

"Oh, don't be stupid. How well do you have to know him? You've known him for over six months now. You two have been pussyfooting around each other all that time. You are driving me crazy. Just do it and get the suspense over with."

"I don't want to just do it."

"Well, why not? Sex is the best thing about being an adult other than payday. *Do it!* You are so stuck in the fifties!"

"You don't have to be insulting. I'll do it when I'm ready."

"Well, seriously. What are you waiting for? What are you worried about?" she asks apologetically.

"I'm not like you. I can't just do it. I am more emotional about it than you are."

"What do you mean—are you looking for a husband—is that it?"

"No, no—I just need to be sure emotionally."

"You mean you need to love him? You need him to love you? Or both? What is it?" she asks sincerely.

"No, I'm just afraid. I haven't done it in over twenty years! What if something goes wrong? What if …"

"Are you afraid he is going to break your heart?"

"No, I'm afraid I might break my own heart. I don't know how I'm going to be when it's all said and done. It's easier to stay on this side of it and wonder about it, rather than to do it and regret it or feel sad about it or wish for something different."

"Virginia Alexandra Parker, you are infuriating! I get it, darlin'. You are afraid it'll make you miss Tony more than you already do. Sweetheart, you can't keep holding onto that. It was over *so* long ago. He would have wanted you to move on. He is probably up there in Heaven, shaking his head that you've waited this long. Not moving on isn't going to change the past. He's not coming home for dinner tonight. He's not going to catch you in the act."

She stops when she sees a lone tear trickle down my cheek. She realizes she's gone too far and said too much. I know she is sorry. She wraps her arms around me, and I put my head on her shoulder. Her hair smells like flowers, and I'm comforted by her touch.

"Look, Ginny," she says, cradling my face in her hands and wiping my tears away with her thumb. "You are not betraying him. He will always be Tony. He will always be the best. Having sex with Mike will not tarnish what you had with Tony. He loved you, and it will be okay if you still love him. I know it's hard for you to let go and forget, but honey, you know as well as I do that you have to. Tony wouldn't want you to waste a chance to have another love in your life or to have some fun with a perfectly great guy. You are allowed to have fun, you know. Besides, you're probably all grown over and virginal again by now, and that's just gross!" she says, averting her eyes and pointing in the general vicinity of my nether region.

I giggle nervously and pull away, shaking my head and hanging it low. I'm scared. After all these years, it's just hard. I've let it go way too long. It's like the elderly couple who've stayed in their house too long, and before they know it, it's too late and too hard to move. It was easier to divert my attention when the girls were growing up. I opened Pangaea, and all my energy went into my store and my daughters. I had Paul, and I had Jessie, and I had my children. I had everything I needed, except for Tony, and I could survive without him as long as I had them. I never needed anything else.

"Well, darlin', I don't know what you are going to do, but I wouldn't let him get away if I were you. You should phone him and invite him to dinner tonight. I can see that Mike likes you a lot. He is a nice man, and he has a great reputation. I'd hate for him to move on because he thinks you aren't interested. Tell him how you feel. Let him know what's going on for you. If he's worth his salt, he'll stick around."

When did Jessie get philosophical?

"Go ahead. Phone him. Don't wait too long. Men need to be needed. They are very insecure, and waiting too long could put him off."

"Okay, I'll phone him. Do you think I should invite him over for dinner—what about lunch? Dinner, I would have to cook, and it will be night time."

"Oh, quit being such a chicken! Invite him for dinner! Make your specialty—it's Christmastime! I'm going for a run now. Want to come?" she asks, slurping down her last drop of coffee.

"No. If I'm cooking dinner tonight, I'd better get started. I'll phone him right away."

"Be sure you do. You want to catch him before he makes other plans."

"Okay. Thanks, Jess." I say with sincerity. She's the closest I've ever had to a sister. I love her with all my heart. "See you later. Can I call for culinary advice and a pep talk?"

"You know you can. Love you," she says, grabbing her coat and kissing me on the cheek.

Closing the door behind her, I lean against it and breathe, contemplating what to do next.

—

I met Jessie in our first year of high school. She sat beside me in our English class. We took one look at each other, and I knew we were going to be friends. When she showed up to join the field hockey team, I smiled at the sight of her. We've been best friends ever since. Over the years, we've probably spent more time together than with anyone else. I was at her house, or she was over at mine. My mom set a place for her at the table every day just as a matter of course. She was probably going to stay for dinner or be there for breakfast.

Jessie comes from a family of five girls, all with names that start with the letter J. They are all buxom and freckled with varying shades of red curly hair, from flaming orange to deep auburn to Jessie's strawberry blonde. She has the best hair of them all and the fewest freckles. They are a loud, happy bunch of women who sing and dance and get along like a house on fire. They play the piano by ear. I took lessons for years, and they are still better at it than I am. They sing like angels, and as sisters often can, they harmonize instinctively. They have vibrant voices that blend to create an incredible sound. Jessie is the second youngest.

Jessie's father was a doctor. I think that's why she was excited when she met Paul. In her mind, she would get her dad's approval if she came home with a doctor for a boyfriend. She grew up in a big, old, rambling house in Dunbar on the west side of Vancouver. The fun that we would have there! The McPherson's was the kind of place that people gravitated. The house was full of girls and boys most any time you were there. Jessie's mom looked perpetually frazzled. That was probably because of the copious amounts of food she was preparing to keep all those kids happy. She wore her hair scrunched up in a bun at the base of her neck, but it was invariably springing out and trying to escape. It seemed that Jessie's house was continuously filled with laughter and music. Saturday nights were the best because their dad would be home, and the Celtic music would be blasting out of the record player, or they would be creating it themselves. Usually, there were a few of us doing a jig in the living room. Dr. McPherson predictably got a tear in his eye when his daughters ended the evening by singing his favourite song. The haunting lyrics and the natural beauty of their voices made for a magical end to a delightful evening.

Sometimes Jessie and I would walk home to my house after school, and she'd end up staying for supper. We didn't live that far apart—just a short bus ride down Alma Street. It would be easy for her to go home if she had to, but she often elected to stay with me. Sometimes we had a basketball or volleyball game, and rather than going home, she'd sleep at my place. Those were usually the nights we'd end up giggling until three in the morning. My mom would finally poke her bleary-eyed head into my room and threaten that she could still tan our hides even if we were big teenaged girls and that we should get to sleep immediately. After all, we had school the next day.

My brother James, who has grown up to be the consummate bachelor, was sweet on Jessie for a long while. I guessed he was secretly in love with her and wanted to marry her. He loved it when she came over. Being friendly the way she is, she could talk easily with boys even though she came from a family of girls. I think she practiced being provocative on James. The poor guy—she'd string him along until he was about ready to bust. Being two years our junior, he was wet behind the ears and innocent. I think she kissed him once at Christmastime when we were all over at her house. I caught them together in the hall as I was making my way to the bathroom. I've never asked her about it. There are some things you just don't want to know.

When we graduated from university, Jessie got a job in junior management with a national hotel chain. When Paul and Tony and I moved up here, she stayed in Vancouver because of her career. Shortly after that, she transferred to Toronto. Long periods would go by that we didn't see one another. We would talk to each other almost every day, but that just wasn't the same, and we rang up some pretty hefty long-distance bills. Phone calls weren't cheap back then like they are now.

I was over-the-moon with excitement when Jessie phoned and told me she was going to move to Whistler. That made my life perfect. I hadn't known that she had been watching her company's expansion plan, and after she worked her way up the corporate ladder, she was ready to pounce on the opportunity when it knocked. When the Whistler townsite started to grow, her company built a hotel here, and she landed the job of running it. It's now one of the most successful hotels in the area. I couldn't believe my ears when she told me she was coming. I didn't have to wait for holidays to see her now—I could see her every day again, and I was ecstatic!

I'm glad I phoned Mike. He sounded happy to hear from me. He seemed even more pleased to be invited for dinner tonight. I know that's a good sign. Kissing him last night took my breath away. He smells good. His scent reminds me of Tony. His lips on mine with his probing tongue—oh my—I can barely stand thinking about it. I might have to run upstairs and take a round out of Bob (so named because he bobs up and down—it's a silly name and a tiny bit gross). It might help me to settle down and control myself better tonight. I think I will. I have time.

I must say I've been pleasantly surprised by my sex drive as I age. I am someone who believed that people stopped having sex at a certain point in life. Like most people, I've never relished the idea of my parents doing it. I never could stomach the thought of that. Therefore, I've had it in my head that older adults don't do it. Now that I'm on the more mature side of life, I can't believe that I still want sex, especially after menopause.

I remember when I was a budding teenager, and our Prime Minister's photograph was splashed across the cover of some magazine cover. He had red lipstick kisses all over his face. I couldn't begin to fathom his sex appeal, and I couldn't imagine what a beautiful woman like his wife, ever saw in a homely older man like him. When it was announced that she was pregnant with his baby, I was utterly repulsed by the thought of her having sex with him. It seemed to me he was in his seventies. Of course, he wasn't, but he sure was old as far as I was concerned.

Tony and I were always horny for each other. We could hardly wait to have sex. I was a child during the sixties sexual revolution, but I was raised to be a virgin on my wedding night, and I was. Tony and I waited until I graduated from university before we got married, but just. I graduated in May, and we got married in June. I wanted to get married on the same day as convocation, but my mother thought that was a ludicrous idea. It would have been far too much planning for one day. I understand that now, but at the time, I couldn't think of a better way to celebrate graduation than by having sex. So we waited one more frustrating month, and we were finally released, into sexual freedom.

Our wedding night was amazing. We did it three times. I hadn't realized you could do it that many times in one day, but I guess I was a fast learner. We caught onto it quickly, and we couldn't get enough of it. We had waited such a long time. There had been so much heavy petting and dry humping. It's not like he hadn't touched me down there, or he hadn't given me an orgasm, it's just that we were extremely pleased to go all the way. We could enjoy our bodies and our love the way it was meant to be enjoyed. We would show up to parties late—bright-eyed, with our faces flushed—as if we knew a secret that no one else did. We'd get teased because everyone knew what we'd been doing. We didn't care. It was glorious.

I usually masturbate at least once a week. For one thing, it helps improve my mood, but the main reason is that I believe in the saying, "Use it or lose it." I don't want my vagina to atrophy. I think it needs regular exercise, just like the rest of my body. I'm pretty sure masturbating must help with that. I heard about a woman with a prolapsed uterus who had to have it surgically removed. I was shocked when I learned that, and it scared me. Imagine your uterus hanging out between your legs! I heard about one elderly lady who had to have moisturizing ointment rubbed on her uterus to prevent it from drying out. Whoever heard of such a thing? I didn't know that could happen. It's another example of things you don't learn about until it's too late. I'm not sure if that condition is preventable, and I don't know if my vagina has anything to do with it or not, but I'll enjoy my self-prescribed prevention therapy.

For years after Tony died, I didn't touch myself. When he died, a part of me died with him. I couldn't bear my life without him. Sex had been such an essential part of our life together that I couldn't think about it anymore. Missing him was agonizing, and my sexual side withered away. I hadn't consciously made it that way, it just happened. I focused my love on my daughters and lost myself in that instead.

Almost ten years went by before things started to wake up for me. I was in my early forties, and my body was craving movement, and I'm not talking about exercise. My body was aching from the inside. I was even having orgasms in my sleep. I'd read about how women in their mid-thirties reach their sexual peak, and I think that's what was happening for me, though I was older than that. I had read about older women and younger men and how they go together like gun powder and matches. I was beginning to understand why.

I told Jessie what was happening to me, and she howled with laughter. Her eyes were shimmering from tears, and she said, "It's about time! I've been worried about you. You haven't talked about sex in so long I thought you'd forgotten all about it!" Of course, she was continually trying to push me out the door to go on a date with so-and-so, this cute beer rep that she knew, or some ski pro, or businessman she had met. I made a deal with her that I would meet the guy for coffee. I never wanted to go, but I did it just to shut her up. I didn't ever get that loving feeling. I *never* felt it. I wasn't interested in any of them. Mainly my heart just wasn't into it.

So when I told her I was about ready to rub up against a post, she said she had just the right treatment for me. We went to Vancouver one day, and she took me shopping to a store full of sex toys. Did I ever get an education that day! There were things in that shop that I'd never heard about or knew existed. I blushed several times as various items were explained to me. There were things there that I'm still unsure of what a person would do with them or why.

The two of us in that store reminded me of the day Tony and I bought the panties in Paris, except this was truly saucy stuff. We laughed and giggled, and I blushed my way through the experience like a schoolgirl. Jessie's eyes popped out of her head when she asked me if I thought a dildo she was considering buying was too big, and I said no. She had it placed down at her crotch, hanging it down as if she was a man, and she was looking at it when I gave my answer. She slowly lifted her head, her eyes comprehending my meaning, especially when she saw my blushing cheeks and sheepish smile. She whacked me a good one on the arm and whispered in a harsh voice, "You bitch! You've been holding out on me all these years! Tony's was that big?" I nodded my reply. Our eyes met, and we dissolved into a fit of giggles as she patted me on the back like a receiver who had just scored a touchdown, "No wonder you couldn't get enough of him!" She bought that dildo just to see what she'd been missing out on all those years.

I ended up buying a vibrating dildo that had a lifelike feel and three different speeds. It was pretty basic as far as dildos go. They've come a long way since then. My current dildo not only has a flesh-like texture, but it heats up and rotates. It has steel balls inside that whirl around in a counterclockwise motion, and I must admit the effect is quite pleasurable. It has ten different settings and six different speeds. It also has a button that presses up against my clitoris and drives me wild.

As I strip down and lie on the bed, turning the ceiling light off so that natural light softly illuminates the room, my thoughts drift to where they unfailingly do at these times. I'm still having sex with Tony after all these years. They say your mind is your most powerful sex organ, and I am living testimony to that. I am still consumed by him when I let my thoughts go. I'm wet before I touch myself, just by the memory of him. My mind drifts back to some of my favourite times with Tony.

We are slow dancing in our living room, playing old rhythm and blues— retro artists who make us feel worldly by listening to them. We wrap ourselves in each other's arms and sway slowly to the music, the rich sounds and the low lights enveloping our bodies. We are instinctive together, and he intoxicates me fully and completely. I remove my blouse and let it drop to the floor. Unbuttoning his shirt, I kiss his neck and follow the trail down his chest, caressing the soft track of hair near his bellybutton. The smell of his sex is musky and sweet. His erection strains against his pants and my mouth waters with anticipation.

Pulling his shirt off, I press my breasts against him. Our gaze is intense, steadfast and full of longing. He lets out a low, soft moan and pulls me closer. Masterfully, he removes my lace, push-up bra and releases my breasts from their confines. They bounce with their freedom, and my nipples tighten under his touch. They ache with the anticipation of his lips suckling me tenderly. I throw back my head and can feel my long hair graze the small of my back. He kisses me down the front of my throat, cupping each breast lightly and rolling my nipples. His feather touch turns me on as he takes my nipple into his hungry mouth and fondles it with his tongue. His mouth tortures me with hot, wet nibbles. The sound from my throat comes from elsewhere, from someone else, a disembodied non-entity—ethereal.

Reaching down, I gently squeeze his balls through the fabric of his trousers. My hand feels his rock-hard penis. It throbs under my touch. His breath catches in his throat as he continues to work his magic on my nipples. Shirtless, we resume our dance, grinding into one another, necking frantically—our tongues wrapped hotly together, flicking and searching.

I hungrily undo his belt, the buttons of his trousers, his zipper. Feeling for my prize, I'm greeted with a grand salute. Pushing himself into my hand, I stroke him. Opening my legs, I rub myself against him, my panties sopping wet and sticky. Our senses are at the brink of delirium as he lifts my skirt and pulls me closer. Our need is urgent.

His pants drop, and I fall to my knees, burying my head in his pubic hair, licking and sucking around his balls—teasing his cock with hot flicks of my tongue. The muscles in his legs tremble, and his breathing becomes ragged. He can't stand it any longer, and I plunge his cock into my mouth, enveloping his length within the grasp of my lips. I drink him in.

Moving me to the floor and cradling my head in his big hands, he kisses my neck and pushes my breasts together. They are full and taut. Straddling me, he slides his glistening cock between my breasts. He is hard again already. Bending over me, he kisses his way past my navel down into the fluff of my pubic mound. My body responds with immediacy, meeting the rhythm of his tongue as I shudder with satisfaction.

He dives into the depths of my body, the depths of my soul. He rocks into me incessantly, moving from side to side, rubbing my clitoris with each thrust. His cock is magnificent. It fills me over and over again. He is relentless, and as I am about to come, he slows down, teasing me. Looking into my eyes, Tony whispers, "Not yet, baby, not yet. I want you to feel me." I can feel nothing else. His touch is all over me. Inside me, outside me, I am him, he is me, we are one.

My voice rings out. Powering into me, he urges me on. "Come for me, baby, come for me!" Following his command, I arch my back and grind into him, exploding around him. My voice is urgent as I make my demand, "Fill me up! Fill me now!" I yell. We writhe in unison as he continues his unrelenting pursuit. My entire body seizes, shudders and convulses. He pumps his final strokes into me as he throws back his head and calls out, "I love you, baby!" He smells like soap and him and me. I die a thousand deaths in his arms.

I lie spent on my bed, glistening in my sweat. The light of the day is waning. A single tear trickles down my cheek as I gaze out the window at the snow-capped mountains.

⏤

Paul had a wife for a short time in the early years. Her name was

Josephine, and we used to call her Josie or Jo. We'd get mixed up between Jessie and Josie, and that could be confusing and funny. She was a nurse at the hospital in Vancouver, where Paul once worked. That's where they met. She was an outsider and never warmed up to us. I guess it was because the rest of us had all known each other for so long, and we were such good friends. Jessie and I are as close as two women can be, so there is no room for anyone else. It must have been hard for her. She wasn't athletic like Paul, so they didn't have that in common. I think she was as bored as could be living up here. She didn't have a job. They didn't have kids as we did, and Paul was either working or outside somewhere in the wilderness. She didn't last long up here, and I understand why she left. She went back to Vancouver, and we never saw or heard from her again—at least I didn't. I don't think Paul has ever been in contact with her. He never speaks of her and has been single ever since.

Shortly after Josephine moved away, Paul and Tony built a duplex. The deal was that one side of the duplex would be theirs, and that would be the medical office. The other side of the duplex would be Paul's home. He was happy with that arrangement because he was close to work. Doctors put in long hours, and he liked the idea of just going next door to be home. Tony and I rented for a while, and then we built the house that I live in now. After Tony died, I used the insurance money to pay out our portion of the loan on the medical office and to pay off my home mortgage. I had enough money left to put a down payment on the building where Pangaea is, and I became self-employed.

I love the word Pangaea. The world together as one—a lofty sentiment I've held since I first learned about the real Pangaea. It all made sense to me. The puzzle pieces of geography and humanity, flora and fauna, melding together. I know there weren't any humans at the time, but it still makes sense in my mind. To me, it's part of the trail that links us all together. I thought it was a perfect name for a store that has items from around the world. I specialize in antiques, collectables, curio items and the like. I have big, chunky furniture that creates an eclectic look—perfect for a ski lodge or chalet. I mostly go to estate sales in Vancouver's wealthy neighbourhoods—places like Shaughnessy, Kerrisdale and Point Grey, to buy items for my store.

It's how I met Mike. He came into my store one day. He was in town checking up on the restaurant he had recently opened. He had heard that my store might be the place to find a unique gift for his mother for her birthday. He was amiable and personable upon first meeting him, and his good looks did not escape me. His icy blue eyes were alive with personality, and he had a good laugh. He was easy to talk to straight away. I noticed his blonde hair was turning steely, and he was developing whitewalls on his temples. His hair was springy as if it might be curly if it were left to grow long. He spent two hours in the store that day looking at everything I had to offer. I am not so out of practice that I didn't notice he was checking me out and flirting.

He wormed out of me that I am single, and he managed to get me to tell him that I am a widow. He learned that I have two grown daughters and that I am a grandmother. I think people who have that sort of ability are like magicians. People who can talk freely and comfortably, as if they've known you forever, and they somehow manage to get all sorts of personal information out of you. Before the encounter was over, I knew that he was a bachelor. The first thing I thought was, how does someone who looks the way he does stay single all his life? I immediately wondered if something was wrong with him, but as I listened, I decided he was harmless and sincere.

That very day he asked me to go for coffee with him. It was almost closing time, and I didn't have anything else to do, so I agreed. Coffee turned into dinner, dinner turned into a nightcap, and before I knew it, it was ten o'clock. By then, I knew a few more things about him. He lives in Toronto. His father had a small chain of restaurants, and when he was ready to retire, he sold the chain to Mike. Mike then took the restaurants nationally. The chain of local restaurants caught on and became a household name across Canada. Now he's opening a restaurant here at Whistler. He comes to town every few weeks to check on his latest enterprise. He looks me up when he is here, and we usually meet for coffee.

He is currently in town for an extended period to oversee his restaurant during its first winter season.

I try to take care of myself the way my mother looks after herself. My mother, now in her late seventies, is one of those impeccably put-together women. She has silver-white hair coiffed within an inch of its life. She goes to the salon once a week to get her hair set, a ritual she has followed for as long as I can remember. She sleeps with a silk scarf carefully wrapped around her head to preserve her hairdo, and her hair manages to look good for the entire week. I'm not sure what my father thinks of that, but it seems to work for Mom.

When my brother and I were small children, my mom's hair was dark brown. She kept it shoulder length, and it was puffy from being back-combed all the time. It flipped up on the ends in a big curl that went all the way around the bottom. People were well-dressed back then. My mom wore a dress every day. She wore flats inside the house, but if she went to the market or out for the day, she put on heels with a matching purse. She wore a coordinating hat and kid gloves, whether it was winter or summer. It was the sixties, but she was a throwback to the fifties.

By the time the seventies rolled around, fashion had become much more casual, and many of the girls I went to school with had mothers who wore hardly any makeup. Their mothers wore a touch of blue eye shadow and natural coloured lip gloss. But my mother wore full makeup—every day. The first thing she did after she got up in the morning was to comb her hair and put on lipstick. She wore blood red lipstick for my entire childhood. I was probably thirteen before I figured out that my mother's lips weren't naturally that colour.

She maintains that a wife should try to look her best for her husband. I'm not sure how the headscarf at night works into that, but that is still her sentiment. She told me that she has never once passed gas in front of my father, and I believe her. I can't imagine her breaking wind alone with herself, never mind in front of someone, especially my father. If a touch of lipstick is all she can manage first thing in the morning, it is better than nothing in my mother's opinion.

47

When my parents celebrated their fiftieth wedding anniversary, my mom showed up to the party in her wedding gown, original shoes and all the accessories. I wore the very same outfit when I got married. She looked magnificent and was both the vision of who she is today and the ghost of who she was many years ago. She was downright beautiful. There weren't many dry eyes after her entry. She knows how to own a room, and in fact, she still fills it right up.

Like my mother, I don't wear blue jeans. They bind and look too casual for me. But, unlike my mother, I'm not particularly dressy. I like casual clothes. A pair of boyfriend trousers and a striped tee is my signature look. Throw a fisher knit sweater over my shoulders, and I'm ready for anything.

I wear very light makeup because it ages me if I'm not careful with its application. It's easy for my skin to look droopy and papery. Fine lines are my worst enemy. I can't wear red lipstick the way my mother can. I have to wear natural-looking lipstick with a red undertone or else I look like a vampire. Like my mother, I believe a woman can go anywhere at any time, as long as she is wearing lipstick.

Tonight, I'm a bit dressed up. I have on a pair of black pencil-leg slacks with a long flowing tunic. The tunic has three-quarter length sleeves and is black with a single red stripe running diagonally across my body. My hair is loose around my face, and I am wearing simple gold jewellery. Dinner is ready to go, and Mike should be here any minute. I quickly go around the living room and light some candles, stoke the fire and select some quiet background music. I am grateful that I remembered to put music on tonight, just in case there are any uncomfortable silences. I hear Mike's tires in the driveway, and I take a deep breath. Not wanting to look overly anxious, I wait until he rings the bell before I open the door.

"You look beautiful tonight," Mike comments. I take his coat as he passes me a bottle of red—a cabernet sauvignon, my favourite. He remembered. He's my kind of fellow.

He kisses me on the cheek as I thank him for the compliment and his gift. Moving into the living room, I ask if I can pour him a beverage.

He requests a Caesar cocktail. That drink happens to be one of my specialties, and my secret ingredient—being well, a secret—is horseradish. I pour myself an aperitif on the rocks with a lemon twist. I place the canapés on the coffee table as we settle in on the couch. Tipping his glass toward mine, he cocks his right eyebrow and says, "To the evening."

I take a sip of my drink and relax into the couch beside him. He has the most luminous blue eyes. They are mesmerizing. They shine with a hint of the devil, and always looks amused by something.

"Dinner smells superb," he comments as his lips twist into a slow grin.

"Lemon-garlic roasted potatoes—just for you," I am much more relaxed than I was last night, and I'm in a good mood. "I hope you like steak. I picked up a couple of fresh New York strip loin at the butcher. The red wine you brought will accompany it perfectly."

"Steak happens to be my favourite—medium-rare, please. You can smell those potatoes outside. My mouth watered when I stepped out of my car, and that was before I set eyes on you."

I squirm at his forward comment, but I am up to sparring. Jessie was right. Inviting him over tonight was the right thing to do.

"I aim to please," I comment, mimicking his statement from the night before. I shrug into myself and giggle. He leans in and kisses me warmly on my lips, holding his kiss long enough to make me catch my breath and want more.

"I bet you do," he whispers, keeping his lips within an inch of mine.

I smell his cologne and fresh breath as my chin brushes his. My heart is pounding in my chest. I pull back to see into his eyes because I can't focus up close anymore. He is looking at me with desire, and I move into him to kiss him deeply. This evening is not going as I had anticipated. I thought I'd be asking him to leave shortly after dinner and pushing him out the door while the night was still young. I did not expect to be this enamoured, nor did I hope to be kissing him deeply within ten minutes of his arrival. He wraps his hand around the back of my head and holds me in place as he slips his tongue between my lips, kissing me longer and harder. My mouth responds before I can control it, and I hear a moan come from deep within me.

"Nice to see you this evening," he comments as he pulls away.

It's shaping up to be quite a night. Aphrodite is dancing like a go-go girl on my shoulder.

"Nice to see you too," I feebly whisper as I scrape around for some composure and try to find my voice.

"I had a very good time last night," he says as he settles himself back down into his spot. I can see the outline of his erection straining against his trousers.

"I did too," I reply, trying to avert my eyes. "I'm happy you were able to make it over this evening."

"I wouldn't have missed it. I'm glad you called."

"Me too," I comment, feeling shy. "I should go and stir the potatoes. We'll eat in about thirty minutes. I hope you can wait that long."

"I do too," he comments slyly, skillfully adjusting himself.

Unable to restrain a giggle, I get up from the couch and move to the kitchen. It is spectacularly weird to feel the way I do. Mike follows me through the swinging doors and is right over my shoulder as I check the potatoes. The steam from the dish is full of rich aroma, and we both say, "Yum!" at the same time. Laughing, I stir the potatoes and close the oven door.

"I made a mixed salad with green goddess dressing for starters. Supper won't be long now."

"I'll open the wine to let it breathe," he says, moving to retrieve it from the living room.

"The bottle opener is on the sideboard," I call to him as he leaves the room. I catch myself looking at his backside in the perfectly fitting pants he has on. My, but that man can wear clothes—he's got the perfect physique. He must look great naked.

I'm not the best cook, but I can put together a decent meal. I know it's hard to mess up a steak, but I'm quite skilled at grilling if I do say so myself. The meal is tasty and is what my mother would consider a good, solid, man-meal. She believes that men should be fed meat and potatoes, which works for me because that's pretty much all I know how to make.

Looking at one another across the table, I catch myself smiling for no particular reason. Mike helps me clear the table. We load the dishwasher and clean up the kitchen, chatting amicably about nothing in particular. After everything is tidy in the kitchen and put away in the dining room, I wipe my hands on a kitchen towel and lead the way back into the dining room.

To my surprise, Mike reaches out to me from behind, captures my hand in his and spins me around into his arms. One of my favourite songs is playing in the background. Our feet move automatically, and we sing along to the lyrics as he dances me around the living room to the rhythm of the song—this song—this happy, cheerful song about falling in love and celebrating it. I have listened to it a million times by myself and danced to around my living room, alone or with a little one in my arms. This song, of all songs, is perfect at this moment. When it comes to an end, he pulls me close and holds my face inches from his own. I can do nothing but look him squarely in the eye.

"Thank you for a beautiful meal," he whispers gently.

"You're welcome," I respond, while our bodies move naturally to the sound of the next song. I put my head on his shoulder and press into him. He wraps his arms around me and moves me smoothly around the floor. My knees are weak. My head is swimming. I haven't let myself be held this way since Tony.

Mike swings me under his arm and spins me around. He pulls me close, and grips my waist firmly, crushing my breasts against him. I am hot and fear I might break into a sweat. We couldn't be any closer. The whole length of his body is pressed against mine as his pelvis moves rhythmically to the music.

He starts kissing me. Small, light kisses on my neck, feathery kisses on my forehead and cheek. He kisses my lips, gently searching and probing with his hot tongue. His breath is warm. My tongue responds to his, and I can't control myself. My heart is about to stop. I can't breathe.

He rubs his hand along the side of my breast, where it begins to swell, teasing me. My stomach is full of butterflies. I trace the top of his ear with my fingernail and tenderly touch the peach fuzz on his earlobe with my thumb. He moans, and I kiss him harder. Aphrodite is on my shoulder, having a conniption, rolling on her back, kicking her legs in the air.

He smells sensational. His cologne is intoxicating. His shirt is fresh and crisp and makes a crinkling sound as he rubs against me. Tipping my head back, inviting more, he kisses me along the base of my neck. He nibbles my earlobe and captures my earring in his mouth, tugging gently. My hair stands on end, and the full length of my body tingles. I might go mad before he returns to my lips and searches for my tongue. My whole body is on fire. I'm not sure if I'm turned on or having a hot flash or both.

He unzips my tunic and begins pushing the sleeves down my arms. My vagina is throbbing, and my panties are sticky. I involuntarily rub against him as I hear my top hit the floor and feel it crumple at my feet. My bra is fully exposed, and the swell of my breasts is glowing in the candlelight.

He kisses the flesh at the top of my bra. Being kissed this way is breathtaking. My vagina quivers, and I gasp as the music swirls around my head. He cups my breasts in his hands and continues caressing my flesh. My eyes catch our image in the mirror on the wall, and my blood runs cold. I see the man kissing me is Tony. The man in the mirror is Tony! I see my half-naked body and partially exposed breasts, and I catch my breath for an entirely different reason. I gasp in horror.

"That's it, Ginny," he murmurs. "Enjoy the feeling."

"No," I whisper with distress, lifting my head and recoiling at his touch.

He continues to kiss me. He is enraptured and hasn't heard me.

"No," I repeat more emphatically, panic coming over me. "No! Don't!"

Looking at me with puzzled eyes, I see his confusion. Following my order, he stops abruptly and pulls away from me.

"Of course," he says. "What's wrong?"

I feel vulnerable in my bra, exposed and misunderstood. I start to cry and turn my head in embarrassment.

"Tell me what's wrong?" he asks in a gentle and concerned voice.

I'm mortified and can barely speak. "It's too complicated," I stammer. "I can't explain. Please don't look at me."

"Of course," he obeys again, picking up my tunic and handing it to me, turning away in one fluid motion.

"Thank you," I whisper, taking my top and slipping it on. I can't look at him. Tears stream down my face, and I am having difficulty controlling my emotions. I retreat to the powder room and lean against the door. Sliding to the floor, I hug my knees and weep silently. My anguish is terrible. My heart is crushed within my chest as I work hard to breathe and collect my composure. I hear a soft tap on the other side of the door.

"Are you all right?" Mike asks. His voice is tender.

"Yes. I'll only be a moment," I reply.

Forcing myself to stand, I lean, wobbly kneed, against the sink and splash cold water onto my face. I pat my skin dry and touch up my lipstick. I don't bother to fix up my look any further before opening the door. Mike is leaning against the wall in the hallway, waiting for me. I can barely lift my head to make eye contact with him. He reaches out a hand, and I take it—I can't control the tears that well up in my eyes. His hand is warm, and he squeezes mine gently. He leads me into the living room and settles me down on the sofa.

"What happened? Are you okay?" he asks carefully.

"I'll be fine," I reply, quickly wiping my tears as they spill from my eyes.

"I'm sorry," he says. "I shouldn't have taken advantage. I didn't mean to make you uncomfortable. I thought you were enjoying it."

"I was enjoying it. You read all the signals correctly. Please don't be sorry. You did nothing wrong. You've been nothing but a gentleman. Thank you for that."

"Can you tell me what happened?"

I wrestle with myself. Mike knows I am a widow, but he doesn't know the circumstances of Tony's death. He doesn't know what kind of marriage we had or how I've spent every day of my life missing Tony. How do I explain that to him? Can I make him understand without hurting him?

53

"No. I'm sorry, but I can't," I reply. Hating myself, I tell him, "I have to call it a night. I've ruined the evening. You should go."

"Of course," he comments quietly. This time he is the one with his head down. He's positively perplexed, I suppose. "I'll just get my jacket and let myself out."

"No, no—I'll get it for you," I say, walking toward the closet. I can hardly control the urgent need I have to push Mike out the door and be alone. I can't get him out of the house fast enough. Rushing, I grab his jacket and thrust it toward him. With my head hung low, I say, "Please don't be mad. I'm not angry. I just can't talk now—I'll explain another time. I'm so sorry."

He takes his coat and slips it on. He steps into his loafers and stands with his hand on the doorknob, looking back at me. His face looks sad, and his eyes are quiet.

"I did have a good time tonight. Thank you for a delicious dinner. I'll be in touch."

Without moving toward him or kissing him goodnight or offering a friendly hug, I reply, "Thank you. I had a good time too. I hope to see you soon."

Hesitating in the doorway, he looks back at me and quietly comments, "I do care about you, Ginny."

Saying nothing more, he steps outside and closes the door behind him. I wait until I hear his car door close before I move. Locking the deadbolt, I lean my forehead on the door and concentrate on breathing. Like an abandoned child, I go morosely up to my bedroom and put myself to bed. This night is so over. Aphrodite is hanging her head even lower than I am.

Chapter 3
Going Steady

"How'd it go?" Jessie's voice chirps over the phone line.

"What time is it?" I question groggily.

"Never mind what time it is. I have to go to work, and I wanted to know what happened last night before I leave. How'd it go?!" she repeats excitedly.

Groaning and yawning, I roll over to check the clock and see it's only six a.m. The memory of the previous evening floods back.

"I saw a ghost," I comment.

"What are you talking about?" she questions sharply. "What do you mean?"

"I saw a ghost," I repeat. "And the night was over before I knew it. I enjoyed every moment of the night—until I saw a ghost."

"Do I have to come over there? What's going on?" Jessie questions frantically.

"We were having such a good time. Dinner was perfect. I made those lemon-garlic potatoes that we like—they were delicious. We kissed, we danced, he took my hand and twirled me around the living room. It felt natural and right. It was the way Tony and I used to dance together. The way he and I used to kiss. It felt so good. It was great," I choke up and can't speak any further. "But, then …"

"What? What happened? Why are you crying?"

"I saw a ghost. It's that simple."

"I don't understand. What are you talking about?"

"It's crazy—why would you understand? I saw a ghost, and you must think I'm nuts! I saw Tony in the mirror! Mike was kissing me, and when I looked in the mirror I saw *Tony*! I saw him, and I freaked out!" I thunder. Tears are streaming down my face now, and I'm starting to snuffle.

"Do you want me to come over?" Jessie asks. "I can push back my first meeting."

"No, no. There's nothing you can do. We don't need to talk about it. I'll be okay. I'm disappointed because I was having such a good time, and I thought I was going to follow through on having sex. Then that happened, and before I knew it, I was throwing Mike out of the house and sending him on his way. He'll probably never speak to me again, and I wouldn't blame him if he didn't. I'm disgusted with myself."

Jessie is silent on the other end. She's trying to put the pieces of my story together, and it sounds as though she's trying to get dressed while listening. She goes running first thing in the morning, comes home to shower and gets dressed inside her walk-in closet, in the dark. I don't understand why she doesn't turn the lights on. It's bad enough that she's half-blind.

"Okay. Let me put two and two together. You had a great time. You kissed, danced, started getting hot and heavy, and then Tony was there in the room with you? I see how that could throw a wrench into the mix. Are you sure you're all right? Has that ever happened to you before?"

"No. It hasn't happened before, but I've never done this with another man. I was half-naked, and I was getting all wobbly kneed and everything. My head was swimming with music and wine and lust. We were having such a good time, but when that happened, it just stopped me dead in my tracks. I couldn't think. I didn't know what to do. I didn't know how to explain, so I just threw him out. I couldn't get alone fast enough."

"Why didn't you call me?" she asks.

"I was mortified. I didn't want to talk to anyone. You couldn't have changed anything or made the ghost disappear or make up for my bad manners or phone Mike for me and tell him how sorry I am."

"No, I guess not. But you had better. Wow. I'm sorry that happened. You looked up, and there Tony was—looking back at you? Ew—freaky."

"Well, he wasn't exactly looking back at me. It was more like Mike was Tony—it was Tony, not Mike, that I saw in the mirror. It startled me, and I didn't know what to do, and all of a sudden, everything we were doing just felt wrong."

"Yeah, I see what you mean. That's too bad—what a way to end a great evening. I was hoping you were gonna get some last night," she comments with a twang and a giggle. I can hear her fingers snap in the background.

"How do I ever explain to him what happened? I can't tell him that! 'Yeah, well, Mike, you were kissing me, and I really liked it and everything, but then you turned into my dead husband, and I just freaked out.' Oh, how ridiculous. I'm not sure if I'm going to get out of bed today. I just want to hide from everyone—including myself! I've blown it, and I'm sure things are over between us."

"Well, maybe that's a self-fulfilling prophecy. Maybe that's what you want. It's probably not too late for damage control. Don't leave it too long, though. Touch base with him and tell him you are okay. Tell him that you had too much to drink or something like that. Keep it light."

"I know I have to talk to him. I'm just not looking forward to it. I exhibited such bad manners. My mother would feel ashamed of me!" I say, laughing.

"What Veronica doesn't know won't hurt her. Your secret is safe with me, and I'll be sure Ronnie never hears about it."

"You have always been my best ally. You'd better get to work. I'm all right. Thanks for calling."

"I'll check in with you later. Don't stay in bed all day. That never solved anything. Get up and go to work. Burying myself in work puts my troubles at bay. That's why I don't have a husband!" she laughs lightheartedly. "Talk to you later."

I groan as I hang up and envision what I have to do today. Talking to Mike about last night is not going to be easy. As I step out of the shower, I can smell coffee. Jessie must have come over after all. She is such a sweetheart. I don't know what I'd do without her. The house is warm because the automatic timer has turned on the furnace. I marvel at modern technology. It's a wonder I had that timer installed, but Paul insisted when I had to get my heater fixed. I step into my slippers and pull my nightie over my head, not bothering to put on my housecoat. I quickly towel my hair dry and scamper downstairs for my morning cup of coffee.

"Hi! You weren't supposed to come over! You were supposed to go to work!" I call as I come down the stairs. "It sure is nice of you to think of me, though. I appreciate it."

"Anything for you," a deep voice calls back.

It's Paul, not Jessie! Instantly, my spirits are lifted. I smile as I turn the corner into the kitchen. He has a coffee ready for me just the way I like it, and he passes it to me as I enter the room. Kissing me good morning, he steps back to assess my look. I know he can tell in one glance that something is wrong.

He looks carefully at me and says, "You've been crying. Why?"

"I have not been crying." I retort in denial, taking a sip of my coffee.

"You have. Why?" he repeats.

I've never been able to pull one over on him. I don't make eye contact and look away too quickly, tears welling up in my eyes, yet again. I'm mad at myself for feeling so emotional about this. Reaching out and touching my face, he turns me gently to see into my eyes. I blink, and a tear drops onto his hand. He reaches a gentle finger and wipes my cheek.

"What's going on?" he asks gently.

I pull my face away from his hand and wipe my cheek. "I just had a bad night. I thought you were Jessie. I just got off the phone with her."

"What happened? I saw Mike's car here last night. Why'd you have a bad night?" he questions with concern.

"It's a long story, and I don't want to talk about it. Can I make you some breakfast?" I ask.

"Thanks. What'll we have? It's cold out this morning—I wouldn't mind something hot."

"How about some oatmeal waffles and hot blueberry compote with maple syrup and yogurt? Doesn't that sound good? I'm just going to run upstairs to change and comb my hair. I'll be right back."

By the time I return, Paul has the waffles mixed, the blueberries bubbling on the stovetop and the table set. We know each other so well, and for so long, we are totally at home in each other's company. The waffle iron is heating up, and I refill my coffee cup.

As Paul pours the first waffle, he persists, "Well? Are you ready to talk yet?"

I sigh heavily because I know there is no getting out of confessing. I'm going to have to confide everything as I always do. He has been my best therapist over the years—that's one thing for sure. I quickly catch him up on all the events of the last couple of days. I don't get into the hot and heavy details because he doesn't need to hear that, but he gets the gist of it all.

"I know it's hard for you," he says, patting my hand.

"It's been a long time for me," I begin. "I haven't …" I can't find the words. I know he'll be able to fill in the blanks on his own.

He is kind as always and doesn't make me say it. "I understand."

"I feel stupid because this shouldn't be so hard. It's such a long time ago," I comment.

"Don't feel stupid. Your feelings are not stupid. They are just feelings," Paul says lovingly.

I settle onto a kitchen chair, and I'm silently grateful to him for his compassion. I let him nurse me. I do, after all, feel like a big baby.

"How can I help?" he asks.

"Could you phone Mike for me and explain to him that I'm not a raving lunatic? Tell him I usually have good manners, and I'm not crazy! But, don't mention anything about the ghost because he might not believe you then!" I laugh as I choke out the words. "I tell you, I've never been in such a predicament with a man before. I don't know what to do.

59

I want to run and hide and pretend it didn't happen, but that isn't going to fly. Dating is hard!"

"Is that what you are doing? Dating?" Paul asks.

I pause before I answer. "Well—I think so," I comment.

"Is that what you want to do—date?"

I don't know how to answer. What is he getting at? "I think so. What do you mean?"

"Maybe dating isn't what you want. Maybe you want to be in love. I think that's the part you miss about Tony. I'm not sure you miss him as much as you miss the thought of him—the being in love with him. I think it's what you've held onto all these years. I think that's what you miss."

I'm quiet and don't reply, ruminating over his words. He's never said anything like that to me before, and I don't know how to take it. However, I've never dated anyone before either, so maybe that's it. I have to think about what he's said. I look at him across the table, holding his stare.

Changing the subject, I ask, "Are you coming over for supper tonight?"

The two of us have dinner together all the time. Jessie usually joins us if she's not caught up in a late meeting or obligations at work. It's just something we've been doing forever. It started back in university—the bunch of us would eat together regularly, often at our parent's houses.

"Sure. That'd be great. It'll give me a chance to do another house call on my favourite patient," he answers with a grin.

"You brat!" I reply as I playfully whack him on the shoulder with my napkin. I retort, "I'm not your patient, and I don't need you to look after me!"

Crossing his arms above his head and shrugging backward to protect himself from the next blow, he laughs and says, "Have mercy! Please don't hit me! I didn't mean it!"

"Oh, shut up," I say with a happy smile. "What time do you think you'll be here?"

"My last appointment today is at five forty-five, which means I'll probably be here around six-thirty," he replies.

"Sounds good. I have no idea what we're having, but it'll be edible.

You should get going—look at the time! I have to muster up some courage and figure out how I'm going to deal with Mike. I'm not sure if I'm going to open the shop today or not."

"You'd better open the shop, Ginny. It is Christmastime, and it'll get your mind off your troubles. Take your time with the call. It's better to be calm and know what you are going to say. Don't feel rushed. You don't owe him anything," Paul comments sensibly. It's absolutely the opposite advice to Jessie's. I'll have to think about that too.

"You're probably right. Christmas music will cheer me up, and I can fuss with bows and boxes and stuff," I say, smiling.

"That's the woman I know and love—the one with a glimmer in her eye just because it's Christmas. See you later." He kisses me on the cheek as he steps toward the door to let himself out.

For the third time in as many days, here I am leaning against the door. Looking down at my feet and concentrating on my breath. I breathe a heavy sigh as I trudge upstairs to get ready for my day.

—

Mike smiles and waves as soon as he sees me. A swoosh of fresh air accompanies him as he enters, and the gust fluffs his hair. The coffee shop is busy and loud, and not many locals hang out here, giving us some anonymity. I am relieved as soon as I see the expression on his face. He doesn't look upset. He seems happy to see me. I'm glad I got here first instead of arriving late and being flustered. He kisses me on the cheek as he shrugs out of his jacket.

"How are you doing?" he asks straightaway.

"I'm good. How are you?" I ask. I'm secretly glad I called him. "Thanks for coming. It's nice to see you."

Without skipping a beat, he says, "I wouldn't have missed it. It's nice to see you too. What are you having? It's cold out today. I think I'll get a hot chocolate."

"I'll have green tea, please."

He smiles and says he'll be right back as he steps away from the table.

I start to relax. My confidence is building, and I practice one more time what I've been planning all day to say to him. I'm going to tell him that I need more time—that things just went too fast for me and put me off balance. That's believable. I think he'll understand.

As he returns with our drinks, I quickly say to him, "I'm sorry about last night."

Caught off guard, he replies, "I thought we might engage in some small talk first, not jump right into it. I accept your apology, but you don't have to say you're sorry. What happened? Can you talk about it today?"

I hesitate, feeling less confident, and blurt out, "My head was spinning. I think I had too much to drink." That wasn't what I was going to say! What happened to my plan?

He chuckles. "Sometimes, alcohol can go straight to a person's head."

Does that mean that he doesn't believe me? What does he mean when he says sometimes? Does he suspect I'm lying? Uh-oh—now what do I say?

"I like to plan. I like to be in control. I felt off-kilter, and suddenly, I felt scared and like I was losing myself. I didn't know what to do," I blurt out. Who is talking? Shut up! I can't stop myself. I go on, "You were kissing me, and it felt so good, and the music was making my head swim, and I felt all wobbly kneed, and before I knew it, I had pushed you out the door and found myself alone in my bed."

Oh, my goodness.

What have I just said? What happened to my rehearsed speech? I'm surprised I haven't told him about the ghost. What has come over me?

He sits silently for a moment before responding. I am beginning to wonder if he heard me. I'm hoping I don't have to repeat myself because that would be even more absurd. I'm trying hard not to squirm, and I'm starting to sweat. Of all the times to break out in a hot flash. I can't say I like menopause. I peel off my sweater and try to discreetly puff my T-shirt out to get some air into it.

He smiles as he comments, "Is that what you want—to go to bed with me?"

Aphrodite's eyes snap open, and she just about gives herself whiplash as she sits up straight on my shoulder and stares at him in disbelief. Feeling shy, I stammer, "Well, I'm not sure. We've never talked about it."

"Let's talk about it then. Is that what you want?" Mike repeats.

I'm starting to have difficulty breathing, and perspiration is popping out on my brow as well as my upper lip. "Yes, it is," I reply quietly.

He looks at me steadily, "Then what's wrong? Why are you nervous? I feel the same way. I want to go to bed with you too."

I don't know what's wrong. I don't know how to answer him, so I retrieve my practiced speech and start spewing some of it.

"I just need more time," I say weakly. I'm not sure my delivery was believable—I'm not buying it myself.

"How much time do you need?" he asks with genuine interest.

"I don't know," I reply pathetically.

"Is that all you need?" he asks.

I'm not sure what he means and look at him quizzically.

"Do you need anything else? Something more?" he asks. "Do you need a commitment from me? Do you need to be my girlfriend? I'm wondering if I need to make it official."

What on earth does that mean, I wonder in alarm? He's not asking me to marry him, is he? I can't think straight.

I manage to squeak out a reply, "Are you asking me to go steady?"

I can't believe I just said that! I'm not fourteen years old. This conversation is going sideways fast, and I am sorely unimpressed with myself.

"If that's what it takes—I guess I am," he replies calmly, looking me straight in the face.

"Oh," I mutter, almost to myself.

What about the logistics of going steady with Mike? How would this be possible? He lives in Toronto! He can't go steady with me if he lives in Toronto. This situation is getting more inane by the minute. I don't know if I want to go steady and can't believe what I've just said to him. He sighs and shifts in his seat. I think he is getting impatient with me. Who could blame him? Aphrodite is whacking me on the head with a caveman club.

We each take a sip of our drink and look out the window. I take a deep breath and look at him. He is so handsome it is easy to get lost in that face. I muster my concentration and focus on what I have to say.

"I'm not sure if that's what I need. I know you don't get it. I don't get it either. I guess I'm just asking you to be patient with me and give me another chance. I know this relationship has moved at a snail's pace, and I can't explain why I can't go faster. I'm appreciative of the time you've already given me. And, yes, I would like to go steady."

Aphrodite faints onto her back with her hand on her forehead. I realize he hasn't asked me. I need to hear him say it.

"Will you ask me, please?" I query.

He laughs outright at my ludicrous behaviour, but gently comments, "Ginny, will you go steady with me?"

I can't help but smile as he says it. I put my head down and peek up at him, "Yes, Mike, I will." I don't know why I needed to hear him say that. It seems foolishly young.

"It's official then," he says as he slaps his hands down on the table and looks me square in the eye. "I have a girlfriend, and her name is Virginia Alexandra Parker. I can't wait to tell the world. No more sneaking around!"

I laugh at his silly statement. How did this happen? I have a boyfriend! All I wanted to do was tell him that I needed more time and then go home to make supper for Paul and Jessie. What have I done?

"When should we have our first official date?" he asks with raised eyebrows.

"I thought we already had it," I laugh.

"I hope our first official date as a newfound couple goes better than our unofficial one," he says with a sly grin.

I visibly squirm in my seat and have a hard time maintaining eye contact with him.

"Well, Saturday night is my tree decorating party, and you are already coming to that. We could announce it that night," I suggest.

"That sounds great," he comments happily. "Are you sure you don't want to keep it a secret for longer? I don't want things to go too fast for you."

I can't tell for sure if he is teasing me or being sincere. "Let's wait and see how the night flows," I suggest with a smile.

"Should I plan to stay overnight?" he asks boldly.

I wasn't expecting that one! His eyes are playful, and he is enjoying making me squirm.

"Let me get back to you on that," I reply. My cheeks start to burn.

—

Munching on a carrot stick and taking a sip of her wine, Jessie asks me, "How'd it go with Mike?" It never takes long for her to get to the point. She's been in the house long enough to settle onto a kitchen chair and wait for the final dinner preparations.

"Well, I went to the coffee shop fully practiced with the story I was going to blab at him, about needing more time and wanting to slow things down and I came out of there with him as my boyfriend," I stated plainly. Paul's hand slipped on the sweet pepper he was dicing for the salad, and I think he nicked his finger. He swore under his breath, but he didn't lift his head. He just kept listening.

"Pssst! Hot stuff!" Jessie comments, licking the tip of her pointer finger and sticking it to her backside. "Tell me everything. What'd he say? What'd you say? Word for word—don't leave anything out."

I sigh heavily and say, "It's like I'm a teenager dealing with this. I had a big speech rehearsed of how the night became overwhelming, and I thought things moved too quickly, and how I was caught off guard and all that. Do you want to hear my exact speech?" She always wants to know all the details.

"No. Keep going," she says, gesturing like a film director telling me to hurry up. She likes everything fast, except maybe for sex. Funny.

"So I get there before he does and settle into my seat to wait for him. He arrived on time, as he always does, gets us a couple of drinks and before I know it, I'm spilling my guts out to him telling him, blah, blah,

blah, what I just told you, and how I found myself getting into my bed all by myself, and asking him to ask me to be his girlfriend! I don't know how that happened!"

Paul puts down the knife, leans his hip against the countertop, wipes his hands on his apron, and watches the two of us, still not saying a word. He is usually the quiet one when the three of us are together, but tonight he is notably silent and listening intently.

"Unbelievable," Jessie states. "Only you could go into a situation like that with an awesome guy and come out snagging him. Is that what you want—to be his girlfriend?"

"No!" I almost shout. "I wanted to slow things down, and I don't think I managed to say that to him. The next time he comes over here, he will be my boyfriend. I will have to have another conversation with him about it before I mess up again and completely wreck this."

"Ew. That's not good. I still don't know why you want to slow things down. I'd do him if I were you. Like I said, get it over and done. It's the suspense that's killing you. You have a boyfriend, and you're right—he's probably going to want sex the next time he sees you," she says, egging me on.

"Oh, shut up!" I reply, annoyed. "I wanted to buy myself some more time. I think he thought that I behaved the way I did because I want a commitment from him before we do it. We didn't even talk about that! We just went into 'Ginny, will you be my girlfriend?' mode. He knew right away I was lying when I said I'd had too much to drink. I'm so muddled up about this. Besides, how can I be his girlfriend when I live here, and he lives in Toronto? We didn't get around to discussing the logistics of that!"

Settling down at the table with our supper, Paul finally says, "Is Saturday night the next time you'll see him?"

Saturday night is my tree decorating party. It's a night I look forward to all year.

"We haven't made any plans, so at this point, yes, and he wants to make a big announcement that we are going steady. Oh, my stomach just turned at the thought of doing that. I have so much to do this week, and I'll have to tell the girls first—I can't just let that bombshell drop on them. What have I done?" I comment frantically, putting down my fork and pushing away from the table.

"Quite a pickle you've gotten yourself into," Paul states. "Why'd you rush into it? I thought you were going to wait to talk to him."

"I told her to hurry and get the air cleared between the two of them," Jessie offers, licking her fingers absentmindedly. Paul's eyes darken and narrow.

"I was embarrassed by my atrocious manners. I felt compelled to talk to him today," I comment, defending myself.

"Ronnie would be proud," he says dryly.

"She would be horrified! And keep my mother out of this," I demand, feeling insulted. I'm my mother's daughter. I flash him a look of warning and see he is studying me carefully. I am blushing, and my upper lip is about to perspire.

I can't believe I just lied to them. I'm not a liar. I don't lie! I can't believe I told them it was Mike who wanted to make the big announcement on Saturday night when it was me who made that suggestion. I don't know why I said that to him because I don't want to do that. I'm not myself. I'm concerned about my behaviour. I don't think I've ever told either of these two people a lie. I hang my head in shame as I think about whether or not I'm losing my mind.

Jessie misconstrues my body language and says in a soothing voice, "Don't worry about it, Ginny. Look at the bright side—you've landed yourself a gorgeous man who happens to be a millionaire, no ex-wife, no kids and someone who appears to be crazy about you. That's rough. I'd be upset too."

"That's not it," I comment quietly. A black cloud forms inside my head, and I push away from the table, putting my plate by the sink. I've barely touched my meal.

"Well, if you want to slow things down, you should tell him before Saturday," Paul states.

"I thought you said there was no rush! What's the rush now? I'm tired of thinking about it," I snap. "I don't know what I'm going to do. Let's talk about something else. The gala was a success on Saturday night. Are any figures in yet for how much money we raised?"

"We don't have final numbers yet, but the silent auction was a big success this year," Paul raises his eyebrows at me as he answers. "That oversized painting brought in a big bid. There was a lot of action for it."

"That's excellent. I'm not surprised. I liked that one, and you know I'm not a fan of that artist's work," proclaimed Jessie, referring to a local artist who is recently gaining in popularity. "Have you heard from the girls? When will Cath be home?"

"I spoke to her yesterday. She'll be home Friday night in time for supper, and she's bringing her friend Danielle. I haven't spoken to Christie in the last few days. I'm not sure when she's coming."

Cath and I are especially close. We talk almost every day. She is going to university right now, but we still keep her bedroom in the house. She comes home fairly often and always for the summer. Christie lives here in town, but we don't talk every day. I see her often, but things haven't been right between us since Eddie was born. If I was honest with myself, I guess things haven't been right for a lot longer than that.

Cath doesn't remember her dad. She was only two years old when he died. I believe she thinks she remembers him because we have pictures of him and the two of them and family photos of us around the house, but I'm pretty sure she doesn't remember him. Christie has some real memories of him. She was six when he passed. I know she's missed her dad. She is just that much older than Cath that she has a real memory, at least in her heart, of the way it felt to be around him. She remembers a few distinct details, but mostly I think it's the feeling of him that she remembers and the sense of us all together. I think it's what has led her down the path she's chosen. She's tried to fill the void his death created in our lives, with things that made her feel something, regardless if it hurt herself or others.

Christie has always been defiant. At a very young age, she was headstrong, and you couldn't very often reason with her. One time, when only four years old, she would not put her bike away. Tony told her that if she didn't take care of her bike, she couldn't have it. Christie wouldn't put it away, so he hung it on the side of the house where she could see it but not reach it. Stubborn as she was, she wouldn't give us the satisfaction of feeling like we had won that round. With hands on hips and bottom lip stuck out, she stomped her foot and traipsed off to her bedroom, refusing to speak to either of us for the remainder of the day. Christie is the spitting image of her father, and I will never forget how she looked that day with her black curls bouncing around her head and her blue eyes blazing.

By the time she got into high school, she was running with the wrong crowd. She didn't like it one bit when I told her that she wasn't allowed to hang around with those kids. That was like telling a girl you don't like her boyfriend, so she sleeps with him to spite you. It's easy for a young person to get into trouble these days. She dabbled in drugs and alcohol, and I spent a lot of restless nights when she was around sixteen. She was not going to do anything I told her to do. I had to settle for keeping a watchful eye and hoping for the best.

Thank goodness for Paul's involvement in her life. She loves him and will listen to him as the voice of reason, rather than me. I involved her in the local ski club since she was about three years old, and skiing with "Uncle Paul" may have been one of the saving graces in her life. The two of them have spent many days together on the mountain. She currently works as a ski patroller. She started as an instructor and then earned her first aid ticket. In the summer, she hangs around. She does a lot of hiking and mountain biking. She used to lead hikes into the backcountry for a local adventure travel group, but she hasn't been able to do that since Eddie arrived. She is my dearest love and my arch-nemesis.

At one point, my parents were so worried about her that they offered to take her and enrol her in private school. They thought the rigidity and high expectations of a school like that might straighten her out. I wasn't having any of that idea. Losing Tony was terrible enough. I wasn't going to lose my daughter as well. I figured the closer she was to me, the better. Things didn't have to be ideal. I can't honestly say why things have been as rough between us as they have been. Maybe we are too much alike. Perhaps we are too different. I'm not sure. It's another thing I can't overthink right now. The long and the short of it is that she'll come over Friday night to welcome her baby sister home.

"She'll be over Friday night, so she can get a good visit in with her sister while the crowd isn't here," Jessie suggests.

"Yes. I love the Saturday night party, but I enjoy the Friday night before even more," I comment. "It's more the way it used to be when we first started doing it—before it got so big."

"I like the Friday night get together the best, too," says Paul. He prefers small, more intimate parties. "It reminds me of those times we'd meet up at your mom and dad's, Jess."

"Yeah—those were fun times. My dad loved those nights the best, too," she states sadly. Her dad died two years ago just before Christmas, and the wound is still easily opened. Her eyes mist over at the mention of him, and she turns her head slightly to dab at them with her napkin.

"We've been through a lot together," I say.

"I can't think of two people I'd rather spend my life with," Jessie says, love evident in her voice.

"We're the modern-day Three Musketeers!" I say, laughing.

"You women are getting out of control—and far too corny for me. I'm going to call it a night. I'll see you tomorrow," Paul says.

He scrapes his chicken bones into the compost and puts his plate in the sink. We don't worry too much about who does dishes—it all works out. Stepping over to give each of us a kiss on the cheek, he waves and says goodnight. I know we'll see him tomorrow, same time, same place.

"Paul wasn't himself tonight," Jessie comments right away. "Did you think he was more quiet than usual?"

"Yes. He seems preoccupied with something."

"What's going on for him? Something at work?" she suggests.

"I don't know. He'll tell us when he's ready."

"So!" she squeals, whacking me a good one on my upper arm. "Now that Paul's gone tell me what's happening with Mike! What are you really thinking?"

There's nothing better than a good girlfriend. Cut to the chase and spill your guts.

"Oh, Jessie. I'm just so mixed up about it all. I don't know what to tell you," I state forlornly. "I'm all over the map with this, and I'm just digging myself in deeper. It sure is easier being single!"

"Well, he's got some great qualities, Gin, so I don't think you have to worry about that. Just get yourself settled down. What do you think is bothering you the most?"

"Seeing Tony in the mirror bothers me! That's never happened to me before. I've never seen Tony just around anywhere like that. It startled me, and I'm not sure what it means."

"I don't think it means anything. Let it go. It's a one-off. Don't get yourself all wound up about it. It's not worth it," Jessie's voice is calm. She's trying her best to comfort me.

"I'm going to try. Do you want to help me make tarts for Saturday? I'm making them tonight," I ask.

"I'd love to," she replies. "Baking is good therapy after a busy day."

We get down to work, and the evening passes. We are a good team working side-by-side, cleaning as we go. We finish around ten o'clock, and she calls it a night. I'll see her for yoga tomorrow after work, and we'll spend another night together, much like this one.

—

It's Wednesday evening, and Mike is coming over soon. I've asked Jessie and Paul not to come for dinner tonight. I should probably invite all of them for supper together, but I am not up to it yet. I've asked Mike to arrive after seven o'clock, and we are just going to hang out. I have one more goodie to make for the party, but it can wait until tomorrow. So, when he asked if I would like to get together, I invited him over to watch a movie. That sounded safe to me. It's nice having him here in town, and

I'm betting he will appreciate the comforts of home.

Is Paul onto something when he says I am in love with being in love? Tony and I were deeply in love, and it started right away at the beginning of our relationship. It was like magical love dust sprinkled down upon our heads, and we were sent on a thrilling trip. People used to ask us what colour love dust is, and we used to say it's like shimmering rose-coloured powder. It gets stuck all over you.

I'm not in love with Mike. He's as hunky as can be, and I can barely take my eyes off him when he's around. He is too handsome for words, but I'm not in love with him. Maybe I'm used to not being in love anymore. Or perhaps I am in love, but with Tony, and my heart doesn't know any other way. I'm also used to being single, and that is not as easy to give up as I thought it might be.

I'm not a woman who has pined for a man. Well, I have done that, but not for just any man. I've only ever pined for Tony, and I haven't wanted to replace him. I haven't wanted a man in my life simply because I didn't want to be alone. Being alone is okay. I don't mind it. I am not alone with the two best friends that I have. But that's not what I mean. I've never wanted to be in another relationship.

I'm not in love with Mike, and that's the problem! I wonder if I ever will be? The sporadic nature of our time together hasn't helped me foster warm feelings of love. It's done the opposite by letting me keep my distance and remain in my world. That feels safe. I wonder if being in love with someone can happen slowly over time? I don't know, because I've only been in love once and that's why I'm worried. I don't know how to make that happen.

Jessie can get into the moment and not worry about all the love stuff. Maybe that comes naturally to women who are pretty like her, with extroverted personalities. They never have to work at it, and men are drawn to them like flies to honey. There is something intuitive, and men know she will have sex with them for fun, without commitment. She's charming, and she can work that to her advantage every time. But, she's never had love in her life for any significant amount of time.

True love has somehow eluded Jessie. She's had a few relationships.

She was with Allen for a couple of years, but they never even got to the living together stage. You'd think that maybe she'd do that, but although Jessie has had many lovers, she is the marrying-type. That staunch religious upbringing of hers runs deep, and women like her never forget that they are expected to get married.

On the other hand, I am apparently in love with love, and tonight I am in love with my most comfortable clothes. I'm wearing the closest thing to blue jeans that I own—my khakis. They are soft and old and broken-in. My black turtle neck and cream coloured wool pullover will keep me warm. I don't set the heat too high at this time of day because I usually light a fire. It will be romantic and keep the two of us toasty.

He'll be here in about five minutes, so I apply my lipstick and scoot downstairs to stoke the fire. I hear his car pull into the driveway. He's right on time, as usual. He is stomping the snow off his boots and shaking the snowflakes from his hair as I open the door to greet him. He looks outrageously sexy. He is carrying a huge bouquet.

"For you m' lady," he says as he offers his flowers with a smile and a kiss to my cheek.

"Thank you! They're beautiful," I reply, duly impressed because flowers like these are costly at this time of year, and I'm wondering where on earth he would have gotten them.

One time over coffee, he told me that he keeps his mom's house in fresh flowers all the time. Once a week, a new delivery comes to her door and replaces the old flower arrangements. I was touched by his sentiment and remember thinking that his mother is one lucky woman to have a son who thinks of such things. I also remember thinking that a man who treats his mother well must also treat his significant other equally. I took it as a good sign, and here I am, with a fresh, out of season, gorgeous bouquet of my own. It's the biggest bouquet I've ever received, and I hope I have a vase large enough to contain it.

"They have some stiff competition in the beauty department," he comments. I take his coat and hang it up while he unties his boots and leaves them on the rubber mat by the door. Smiling, he asks, "How are you this evening?"

"I'm fine, thanks. How about yourself?"

"I'm all the better for being here with you."

Rummaging around in the back of my cupboards, I find an old vase big enough to hold the bouquet. I'll keep it in the kitchen for now where the heat from the fire won't wilt it.

"What can I get you?" I ask. "Do you want a glass of wine or a drink of some sort?"

"I'll just have a nice hot cup of tea if you have one."

"Tea, I've got!"

He knows I'm a tea granny. I have every variety under the sun. We settle in on the sofa and look at one another, clinking our mugs together as if they are wine glasses. It's our first meeting since I became his girlfriend.

"I have an invitation for you," he begins. "I know you want to take things slowly, and that's alright with me. If you are not ready for this idea, let me know. We can do it another time. New Year's Eve is coming, and if we are going to do something that night, we should book it. I want to take you to Vancouver for a few days to ring in the New Year. What do you think? Would you like to do that?"

I haven't given New Year's Eve a single thought. It's been so many years since I've gone out that night I can't count them all. It would have been before Tony died and probably before Christie was born. That's a long time ago now. Jessie usually works on New Year's Eve, while Paul and I snuggle into the couch to watch a movie.

"I haven't gone out for New Year's in a long time. What do you have in mind?"

"I want to book the penthouse at my favourite hotel. It's a classic. I stay there when I go to Vancouver for business. They know me well," he replies offhandedly. I forget he is wealthy and lives differently than I do. He lives at the hotel that Jessie runs. The only time I ever stayed in a hotel in Vancouver was on my wedding night.

"I'm impressed," I comment before I can edit my thoughts. "That would be lovely."

"I have a few favourites in Vancouver. There's a restaurant I'd like to wine and dine you at, although I may have to use my influence to get us a good table with a late booking like this."

I'm not sure if he's talking about his restaurant or another, but I giggle and reply, "Being influential the way you are, you can probably find us a table. You must know someone."

He laughs and shifts in his seat to face me square on.

"I am hoping—if you are ready—that we can consummate our love affair that night."

Our love affair! Consummate our love affair! There's no beating around the bush. My throat constricts, and I have difficulty swallowing. My vagina gives an involuntary squeeze in anticipation, and it surprises me. Aphrodite gives her sleepy head a shake and flicks open her eyes. She nudges me and encourages me to say yes. Instead, I tip my head away from him slightly and cast my eyes to the floor.

When my confidence returns, I lift my head and meet his gaze, "In my fantasy about us, your invitation sounds incredible. I'd love to go to Vancouver to do that with you. However, the real-life me doesn't want to get into a situation where we will both be disappointed. I don't want you to spend all that money on me and then have me behave the way I did the other night. I'm just concerned that it might be too much too soon."

"Fair enough," he replies. "What if I told you that the penthouse has more than one private bedroom? You could have your room. We could still go. You could let me show you a night on the town, and we see how the evening unfolds. If you are more comfortable being in your room, then you can be. If you want to join me in my room, then you know the door is open."

This invitation is too good to say no. Aphrodite has already changed into her showgirl gown and is go-go dancing on my shoulder. I have to work hard to shush her into submission.

"How can I resist an offer like that? Are you sure?" I ask.

Mike looks at me seriously and says, "First of all, let's get something straight. You could never disappoint me. Second of all, money is not an issue. I want things to be good between us. I want it to be the best it can be for you. The better it is for you, then the better it will be for me. I understand that you want things to move slowly. I'm not exactly sure how slowly, and I don't want to offend you, but you should know I am anxious to move forward with our relationship. I have been single for a long time too, and I haven't found anyone who I want to be with, the way I want to be with you."

I sit quietly with my head down, not believing my ears. This man is special. He once told me about a girl he loved long ago. He was very young, and she was even younger. As often happens with the young and in love, she became pregnant. He wanted to marry her, but before that day came, she miscarried. That's when her parents learned of the situation. They were scandalized and forbade the two of them to continue their love affair. Her parents moved her across the country to live with her grandparents, breaking the hearts of the young lovers. Mike's father urged him to let her go and encouraged him not to follow her, insisting that it would be for the best in the long run. Mike told me about how hard it's been to find someone to love, and he hasn't been in love since. He said to me that a love life requires time and effort, and simply put, he is busy. I wonder if Mike can succeed at being my boyfriend? He is taking a chance, too. Maybe his next love will be me. Without further hesitation, I make my decision.

"I'd love to," I say. "It sounds wonderful. Thank you. I'll look forward to it."

"You won't be disappointed. I'll make sure you have the time of your life," he says, leaning in to kiss me on my cheek.

I position myself so that his lips miss my cheek and land squarely on my mouth. He lets out a sound of pleasure as his lips touch mine. Warmth spreads over my body. My lips are hungry for his, and I am kissing him full-on, tongue and all. My shy self is forgotten as I wrap my arms around his neck and push him back in his seat. I don't know why I am doing this. I want to take things slowly, but I can't stop myself. I press into him and kiss him harder. His blue eyes glitter with delight.

"You are full of surprises," he says as he plants a slow, tender kiss on my lips. He unwraps himself from my grasp and sets me back into my spot before reaching for his tea. "What are we watching tonight?"

I'd completely forgotten about the movie. I thought we could surf through the channels and find something that appeals to both of us. The girls convinced me to buy a flat-screen TV that hangs on the wall, and they made me get rid of the old box-style television that I had. I found I wasn't even able to give it away, although it was a perfectly good television! I took it to my store to try to sell it there. You never know when someone will be looking for an old relic. I now have all the gadgets and gizmos that go with modern TV. The girls told me they were embarrassed by my dinosaur television situation and that neither of them enjoyed watching TV at my house. I gave in and let them guide me into what to buy. Now I have a big, modern, fifty-inch television that I barely know how to operate.

Swallowing hard and pushing my hair back into its place, realizing he has stopped me from further embarrassing myself, I reply, "I don't know. I thought maybe we could browse and find something we both like. Do you want to watch something fluffy or serious? I like a good docudrama if we can find one."

"Let's get her fired up and have a look," he quickly takes the controls and has the TV going in no time. I didn't even have to tell him how to turn it on—he just knew. This is excellent!

"Do you want anything to eat?" I ask him. "I have Christmas cookies."

"No, thanks. It's hard enough eating in restaurants as often as I do, but you combine that with Christmas, and I have to be very careful. It's a dynamite combination," he said, patting his tummy.

"It's a challenging time, that's for sure—on the pocketbook and the waistline," I answer. Mike can't ever have eaten very many cookies by the look of him.

We settle into the movie, and I manage to stop behaving like I am in high school. We snuggle on the couch and hold hands. It's delightful. Mike is gently rubbing my thumb and wrist in a way that feels very endearing. It's all I can do to resist pressing myself up against him again and kissing his face off. At the end of the night, I finally get my wish. Standing in the doorway, ready to say goodbye for the evening, he kisses me goodnight. He looks at me and thanks me for a pleasant evening, kissing me again, softly and slowly.

"You're a doll," he replies as he zeroes in for another round.

"I think the same about you," I respond automatically. My mouth finds his, and I kiss him long and hard, with serious intent. It's delightful.

"If you keep kissing me like that, I'll have to pick you up and carry you upstairs to make some serious love with you," he whispers huskily into my ear. I hear myself moan softly in reply and continue kissing him in earnest. He said he would make love *with* me, not *to* me. I like that.

I reach down and touch him on the outside of his trousers. I mean, I'm feeling his erection. I am lost from myself again, and I am out of control. This man has a spell over me. I can't believe what I am doing with my hand! I want to slow things down, remember? His erection is exquisite, and I find myself positively hungry for him. I have never touched him there before. I am feeling very bold and resist the urge to open his zipper and stroke his bare flesh.

His body tightens, and I hear his breath catch in his throat. "I love that," he says, pressing into me and continuing his kisses. His lips move from my mouth to my neck, then to my ear and back to my mouth. He rhythmically grinds his pelvis into my hand.

This time it is he who is bold, letting me know exactly what he wants. Pinning me to the wall, he bends his knees, so he is more my height, and rubs himself against me. He runs his hand inside my top and unhooks my bra before I am aware of what he has done. He is good. Rubbing my nipple while kissing my neck, he continues to grind into me. I cannot escape his grasp, and I naturally grind back. Aphrodite is delirious with delight and about ready to pass out. I moan with exquisite pleasure at his touch.

"I'd better go," he whispers into my ear, taking a nibble and pulling away from me.

"Yes," I whisper back, not very convincingly. I am positively breathless. I push my hair back and lean my head against the wall, more to steady myself than anything else.

"You look sexy when you do that," he comments, leaning in to kiss me again. It's very chaste and controlled, telling me the kissing is over for the evening.

"I'll book New Year's Eve. I'm looking forward to it more and more," anticipation thick in his voice. "It's going to take all my resolve to wait that long."

Still feeling unsteady, but starting to recover, I smile at him and repeat myself, saying "yes" again. He gives me a peck on the cheek and makes his way out the door. He thanks me again and tells me he'll call me tomorrow. I know he's quite busy the next couple of days, and I probably won't see him until Saturday. I don't want him to go as I watch him get into his car and drive away. But something is missing, and as my body aches with sexual longing, my heart trembles with fear.

—

As Jessie and I put the final touches on one of the treats for Saturday night, she interrogates me about my movie night with Mike. We haven't spoken to one another all day, and she had a dinner meeting tonight, making this our first opportunity to catch up.

"How'd it go? What did you do?" she asks eagerly, her eyes all lit up with curiosity. For once, she's living vicariously through me. That's a switch! I've listened to her sexual exploits over the years, but never the other way around.

"We watched a movie," I say quietly, knowing that my answer will annoy her. It's not what she wants to hear at all.

"Oh, don't be nauseating. I know that!" Jessie says as she whacks me a good one on the shoulder. "What happened? Give me the update!" she demands.

Deciding not to tease her any further, I tell her what she wants to know. "Mike wants to make a date for New Year's Eve. He asked to take me to Vancouver and book the penthouse suite at his favourite hotel and take me out on the town. He wants to make it the night that we do it for the first time."

"Nice. You said yes, of course. Please tell me that you said yes," Jessie turns her head sharply to look at me. I can hear the alarm in her voice as if I'd be nuts if I were to say no. Jessie and Aphrodite are one and the same.

"I said, yes. I'm terrified deep inside, but I said yes. It's time to move past this stage I've been stuck in, and I'm going to have to bite the bullet and do it. It's kind of nice having a date in mind. It takes the guesswork out of it."

"You like that—being the planner. You could be called a control freak, you know," she teases.

I laugh at myself because I know she's right. I do like to plan and be in control of things.

"It's something to look forward to since Christmas will be over. I can't remember the last time I went out for New Year's Eve. I think it was before Christie was born. It may have been that night that you had us all over to your apartment—remember when you were with Allen—I think that was New Year's Eve. I seem to recall we had sparklers for some reason. Francie and Robert came too. We haven't seen them in years."

"That was a long time ago. I can't believe you remember those people. I had to think for a second who you meant. The penthouse sounds impressive. He is going to sweep you off your feet that night. Let him give you the moon, Gin," she encourages me.

"It'll be fun. It's out of my comfort zone, but it's something good to look forward to."

"We'll have to go shopping to get you something to wear. You can borrow from me if you want, but it's nice to have something new. What else happened last night?"

I know she wants to get to the sexual stuff. I don't make her wait any longer. "We had a full-on kissing session straight away after he invited me out for New Year's Eve. Then we necked our faces off at the door before he left. It got pretty steamy. I don't know what came over me. I could barely keep my hands off him all night. When I was kissing him goodbye, I reached down and touched his penis!"

"Good girl! Way to go! Is it going to be worth the wait?" she asks, never delicate about affairs of the heart or otherwise.

"It's going to be worth the wait. Oh, Jessie—he pressed himself up against me. He had my back up against the wall, and before I knew it, I was grinding into him. It felt incredible. It was all I could do to not run upstairs with him."

"Nice," she contemplates. I can see her trying to imagine it and also figure out why I hadn't done just that.

There is a moment of silence between us while we work.

Then she asks, "So what's wrong?"

I pause before answering, "I don't know. Mike left, and I was hot and bothered, and part of me wanted him to stay. But I was glad he didn't. I felt scared and unfulfilled."

"Because you were unfulfilled, you stupid woman!" she jibes.

I giggle, "My body wanted more, but that's not it. It just didn't feel right somehow—like something was missing."

"Oh, probably love," she says almost sarcastically as she rolls her eyeballs.

"Well, definitely love. I don't love Mike. Not yet, anyway."

"Did you see any ghosts?" she asks.

"No! There were no ghosts last night. That was one good thing," I say with relief in my voice. I was kind of nervous about that and glad that it hadn't happened again.

"That's a relief. Maybe you're not going nuts after all," she laughs.

We finish up and clean off the counter. Jessie wipes her hands and says that she'd better get going. I ask her if she'd like a cup of tea before she goes, but she declines. She has an early morning tomorrow. She lives in a condo on the other side of town, about ten minutes from here. She sits on the floor to put on her boots, and I think for a moment that she's right—I'll have to get something to sit on for this spot. We're all a tad long in the tooth to sit on the floor to put our boots on. She wraps herself up in a pink scarf and zips up her cream coloured parka. She looks fresh and young, with her hair springing out from under her hood.

"Well, my darlin', I'll see you tomorrow. I'm sure looking forward to it. I can hardly wait to see Cath!" she says as she puts her hand on the doorknob.

"I can't wait too. Her classes finish tomorrow, and she's got two more weeks of exams before the holidays begin. I haven't told the girls about Mike yet. I'm not sure where or when. I know I have to tell them tomorrow night, but I'm nervous, and I don't want to wreck the night."

"That information shouldn't wreck the night. This announcement is good news. Won't Mike be here tomorrow evening? That should be a big hint."

"He won't be here until Saturday night in time for the party. I don't want it to upset them. I want them to be happy about it. Maybe I should tell them on the phone before they get here tomorrow."

"No, you should tell them in person, and it should be tomorrow night. It'll be good with us all together. Are you still planning on announcing it on Saturday to the big group?"

"I don't know. If I tell the girls tomorrow night, that's probably enough announcing for the time being. Other people can figure it out on their own. It's not their business anyway."

"You're right. Don't draw too much attention to it until you've done the deed!" Jessie teases. "Every woman in town will be green with envy," she says. "On second thought, maybe you should say something, then women will know to keep their hands off him!"

"Shut up!" I laugh and put my head down, rubbing the toe of my slipper into the floor.

"Oh—I've gone and embarrassed you! I'm kidding. I only mean until you are more sure of things. You don't have to make a big, formal announcement—it's not like you are announcing your engagement. Just lie low."

"That's what we'll do. I want to tell the girls and then settle into the feeling of it. Try it on for size," I laugh devilishly at my double entendre.

She whacks me on the shoulder and giggles, "Get busy on that, and I want all the details—don't forget that! I'm going. See you tomorrow."

We have a quick hug at the door, and she lets herself out. I can hear the engine of her vehicle warming up. As she puts it into gear and backs out of the driveway, I turn off the outside light.

Chapter 4
The Announcement

"Hi, Mom!" It's Christie, letting herself in. "We're here! Supper smells delicious—what are we having?"

Eddie jumps into my arms as I come into the foyer to greet them. He kisses me on my cheek and says, "Hi Gwamma! How aww you today?" He hasn't quite mastered his "r's" yet. Looking gorgeous with his black curly hair bobbing and his blue eyes sparkling, he's the picture of his mother at that age.

"I'm great, sweetheart! I love you," I say automatically, kissing him on the face and giving him a squeeze. He brings out the best in me. Wriggling out of my arms and dropping to the ground, he goes right to his toy box.

"How's my other sweetheart?" I ask as Christie offers me her cheek. We're still affectionate considering all the trouble we've had over the years.

"I'm good," she comments. "What are you making for supper? It smells amazing! Is it lasagna?"

"Good nose!" I reply. "You recognize the smell, and you know my repertoire of dinner selections!" I say with a laugh.

I can't get used to all her piercings. On her left ear, she has piercings

84

up to the top of her ear. I've lost count, probably about five of them. She has a diamond stud in her nose. I was shocked when she came home with that. She also has a pierced belly button. She wears a pink crystal in it. I think she regretted getting that one because it got infected and took a long time to heal. It seemed pretty painful. Thank goodness I've been able to talk her out of getting her face pierced. Paul may have had more of an influence on that than me, but I like to think that I've had something to do with making her see the sense of it. I told her she would regret it when she is older. I couldn't stand the idea of her destroying her beautiful face and skin.

I haven't been as successful with the tattoos. She started with a butterfly on her backside, just above the bikini line. She then got that embellished and added to the wings, making them spread out like a phoenix. A tiny fairy sits on her ankle, waving her sparkling wand at the world, and a cloud of fairy dust travels up her leg in a cosmic swirl. After she got the fairy, she got an armband. She has buff arms, and it's alright now because she is firm and slim. I've tried to warn her about what's coming, but she doesn't listen. Even though she has a strand of ivy adorning the back of her neck, thus far, I've been successful convincing her not to tattoo her face or hands. I hope it stays that way.

"How's my girl?" Paul calls as he comes around the corner from the kitchen where he's been making a salad. He bends down and kisses Christie on her cheek.

"I'm good," she smiles as Eddie tears around the corner.

Jumping into Paul's arms, he yells, "Uncle Paul! I'm so glad to see you!"

"I'm glad to see you too, squirt!" Paul says as he kisses him on the forehead. "How's my favourite boy?"

"I'm gweat! I'm thiwsty and hungwy!" Eddie announces in his high pitched, four-year-old voice.

"Well, you've come to the right place because we have food and water!" Paul says, putting Eddie down and leading him to the kitchen. "Follow me. I've got just what you need."

Eddie obliges and follows Paul happily into the kitchen, leaving us two women giggling at the sight and sound of the two of them together.

"Don't you just love that?" Christie comments. She knows that Paul is the closest thing to a grandpa that Eddie has. His only living grandpa lives in Australia and has never met him. Eddie's father is Australian. He came here to work as a ski technician.

"I do," I say, looking at my beautiful daughter and brushing her hair out of her eyes. "They are pretty sweet together."

"Cath's not here yet?" she asks, glancing around. "I thought she might be here by now."

"Not yet, though I think she'll be here any minute. Come to the kitchen while we finish getting things ready for dinner. Aunt Jessie isn't here yet either."

Paul has Eddie entertained at the kitchen table with a bowl of carrot sticks and cucumbers and some toy cars. Veggies go down better with cars. They are currently racing the red sports car (Eddie's) against the fire truck (Paul's). Paul's is terribly slow, but it makes a convincing putting sound.

As I get back to work, I hear the door open, and Jessie shouts to us, "Look who I found lurking around your driveway!"

With a hoot and a holler, we rush to the foyer to welcome them because we know she means Cath and her roommate Danielle. In a flurry of kisses and hugs, we greet each other enthusiastically. Coats and boots get put away, and Paul takes the girls' suitcases upstairs to Cath's room before we congregate in the kitchen for drinks and nibbles. Supper is almost ready.

"It is *so* good to be home!" Cath exclaims. "I can hardly wait for exams to be over."

She looks tired, but nothing out of the ordinary for a university student starting exams.

"Did you have a good trip up?" Paul asks as he enters the room.

"Yeah! Good conditions and the moon was lighting up the road. It looked so pretty, especially once we got closer to home and into the snow!"

"You've got winter tires for your vehicle, right?" Paul inquires, with a firm male voice of authority.

"Yes, Uncle Paul—I've got winter tires on my vehicle. You know that. You had them ordered and put on for me!" she replies.

"Good girl. Just making sure you weren't remiss in following through on that."

"I'm not remiss. Thanks very much. That was super nice of you."

Paul nods at her in acknowledgement of the compliment. Their eyes meet, and the love between them is palpable. Cath adores Paul. Paul's eyes are smiling at her.

"We should eat up so we can get started on playing cards," he comments. The girls giggle and look at one another. I think the three of them have other plans. We'll see if they entertain Paul's suggestion or not, but I'm sure they've organized a night on the town.

"Dinna is sewved," I announce in my best drawl, trying to mimic Eddie's r's. Gesturing with my hands, I direct them to the dining room where the food is out on the table. Bringing their drinks, they all settle into their spots, leaving me the seat closest to the kitchen. We dish up our plates and relish in each other's camaraderie. It feels good to be together.

Mom and Dad took Cath in during her first year of university. She was happy to live with them while she transitioned from high school to post-secondary. That first year can be overwhelming, especially for a kid from a small town. The university campus is large and intimidating, so it was good for her to have some familiarity and stability.

She was more confident upon entering her second year. She thought she'd like to try living in residence. She met Danielle that year. Danielle is from Chilliwack, a town in the Fraser Valley, and she'd also been living in student housing. They became friends and requested to be roommates for their third year. Danielle is a nice girl. I like her. She is fresh-faced and freckled, a petite blonde who is full of fun. The two of them both study business and spend a tremendous amount of time together.

"What time are people coming over tomorrow night, Mom?" Cath asks.

"The first guests should start arriving around seven. I hope everyone has arrived by eight," I answer.

"The usual guest list?" she asks. She knows who to expect—neighbours, locals from the business sector that we've become friends with over the years, and some friends from the ski club.

"Yes. All the usuals," I comment.

Jessie coughs into her hand, trying to catch my eye. I ignore her.

"Jorrie and Ben will be here first," Cath says with a grin. "They always get here first after all us guys," she says, moving her hand in a circle to indicate everyone present at the table.

"All us guys," Christie pokes her. "Good thing you're studying business, not English. I hope you don't write like that in your essays." I think she's envious of the path that Cath has taken. Christie is an intelligent young woman but has never lived up to her potential.

"Never mind," I say soothingly. "You are probably correct. They are usually right on time."

Jorrie and Ben are my next-door neighbours. Whatever you invite them to, they are reliably punctual. When you tell them what time to arrive, they are so precise that you had better mean it. If you say seven, but expect that people won't show up until seven-thirty, then you had better tell the two of them seven-thirty and everybody else seven. They've never been late for anything—ever. They are as dependable as clockwork.

"Let's lay wagers on who'll be here and when!" Cath jokes. Laughing, she says, "Lola and Scout will be here dead last."

"Anybody with names like that never did have a chance at being punctual," Paul adds, smiling.

Lola and Scout are buddies from our ski club. They live in Vancouver but come up most weekends to ski. They are a couple of hippie-types who wear sandals all year long. In the summer, they wear them in bare feet. In the winter, they wear them with grey wool socks. Their wardrobe consists basically of fleece jackets and zip-off pants.

"Any newbies?" Jessie asks.

I scowl at her. She is pushing. I guess there is no time like the present, so I take a deep breath and jump right in.

"Well, yes, there is. I've invited someone that not everyone at this table knows yet." I make eye contact with my daughters, and I say, "I've invited my friend, Mike."

"Mike? Do you mean Mike Monroe? That guy who owns Monroe's Restaurants?" Christie asks. "I heard he was back in town." Being the local, she is more in the know than Cath. I've mentioned Mike to both of them before, they know we are friends.

"Yes. That's the one," I confirm. "Mike will be among the first to arrive."

"How do you know that?" Christie asks.

"Well—he's my special guest. That's why I know he'll be here early," I reply.

They all make eye contact around the table while they try to deduce what I've suggested. Paul starts clearing plates and moves into the kitchen while Jessie hangs on at the table.

"What are you saying, Mom? What do you mean, your special guest?" Christie asks.

"Well, girls—there's something I need you to know. Mike and I have been spending quite a lot of time together lately, and we've decided to become more serious about one another. I guess you could call him my boyfriend. Mike is coming to the party as my boyfriend." I hear the words come out of my mouth, and it sounds strange. First of all, I think the word boyfriend describes someone who is under twenty-five years of age, making it odd to refer to Mike as such. I ramble on, knowing that I am speaking far too quickly and an octave too high, "I know he'll be among the first to arrive because I've asked him to come early to help greet guests and meet the two of you before the others get here."

There is silence around the table. Even Jessie is quiet. I hear some cutlery hit the floor in the kitchen, and Paul's voice mutters something unintelligible.

Jessie says, "Come on, Danielle. Let's see if we can help Uncle Paul with the dishes."

She and Danielle scurry into the kitchen, the double doors swinging behind them as they chatter in a friendly manner about what they might find for dessert.

"You have a boyfriend?" Christie says incredulously.

Cath's eyes are quiet and cautious and follow back and forth between Christie and me.

"Yes, I suppose I do," I answer.

"When did this happen?" she asks. "Why is now the first we're hearing about it?"

"Well, it happened rather quickly," I reply. "Just this week. You don't need to sound so surprised. It's not like you didn't know we've been seeing one another. We've had dates!" I say defensively.

"He's your boyfriend?" Christie's voice is starting to get sharper as she formulates the idea in her mind and digests the information. She's never been good at accepting surprises. She likes the status quo and is easily tilted.

"Yes. Mike's my boyfriend, and I hope you'll be gracious toward him," I say quietly. "I hope you'll welcome him into the family."

"Welcome him into the family!" she retorts. "What are you talking about? Welcome him into the family. He's your boyfriend, and you want us to welcome him into the family? What do you mean you've had dates? When have you had dates? You told me you met him for coffee once in a while—that's not a date! We've never met the guy! What's going on here? Are you getting married or something? Welcome him into the family—pfft!"

"Lower your voice and calm down," I say to her. She is predictably dramatic and overreacts easily. "There is no reason to be upset. I thought you might be happy for me."

Silence encompasses the room. Being happy for me is not within the realm of experience my daughters have had. There is a lot of history in this room. There have been happy times, but there's been an equal amount of heartache. The history made in this room has involved Christie, Cath, Paul, Jessie and me. It has never affected anyone else. We have never welcomed anyone new into our inner circle. Cath gathers up the remaining plates and scrapes them clean, piling them on top of one another. She has yet to say a word, and her eyes are cast down.

"I'm happy for you, Mom," she says quietly. "You've mentioned Mike before. We knew you were friends. We just didn't know it had become more serious."

"Well, it hasn't been serious, but things have changed rather quickly—just this week, as I said. We've decided we would like it to become serious. We've taken things very slowly, and we would like to move forward in our relationship. We want to be a couple," I explain.

"Oh, just stop talking," Christie says with a growl, pushing her chair away from the table. "Ew."

"Christie—stop!" Cath looks sternly at her sister. Cath is as meek as Christie is feisty. She rarely speaks harshly to anyone.

"Just stop it!" she continues. "This is wonderful news. Don't wreck it for Mom. You don't have to make it difficult. Just be happy for her." Turning to me, Cath says, "I'm happy for you, Mom. Way to go."

Christie sniffs and pushes further away from the table. "Do Aunt Jess and Uncle Paul know about this?" she asks.

"Yes, they do," I admit. "I told them the other night."

"So we are the last to know," she comments angrily.

"Christie, it doesn't matter who knew first. Don't be stupid. Mom sees Uncle Paul and Aunt Jess every day."

"Don't call me stupid! I'm not!" Christie glowers.

Even Eddie has snuck off to the kitchen by now.

"I didn't call you stupid. But, you don't have to act this way. It's Christmas, and Mom has a boyfriend! What could be more wonderful?" Cath asks.

"Pollyanna."

Sighing, I interject, "Girls, I've been very nervous to tell you. This is important to me. Mike is nervous too. We want this to work for everyone."

"What do Aunt Jess and Uncle Paul think?" Christie asks.

"They are happy for me."

As if they were listening at the door for their cue, the others all enter the room, carrying dessert plates and dessert. There is a strong Australian influence in this town, and I've learned how to make a pavlova. It's delicious and easy to make. I've made a large one, billowing with whipped cream and fruit. It looks festive and beautiful. My eyes meet Jessie's, telling her with a thankful look that her timing couldn't have been better. She winks at me in acknowledgement.

"I put the coffee on," she announces, gesturing toward the kitchen. "It'll be ready in a moment and will go perfectly with this whipped cream!"

⁓

"Well, that didn't go so well," Paul commiserates. He hands me another wet dish, and I polish it dry.

I sigh heavily before commenting, "Not as well as I'd hoped it would."

There is a silence between us for a few moments while we routinely do the dishes. The only sound is the tinkling of cutlery and the stacking of plates. The girls excused themselves after dessert with a burst of energy that propelled them off to one of the local nightclubs. It was delightful listening to the giggling and sound of hair spray pumping coming from the bathroom as they prepared for their evening. They likely plan to drown their sorrows, Christie anyway, and dance the night away. I don't worry about them anymore—I know they'll take care of each other. The pouting and heavy sighing was almost intolerable for the duration of dessert, as Christie made it abundantly clear she was not happy about my announcement. A night at the card table was out of the question. Jessie retired early after a long day at work, and Paul, bless his heart, stayed behind to help me clean up.

"I'm honestly not sure why she is not happy for me about this," I reply with frustration.

"You know Christie. She needs time to digest new information. She'll come around."

"Do you think so? I feel defeated. I haven't had practice telling them about boyfriends, but I didn't think it would go that badly," I moan, feeling exasperated. Silence fills the room as we companionably wash and dry the dishes together.

"Are you happy?" Paul asks me out of the blue.

"What do you mean? Of course I'm happy! It's Christmas, and my girls are home, and my favourite party of the entire year is tomorrow night, and I am happy."

What is he trying to get at?

"That's not what I mean, and you know it," he says, putting down the pan he is scrubbing and turning to look at me. "Are you happy about the decision you've made to be with Mike?"

I squirm under his intense gaze and look at my slipper. "Well, I guess so," I say in a small voice.

"Do you think maybe that's it?" he asks.

"What do you mean?"

"Christie's reaction—do you think that maybe she knows you are only lukewarm about having a boyfriend? Listen to yourself. You've got a boyfriend for the first time in decades, and you just told me that you 'guess' you are happy about it. Christie is very compassionate and intuitive about your needs, though you don't give her credit."

I think about what he has said. I'm not sure how to reply. Does Christie understand me that well?

"Furthermore, you are not aware of it, but she is protective of you. You are everything to her."

"Do you think she's mad at me because I didn't tell her first—by ourselves?" I ask. "Damn! I knew I should have called her and had some alone time with her to break the news. Things have been busy this week, and it all happened so fast. I am such a bad mother. I should have considered her feelings more carefully."

"You've done nothing wrong, and she'll get over it. Once she drinks herself into oblivion and you nurse her through her hangover tomorrow, she'll forgive you."

"I've made such a mess of things."

"Nah, not so much," he says quietly, returning to the pan he is scrubbing.

He looks endearing at the kitchen sink, wearing rubber gloves while he washes dishes. I'm not sure if it's because he's a doctor that he does that or what. He also wears an apron. I bought it for him, and he keeps it here at the house. It says, "Skiers do it with finesse." I know it's a silly play on words, but I liked it when I saw it, and he laughed when he opened it. It was one of those "just because" presents. I found it when I was in a shop in Vancouver, so I picked it up and gave it to him one night when we were barbecuing. He put it on straight away, and it has a special hook on my kitchen wall where it's handy for him to use. He doesn't like having to dig around in a cupboard to find something.

"You're so sweet to me," I say, reflecting his quiet mood.

"Sweets for the sweet," he says without looking at me.

With a flood of emotion, I realize how much I love this man standing in my kitchen. I love him with all my heart. He's been part of my life almost every day for over thirty years. He has never once acted dishonourably toward me. He is the friend that I trust with my life. Reaching up, I wrap my arms around his neck, accidentally dropping my dishtowel on the floor behind him. I press my head into his chest and hug him tightly, breathing in his scent. He works his hands out of the rubber gloves. I hear them snap and fall to the counter. He wraps his arms around me, returning my embrace while resting his chin on the top of my head. We exchange no words. We don't look into each other's eyes. We stand in the kitchen by the sink and hug each other like we are never going to let go. A lump forms in my throat, and I silently swallow it back.

⸻

Eddie gets up early in the morning and young ladies who have danced the night away—even mothers—don't. Christie knows I will tend to Eddie's needs and allow her to sleep. By the time the first girl emerges from her bedroom, it is afternoon. I am surprised to see that it's Christie. She looks worse for the wear with her dishevelled hair and old pyjamas, but she is standing.

Eddie and I are cutting out cookies on the kitchen table. There is a big bowl of green icing, and a shaker full of Santa sprinkles that he is using to decorate. He has more icing on his face and in his hair than on the cookies, but it doesn't matter. He is adorable, and we are having a lovely time together.

Christie pours herself a cup of coffee and sits down at the table beside us. She takes a cookie and starts to eat it between sips of coffee. I learned a long time ago to wait for Christie to start the morning conversation. It may not be morning, but it is for her. It takes her a while to wake up, and she's usually not ready to start talking until she is about three-quarters of the way through her first coffee. Eddie is chattering away and singing Christmas songs to himself while creating his decorative masterpieces. I don't try to direct him. I just let him fly with it.

"I am sorry about my attitude last night," Christie says quietly, not looking up from her cup and taking a second cookie.

"I accept your apology. Thank you," I say sincerely, without offering more. It's best to follow her lead in these situations. She eventually works her way out of it.

"I am happy for you, Mom," she reassures me. "Really. I was just surprised to hear you say those words. It's not something I ever expected to hear you say. Aunt Jess, yes, but not you!"

She smiles and looks up at me, searching my eyes, hoping to see forgiveness. She is so lovely. My heart melts at the sight of her sapphire eyes, looking pleadingly into mine. I move toward her and open my arms to her, inviting her for a hug. She stands up from the table and buries her head in my chest.

"Forgive me," I hear her whisper, while I squeeze her hard and kiss the top of her head.

"Always," I reply as we release one another. I squeeze her hands before letting go.

"What time is Mike coming over?" she asks.

"He'll be here around six—after supper, but before the party. He is looking forward to meeting you. He doesn't have any children of his own."

"Darn, I was hoping he had a son," she replies, laughing.

"Well, he doesn't!" I say, laughing along with her. She has a relationship with Eddie's father, but it's not rock solid. They are on-again-off-again, and I think it wears her down. I'm pretty sure she would like something more steadfast.

"At least I don't have to rely on my mother to find me a boyfriend. That would be pathetic." She giggles as she refills her coffee.

"Yep, that's a relief. It takes the pressure off of me too. I only know old guys!"

"Are you excited about it?" she asks.

"I suppose I am," I answer pensively. "I'll admit I'm more scared than anything."

"I bet," she says without expanding. Pouring herself a bowl of cereal, she asks, "What's Mike like? I've heard he's super-rich."

"Well, he is rich, but money doesn't make a man. It doesn't say anything about who he is as a person. Mike is very nice. Better than that, he's a good-hearted, solid man. Even though he has a lot more money than we will ever have, he isn't a player. He has been nothing but a gentleman toward me. I like him a lot, and I think you will too."

"Don't worry. I'll behave myself. I'll give him a chance," she says, looking at me with shy eyes. "I know you wouldn't bring him home to us if he weren't magnificent."

It's times like this that I see Christie is my daughter, too, not just her father's. She is the spitting image of him and reminds me of him through and through, but those shy eyes and the way she uses them, are all mine.

"Thank you," I reply with relief. "You will like Mike. He is nervous about meeting you all. He's met Aunt Jess and Uncle Paul already. He doesn't have any family around here, or as I said before, kids of his own, so he's anxious to make a good impression. He's a great dancer!"

"Ah! That's the way to your heart! He's got the moves, does he?" she says with a laugh. "Ew—that's just gross, Mom!"

"I suppose it is," I admit.

"I can't imagine you with another man," she blurts out.

There is a silence between us while we listen to Eddie sing to himself. I take the latest pan of cookies out of the oven and put them onto a cooling rack before I reply.

"I can't either, honey. I've had a tough time with it."

"What's it like? What's going on for you?" she probes.

"It's scary, is what it's like. I'm petrified! I haven't dated anyone since your father. It's an understatement saying that I'm rusty at this. I'm completely out of my comfort zone, and I feel like I'm cheating on your dad."

There. I said it out loud. It's the core of what is causing me such anguish.

"It's been a long time," she replies slowly. "What does Uncle Paul think of all this?"

Just then, Cath and Danielle come down the stairs, and our woman-to-woman talk abruptly ends as they enter the kitchen.

"Thank goodness there is coffee on!" Cath moans as she gets a cup for herself and her friend. She is oblivious of the mood in the kitchen. My eyes meet Christie's, and a silent message passes between us. We say no more. I realize that my eldest is growing up.

The rest of the day is taken up with preparation for the party. The girls help me put together trays of food and goodies. Danielle works alongside us and fits right in. We set out dishes and cutlery and holiday napkins. Cath makes sure the music is queued up—she knows the playlist. We tidy and fuss and make sure everything is just right. Before we know it, supper is over, and it is just about time for guests to start arriving. As usual, Mike shows up right on schedule. I am at the door and greet him outside before he comes in.

Looking at me from head to toe, he whistles and replies, "You look fantastic!"

"Thanks!" I say, twirling around to show him how my skirt flounces. I pull this dress out of my closet once a year just for this occasion. It is black taffeta with a fitted bodice, a sweetheart neckline and a full skirt. The skirt flares out in a big circle when I spin around. It is one of the few sleeveless dresses I have. I am wearing my pearl necklace and earrings.

I have on Cath's slingbacks that I wore to the gala. I know my eyes are shining, and I have more makeup on tonight than usual. I let the girls convince me to put on a darker shade of lipstick in celebration of the season. It is deep red. After I blotted it and let them put gloss on my lips, it looked just right. I am looking very festive and feeling flirtatious.

I offer him my cheek for a kiss, and he obliges willingly. Taking his hand and pulling him into the house, I say, "Let's go in! The girls are anxious to meet you!"

All three of them are standing in the foyer, waiting, and I make introductions.

"Mike, these are my daughters. This lovely lady is Christie, my oldest," I say as she steps forward slightly, "and this is Catherine." Cath nods her head in acknowledgement. "This young lady is Cath's friend, Danielle," I say, making a slight gesture.

"It's very nice to meet you all," Mike says.

"It's nice to meet you too," Christie says with a smile on her face. She steps toward him and reaches out her hand, trying to make things smooth for me. Looking stunning tonight with her curly hair pinned up, she is wearing a long, dark green iridescent shift with sequins, beads and a frayed hemline. Draped around her neck is a fringed, lacy scarf. Her outfit has a bohemian flare, but is festive and befits the season. "Mom has told us a lot about you," she lies. "All good!" she adds, winking at him and making a clicking sound with her mouth. Her casual, friendly gesture relaxes us, and we all giggle a sigh of relief.

Eddie dashes into the foyer and jumps into her arms, followed in hot pursuit by his father. Laughing, Christie says, "This is my son, Eddie, and this is his father, Bradley." She tips her head in Bradley's direction, meeting Mike's eyes as the two men shake hands.

Cath steps forward and reaches for Mike's hand, "Allow me to take your coat, Mike. Thanks for coming tonight. It means a lot to us." My daughters have such good manners. Their kindness and congeniality touch me. It's as though I had paid for finishing school. They are doing everything right. Relaxation settles over my body.

"I've brought a bottle of bubbly for the occasion," he says, handing me a bottle. "There's a case in the car," he whispers in my ear. "I thought you might like to offer it to the crowd." It's his way of contributing to the party. It is genuine champagne, and he brought a whole case! Accepting the bottle from him and thanking him, I bustle into the kitchen and nestle it away in the fridge.

Jessie and Paul arrive next. They usually have supper with us on this night, but this time, they intentionally came later. We settle ourselves in with a cocktail and begin to let the night unfold. Just as predicted, Jorrie and Ben knock on the door at seven o'clock sharp. We laugh as we make eye contact around the room. Soon, the house is full and roaring with sound. The smells and tastes of the season fill up the rooms. I am happy and enjoying myself immensely.

Years ago, when this tradition started, people used to bring a decoration for the tree, and I would purchase everyone a tree decoration in exchange. Over time, there got to be too many decorations, so we stopped doing the ornament exchange. There is an over height, cathedral ceiling in my living room, which accommodates a huge tree. It's loaded with lights and dripping with decorations by the time we are done. Christie has the honour of putting the star at the top. When she was a girl, Uncle Paul used to be the one who would stand on a step ladder and hold her up high so she could reach. Now it's Bradley who has that honour, at least for the time being. It's crowded on the step ladder, but she is tiny, and he can easily support her. With the tree fully adorned, we all cheer and hoot.

The food and drinks just keep coming during this party. I rush into the kitchen to check on a hot dip that's in the oven warming. When I open the oven door, flames burst out at me! Hollering and stepping back, I see that I've left a potholder inside the oven, and it has caught on fire. Reaching in with some tongs, I grab the burning potholder and start flicking it around, trying to extinguish the flame. Paul comes through the swinging kitchen doors just at that moment and lets out a yelp of surprise. Rushing toward me, he grabs my arm from behind and directs me toward the sink where he reaches past me and turns the water onto the flaming cloth. He wraps his arms around me and turns me to face him.

"What on earth happened in here?" he exclaims, raising his voice over the music.

Gasping for air between fits of laughter, I tell him what happened. I'm not sure why I think this is funny. It's nervous laughter, I suspect. I'm grateful I didn't light the house on fire! That would make for a memorable party. He is looking at me as if trying to determine if I've had too much to drink. He moves a strand of hair off of my face to look into my eyes.

Mike enters the room and asks, "I'm wondering if you'd like to offer your guests a round of the champagne I brought? I could go out to the car and get it."

Stopping in his tracks, he looks back and forth between Paul and me. I am in Paul's arms, and it appears as though we are having a tender moment. The look of surprise on Mike's face is unmistakable. I squirm out of Paul's grasp, straightening my hair and dress.

"It's not what it looks like," I say, laughing and waving Paul off. "Paul was just preventing me from burning down my house." I quickly explain the story, and Paul reaches into the sink to show the soaked rag as evidence of the truth. "This is probably a perfect time to offer a round of champagne. I'd better get that dip out of the oven before it burns too. Do you mind going to your car to get the champagne? It should be well-chilled by now!"

"I don't mind at all. I'll get it now. I'll be back in a moment," Mike says as he leaves the kitchen and goes out the back door.

I burst out laughing again as Mike heads out of earshot. Paul retrieves the warmed dip from the oven and puts it on a trivet on the counter. I think he doesn't trust my judgment at this point. Jessie comes into the kitchen, wondering what we are doing. We retell the story, and once again, I burst into giggles. I am having a hard time controlling myself.

Mike comes in the back door with the case of champagne. Ever discrete, he is. He doesn't want to draw attention to his gift. Jessie gets the champagne glasses that we had set out on a tray earlier in the day. Popping corks, we tip the glasses and fill them two-thirds full. Mike holds one of the swinging doors for me while Paul holds the other, allowing me to graciously enter the living room with a fully loaded tray of champagne. The crisp, cold bubbles top off our evening perfectly, and the guests express their appreciation of the delicious treat. The celebration continues in full-swing once we've toasted the season.

The final guests leave shortly after two in the morning. Eddie is curled up in a ball on a pillow under the Christmas tree. He had managed to last until almost midnight before running out of steam. Bradley gently picks him up and carries him to his bed, tucking him in for the night. Christie says goodnight to us and follows them up. By the look of the room, I think the party was a success.

"You sure know how to put on a party," Mike comments, putting his feet up on the coffee table.

Kicking off my shoes and groaning in agony, I rub my toes and wince as I sit on the couch beside him.

"This party is an institution. We've been hosting it so long it runs itself."

"I think it gets better every year," Jessie chimes in as she comes around the corner from the kitchen. Her face is flushed from all the dancing, and her hair is damp around her brow. She looks twenty years old as she pads into the room in her stockinged feet. "Are your feet sore?" she asks.

"Eff!" I say, as she sits down on the floor in front of me and starts rubbing one of my feet.

"She can't say f-u-c-k," Jessie whispers to Mike, as she spells out the word when she sees he doesn't get what I've just said. "She only says the first letter. It's much more ladylike."

"Shut up!" I retort, whacking her with a stray napkin.

"I see," Mike replies, with amused eyes. "Would you like me to rub the other one?"

"That would be divine."

Paul comes in from the kitchen and announces that he has done the first round of cleaning. "Well done on another successful Christmas party! That was a lot of fun."

He flops onto the overstuffed chair I have in the corner. Taking in the sight of me splayed on the couch, getting my feet rubbed, he says, "Don't you look like royalty."

"All my servants before me," I retort.

"I'm going to bed," Jessie announces, pushing back her hair and gently placing my foot onto the floor. Mike keeps rubbing the ball of my foot and my arch. He is sending electricity up my leg. Aphrodite has one eye open and is waiting with bated breath for his next move.

"Me too, but I'll be heading home," Paul says matter-of-factly. Usually, he stays the night when we have this party. "Don't get up. I'll let myself out."

"Are you sure you don't want to stay?" I ask. "You know we have room."

"Nope," he replies firmly. "I'm sleeping in my bed tonight, where I won't be woken by a four-year-old three hours from now. I'm going to ski a half-day tomorrow afternoon, so I want a good sleep."

"I don't blame you," I say quietly. I am surprised by how disappointed I am that Paul is not going to stay overnight. He always stays overnight after this party. It's a tradition.

Pushing himself up from his chair, Paul makes his way toward the coat closet at the same time that Jessie moves toward the guest room. It's really her room as she is just about the only person who ever stays in it.

"G'night, Jess," he says as he puts on his shoes. "Have a good sleep."

"Good night, everyone," Jessie says as she blows us all a kiss and goes down the hall.

"I'll see the both of you soon," Paul says as he moves toward the door. "Thanks for a great night, Ginny."

"My pleasure," I reply. "Sleep well."

"I will."

And he is gone.

Paul's departure leaves Mike and me alone in the room. It's uncomfortably quiet for a moment. Paul's vehicle idles outside. For the longest time, it's the only thing that I hear. My attention returns when Mike stops rubbing my foot. My feet are aching and swollen. I need a drink of water, but I can't bear the thought of walking across the room to the kitchen.

"You are good friends," he says.

"Hmm," I reply, distracted. "The best. Paul's always been there for me."

"Have you ever been more than friends?" he asks quietly.

I look down and shake my head, "No. Our relationship has never been like that."

"Why not? You are so close," he continues.

"I'm not sure. I've never thought of him that way. He was Tony's best friend, and he became Uncle Paul to the girls. That's where it started, and that's where it ended. He's been a part of my life almost since the day I met him. I'm not sure why it's never been anything more."

"Do you like it that way … the not 'anything more' part?" he asks.

I shift uncomfortably in my seat. Why is Mike asking me these questions? Is he worried that I have a relationship with Paul that I am hiding from him? I look at the floor and furrow my brow.

"I like having Paul in my life. If it means 'not anything more' to have him in my life—then yes—I like it that way."

"Have you thought about how things might change between you and Paul as our relationship grows?"

Why would anything have to change between Paul and me as I get closer to Mike? Things won't change between Jessie and me. What's he suggesting?

"No, I haven't. I believe that things will not change," I reply crisply. Fatigue rushes through my body, and I'm feeling ornery as I recognize that things have already changed. Paul is sleeping at his own house tonight, not mine, and I'm not happy about that.

"I just think your relationship with him might naturally shift."

"I never thought about it. Are you worried about Paul and me?" I ask. I can hear my voice getting higher, almost shrill. I am irritated by this conversation.

"Should I be?" he questions.

"No!" I say emphatically. "Listen, I'm tired. I desperately need a drink of water, and my feet are killing me. I'm going to hobble into the kitchen, and then I think I had better get to bed. Eddie will be up early." I want him to think it will be me looking after Eddie in the morning, even though I know it will be Christie and Bradley.

"I had better get going anyway. It's late," Mike says as he disentangles himself from my leg and releases my foot. He stands up from his seat and stretches, letting out a low moan. "I'm tired too. You put on quite a party, Ms. Parker. That was fun."

"Thanks. I'm glad you had a good time."

For reasons I'm not clear about, I'm not unhappy that he is leaving.

"I'll get you a drink of water before I go," he says, retreating into the kitchen.

I look down at my feet and see the swell marks imprinted into my skin. My feet are red at the pressure points of the shoes. High heels are the Devil's work. Slaves to fashion have painful needs. I chuckle to myself at the irony of that thought, considering it's me who has sore feet from wearing heels.

Mike returns with a tall glass of ice water. Handing it to me, he says, "I'm not mad, you know."

"Mad? About what?" I ask.

"About what I saw in the kitchen."

"In the kitchen?" I say, not following his gist. Then it dawns on me. "You mean when you walked in, and Paul had his arms around me? Then I'm glad you're not mad because that is no reason. It wasn't what it looked like."

"So you say."

I'm feeling exasperated and defensive, as sweat pops out on my upper lip. That's just what I need. I'm agitated and can't think of anything civil to say. I look at the floor and don't reply. I think we are having our first fight! It's too early in our relationship to be fighting over anything—we haven't even had sex yet.

"Look, I'm going to call it a night. I think I've overstayed my welcome," Mike says as he walks toward the closet.

"Don't be silly. You are very welcome here." Trying to change the subject, I remind him of how my girls greeted him. "I think it went well with my daughters, don't you?"

"They are very well-mannered."

"I agree. Thank you. They'll warm up as they get to know you better."

"I'm sure they will," he says as he puts on his coat and shoes. Standing at the door, looking back at me, sprawled on the couch with my feet up, he says, "Good night, Ginny. It was a great evening."

"Good night, Mike."

He lets himself out, and as I hear the door click, it registers that I didn't go to the door to say a proper goodbye. He didn't cross the living room to kiss me. I didn't even receive a peck on the cheek. I also don't care.

Chapter 5
Wet Dreaming

A dark head is looming in my vision. I look up and see it's Tony! I'm surprised to see him—we've been apart for so long. He looks young and vital. He is walking toward me with that confident swagger he has when he is feeling playful. He smiles at me, and his face lights up. He is glad to see me too. Rushing into his arms, he wraps me in his embrace. I bury my head in his shoulder and breathe him in, closing my eyes and relishing the moment.

His lips find mine, and we kiss passionately. The warmth of his love floods my body. It's been an eternity since we've done this. The sun is shining on our heads. Laying me down in the grass, he moves his hand to my breast. My body responds immediately, and I press myself into him. He kisses me, and I moan with pleasure. My hand reaches down between my legs and rubs my clitoris gently. I am on the brink of coming. He moves into position to make love to me, right then and there in the field, in the sunshine, among the daisies.

I am aching with desire, and my pelvis bucks with joy as our bodies meet. I've missed him desperately. I love him as much as ever. Where has he been all this time? It's good to have him inside me where he belongs. My hand is working harder now, and I let out a low groan of pleasure as my vagina bursts into rhythmic spasms. He's kissing my neck and breathing into my ear, encouraging me to come again, to come more, to move with him and enjoy it.

"Ginny," he says. "You're all mine."

My body responds, and I convulse again into bliss. My fingers press harder and rub faster. My orgasm is stronger this time, and I moan deeply with satisfaction. I open my eyes to look at him—to take in the glory of his beautiful face. But it's not Tony making love to me. In my dream, I see that it's Paul! Paul—who has loved me forever. I'm pleased to discover that Paul is such a good lover. Why haven't I done this with him sooner? I touch myself again, and my hand lingers between my legs, my vagina languishing in its mood. I turn my face, and my lips search for his. We kiss deeply, passionately, again. Our bodies move together as one and explode as we climax together.

My vagina is throbbing and convulsing, and I am wriggling under the sheets in my pleasure. I stop rubbing myself and move my hand away from my crotch. I am in my sheets, not in a field of daisies. I am in my bed—not with Tony—not with Mike. In my fantasy, I am in my bed with Paul.

Chapter 6
Forever and Always

Jessie crawls into bed with me at some ungodly hour. It is still dark out. I'm guessing it's around six. She cuddles into my back. We sleep like that for a good long while. Sometime later, I wake from my slumber with a groggy head and pad my way to the bathroom. I wince as my feet hit the floor. The first few steps are agony. As I sit on the toilet, I recount the events of the night before. That was possibly the best party yet. I catch a look at myself in the mirror and see that it's obvious I've been up late partying. I look rough, and every bit my age.

As I slip back into bed, Jessie asks, "How was your night?"

She's really asking how things went with Mike once we were alone. I ignore her curiosity and reply, "Great. I think it was the best party ever. I had such a fun time dancing."

"The dancing was the best part of last night. People were into partying. Any highlights of your evening?" She definitely wants to know about what happened with Mike, although she's not usually this subtle.

"Yes. Me trying to burn the house down! Can you believe I did that? That was a real senior's moment—leaving the potholder in the oven. Have you ever done anything like that?" I ask in a worried voice. "If Paul hadn't been there to save us all, we might be waking up at the community centre this morning, sleeping on the floor with a mat and a donated blanket! If a spark had hit the curtains, I might have caused serious damage. I can't believe I did that. It scares me."

"Don't be silly—you are not a senior. You just had too many things to do. Did you drink too much?"

"I drank, but I didn't drink too much. I didn't know where my glass was half the night."

"Did Mike have a good time?" There it is. She can't wait any longer.

"He said he did."

"Oh, come on! Give me more than that!" she says, whacking me on the arm. "What happened after Paul left?"

I can't believe how annoyed I still am that Paul isn't in the house this morning. My mind flashes back to my wet dream during the night. I roll toward her and rub my eyes.

"Nothing."

"You piss me off! Don't tease me. Give me the goods. What happened?"

"Honestly, nothing happened. Mike just went home. I didn't even get a peck on the cheek good night."

"What?" she exclaims. "Lover-boy just went home? You're not telling me everything. What happened?"

"Well, I think he is suspicious of Paul and me. He walked into the kitchen right as Paul was saving the day. He had his arms around me, and we were laughing. I guess it looked like something else was going on. Anyway, Mike interrogated me about what he saw and wondered if there was more to my relationship with Paul that he should know. Do you think that things will change with you guys if Mike and I continue this relationship?" I ask.

"Well—maybe. Mike might not want to share your life as a couple with the two of us. For example, he may not want to have dinner with us every night. And, you might not be here—you might be in Toronto—that would certainly change things. He might want to have you all to himself, so he can exhaust you with sex and dress you up in nothing but diamonds!" she adds jokingly.

"Don't be ridiculous!" I laugh. A flutter of panic rises in my stomach. I hadn't thought about changing my location. "Seriously—do you think things will change?"

"I don't know. I think it could. I guess it depends on how you go about it. You know—being clear with your expectations."

"One thing I know for sure is that I'm not giving up my relationship with Paul to have one with Mike. I was thinking about that last night when he was talking to me about it—with an accusatory tone I might add. My relationship with you won't change, so why would it have to change with Paul? Just because he's a man? Mike better not be the jealous type because that would make me crazy and destroy our relationship!"

"You mean it would make you more nuts than you are now, Ms. Pot-Holder-in-the-Oven!" she laughs, whacking me on the shoulder.

"I'm never going to live that one down! That was bad!"

"Seriously Ginny, if he doesn't already get how close we all are, you had better clue him in fast. He'll have expectations of what he wants your relationship with him to be like too. You'll have to consider that. I know you've been worried about the sex part, but it's not just about that—it's also about the day-to-day relationship stuff. When we were young, it was easier to adjust to each other's lives because that *was* our life—just hanging out together. But, Mike's life is separate from ours, and he didn't grow up with us. There will be adjusting to do, and it might not be easy for either one of you. You've had it your way for a very long time now."

"What do you mean I've had it my way?"

"I mean, you haven't had to consider anyone else. Life has been about your life and your children's lives. Paul and I fit into that because we've been a part of it since the beginning. You've never had to consider anyone else."

"I've never thought about any of that. I've only been obsessing about how scared I am to have sex." My thoughts flashback to last night's dream. What is happening to me? That was Paul in my dream. And it was good.

I say out loud, "I've got to think about that for a while. I'd like to get some more rest before the whole household starts to come alive."

"That works for me. I'm tired this morning. It was fun last night," she adds, muttering into her pillow. I think she's already half asleep.

"Mmm, it was," I say, remembering my dream again and rolling over.

—

Tony and I never once turned away from one another. If we were hopping mad at each other, we worked it out before the end of the day. We never just left or walked out. I am not sure how to deal with what has happened between Mike and me.

Tony and I had sex every day of our married life. Jessie had a hard time believing that, but we did. Other than when we weren't in the same place, or one of us was ill, or something like that. Otherwise, we did it every day, at least once. Jessie was in awe of that, and I think jealous. She would have liked nothing more.

It was just part of our repertoire. It was what we did. It became what we expected from one another, but it was mostly about love and pleasure. We enjoyed sex. It was fun and loving and nurturing, and it helped us to build a solid bond. We communicated through sex. Sex was a cornerstone of our relationship. I think it's why I've missed him the way I have.

He used to like to give me multiple orgasms. He worked hard at pleasing me, and that was one of his favourite things. He had this routine he would do with his fingers and wrist that was better than any vibrator I've ever come to know. He would get his fingers inside me and vibrate the heel of his hand on my clitoris, and it would drive me wild. If he suckled my nipple at the same time, I would orgasm forever. One time we watched the clock, and he was immensely pleased with himself because he made me come for twenty-five minutes just with his hand. He was beyond boastful when he eventually penetrated me with his penis and made me come even more.

I'm out of sorts today because of my dream. I'm jumpy as we go through our routine post-party house chores. Only when someone speaks directly to me, do I snap out of my preoccupation. Jessie thinks it's because of Mike, and the girls think I had too much to drink last night. Only I know the truth. I'm trying to figure out that damn dream.

I've never dreamt about Paul like that before. I've had plenty of orgasms in my sleep—that seems to happen to me when my bladder is full. Jessie just said "lucky you" when I told her about it years ago. I think she has to work pretty hard to achieve an orgasm, and even then, it doesn't necessarily happen for her. To make her feel better, I jokingly told her it's just because I have a big clitoris. She laughed and whacked me on the arm when I said that. Oh, and then she called me a bitch.

I love her.

But what is going on here with Paul? The intimation of my subconscious confounds me. Is Mike right? Is there more going on here than I've been aware of? Paul has just always been around, and I tell myself that it's only the fear of losing him in my everyday life that made that dream happen.

But it was so good.

I haven't had sex like that since Tony.

Oh, my goodness.

I love him.

But, that is not any different. I've loved Paul for years.

Last night I just stepped out of my party dress and fell into bed, and all my clothes and accessories are scattered around the floor. I hang up my dress and put my stockings into the lingerie bag for washing. I gently put my pearls into their velvet pouch. The fabric is luxurious. The beads have such lustre.

Tony gave them to me the night before our wedding, a gift to be worn on our wedding day. I cherish them. We were sitting on the front porch swing at my mom's and dad's place, and all the guests for the rehearsal party were inside. My parents were schmoozing them all, and plying them with alcohol. We stole away for a private moment. I gasped when I opened the box because the necklace glowed in the twilight. I didn't know much about pearls at the time, but my untrained eye could tell that they were exquisite. I thought he must have spent his last dollar on them, the way they shone in the evening light.

My engagement ring was not expensive. It was just a young person's "all I can afford" type of ring. It was pretty but small and ordinary, a quarter-carat diamond set into an unadorned ten-karat gold setting along with a plain gold wedding band. I assumed he had saved all his money to be able to afford these pearls as well.

"They were my grandmother's," he said quietly, trying to peer into my eyes. I was overcome with emotion and had my head down. "My grandfather gave them to her on their wedding day. It was one of the few things they brought with them from the old country."

It was quaint how he referred to Italy as the old country. His maternal grandparents were from there. They moved to Canada just before World War II broke out. They left with the clothes on their backs and the few treasures they could squirrel away in their pockets and carry bags. They did not have trunks full of exorbitant mementos.

"My mother told me that I could give them to my wife on my wedding day. I know it's not our wedding day, but I wanted you to have them for tomorrow, and I hope you'll wear them. I know I won't be seeing you tomorrow until the ceremony, so I thought this would be my last chance to give them to you."

I was so overwhelmed I couldn't speak. Hearing the story from Tony, I knew how much these pearls must have meant to his mother. I knew she must love me to give them to me. This gift was a symbol of her ultimate blessing of our nuptials. She had been vexed at me when I announced that I intended to keep my maiden name. Her life was steeped in tradition, and women did not do that in her world. She took my wishes as an insult. Tony explained to her that it was important to me to keep my identity and that it was what more and more women were doing these days. This gift was representative of her forgiveness and acceptance of my decision.

"They are lovely," I managed to whisper. "Thank you. I'll treasure them."

"You are welcome. Can I put them around your neck?" Tony asked gently.

"Please," I said, holding up my hair and turning my back to him. Once he had them clasped, I turned toward him to ask him how they looked, but my answer was in his eyes, and I needed no words.

"You are so beautiful," he leaned in and kissed me gently on my mouth.

Not a probing, sexual kiss, but a passionate, loving one. Our lips lingered in that precious moment.

Just then, Jessie burst out onto the porch. She was in high gear that night. She caught the scene before her and shouted inside the house, "I found them! They are out here making out. They can't wait until tomorrow!" she added with a big laugh. "Come on in, and join the party! People are wondering about you. You don't have cold feet, do you?"

"No. No cold feet out here," I replied calmly. "Look at what Tony just gave me," I said, showing her the pearls.

She let out a low whistle and threw her head back. "Wow! Those are beauties. That's what has been going on out here. How romantic. Sorry to interrupt you."

"It's alright. We should get back inside anyway. We'll be right in," I said quietly.

She's not always the most perceptive person, but she knew to excuse herself at that moment.

"See you in a while," she said as she went back inside.

Turning to Tony, I said, "I know how much this means to you, giving this gift to me. I want you to know how much I love you and that I can hardly wait to spend the rest of my life with you. Tomorrow can't come fast enough."

"You're my girl," he said lightly. "You always will be. It feels like I've loved you forever. I can't wait for you to become my wife."

He wrapped his arms around me, picked me up, and twirled me around the porch. I squealed with delight and tossed my head back, my long hair flowing behind me. I could feel the coolness of the pearls on my skin, and I knew this love would be forever. Wiping the tears from my eyes, we joined hands and went back into the party.

"Whatcha doin', Mom?" Christie asks, tiptoeing into my room. My head is down, and I have a tear in my eye. I turn my head away from her, not wanting her to see me cry.

"Oh, I'm reminiscing," I answer. Not looking up, I say, "I remember the day your father gave me these pearls."

"Mmm," she replies cautiously, not sure of my mood. "The night before you got married."

"Yes. They'll be yours one day, you know," I say, looking up at her.

"You haven't given up hope on me yet?" she asks.

"I'll never give up hope on you."

"I know, Mom," she says, waving her hand in front of her face. "Stop it, or you are going to make me cry. Come on. Put those silly pearls away, and come downstairs. Cath is just about ready to go. The house is all cleaned up."

I am surprised to see that it is starting to get dark. I don't like it when Cath leaves late in the day. She should have left a couple of hours ago so she would have light for the whole drive. Now there will be crazy drivers rallying down the road after a day of skiing. My stomach flips with fear. She and Danielle have their bags waiting at the door, and they are bundling into their coats and boots.

"I'll see you in less than two weeks, Mom. My last exam is ten days away. I can't wait to finish! I'll probably come home on the Saturday before Christmas."

I knew she would want to party with her friends from university before they all go home for Christmas. It will be the twenty-second by then. The big day will be almost upon us.

"That sounds good to me, honey. It's late. You should have left earlier. Are you sure you don't want to stay until morning?" I ask pleadingly.

"Oh, Mom, we can't. Danielle has to work in the morning, and we both have to study. You know I will drive safely. Nothing bad is going to happen," she says with the confidence of youth.

"Just drive carefully," I say, quietly swallowing the lump in my throat and hoping she doesn't sense my fear. Kissing me on the cheek, she grabs her bag and turns to the door.

"Thanks for a great weekend, Ms. Parker," Danielle comments. "I had a fun time."

"You are welcome to visit any time," I say, reaching in and giving her a peck on the cheek. She is a lovely girl.

"I'm going to go home too, Mom," Christie replies. She has Eddie's things all packed up at the door. "Bradley should be home from work soon, and I want to have supper ready."

"Take some leftovers. You know that, right?"

"Got 'em," she says, nodding her head toward one of her bags. "I raided the fridge and took all my faves!"

"Good girl," I say happily. Mothers love feeding their children. It doesn't matter how grown up they are.

"Well, girls, thanks for helping with the cleanup and thanks for staying over. I don't know about you, but I had a good time," I comment cheerfully.

"Christmas is your time, Mom. We wouldn't have missed it for anything." Christie plants a kiss on my cheek as she tucks Eddie onto her hip. "I'll call you later," she adds as she leaves.

I'm alone in my empty house. Jessie left a while ago, choosing to walk home. No one has made mention of the fact that Mike hasn't called today. It's bothering me, but not enough to pick up the phone to call him. If he has a bee in his bonnet about this topic, he will have to work it out for himself. I lie down on the couch and stretch out. The Christmas tree lights are on, as they have been all day, and they create the only light in the house. They shimmer and promise joy, but my mood is melancholy after all the fun and excitement. I'm tired.

Tony and I started this tree decorating tradition the year we got married. We didn't have extra money back then for extravagances like tree decorations. My mom gave us a box of old ones from when I was a kid to tide us over, but I wanted something shiny and new on my tree. When we came up with this idea, we invited all our friends, and the party caught on. Before we knew it, we had created a tradition. It's only been the last few years that my parents stopped travelling up for it. I think the drive is too hard for them now.

The first Christmas after Tony's death was hell. I thought I would lose my mind before the season was over. I was wracked with grief. Everywhere I turned, and everywhere I went, reminded me of him. Jessie and Paul made me have the party that year. They said they would help and that we should do it as a tribute to Tony. They said that we could think of it as a wake. My parents thought it was tasteless, yet the idea appealed to my mom's Irish ancestry. I wasn't sure I could do it, I felt so weak. It seemed like I was constantly crying. Jessie and Paul said that if I didn't do it, I probably would never do it again, and I knew they were right.

The long and the short of it is that we put on the party. It turned out to be great fun and was a welcome distraction from my desperate mood. Everyone brought something to eat and drink, lightening the workload for me. People went out of their way that year to exchange extraordinary tree decorations. Every year when those decorations go onto the tree, I remember my friends' generosity and love as they helped me navigate that awful time. People do care.

My daughters were so small and cute back then. They were oblivious to what was going on. They just didn't understand why Daddy wasn't coming home from work every day. It was hard to explain to them in a way they could understand. They were a pure joy to have in my life, that Christmas in particular. I think focusing on them is the only thing that kept me sane.

I'll never forget the night that Paul came to my door with the news. He was stricken. I could see that he had been crying. It was evident something horrible had happened. It was almost eleven at night when he showed up at my house. The girls were all tucked into bed, and I was unwinding with a glass of wine. I was feeling edgy because of the late hour. I hadn't heard from Tony and was wondering why he wasn't home yet. Doctors are often late getting home—it's the worst plight for the spouse of a doctor. I thought maybe he'd gone to the office to wrap up loose ends before the end of the workday. Work didn't usually bother Paul, though, and I was ill at ease seeing his bleary eyes and red face.

The police had gone to Paul first. Being the wife of a local doctor, they didn't want to show up at my door. Tony and Paul knew all the police officers in town, and the RCMP captain in charge of the station that night decided they should tell Paul first, knowing he would break the news to me. It was rightly so. It would have been far worse seeing a police car enter my driveway on a rainy November night. A person knows something terrible has happened. However, I didn't immediately know why Paul was here or why he was crying. He couldn't get words out. He couldn't look at me.

Trying to take his coat and rubbing his arm, I asked, "What is it, Paul? What's wrong?"

I had never before seen him like this.

"There was an accident," he choked out.

"Oh, it must have been a bad one. I was wondering why Tony was overly late getting home. I figured it was something like that. Is he coming behind you?" I asked, looking toward the door, expecting his headlights to shine into the front room window as he entered the driveway.

"No. No, Tony's not behind me," Paul said. "He's at the hospital."

"It must have been a terrible accident. What happened? Why are you here, and he is still working?" As I asked the question, I knew the answer. He wasn't working—he was the patient—it was Tony in the accident.

"He's not working, is he?" I asked quietly without looking up.

"No—he's not," Paul replied solemnly.

"Oh, my God! I've got to get to him!" I screamed as I lunged toward the closet for my coat. "Call Jessie! Get her over here to watch the kids!"

Grabbing my arm to slow me down and forcing my eyes to look into his, he said, "Ginny, there's something you need to know."

"No! No! Please don't say it! No! There is nothing I need to know! Let me go and let me get to him!"

"Ginny, slow down. Ginny, he's badly hurt. He's unconscious. He's had a serious head injury. He's in critical condition in ICU."

"Don't say that! Stop talking! Let me go! I have to go!" I bellowed at him, breaking into sobs. I could barely breathe. "Call Jessie right now!"

"I've already called her. She's on her way. She should be here any moment," he paused. Uncomfortably, he continued, "Ginny, I want you to prepare yourself for what you are going to see. He's in bad shape."

A car that should have been Tony's pulled into the drive. It was Jessie. I could hear her run up the stairs to the door. She burst in and ran to me, her eyes full of tears, and she wrapped her arms tightly around me.

"Go!" she said. "Get out of here! Go! Aunt Jess is here!"

Paul grabbed my hand and steered me out the door. It was the longest ride of my life. We only live a few minutes from the hospital, but the trip took an eternity. On the way, Paul filled me in on the details as he knew them. It was a single-car accident. No one else was hurt, only my Tony.

Pulling into the emergency department, I hopped out of the car before it came to a complete stop. I ran blindly to the admissions desk. The head ER nurse had been expecting me, and she escorted me right up to Tony's bed in intensive care.

His face was swollen beyond recognition. I told the nurse, "No. This man is not Tony. You've put me with the wrong patient. I want to see Tony."

From the tears in her eyes, I knew she had brought me to the right patient. Without words, she directed me to his bedside. I was filled with horror as I observed the sight before me. My beautiful Tony was mangled. He had a blood-soaked bandage around his head, and I could see a path of stitches leading up from his temple, across his forehead and up underneath the swaddled cloth. Both his eyes were swollen shut and were black and purple with bruising. His lower lip had stitches in it, where I learned afterward his teeth had gone through. His left arm was in a cast and slung up over his body, and his left leg was also in a cast. His leg was broken in four places. He had four broken ribs and multiple internal injuries. The tubes up his nose and down his throat confirmed he was not breathing on his own.

"No! You are lying! No!" I growled at her. "Take me to Tony right now!!"

Paul entered the room, and his eyes met mine. I knew that the nurse was not lying. I knew that this was Tony. My knees buckled underneath me, and I collapsed to the floor. I peed my pants.

"Ginny," Paul soothed as he rubbed my back. I could hear him choking back his tears. "Ginny, get up. Tony needs you. He needs to know that you are here and that you are okay. Let him know that, Gin."

Pulling me up from the hospital floor, he held my hand and guided me to the side of the bed. "His brain is very swollen. He's unconscious, but tell him you are here. Tell him."

My eyes wild with fear, I stabilized myself against the bed. I took Tony's right hand and told him I was there. I assured him that I would take care of him and that he would be alright. I let him know that he had been in a car accident and that he was recovering in the hospital. I told him he would be fine in no time flat and that I would take him home.

I was like a robot. My voice was empty and devoid of emotion. Separated from my body, I watched us from a corner of the ceiling, taking in the tableau below. A scared young wife, holding her sweetheart's hand, their best friend standing behind them, his hands on her shoulders, steadying her.

"What happened?" I asked later. Looking pleadingly into Paul's eyes, I asked him again, "What happened?"

"He was in a single-vehicle accident. He was coming up the hill where the big bend is. Remember I told you? The police say they don't know why his car went out of control."

"No. Please say this is not happening," I said to Paul in disbelief.

But, when my mother and father entered the small room, I knew it was all real. My Tony was in critical condition and might die. My mother kissed my head and rubbed my back while I wept into her shoulder. She passed me off to my father, and he did the same. Someone helped to clean me up and change me into a pair of scrubs.

It was an endless night. The thing I remember the most is the glaring hospital lights. The brightness of those lights is emblazoned in my memory. Maybe it was because I had been crying that the light bothered my eyes the way it did, but it was like there were blinding silver halos around all of the lights. They made me squint. I just wanted to turn the lights down and go to sleep. I wanted to wake up to a new day where my life was perfect again.

Tony's mother arrived the next day. My brother picked her up at the airport in Vancouver and brought her to us. After Tony's dad died a couple of years beforehand, she sold the farm in Delta and moved back to the town of Oliver, where her family was from, to live at the family vineyard. They have a big extended family with whom she now lives. She had been alone in her house on the blueberry farm in Delta, and I knew she felt lonely. I couldn't blame her for wanting to surround herself with her family. She caught the first flight out *in the morning and got to us as fast as she could.*

Paul had prepped James and told him to be sure to find him first upon Rosa's arrival. He wanted to be the one to prepare her for what she would see. It was one thing to hear about Tony's condition on the phone, but it was another thing to see the destruction with your own eyes. When Rosa entered Tony's room, she gasped in surprise at the sight of him and fell to her knees at his bedside. She buried her head in his side and whispered something in Italian. I can't imagine seeing my baby in the same condition as Tony. I can only imagine how she must have felt, looking at him that day.

He was more swollen, and if it were possible, more black and blue, with tinges of green and yellow and purple. His condition was dire. He was not expected to live, and he didn't. It was two more days of waiting for him to die. I never left his side once. My mother wanted me to go home to take a shower and get some sleep. She said I'd feel better. But, there was no hope in hell that sleeping and showering would make me feel better, and I was not leaving that room. Instead, my mom brought me some fresh clothes from home, and I made do with that. I asked that a cot be put beside his bed so I could lay beside him and hold his good hand. I never let go.

It was about two a.m. on the third night when I woke up to find that we were alone. There had been a bedside vigil, as no one wanted to venture very far from his side. I sat up and stretched. I looked past his injuries into his beautiful face and felt a tear trickle down my cheek. I was too tired to bother wiping it away. It just didn't matter. I remember watching it fall and splash onto his arm. I hoped it hadn't disturbed him in his deep slumber. I rubbed my thumb along the side of his hand and cried as I had never cried before. I knew he was leaving me. I knew there was nothing to be done except wait and let nature take its course. We had a clause in our living wills indicating that we were not to be kept alive artificially for more than three days, and the life support was coming off in the morning.

I knew I wasn't supposed to, but I couldn't stop myself. I climbed into Tony's bed, rested my head on his shoulder, and kissed his neck. Placing my arm around his torso, I started to talk to him, ramble, really, but talk to him I did. I said anything I could think of, anything that could make him feel better.

He had to know how much I loved him and that he wasn't alone. He had to know how badly I wanted him to stay. I started reminiscing. I babbled about the day we met, our first date, partying with our friends, our wedding day and how Paul had misplaced the wedding bands and had a last-minute frenzied panic looking for them, all our times dancing in the living room, the birth of our first child, our second child, the trip we took to Hawaii. Anything I could think of—anything fun and happy and light —anything good.

"You are my love, Tony," I whispered in his ear. "You are my only love. I love you with all of my heart. I will never forget you. You have been the best thing that ever came into my life, and I will always honour that. I will raise our daughters to know you, and they will never forget their daddy. I promise you that, my sweetheart. I said I would be your wife until death do us part, but I will be your wife forever—like we said that night on my mom and dad's porch. You are mine, and I am yours, and that's the way it will always be."

I closed my eyes and slept for one last time with my husband. When the hospital staff came in the next morning, they found me curled around him. I knew I had broken hospital protocol, but I didn't care. The night nurse turned a blind eye to my behaviour because I know she regularly checked his status. I've sometimes wondered what she thought when she peeked in that night. She just closed the door and let us be together one last night.

I rubbed my bloodshot eyes, climbed out of his bed, and was careful not to drag any of his attachments with me or bump him in any way. It seemed like it was only minutes before our family showed up in his room. We were all standing around his bed, holding hands when the life support equipment was turned off.

It was the strangest thing to witness. I had a vision in my mind of how it was going to go. I thought that his body would die immediately, but it didn't happen that way for Tony. For a fleeting second, I thought maybe he would continue to breathe on his own. I remember my eyes searching Paul's, and I'm still not sure if I imagined it or not, but I think he shook his head almost imperceptibly. No, Tony wasn't going to live. This is how it goes. Because his breathing had stopped, his organs would start to shut down. His brain function was already lost. Eventually, his heart would give in. In his final moment, his body convulsed, and he was gone.

I'm not sure how long we stood that way, waiting. I don't know how long it took. The room was filled with love and sorrow. Everyone who loved him was there the day he died. Well, except for his babies. They were home with Jorrie and Ben. Bless their great big hearts.

Rosa was a class act that day. She was stoic, and it helped me. She didn't cry like the crazed Italian mamas in the movies when they are overcome with grief. She crossed herself, and I could see her lips moving in silent prayer. I can only guess what her thoughts were. Possibly, she remembered the day Tony was born. This fine boy she had given birth to, this wonderful son who had made her infinitely proud. She crossed herself, and then she came to me and wrapped her arms around me. Holding me in her loving arms, she never said a word, she just embraced me and let me cry. All of the love she had for Tony poured into me, and she was my mama too. She held me that way until my tears were spent. Kissing me on my forehead, she laid me down on my cot beside Tony and tucked me into my bed. She sat silently on the edge of the cot beside me and held my hand.

I could hear others around us, but I was oblivious. A doctor came in and officially pronounced Tony dead. They unhooked him from the traction and all his tubes. People were buzzing around the room, but no one was bothering us. They let us be there with him. I didn't sleep, but it felt good to rest. I lay there and let Rosa love me. I needed it as much as she did.

Shaking my head and wiping my eyes, I pick myself up from the couch and turn the Christmas tree lights off. Streetlight illuminates the foyer and guides my path upstairs. Without turning on any lights, I strip down and search around for my nightgown. Slipping silently into bed, I pull the covers to my chin and close my eyes on that grim memory from so long ago.

Chapter 7
Growing Pains

"We have some work to do."

I jump in my seat. I was engrossed in my job and hadn't heard the door to the shop open, even though it has a bell at the top that tinkles when someone enters. I guess the Christmas music drowned it out. I'm sitting at the service desk, which happens to be at the back of the store, and I look up to see Mike. I must have a blank look on my face because he repeats himself.

"What?" I ask. I am cloudy minded and disoriented, tired from the weekend and in a dark mood. I woke up this morning with smeared mascara from crying myself to sleep. I had a kink in my neck, and I'd hurried out of the house without breakfast because I was late. I'm not sure what time it is now. I rub my eyes and glance at my wristwatch—it's eleven-thirty. I have been consumed in my paperwork for about an hour.

If I understand him correctly, he is talking about our relationship and not about my paperwork. It seems far too early in our courtship to have any work to do. Shouldn't it just be all about fun at this point? I don't have the energy for this conversation. I continue to stare at him blankly.

"Ginny," Mike replies calmly, getting to the point. "I'm sorry about Saturday night."

"Oh," I reply quietly. I put my head down and look away. Do I accept his apology? Do I say I am sorry too? Am I? I'm not sure. A lump starts to grow in my throat, and my eyes begin to tear up. "What do you mean, we have some work to do?"

"I mean that we should talk about what happened at the end of the night on Saturday."

"Oh," I repeat lamely. There is a pregnant pause as we both search for what to say next.

"The shop looks festive," he says—filling the silence.

"Thanks," I reply, looking around my tastefully decorated room. It does look lovely. I am exhausted this morning and thankful the shop isn't busy. My store gets lots of customers at Christmas, but this day has started slowly. I stretch and stifle a yawn. I'm not in a good mood.

"Can I take you out for lunch? Maybe we could talk it out."

He is trying, but I don't feel like conversing. I have such mixed emotions. I am raw from the memories of last night and the conflict of the night before. I keep my head down and avoid eye contact.

"I'm not trying to put you off, but I'm sorry, I can't go for lunch. I have too much paperwork to sift through this morning, and I want to take advantage of this slow start to the day."

It is snowing quite vigorously outside, which sometimes keeps customers hunkered down in their condos enjoying warm beverages, rather than poking around in shops.

He looks chastised, and I feel bad.

"Ginny ..." he begins. His eyes search my face.

"Mike, don't," I cut him off. "It's not that I don't want to talk. You are right—we need to. I just don't want to right now. I'm tired and disheartened this morning."

He shifts his body and looks away, "It's not the right place and time."

"That's right—it's not," I say. There is an uneasy pause, and we both start talking at the same time. "I apologize, you go first."

"It's a lot of competition."

"What do you mean? What is?" I question.

125

"Your friendship with Jessie and Paul—it's a lot of competition," he comments quietly. This time he is the one looking down at the floor.

"You don't have to compete with them. There is no contest," I say firmly. "Jessie and Paul are as much a part of me as my daughters are. They are my family!"

"I know. I see that. It's just an unusual relationship. I don't have a close friendship bond like that with anyone. My brother would be the closest, but it's not like what you have."

"I'm extremely fortunate to have them in my life. They mean the world to me." I am defensive.

"I know. I'm sorry. I'm not used to friendships like that. Over the years, I have spent a lot of time on the road and away from home. I don't have anything like that in my life."

I can tell he is sincere in his apology.

"If you are the jealous type, this relationship will probably not work, and we should probably cut ourselves loose from it right now." I can't believe the boldness of my statement, and I certainly hadn't meant to blurt it out in such a hurtful manner. I surprise myself. I'm more surprised by the massive sense of relief I feel once I've said it.

"Whoa. Slow down," Mike says, reaching for my hand and searching my eyes again. I let him take my hand. His is warm and comforting. My fingers are cold, and it feels good to have my hand held. He rubs his thumb over the back of my hand. "I don't know if I'm the jealous type. I don't think I am. That side of me has never been challenged before."

What is that supposed to mean? Does he always get what he wants? He is wealthy and privileged, so maybe. The door to the store chimes as someone enters the shop. We both look up. I automatically put a smile on my face and greet the person.

"Listen," I whisper, needing a quick conclusion to our conversation. "I can't go for lunch. I'm too tired, and I have too much to do. Jessie and Paul aren't coming over tonight as I want a quiet night at home by myself. How would you like to come over for supper tomorrow evening and join us then?"

126

"I understand," he comments. "I'd love to do that. What time?"

"Around six o'clock. Don't bring anything. Just come and hang out with us. It will be completely casual. I might put you to work peeling carrots," I smile bashfully, hoping we have partial resolution and have called a truce.

"Deal," he says firmly, that slow, sexy grin of his returns to his handsome face. He looks hopeful. "I'll see you then."

"Okay."

He starts to move toward the door and stops midway, looking back at me as if he wants to say something more. He mouths a silent "thank you" as our eyes meet across the room, and he lifts his hand in a wave as he braces himself for the storm. I catch a glimpse of him raising his collar and shrugging down into his coat as I walk toward my customer with a smile and a greeting.

—

It's been a long day. I didn't think five o'clock would ever come. I am thankful that the lack of customers persisted because it allowed me to get ahead of the game at work. It's one good thing that has come out of today. It has snowed almost two feet, but our winter roads are kept in top condition, and it's an easy drive home. I am anxious to get into my nightie and call it a day. The outdoor Christmas lights uplift me as I enter the driveway.

Letting myself into the house, I am silently grateful for programmable thermostats and light timers. They are two more modern conveniences I never dreamed I'd get. The house is dark inside, but toasty warm. I turn the kitchen light on and pour myself a glass of wine. I make my way into the living room to turn on the Christmas tree lights. Standing back and admiring the festive beauty of my gorgeous tree, my eye goes to a crystal snowflake. It's a collectable—a new one is released every year, and this is the only one I have. Tony gave it to me on what turned out to be his last Christmas, almost a full year before he died. I hold it gently and turn it over in my hand, patting it with loving tenderness. That old familiar sadness wells up inside me—that feeling that never really goes away.

Going upstairs to change my clothes, I decide to have a bath rather than jump right into my nightie. I tie my hair in a ponytail and remove my makeup while waiting for the tub to fill. Slipping into the bath, I take a sip of my wine. My mind wanders back, and I allow myself to remember that hideous day.

"You're going to be late! Hurry up!" I demanded. I was short-tempered that morning. The girls both had chest colds, and I was seriously concerned about them. I was tired because I'd been looking after them non-stop for the last few days.

"Settle down! I know I'm late!" Tony called to me in a stressed voice. He was agitated too. He came out of our bathroom, adjusting his tie, swiping his hair back and tucking in his shirt all at the same time. He was rushing to sit down on the bed to put on his shoes. He had become involved with a cohort of doctors in North Vancouver and had an important meeting with them that day. He was running late.

"You should have gotten yourself organized last night," I sounded like an old fishwife.

"You should have gotten yourself organized last night," he mimicked me under his breath, thinking I hadn't heard. I'm pretty sure I saw him roll his eyeballs.

"Did you just mimic me?" I questioned. I remember stopping mid-stride as I was trying to collect some of his things for him. My head snapped back, I halted and dropped his stuff on the floor. Putting my hands on my hips, I felt exasperated.

We usually got up early. As a matter of course, we set our alarm for five in the morning, rolled toward each other, made love and began our day. However, this particular morning, our alarm clock hadn't gone off. We had both overslept. It was ten-to-seven before I woke up and realized he was still sleeping. I knew he had to be on the road by seven o'clock, and it was seven-fifteen now, and he had to stop by his office before making his way into the city.

"Yes, I just mimicked you, Ginny! What good does it do telling me I should have gotten myself organized last night? Do you think I don't know that?

Leave me alone, and let me get ready," he yelled at me.

I could hear one of the girls crying. I looked at him with tears in my eyes. He never spoke to me that way, and I felt hurt by his words. I was silent and gave him a long, hard look. I know my bottom lip was quivering, but I worked to set my jaw and not cry. I stepped over his coat and briefcase and stomped off to the girls' room. A few minutes later, I heard the garage door open and his car leave.

We hadn't said goodbye to one another. We hadn't made love. We hadn't even kissed each other that morning. The next time I saw him was in his hospital bed that night. After that brutal day of dealing with the girls being fractious, and the simmering, residual anger I felt because of our behaviour that morning, the next time I saw him was after the accident—the accident that ultimately took his life.

I wipe my face with a facecloth and contemplate the colossal misfortune of that day. Tony and I rarely fought. Our alarm clock always went off. He was always organized for work. The girls were never both ill at the same time. I knew his day was long, and I knew I should have just been quiet and left him alone to get ready. But I was aggravated that morning and couldn't stop myself from badgering him. I was a mother with two sick kids. A long day of caretaking was ahead of me. I knew the two of us would make up the moment he walked through the door that night. All would be forgiven, and we would carry on. Our love would prevail, as it always did. But, it didn't happen that way.

Holding my breath, I lie back in the tub, submerging myself and soaking my hair. I have to wash this day off, and the indelible memory of that awful day, so very long ago. I scrub the shampoo into my scalp and sink under the water for a rinse. The lump in my throat that has been building all day dissolves, and I come up gasping for air. The tears that have threatened me throughout the day come pouring out. I hear my voice resonate on the walls of the bathroom. At first, I don't recognize the sound of my crying. It sounds empty and desolate and echoes my feeling of being unforgiven. Then I realize it sounds just like me.

—

"Private Mike is reporting for carrot peeling duty—ma'am!" Mike announces, with a click of his heels and a military salute. His back is poker straight, and his eyes are looking ahead at nothing. He is really putting it on.

I laugh as I wipe my hands on my apron and pull him into the house. "That's funny!" I say. "Carrot-peeling duty is already taken, but I have some potatoes that need to be peeled. How are your skills at that?"

"My skills are expert, ma'am! My father owned a chain of restaurants. I've peeled millions of potatoes in my day!" he replies, continuing his parody and standing taller while puffing out his chest. His voice is clipped, and his eyes are laughing.

"Fantastic. Get to it then!" I order with a giggle, pointing to the kitchen.

I purposefully don't take his coat. I figure if he is going to be part of the gang, he will have to learn to be self-sufficient. I turn and go back to the kitchen, letting him figure out what to do next.

When he gets into the kitchen, Jessie tosses him an apron and says, "Pull up a stool, man! I have a paring knife ready for you, and there's your pile of potatoes. Better get busy!"

Thank goodness for Jessie. She is excellent at helping people feel comfortable. I guess she too figures that if he is going to be part of this group, the sooner he develops a communal work ethic, the better. She pats a stool at the kitchen island, inviting him to sit beside her.

"Your wish is my command," he says, bowing to her. She laughs and whacks him on the arm. Good old Jessie. What would I do without her?

"I hope you like pork chops," I announce. "We have grilled chops with a side salad, carrots, sautéed broccoli, and potatoes."

"That sounds delicious!" he replies enthusiastically, tying his apron around himself and settling into his seat. He has on a pair of black designer jeans and a black, long-sleeved T-shirt. He looks delicious, and I hate to see him cover up with the apron.

"Paul won't be here for another half hour," Jessie informs him. "Want some wine?"

"Sure. Thanks," Mike comments, waiting to be served.

Jessie continues peeling carrots. She never was one for serving a man. She has a thing about letting them look after themselves. I don't know if that has anything to do with growing up in a house full of women or not. After a moment, she sees that Mike has not moved.

"Glasses are in the cupboard—help yourself. There's white in the fridge if you prefer that," she nods her head in the direction of the wine bottle.

"Or I can make you a cocktail if you like. Would you prefer a martini or a Caesar?" I ask while chopping veggies for the salad.

"No, no—this is great. Thanks," he says, filling his glass and taking a sip.

"Tell me—how's everything?" Jessie asks him as he seats himself back down. "Did you have a good day?"

"I did, yes. Thank you. Operations at the restaurant are in good shape. Launching our opening in the summer has paid off as we have the kinks all worked out in time for the holiday season. All systems are go and ticking along nicely."

"Right on," Jessie says. She knows the importance of being ready for the winter season. Businesses located in a world-renowned ski town, have to be on top of their game with top-notch training systems and standards for their employees.

"How about you, ladies? Did you have a good day?" he asks us, looking first at me and then at Jessie.

"I did," I announce. I had a sound sleep last night after going to bed early, and I'm feeling much better than yesterday. After my bath, I made myself a peanut butter sandwich and crawled under the sheets. I think I fell asleep by seven-thirty. "Work was busier today than yesterday. People were venturing out after yesterday's storm. I sold that sofa I picked up at that old house in Point Grey! Remember the estate sale we went to, Jess?"

"That's great! It was a nice piece," she comments. "I hope you picked up a good bit of coin for it."

"I did all right," I say quietly, putting my head down and shying away.

We never talk about finances. She never asks me how much money I make at the store, and I never ask her how much money she makes at the hotel.

"We had fun that day," she comments. We met Catherine and Danielle for a late lunch and had a walk along Kitsilano Beach before heading back home. We had some good laughs with the girls—it was a happy day.

"I had a good day today, too," Jessie shares. "We are ramped up for the holiday season. The hotel is looking gorgeous with all the lights and decorations. You should come on by and have a look at the gingerbread village. It's better than usual this year."

"I will. I'd like that," I say. "You should come with me, Mike. Maybe some evening this week, we can go over and take a look."

His eyes meet mine, and my knees weaken as he gives me an intense, smouldering look. He raises his right eyebrow and grins that sexy grin.

"I'd love to," he comments cheerfully. His gaze lingers, and his eyes roam my face and neck. I hope he didn't see me squirm, and I'm glad I have a turtleneck on, so they can't see the blush that is rising on my décolletage. I look away to avoid his gaze. He continues to look at me as if drinking me in.

I hear someone cleaning their boots on the front porch. Bradley calls it the Canadian foot-stomp because everyone here automatically kicks the snow off their boots before entering a building. Paul enters the house and comes around the corner into the kitchen carrying a brown paper bag of groceries while removing his scarf. His hair is tousled, and he has snow on his coat.

"I brought a few things from the store," he comments, pulling out a carton of milk, some eggs and a box of cereal. "I figure your shelves might be empty after the weekend eating frenzy."

Jessie and Paul are good about helping out with groceries. Because we eat together as often as we do, they just come over with food whenever they see something on sale or crave their favourites. It works out. It's my house, but it's our food. We share.

"You're here early," Jessie comments.

"Yeah—my last patient didn't show up. I had time to swing by the store to pick up a few things on my way," he informs us as he removes his coat and hangs it on a hook in the hall.

As he enters the room, I pass him a glass of wine and say, "I was just about to put the chops on, your timing is perfect."

Taking an appreciative sip, he thanks me and shakes hands with Mike. Everyone seems comfortable. I've decided that Mike will have to sink or swim.

"We were just talking about what a good day we each had," Jessie comments. "How was yours?"

"It was good, thanks. It's the calm before the storm," Paul replies.

Jessie and I both know what he means. School is out in less than two weeks, and Paul knows that once that happens, the ski hills will be jam-packed with people, and his office will flood with injured people. He offers a walk-in medical service during the holiday season. If the first aid station on the mountain gets inundated with sprained wrists and pulled muscles, they often refer patients to him. It helps to take the pressure off of the ER and leaves them to deal with the more severe injuries, like broken legs and arms, or worse. Running his hands through his hair, he sits down on a chair at the kitchen table.

Looking around, he asks, "Anything I can do to help?"

"You could set the table, I suppose. That would be great," I answer. "Supper won't be long now."

Getting up from his spot, he goes to the drawer that stores the placemats. He knows I like to protect my table. Tucking placemats and napkins under his arm, he moves to the cutlery drawer. He has set the table a million times and has a routine. I am surprised he asked if there is a job to be done. He always pushes up his sleeves and pitches in, knowing exactly what to do.

"Supper's ready," I announce. "Mike, we serve ourselves from the stove. We don't usually get too fancy. There are fewer dishes that way."

"That's right!" offers Paul. "And since I do most of the dishes around here, we like to use as few as possible."

It's a jibe at Jessie, who hates doing dishes. Being one of the youngest in her family, washing up was one of her jobs. She detested it, especially at big family events, when everyone seemed to revert to old-fashioned ways, with the men and boys retiring to the living room to relax after a meal, leaving the women and girls to clean up and do the dishes.

"Hey! I do my part around here!" she laughs, knowing she is being teased. "I peel carrots regularly!"

"And now that you've got Mike to help you with that, you can retire," retorts Paul.

"Oh, shut up!" she laughs, whacking him on the arm as we line up at the stove.

They let me serve myself first. It's a sweet gesture, and I secretly like it. I am the matron of the home. It's my kitchen, and I am responsible for most of the meals, which earns me the right to go first. Mike falls in line behind me, and we all dish up.

"Now that Ginny has a boyfriend—does this mean that you and I will be getting together?" With wide-eyed innocence, Jessie looks at Paul. Her questioning face is mischievous, and she is stifling a laugh.

Paul nearly gags on his first bite and lets out a laugh. "You'd like that, wouldn't you, you vixen, you," he teases.

"My daddy would be doing a jig in Heaven if he looked down and saw me with the honourable Dr. Tate," she swoons—hamming it up for Mike, who seems to be mystified by the conversation.

"Oh, you're more woman than I would ever want to handle," Paul says jokingly, looking at her fondly.

"Come on, Uncle Paul, loosen up—what's wrong with me anyway?" she pouts, sticking out her lower lip. She is using a cartoonish voice, and it cracks me up.

"All right, you two—quit putting on a show for Mike," I demand. "We don't have to act like we are in high school again. I think the two of you have lost your minds!"

"I'm not putting on a show, I'm serious—Jess is too much woman for me!" Paul reinforces with a laugh.

Jessie, a chronic fast eater, puts her knife and fork on her plate and flounces to the kitchen sink, pretending her pride is hurt. "Humph!" she snorts. "I'll take that as a backhanded compliment."

They are both grinning at each other. It is good to see them spar this way. For an instant, I wonder why they have never become a couple. I've never considered that before, but it would have made good sense.

After supper, Jessie and Paul both excuse themselves with things they have to do at home. It was a fun evening, and this entire arrangement feels promising to me. Now it is just Mike and me standing at the door. I get his coat from the front closet and hold it for him as he puts on his boots.

"So, that's how it goes around here."

"Yes," I reply. "That's pretty much it. We eat, visit, check-in with each other, and call it a night."

"It was fun," he says plainly. "You're lucky to have such close friends."

"I know I am. I think I could not have endured my life without them."

"They are good friends to you, and I can tell they love you very much."

"I love them too."

Putting his coat on and zipping it up, he reaches for me and gently kisses me. "I had a great time tonight. Thank you for inviting me. I hope I fit in."

He put his hand on the door handle, and just as he is about to turn it, I reach for his free hand and stop him.

"You fit in," I say, looking directly into his eyes.

Encouraged by my words, he lets go of the door handle and wraps his arms around me, encompassing my whole body with his embrace. I am small in his arms. He bends his head down and tips my chin up toward him. His lips find mine, soft and warm and gentle. His tongue probes my mouth, and I automatically press my body against his. Every bit of me is alive and tingling. Aphrodite is sitting cross-legged, floating three feet above my shoulder. I don't try to shush her. I wrap my arms around Mike's neck and draw him closer to me, our lips hot and wet and searching.

135

"I'd better be on my way," he breathes huskily into my ear while releasing himself from our embrace. "Will I see you tomorrow? Should we go to the hotel and look at the gingerbread houses? I'll be going home to see my folks on Saturday."

It is sweet of him to ask. I don't suppose it's something that he really wants to do, but he knows enough about me by now to know that I would want to see the display.

"I can't tomorrow because Jessie and I are going to yoga tomorrow night. We missed our class this evening. How about we have a regular supper here Thursday night with Jessie and Paul, and then on Friday night, we go over to look at the display? Maybe we can make a night of it and have a cocktail in the lounge afterward."

"That sounds like a date," he grins. "Would you like to have dinner in my suite?"

I forget that he lives at the hotel. In my mind, people don't live in hotels. "That would be a treat!" I exclaim. "That sounds better than the usual Friday night toast and eggs before flopping on the couch with a bowl of popcorn!"

"That's great then. I'll arrange it. Would you like me to pre-order, or would you like to order for yourself?"

"Ooh—surprise me," I say, clapping my hands together. "The possibilities are endless!"

"I hope so," he looks at me with intense, searching eyes. I can see the longing in his expression, and I am impressed by his self-control. He gives me a peck on the cheek and stands in the open doorway.

"Until Thursday," I say to him with a smile.

"Until Thursday," he repeats, giving me one last long look before closing the door behind him. I lean my back against the door and close my eyes, focussing on my breath as I hear his car drive away.

⟶

"Okay. Yes—okay," I am fiddling with the telephone cord as I speak to Jessie. "Yes, I can bring that to you. Alright—see you there." I wave to

Paul as I hang up the phone. He is coming in with more groceries in his arms. He shakes his head as he takes his coat off and hangs it up in the hall closet.

"You're early! I didn't expect you for a while yet." I exclaim as he enters the kitchen. "That was Jessie. She won't be joining us for supper tonight. She has something she has to take care of at work, and she is going to meet me at spin class later. Did you see her scarf around anywhere? She says she thinks she left it here."

"I just saw it in the coat closet, hanging on a hanger." Jessie's clothes are easy to identify because she usually wears coral or peach or some shade of orange. If he had never seen her scarf before, he would have known it was hers because I never wear those colours.

"Okay, good. I'll get it and put it with my gym bag." Stepping out to the foyer, I rummage through the closet and call back to him, "We have eggs for supper tonight. I'm going out tomorrow night, so I thought I'd do our usual Friday night supper this evening. Sorry to disappoint!"

"No problem," he calls back as he puts away the groceries he brought. "What's up? Where are you going?"

I go to the fridge and get out the carton of eggs as I answer him, "Mike is taking me out for dinner and then we are going to see the gingerbread house display at the hotel."

My comment seems to fall into dead air. I'm not sure if I imagined it, but it seems to be still between us for a moment longer than it should be. There's a pause, and neither of us speaks.

"I see," he comments, sounding hollow.

I put my head down and rub my toe into the floor—feeling self-conscious, and holding onto the counter to steady myself. This situation is weird for me, so I suppose it is equally strange to Paul.

"Thanks for the other night," I say. A lump rises in my throat, and sweat starts to pop out on my upper lip. I pray to God that I won't cry, and I set my jaw stubbornly. This is Paul. I can be honest with Paul, and I don't have to feel embarrassed. He hasn't answered me, and I look up to see him watching me.

"I said thanks for the other night," I repeat.

"You're welcome. But, there's nothing to thank me for," he comments quietly, still looking at me steadily.

"Oh, there is. You—"

"Ginny—I would do anything for you," he interrupts me. "You don't have to thank me for doing something routine like that. If this is something you want, then—"

It's my turn to interrupt. "Still—it must be difficult for you. I mean, I know we've never been an item, but it's strange having a fourth in our circle. Thanks for being gracious and welcoming toward Mike."

Rushing toward him, I wrap my arms around his neck, hugging him tightly. I wish I could repay him for every kindness he has ever shown me. I don't want things to be difficult for him, and I need him to know how much I don't want to lose him. His arms are around me, holding me tight. I am acutely aware of the warmth of his neck and the smell of his hair. Turning away, I swiftly wipe a tear from my eye as I free myself. If he has noticed my tears, he doesn't comment. Taking my hand, he turns me to face him.

His voice catches as he quietly repeats, "I would do anything for you."

The air is still between us, and neither of us moves. We stand looking at one another and are both startled when we hear a knock at the door. Paul clears his throat and rubs his eyes as if shaking himself out of a trance. I pull my sweater down further onto my hips and pat my hair as if my mother has just walked in on me, making out with a boy.

Looking down and clearing my throat, I say, "I'll get that."

I move quickly to the door and paint a smile on my face. The interchange with Paul has shaken me. I am uncertain of its meaning, and I'm not sure what he is telling me. I greet Mike with a blazing smile.

"Hi! Come on in!" I say, gesturing for him to hurry and closing the door behind him.

He reaches in and gives me a peck on my cheek. "Hello, gorgeous!" he says with a grin.

Laughing, I reach out to help him take off his coat. He removes his boots and puts them on the rubber mat by the door.

"It's cold out there tonight! Come on in—do you want a cup of coffee?" I ask, hoping to sound natural.

"Sure—thanks—that would be nice," he agrees, rubbing his hands together briskly. "It will help to take the chill off."

"For sure. Come on into the kitchen. Help yourself to coffee. I'm just getting the eggs on."

We spoke to each other earlier today, so he knows we are having a quick supper tonight, and that Jessie and I are heading off together in time for our seven-thirty class. I am happy that he is trying to get into the routine of things with us. I suspect a quick divergence like dinner tonight probably isn't right up his alley—especially now, knowing that all he is getting is eggs. Mike is making an effort to fit in, and I appreciate it. The sooner he learns my routines, the sooner he will be able to adapt to my lifestyle—or not. I purposefully don't think about whether I will have to adjust to his.

Paul is busy slicing up a beautiful loaf of artisan bread that he brought. It is from one of our local bakeries. He would have gone early in the day to snag this particular loaf, because of its popularity, it sells out fast. He has the toaster out and is about to get started on making the toast. The men greet each other while Mike pours himself a coffee.

"I hope you men don't mind if I fry these eggs. I was going to poach them, but I think I want fried instead. I have to let my supper settle before I get on that bike, so I want to eat right away."

"No hurling allowed," Paul commands.

"Yuck. That's for sure," I comment. Worse than the hurling idea is the heartburn I am getting more and more often as I age. If my food doesn't have time to digest before I get on that bike, I will suffer later.

The toast is made, the eggs are ready, and we settle around the table with our plates. I remember the cheese platter I prepared earlier, so I retrieve it from the fridge. Jessie recommends letting cheese sit out for a while to warm a bit. She says it tastes better, that it mellows and opens up the flavours like a good wine, but I can't let myself do that. To me, cheese needs to be refrigerated.

"Jessie begged off at the last minute," I tell Mike. "Something came up at work that she has to take care of. I'll be catching up with her at spin class."

The conversation is more stilted than the other night when Jessie was here. I wish she would show up at the door. Paul and I haven't made eye contact since Mike arrived on the scene. Thank goodness, Paul isn't entirely without social skills. He picks up the conversation and starts to make small talk with Mike.

"What are your plans for Christmas, Mike? Are you sticking around town?" he asks amiably. Paul can turn on the gift of the gab when it is necessary.

Shifting in his seat, Mike answers, "No, I'll be heading back to Toronto on Saturday to see my folks. I have some business to catch up on at my head office, so I'm giving myself extra time before the big day. My parents live in Toronto. They are getting quite elderly. I spend time with them at Christmas because it means a lot to my mother."

I'm touched by how dear his mother is to him. He treasures her and shows her how much she means to him every chance he gets. I think Mike is a good son, and she is probably looking forward to seeing him. I secretly wonder about her and decide she must be an upstanding woman to have raised a man like Mike.

"Mmm, yes—Christmas can have that effect on women," Paul says as he winks at me. This friendly gesture relaxes me. He knows I am tense and worried. "Is that where you grew up? Toronto?"

"Yes, it is. My dad's family are long-time residents. How about you? Will you be going anywhere for the holidays?"

Being a West Coast girl, I've only been to Toronto a couple of times when Jessie lived there. I don't know much about that city, so I only half-listen when Mike talks about it, but I know he grew up in the neighbour-hood of Rosedale. His parents live in the same house where his dad grew up. Mike grew up there too, but he lives in a condo downtown now.

"No, no—I don't go anywhere at Christmas. I'm needed here," Paul says. I'm not sure if he is referring to my house or his job.

"Paul offers a walk-in medical service over the Christmas break. It keeps him very busy. We don't usually see much of him," I offer as I refill our coffee cups.

"Thanks, Gin," Paul says automatically. "Yes, it certainly takes up my time."

"Where are you from, Paul?" Mike asks.

"I grew up in Kamloops, but I don't ever get back there. My folks passed away a few years ago, so there is no reason for me to visit."

"I'm sorry to hear that. Do you have other family members?"

"No, I don't. I'm one of those stereotypical spoiled brats—an only child," he says with a smile.

"I see," Mike comments quietly, looking pensive.

There is a pause in the conversation, while the two men digest their newfound information about one another. Paul is possibly glad to hear that Mike won't be around for the Christmas season, and Mike might feel worried that Paul will be. I am surprised by the amount of information Paul has offered to Mike. He doesn't usually tell much about himself, especially to someone he barely knows.

Years ago, a bunch of us went down to Locarno Beach one warm summer night. We thought we were cool—almost rebels because we took with us a couple of bottles of red wine, a baguette and some cheese. It's against the law to drink alcohol in public areas, so it would have been a big deal to get caught. That aside, we felt pretty grown up taking along wine and cheese, rather than beer.

We were pouring the wine into plastic cups when Jessie commented on how disappointed her dad would be if he knew she was drinking in a public place. I agreed and said something along the same line as Jessie. My dad used to be a business professor at the university I attended. He's always been pretty straight and narrow. He would not have been happy with me if he had known about our beach party. Some of the other girls in the crowd concurred, and I heard Paul snicker. He said that his dad wouldn't have noticed that he wasn't home.

I remember that moment because we all got quiet and looked at him. He was lying on his back, resting his head on his hand. His long body was stretched out, and his sleeveless T-shirt was riding up at the waist, revealing his lean, muscled torso. I could see some of the girls trying not to look, but not being able to stop themselves. He never had to try very hard with girls. They did the work for him. His bare feet dug into the sand, and his free hand was running sand through his fingers. He was looking up at the twilight sky, and at that moment, with those words hanging over us, he was alone in the crowd. Our dads knew where we were and what we were doing. We often wished they didn't know as much about our activities so that we could have more freedom.

Tony was working at his summer job that night. He worked on his mom and dad's blueberry farm during the summer. It was harvest time, and he had to work late. Once we got the fire going, kids started to pair off. I remember moving over to sit beside Paul. I just wanted to be near him that night. Jessie was flirting with some boys who were hanging around playing beach volleyball and had migrated our way. We sat quietly for the longest time, just looking at the fire.

"My old man doesn't give two shits about me," he said out of the blue.

"Oh," I said feebly. It was such an unexpected comment, and I had a hard time believing such a statement. "I'm sure that's not true."

"It's true," he said, turning to look at me.

I looked into his eyes, and I saw real sadness that I hadn't noticed before. Paul was always composed. He was friendly but aloof, was there but at the periphery. He was participating, but not.

"I'm sorry."

"Don't be. I'm all right. My life is better without him," he said, looking back at the fire.

It dawned on me that Paul never went home. We knew that his dad worked as a mechanic for one of the railways. Paul could have easily got on with the railway and pulled in some big money over the summer. He was on scholarship, so he didn't need to work in the summer like the rest of us, but he did. He spent his summers in a research lab working for one of the doctors at the hospital.

"My dad is an alcoholic," he said as if he needed to explain.

"Oh," I replied, once again feeling at a loss for words and not knowing how to respond. I quickly ran through all the parents in my life, and I couldn't think of anyone I knew that was an alcoholic. My dad liked his martini on a Friday night, but that was about the extent of it. I had never once seen him drunk.

"He used to kick the crap out of me every chance he got until I got too big," he said as if speaking to himself. "Better me than my mom."

He got up and left me to sit at the fire by myself. I watched him walk to the water's edge, where he waded for a while before coming back and joining the crowd. He didn't sit back down beside me. He placed himself among some of the other girls who were there that night. He could be quite charming, and I could hear his voice amongst the tittering of the girls.

It was then that I knew Paul and I were friends. I mean friends in a way that isn't usual for a young man and woman. In a way that was different than what I thought it was. I had never heard this information from Tony. If Tony had known, he would have told me. He pretty much told me everything. Paul had just confided in me and told me something that he had probably never shared with anyone else.

I also understood that I had been born into a charmed life. My parents were upper-middle class, living on the west side of Vancouver, historically one of the most expensive places to live in Canada. My dad had tenure at a local post-secondary institution. He was a business professor, which was why I was studying business. My mom didn't work outside the home because she didn't have to. She looked after all of us—a big job in itself—and she did it effortlessly.

I was cared for and sheltered and loved. My parents were happy the day I was born, and my existence enriched their lives. It wasn't that I didn't realize that this wasn't how it was for all people. It was just that it was all I had ever known. It was all that my friends had ever known. We never thought very much about how other people lived. We were young and self-absorbed, as only the young can be. We certainly never thought there were kids amongst us who may have been raised otherwise. It was at that moment that I understood how privileged and indulged and entitled I was.

"Ginny? Gin!" I hear Paul say my name. He is trying to get my attention. "Where'd you go? Thinking about Santa?"

"Oh, sorry! You caught me in a daydream. Did you ask me something?"

"I asked you when your mom and dad are coming up," he says, looking at me carefully.

"Oh, I'm sorry. I didn't hear you. James is bringing them up on the twenty-third."

It has been a few years since my dad stopped driving the Sea-to-Sky Highway, and my mother simply refuses. For one thing, my parents know it consumes me with worry when they drive up, especially if it's raining. My parents are getting old, and I don't think they do much driving at all anymore.

"That will be fun for you," Mike replies.

"Yes, it will. We have such a good time together. We love having Christmas up here. Sometimes I wonder how many more years they will be able to make the trip."

"Oh, it will be a while yet. Your parents aren't that old, and I think they are in love with Christmas at your house as much as you are," Paul states.

We are cleaning up the last of the dishes as I down the remainder of my coffee and stick my cup into the dishwasher.

"I'm sorry to have such a basic meal and be on the run," I say, looking at Mike. Paul knows the routine, Tuesday night is yoga, and Thursday night is spin class. It can get muddled up during the Christmas season, but Jessie and I try hard to keep up our exercise regime. I think it's the only thing that keeps me sane.

"Restaurant workers call it dine-and-dash," Mike laughs. "No, seriously, it doesn't bother me. I have some things to attend to at the restaurant tonight, so it gives me a head start on tomorrow. There are a bunch of things I need to wrap up before Saturday."

We are all getting our coats, preparing to leave at the same time. I am thankful that there will be no chance for another tricky moment between Paul and me. I don't think I can handle any more drama this week. I am looking forward to working out some of my frustration on the spin bike.

"I'll see you tomorrow," I say, looking at Mike. Turning to Paul, I say, "When do I see you next—Saturday?"

"Probably not," he answers. "I'll probably be too busy with work that day, and I might go ice climbing on Sunday, so it'll be a few days before I can get over again. I'll call you once I get it all worked out."

"Okay," I say, leaning in to kiss Paul on the cheek. Turning to Mike, I say, "We can talk later. I'll call you after I get home tonight."

He seems happy with that plan. He leans in and kisses me on the lips. I hope neither of them notices me squirm. I can't believe how uncomfortable I feel being kissed in front of Paul. I can't wait to get away from them both.

"Okay, you two—out the door, you go!" I push them both out and lock the door behind them. I grab my gym bag and make my way through the inside door to the garage. Driving away, I wonder how my life has managed to get so complicated.

—

I am lying on my back, naked, in the seclusion of the steam room. It is dark except for the small lights that guide the way, and it's forty degrees Celsius with one hundred percent humidity. I am dripping with sweat, and it feels fantastic after our strenuous workout. Tonight's class has exhausted me. The muscles in my thighs shake as I try to relax them.

"I'm wrecked," I say to Jessie, who is lying on the bench across from me. It's ladies' night at the gym, and we are safe to relax in our nudity. The steam room is "Adults Only" after nine p.m., meaning clothes are optional, but I never want to do that with men around. No other women are in here with us tonight, which makes it very comfortable. I adjust my towel underneath my bottom. The thought of someone else's bare bottom in the same spot as mine makes me queasy.

"I'm tired too," she says. "That was more intense than usual tonight."

"I'm glad to hear you say that. I thought it was me. I could barely keep up," I say, rubbing the sweat from my face and taking a deep breath. "Have you decided which day you are going home for Christmas?"

"I'm heading out on the twenty-third," she answers. "My mom is very excited that we will all be home this year. Even all the grandkids are coming!"

Jessie always goes home for Christmas. Being raised in a religious home, this is the premier event of the year for her family, as I suppose it is for many of us around here. I know she has a pile of baking that she is planning to contribute. She has been working on it for weeks in her spare time. Her mom cooks up the best turkey and ham. All the girls help by bringing veggie dishes and appetizers and alcohol. It is a complete feast at the McPherson residence at Christmastime.

Jessie's oldest sister married a pilot and moved to Calgary. It has been a couple of years since she has been home for Christmas. Her baby sister lives in Oregon. She is a professor at a college in Portland. I am pleased to hear that they are all making the journey home. The last we talked about this, it was just going to be Jessie and her two sisters who live in Vancouver. I can envision the joy on Patti McPherson's face with all her children and grandchildren in her big house.

"That's great. It will be good fun. I wish I could be there to hear you all sing together."

"I know, hey! All crowded around the piano like old times." Her voice falters, and I know she is thinking of her dad.

She tries to put some enthusiasm into her tone, but this is the third Christmas without him, and she still isn't used to it. I know she misses him deeply. Somehow or other, among all those girls in that great big house, she ended up being "daddy's girl." When we were in our twenties, she was still sitting on his knee, getting a cuddle from him. Her sisters used to tease her and call her a sissy, but I knew she didn't care. If anything, she was smug about it. To her, sitting on her dad's knee was like sitting on a throne.

"It'll be all right," I say quietly into the darkness of the room. The steam envelops us both, and it is easy to feel as if you are alone, with just the closeness of the air hugging you.

"I miss him so much," she sobs. I can't see her, and I am thankful for that. Sometimes a woman just needs to cry and not worry about how she looks with her face all screwed up as she gasps for air.

"I know," I reply gently. We sit in the darkness, and I let her cry. When I can hear that she has composed herself, I change the subject.

"Mike and I are going to see the gingerbread display tomorrow night. He has asked me to dinner at his suite."

This comment gets her attention, and she quickly changes her tone. I can hear her rub her nose and suck back a sniffle. Talking about sex and men is her favourite topic, and she wants to know more. I hear a low whistle of approval.

"Woohoo!" she exclaims. Our tender moment has passed. "What are you going to wear? What time? Tell me everything!"

"I don't know what time yet, and I'm not sure what I'm going to wear. I'm going to be talking to Mike later tonight after I get home."

"You should wear that red wool jersey dress. You look good in it, and you could wear it with a pair of boots. It's a good colour for you. Will you wear your hair up or down?"

"Probably up. I get unbearably hot these days. I might die of heat exhaustion in that wool dress," I say, finding it ironic that I am lazing about in the steam room, perfectly fine with the heat and enjoying it very much. "I like your idea, though. I like that dress too. It's comfortable."

"I'd come and help you with your hair, but I work tomorrow night," she says. It isn't very often that she works on a Friday night anymore, but this is high season.

"That's okay. I'll manage on my own."

"What are you going to do about birth control?"

That's a question I wasn't expecting. I am surprised to hear it and not sure how to respond because I haven't given birth control a single thought.

I guess I didn't respond fast enough because she continues, "You have to have a plan, you know. Getting pregnant at this age would be disastrous."

Sheepishly, I confess, "I haven't had my period in over a year. I'm pretty sure I don't need to be concerned about pregnancy."

"What?" she hollers. I know she would have whacked me a good one if I had been sitting beside her. "Why haven't you told me? Lucky you! I'm still getting mine. That's not fair—I started before you, and I should be finishing first!"

"I'm not sure why I haven't told you. I wasn't trying to keep it a secret. I just never thought to mention it. All part of the process I guess—forgetfulness, I mean!" I add with a nervous laugh. "Honestly, I've been so preoccupied with the idea of having sex again, I never thought about anything else."

"You should use protection. You know—a condom. STI's are rampant out there. I never have sex without one."

"I've never used one!"

"You've never used a condom?" she almost screamed her response.

"Shh! I think the front desk clerk heard you!" I say, giggling. "No! Of course, I've never used one. Remember, the first time I ever had sex was the night I got married."

"Yeah, but," she said dumbfounded. "Didn't you ever use them for birth control or anything?"

"No. I used the birth control pill. You know that!"

"Well, I know, but it just never crossed my mind that you had never used the other. Wow!" she says, ruminating over this new information. "Well, what are you going to do about that? Will you use a condom? You have to insist upon using a condom. I could give you a lesson."

"I don't think that will be necessary!" I exclaim.

I envision Jessie peeling a condom open and slipping it over a cucumber while explaining that she hoped his penis is this big in real life. *Horrifying.* I shake my head. I wonder if this is a conversation people still have with one another before they do it. I'm more nervous than ever.

Feeling shy, I say, "I don't know. I guess he and I will have to talk about it and decide. How do I broach the subject?"

"You just say, 'Hey, Mike, if you wanna 'eff' me, slip this on first!'" she is giggling uncontrollably at her joke. By now, she has brought her towel and moved over beside me. I am starting to get a renewed cramp in my stomach at the thought of this whole process. The heat of the steam room is too much, and I have had enough.

"I have to get out. I'm overheating," I say desperately.

"You're overheating, alright, girl! You are going to be on fire tomorrow night!" she teases.

"Shut up!" I say, whacking her on the shoulder as we wrap our towels around ourselves and open the door to the steam room. "We aren't doing it tomorrow night, so I don't have to worry about it right now."

"You don't think he is going to invite you to his suite and not make a move on you, do you? You are more naïve than I thought. He is going to have you alone on his turf for the first time. Be prepared, my darlin'. He is going to seduce you."

I get into the shower and dunk my head under the nozzle, trying to drown out her words. It hadn't crossed my mind that he might try to seduce me tomorrow night. We have made our plan. He knows I am comfortable with it. What am I going to do now? Even though my head is soaked from the shower, sweat is popping out on my upper lip. There is an inferno raging inside me. I have to turn the hot water off. I stand there in the cold shower for an eternity. I put my face up toward the water and hold my breath.

—

"Yes, I did have a good workout. It was hard tonight. I don't remember ever feeling this out of shape. I guess I've been eating too many Christmas cookies," I laugh as I fiddle with the phone cord.

"Oh, I doubt that—you look amazing. That's something I like about you. You eat real food. It's great to see a woman with an appetite. I admire how you look after yourself and how exercise is part of your life. That's pretty hard for most people—at least it is for me. I have to work at it and build it into my day. I have to schedule it," Mike says with sincerity.

"Well, it's not like I'm an athlete or anything," I say matter-of-factly, but thinking he must be excellent at scheduling because he looks incredible. "It's because Jessie lives here, and it's something we've habitually done together. Ever since we were kids, we've been riding bikes and playing tennis and things like that."

"Well, I think it's great. As I said, I admire you for it. It doesn't hurt that it makes you pretty easy on the eyes," Mike flirts.

I blush and remain quiet.

"You don't have to act shy. You must have some idea of how good-looking you are," he prompts.

"Honesty, I never thought about it. I'm just a mother and a grand-mother and someone who has good genes. Stop it, please. You're embarrassing me," I reply shyly.

"Well, you are a beautiful woman and good genes or not, you look good in your jeans," Mike says with a laugh.

I guess he hasn't noticed that I never wear jeans, but I giggle and accept his compliment, "Thank you. That's nice of you to say." After such a hard workout, it feels good to be complimented. My hard work is paying off. "What time do you want me to come over tomorrow?"

"I will come to pick you up. I don't want you to come over unattended. I'll come and get you," he states firmly.

"Okay, that will be lovely!" I reply enthusiastically. Mike is a gentleman. It feels good to be picked up for a date. "In that case, what time should I be ready?"

"I was hoping that we could have a late dinner. I want to stay at the restaurant until around seven o'clock. Can I pick you up at eight? Is that too late?"

"No, that will work," I comment. I keep my shop open until seven on Friday nights, and since it is Christmastime, it should get pretty steady traffic. The village buzzes in the evening with tourists who have open wallets.

"It's set then. I'll say goodnight to you, and I'll see you tomorrow evening."

"I look forward to it," I say honestly, realizing how much this is true. "Good night. See you tomorrow. Have a good sleep."

"Sweet dreams, my darling," he says quietly and disconnects the call.

I put the phone down and lie quietly in my bed, snuggled under the covers. I still have my socks on because my feet are cold. Stretching out, I feel the sore muscles in my legs twitching—and I wonder why tonight's workout was so hard. Maybe our instructor thought we had to work harder to earn our Christmas treats. I am startled out of my semi-slumber when the phone rings again. I pick it up quickly, thinking it is Mike.

"Couldn't get enough of me? Needed to talk to me a little more?" I ask cheekily.

There is a pause on the other end, and then the caller identifies himself, "Uhh—it's me, Paul. Were you expecting someone else?"

"Oh! Hi, Paul! You surprised me. I thought it was Jessie—I just got off the phone with her," I lie, and it shocks me again that I lied so quickly. Why didn't I say that I thought it was Mike? I am allowed to say that—he is my boyfriend. What a strange term for a grown man. "What's up? You don't usually call at this hour."

"I'm sorry for calling so late," he says. "I hope I'm not disturbing you."

"No, you're not disturbing me. I am just lying here in my bed, considering turning the light out."

"That's good." There is a pause as he seems to be searching for words. I wait. Clearing his throat, he says, "Gin, I wanted to talk to you about what happened between us tonight."

"I'm fine. It's all right." I lie again, answering too quickly. This lying thing is becoming a habit.

"I can tell from your voice that is not true."

Damn! He knows me so well. When I get nervous, I speak too quickly, and my voice gets higher. It is my turn to pause. I purposefully control my voice before I comment, "Well, okay, maybe I was uncomfortable. It's just such a weird situation. We'll get used to it."

"I won't," he says plainly.

What is that supposed to mean? I'm glad he can't see me squirm under my sheets. My feet have warmed up, and I have to kick off my socks and throw back the covers. I am starting to heat up all over.

"Ginny," he continues. "You mean the world to me. I know you know that, but maybe I don't tell you often enough."

He pauses again and stumbles with his words. My eyes are filling with tears, and a lump is forming in my throat.

"You mean the world to me too. I never want to hurt you—ever! You've been the best friend to me my whole life, and I don't know what I would ever do without you. You tell me if you can't handle it and I'll break up with him. I'll do whatever it takes!" the words tumble out of me.

Where did that come from? I am losing my marbles. Why can't I make my mouth stop? I hadn't intended to say any of that. Is this fear speaking, and making me act insane? Do I want to sabotage my relationship with Mike?

"Whoa, slow down, Gin. I just wanted to check in with you and let you know I am okay, and I'm hoping you are too. It was a difficult moment in the kitchen only because we were interrupted. I am not going anywhere, so relax. I am also calling because I wanted to know if you would like to come over to my house for supper on Boxing Day."

Wiping the sweat from my upper lip, I freeze when he says these words. I sit up straighter in my bed and push my damp hair off my face. We never have dinner at Paul's place. We eat at my house. What is he going on about? I am at a loss for words.

"Look," he continues as if reading my mind. "I know it's a busy time and that it's an unusual request. But, it might be one of the last times we get to be alone together, and wouldn't it be nice to spend some time together, just the two of us. Your mom usually cooks a ham on Boxing Day, so you know the family will be well fed. Everyone will understand."

Pondering his words, I realize he is right. I hadn't considered that we might not ever be alone with one another again. My heart feels heavy at the thought.

"I'd love to," I say quietly. "What a nice idea."

"Okay, it's settled then. Let's talk about the details closer to the time. I'll let you go so you can get some sleep. Morning comes early."

"Yes, it does," I reply automatically. "Paul?"

"Yes, Ginny?"

"Thanks."

"My pleasure," I can almost hear him smile through the phone. I imagine the wrinkles around his eyes scrunching up, and I can feel the warmth in his expression. "Good night, Gin."

"Good night, Paul."

I hang up the phone and roll over, looking out the window. I don't sleep with my curtains closed. I like to wake up with the morning sun, not that there is any sun when I'm waking up these days with our dark winter mornings. I enjoy looking out the window at the moon and stars. I like the light of the town coming into my room and comforting me.

The sky is clear tonight. It is much more uncomplicated than my thoughts are. I'm scared and unsure of myself, more so than ever before. Hugging my pillow tight to my body, I hold my gaze on the mountaintops in the distance. Their outline can barely be made out in the night sky. I wonder if bears, cougars and other wild things ever feel confused, and I decide there is no way on earth that any living creature could feel as mixed up as I do right now.

Chapter 8
New Age

I gaze around Mike's suite and wait as he clears the supper dishes and sets the room service cart out into the hall. I am comfortably snuggled into the corner of the sofa. I have never been to a penthouse suite before. Well, that's not true. I have been in this penthouse suite once when Jessie first acquired her job at this hotel. She was vibrating with excitement when she took us all on the grand tour of "her" hotel. She was adorable, all pink and blushing and proud of herself, as she deserved to be. It was quite an accomplishment to be the general manager of a first-class hotel like this one—especially for a young woman and especially in the early nineties.

We were happy for her. Tony and I put on a party for her after she landed her job and got settled. We made a big banner that said "Boss" in giant block letters. We figured that about summed it up. Beside it, we had a gigantic poster of Jessie. It was a blown-up snapshot someone had taken of her at a party. Decked out in a slinky dress, she was laughing with her head tipped back, and her curls were glowing like a nimbus around her head. Despite the posters on the wall, we felt like it was a real grown-up party because we served martinis and canapés. Jessie's and my parents both came up for the weekend. It was such a fun time. We were thrilled to be together again and have our darling Jessie back with us on the West Coast.

I remember being impressed with the penthouse suite back then, but I don't remember it being as fancy. The hotel did a major upgrade a few years back, and it looks as though they spared no expense. The bathroom impresses me the most. It is designed with wall-to-wall marble. The floor is marble, the walls are marble, the double sinks are marble, and the shower is marble. The shower has glass doors on each side, making it possible to walk right through to the soaker tub that perches in a bay window overlooking the mountains. It has two shower heads, one on each side, one detachable and the other fixed. It also has shower nozzles that run the length of your body—one at the top around the shoulder area, one at the middle and one at the bottom about knee height—ensuring that your body gets sprayed from top to bottom and everywhere in-between. It looks enticing in a very sensual way. Mirrors cover the entire wall surface above the length of the sinks and up to the ceiling. I can't imagine that one person gets to enjoy this kind of opulence. And that is just the ensuite bathroom.

There are two bedrooms outfitted with king-size beds. They are both dressed with puffy, white hotel duvets. Four giant pillows are expertly placed and propped up against the leather headboard. Sumptuous steel grey towels are fanned out at the foot of the bed, along with all the personal sundries a person might need for a penthouse sleepover. The master bedroom has a dark grey chaise lounge situated in front of the floor-to-ceiling window that looks out at the mountains.

Floor-to-ceiling windows also allow the enormous great room to have the most magnificent view. They encapsulate the room, and the ceiling must be at least twelve feet high. Plush carpet covers the floor and kisses your toes as you walk—it feels like it has an inch of padding underneath. To the right is a gleaming mahogany dining table big enough for eight people to sit comfortably. A chandelier with just the right combination of sparkle and light hangs over the table. It is perfection in its subtlety. I blush as I imagine making love on that table.

To the left of the dining area is the living room. Two couches and two swivelling chairs flank an understated mahogany coffee table. The sofas are dark grey in colour and contemporary in their styling. Some of the walls are dove grey, and some are like a vanilla milkshake, smooth and velvety-looking. The throw pillows have steel grey, beige and teal colours patterned into them. The decor is simple and yet simply outstanding. The suite must be at least 2500 square feet—almost as big as my house. Never could I have imagined such a place, and never in a million years did I ever dream that I'd be a guest in one. I can't guess how much it must cost to rent a suite like this. It must be thousands per night. I'll have to ask Jessie. I secretly hope that Mike gets a good deal on a monthly rate.

I walk across to the window and lean against one of the braces to gaze at the vista outside. The ski hill and the village look lovely at night. The merry lights of the season are twinkling.

"Beautiful, isn't it?" says Mike from behind me. He hands me a warm snifter of cognac, slips his free hand around my waist, and holds me from behind. I hadn't heard him approach, nor had I expected him to embrace me in such a way. We aren't lovers. Not yet.

"It's breathtaking," I reply, sipping my drink. It makes my eyes water. I'm not much for cognac.

"Just like you," he says, moving around to face me, and leaning in to kiss me warmly. "You look terrific in that dress. I love it." I make a mental note to thank Jessie for the recommendation. He kisses me again so quickly I don't have time to reply. His tongue gently opens my lips and probes my mouth. His hand is on the small of my back, pulling me toward him and holding me tight. My knees weaken, and I steady myself against the window brace. I kiss him back with surprising urgency.

"Don't worry. I've got you," he says. My transparency makes me blush. "You look gorgeous when you blush."

I'm so embarrassed I blush even more. He leans in and kisses me again. Not stopping, he kisses me more. Aphrodite has eyes as round as an owl's and is sitting up very straight, observing intently. He moves his lips down the nape of my neck, pushing my hair gently to the side. I start to perspire. I should have worn my hair up as I had planned, but I had to get ready in a hurry. His kisses are slow and intentional, working their way back to my ear. He takes my earlobe into his mouth and breathes gently into my ear. His warm breath makes my heart race and my body yearn. I tip my head back, wanting more. Aphrodite gets up and puts her go-go dress on.

I moan as his lips travel down my throat and rest at the hollow of my neck. I am hungry for kisses, just like this. He is kissing me gently and patiently. I am twitching down to that warm spot between my legs. I must have squirmed because he pulls me closer and presses the length of his body against mine. Oh my. He is luscious.

I turn my face toward his mouth and kiss him with serious intent. I can't stop myself. I had only meant to thank him for a lovely dinner and tell him how much I enjoyed the coq au vin. Instead, I can't find my voice. I have my arms wrapped around him now, one hand holding steadfast to the glass of cognac and the other at the back of his neck, running my fingers through his hair and bringing his head toward mine, inviting more. Breathing him in, I appreciate his intoxicating scent. I want him desperately.

He steps back and takes my drink from my hand. Placing our two glasses on the coffee table, he leads me across the room toward his bedroom. What is he doing? It appears that Jessie was right. He plans to seduce me! I can't stop myself from following him. I let him lead me to his bed. I am about to protest when he leans in and continues kissing me. My body aches for this kind of attention. I want him badly. I kiss him back, and I allow him to lay me down.

"I—," I begin a weak protest.

"Shh—relax," Mike whispers in my ear. "Just enjoy it."

I spread myself out while he continues his pursuit of pleasure. I can't help but kiss him back. I can't help but let him continue to kiss me. His hands are all over me. He is touching the length of my body, rubbing my legs and stomach, finally finding his way to my aching breasts. He puts one hand behind my back and encourages me to arch while he feels my nipples with his free hand. He bends his head and kisses each one, breathing in my scent. It is exquisite to be touched this way, even through the fabric of my clothes.

His hand travels to my bottom and gently rubs my thighs and buttocks. He reaches under my dress and undoes the fastener to my bra. My breasts spring loose, and I instinctively push my body into him. He fondles my nipples, and I moan in delight, kissing him deeply and luxuriating in his touch.

I help him push my dress over my head. He slips the straps of my beautiful purple bra off my shoulders and removes it. I am topless on his bed, leaving me in my stockings, my purple silk panties and a long gold chain. My head is swimming with delight.

Bending his head again, he continues his work on my nipples. He suckles each one gently, paying them equal attention. I arch back and continue to press myself into him. He pushes against me, and I can feel his erection against my leg. I am thoroughly wet, and I want him badly. In my mind, I hadn't felt ready to have sex, but my body is telling me otherwise, and I can't stop what I am doing.

"I—," I try once more to speak.

"Shh—don't talk," he says, between nibbles. "I want to feel you. We can stop anytime. Just lie back and let me touch you."

Mike's voice is thick with desire as he continues his journey around my body. I sigh and relax onto the bed. He whispers into my ear how good I smell. I writhe under his touch as his hand moves to my stomach and down my legs. Looking steadily at me, he unbuckles each of my stockings slowly and deliberately, gently rolling them off of my legs. He lifts one of my feet and puts my toes into his mouth, one by one. His gaze never wavers from mine. Licking and suckling each toe like a nipple, his touch sends shock waves up my leg.

Undoing the clasp of my garter belt, he bends his head and kisses my belly button. He licks my tummy with a featherlight touch. The heal of his hand presses my mound, pushing firmly against the outside of my panties. He runs his fingers along the length of my crotch and smiles with satisfaction when he feels my warmth. An involuntary moan slips from the back of my throat, and I hear his contented sigh as he rubs me.

His eyes roam the length of my body, drinking in every detail. Turning me over, he kisses my bottom, moving gently back and forth from one cheek to the other, lingering in the middle. His kisses move to the small of my back and follow my spine up to my shoulders. His entire length is pressed against me as he kisses my back. As he nuzzles into my neck, I think I might pass out from pure rapture. He moves back to my buttocks and nestles between my legs. His kisses move down and rest on the back of my knees. Tickling me with his tongue, he kisses me until I squirm with delight and can barely take any more of this teasing.

Looking into my eyes, he rolls me over and lies down beside me. He smiles, kissing me again, and I press my body toward him as he massages my buttocks. At long last, he puts his hand inside my panties and touches the skin on my bottom. His fingers work the garment down my legs and off onto the floor. I am fully exposed. I can't believe I am naked on a man's bed. I close my eyes and let him touch me. He reaches up between my legs, his fingers exploring between my labia and running along the silky softness of my most private part.

"You're so wet," he whispers in a gravelly voice, thick with lust.

I moan in delight. I push toward him to meet his touch. My body wants more from him. He slips his middle finger into my vagina. My eyes roll into the back of my head, and I bite my lower lip.

"You are so sexy," he says with satisfaction. "Do you like that?"

I can't speak. I nod in agreement. Mike smiles at me and puts his finger deeper into my body, moving it back and forth, in and out. I grind myself into his hand.

"That's it," he growls. "Let me make you come."

Speechless, I nod and keep biting my lip. My vagina trembles as Mike places the heel of his hand on my mound and slips another finger inside me. Rhythmically rubbing his fingers in and out, I move with him. He kisses my mouth and vibrates his hand as he presses into me. My body goes wild and responds naturally to this motion. The only person who's ever done this to me is Tony. I didn't know that other people knew this move. It's like smiling at an old friend you haven't seen in a long time. It's just normal.

"You like that, do you?" he questions softly. "Do you want more?"

"Yes," I manage to choke out.

He stops the vibrating motion and returns to relentlessly moving his fingers in and out, over and over again—digging upward, gently rubbing my G-spot. When my body adapts to the rhythm of his motion, he moves the heel of his hand back to my pubis and vibrates me some more. He bends his head to my breasts and nibbles each nipple as he works my vagina.

This combination puts me over the edge. My orgasm is building deep inside me, and with every grind of his hand, it gets stronger. My back arches naturally, and my head tips back. I moan as I buck myself into his hand. His mouth keeps working my nipples, and I can hear him say, "That's it—move into me—enjoy it—let me make you happy—let me make you come—that's it—come for me."

Wild with passion, my orgasm continues to build and is almost complete. Moving rhythmically into his hand, I am in paradise. He smells so good, his body is so hard, and he is making this all about me. He wants to give me pleasure, and it is working. My body bucks into a full climax, and I ride his hand wildly. He starts vibrating my clitoris with the heel of his hand and bites my nipple gently at the same time. I close my eyes and throw back my head as my voice rings out. I see stars. My vagina is grabbing his fingers and sucking his hand into my body. His fingers work their magic, and I continue to moan and move on his hand.

My breathing returns to normal as my orgasm subsides. My eyes are closed, and my back is beginning to relax. Mike's hand slows but has not stopped as he pushes my legs apart. *This is it.* I expect to hear his belt buckle and his zipper. I hope he will lower himself on top of me and make love to me.

Still moving his fingers gently inside me, I gasp when something warm, soft and wet touches my clitoris. It's his mouth! His fingers are moving deep inside me now, rubbing my G-spot slowly and rhythmically. His mouth is firm on my clitoris. I groan and drive into him as another shock wave runs through my body. His tongue moves in a steady, swirling motion, around and around. I think I am going to go mad. His fingers work in and out relentlessly, and his tongue is an endless probe. Unable to stand it any longer, I throw my head back and convulse with delight. The sound that emanates from me is deep and throaty.

"That's it," he says. "Scream for me. Let me hear you beg. That's it. I was hoping you were a screamer. Keep coming for me—that's it—move into me."

As my climax reaches its pinnacle, he returns his mouth to my clitoris and continues his magic. My orgasm is even more intense than the first one, and I roar with delight as I ride his hand like a madwoman. I don't want him to stop. As my orgasm subsides, he vibrates his hand more and brings me to delight one more time. Finally, I collapse on the bed in a puddle of perspiration and spent desire. I am overcome with satisfaction. He holds me in his arms and wipes my sweaty hair away from my face. He kisses my lips. I can taste myself on them. I kiss him back and let him hold me. I fall into a warm state of being and feel like I am floating. Aphrodite is holding onto a strand of my hair and floating beside me in blissful surrender. I gaze out the window and fall asleep.

—

Jessie grabs me by the elbow and steers me away from Mike. She has an earnest look on her face.

"Excuse us, Mike," she says directly to him, not waiting for him to respond. "I need to speak to Virginia alone for a moment."

Virginia! I wonder what has happened. She only uses my full name when something serious has taken place. I hope everything is alright. I have to quell the momentary sense of fear that strikes me. Mike and I ran into her in the great hall of the hotel as we were perusing the gingerbread display—which is phenomenal. It is quite late, and she must be on her way out after her shift. Jessie looks festive and businesslike dressed in her maxi length, winter white cashmere coat, accessorized with a dark orange scarf and matching gloves. I can't imagine what is so urgent that she has to lead me to the ladies' room.

Practically dragging me, she finally gets me into the confines of the bathroom. Giving me an excited look and whacking me on the arm, she says sharply into my ear, "You've had sex!"

I whack her back. I am honestly cross with her. It's the second time in less than a month that I have had to rush to check under the toilet stall to make sure we are alone. This time, there is someone in there! I put my finger to my lips and give her a hard look, warning her not to speak.

I move to the sink and start washing my hands. The toilet flushes, and I hear the woman pulling up her pants. I take my time and wait, the whole while glaring at Jessie. Jessie comes to the sink and removes her gloves. She also begins washing her hands. We make eye contact in the mirror. I glare at her once again. I dry my hands, then check my hair and lipstick in the mirror. The woman opens the door to the stall and stands there looking at us.

She gives us a grin and says, "Beautiful night, isn't it?"

Softening my gaze, I look at her and smile, "Yes, it's just lovely. It's not too cold tonight."

Jessie opens her purse and takes out her lipstick. She freshens her already perfect lips and smiles at the woman while she waits impatiently. She is veritably vibrating with the anticipation of my answer. The woman takes her time. She carefully washes her hands. She, too, reapplies her lipstick and brushes her hair. She takes the time to adjust her scarf and straighten her coat. She steps back from the mirror and assesses herself.

"That should do it," she comments.

"Enjoy the rest of your night," Jessie offers. I think she might just push the woman out the door.

"Thanks. You too," the woman says, giving me a long, curious look, running her eyes up and down my length. As she walks out the door, she wishes us a Merry Christmas and tells us she hopes all our Christmas wishes come true.

"Bitch," Jessie says, too loudly, as she locks the door behind her. Leaning against the door, she surveys me carefully. I start to blush.

"You've had sex! I was right!" she squeals, rushing toward me and bursting into laughter.

"Shut up! Keep your voice down!" I answer sharply. "I have not!"

"You have too! You have that freshly fucked look! Your cheeks are all rosy and flushed. Your eyes are all glazed." Whacking me on the arm again, she leans against the sink and says, "Tell me everything! Don't leave anything out!"

"Oh, my goodness—this is ridiculous!" I say, making my way toward the door, although I know escape is impossible.

"Oh, no, you don't!" Jessie says, jumping in front of me and blocking the door. "Confess! What's going on? You know you are not going to get out of this! You have the same look on your face that you used to get when you came to parties late after you and Tony had spent the whole night screwing! I know you've had sex!"

She is gleeful! She is bouncing up and down on the balls of her feet and clapping her hands. The look on her face is pure joy. Silently cursing my shy nature and my telltale cheeks, I know I have no choice. I have to put her out of her misery.

"Well," I start. "I didn't exactly have sex."

"What do you mean?" she asks excitedly. Then with a knowing look, she tips her head back and says, "Oh! I know what happened! He got you into his bed, and you two were making out, and then you didn't want to go all the way with him, so here you are in the bathroom of my hotel!"

I can tell she is teasing me, but I also know she is familiar enough with the look on my face that I have to give her some details.

"Oh, hurry up! Tell me what happened!" she exclaims, reaching out and whacking me again.

"Stop it!" I laugh. "You'll give me a bruise! That's three times you've hit me!"

I decide to tell her what she wants to know.

"Well, it went kind of like this. Mike ordered the coq au vin. We had a lovely dinner, by the way. Please give our compliments to the chef." She rolls her eyeballs and rotates her hands in a circular motion, indicating that I should get on with my story. Laughing, I continue, "I was gazing

163

out the window in the living room, looking at the mountains, when he came up behind me and started kissing me. Before I knew it, he had me on his bed and stripped down to nothing, and he was doing the most delicious things to my body."

She was clapping her hands together again. "And you let him! Good girl! I'm so proud of you! I told you he was going to seduce you! Then what happened? What did he do? Did you have intercourse? Did you use protection?"

The questions are coming at me fast and furious. "No, we didn't use protection because we didn't have intercourse. He just—you know ...." I let my voice trail off, and I let her put two and two together.

"You bitch!" she exclaims, whacking me a fourth time. Her eyes are excited, and she has a big smile on her face. "Only you could land a gorgeous millionaire who made your first sexual encounter all about you! Are you telling me that you didn't have intercourse and that he didn't want you to do something to him in return?!"

"Well, you're right, I guess it was all about me. I couldn't believe it either. After my fourth orgasm, I fell asleep in his arms, and when I woke up, Mike was still holding me. It was sweet."

"Unbelievable. Four orgasms. Sweet. I really hate you!" Jessie comments almost to herself while pacing the floor. Looking up at me, she asks, "He didn't even ask you for a blow job?"

Laughing, I shake my head back and forth to answer. Embarrassed, I put my head down and rub the toe of my boot into the bathroom floor. I have just had the most incredible sexual experience that I've had in an eternity, and here I am talking about it in the bathroom like a teenager. The memory of it makes Aphrodite's head spin around on her shoulders as if she is possessed. I shush her and blush.

Leaning against the wall of the bathroom, Jessie stops pacing and looks at me. "Ginny," she says. "I am unbelievably happy for you. You have done something monumental tonight. This is incredible. I am bursting with happiness for you."

She steps toward me and wraps her arms around me, hugging me hard. Pulling away, she looks at me and says, "It couldn't have been easy for you. I am exceptionally proud of you and truly, truly happy for you."

She kisses me on both cheeks as her eyes well up with tears. I am astonished by the fact that I didn't find it that hard to do. I am wondering why I've waited this long. Maybe it was the change of location. Maybe it was the martini before dinner. I don't know. I just felt relaxed and, admittedly, horny. I, too, am happy that I've done it. It takes the pressure off of New Year's Eve and gives me something to anticipate in the coming days.

"You don't have to cry," I say, reaching out to her, taking her hand. Trying to joke and make light of the situation, I comment, "It's not like I lost my virginity or anything."

"I'm just so darned happy for you! I like Mike more and more all the time! What a man you've got!" she says, wiping her eyes. "We'd better go. Mike will be worried. You can tell me all the rest of the dirty details tomorrow!"

Hugging me again, she pats her hair and straightens her coat before unlocking the bathroom door. Two women are standing outside waiting. They give us a quizzical look as we walk out of the washroom. Jessie doesn't make eye contact with them, and I am pretty sure I heard her mutter, "my bathroom" under her breath. She holds her head high and shakes her curls back off her face, raising her chin. I am blushing and put my head down slightly, turning away from the two women and their questioning looks. I try to locate Mike. He is across the room, talking to someone he knows. Our eyes meet, and I wave, smiling at him, conveying that everything is okay.

⸺

We are seated in his car outside my house. The motor is running, and Christmas music is playing quietly. I am cozy in my coat and scarf. The seat warmer is on, and the heater is purring inside the car. We are both looking at the Christmas lights on my house.

"Thank you for a lovely evening," I blush as soon as I say it, and I am thankful for the dim light. I turn my head down and away, sneaking a look at him from the corner of my eye.

His eyes are on the Christmas lights, but a slow grin is spreading across his face. Without looking at me, he comments, "The pleasure was all mine. I'm glad you enjoyed yourself."

I can't tell if he is teasing me or not, and I resist the urge to whack him on his arm. I stifle a giggle while stealing another peek. My giggle makes him laugh, and before we know it, the two of us are having a good chuckle. Clearly, we both had a good time this evening.

I turn my body to face him. His eyes search my face, and he kisses me gently. It's a soft, loving kiss. The kind of kiss that shows affection. A kiss that settles warm on your lips, promising more but not asking for it.

"Ginny," he says quietly. "I want to thank you for tonight and this week. Thank you for inviting me into your life and allowing yourself to come into mine. It means a lot to me. You mean a lot to me."

I look away, my eyelids downcast. We sit without speaking. It *has* been a good week. For the first time, I believe *we can do this*. I can give this a chance. We can make this work. Tonight, I feel like a young lover. We sit and listen to the Christmas music playing on the radio. He takes my hand and lifts my gloved fingers to his mouth and kisses them.

"I have something important to tell you," he says. "I've kept this under my hat until now, but it's time to let you know that I'm moving my head office to Vancouver. That's the real reason I'm here over the winter, not to oversee operations at my new location. I'm staying here in Whistler rather than Vancouver because I wanted to be closer to you. I've been hoping for things to go well between us."

I say nothing, but allow him to keep holding my hand. My throat is tight, and sweat pops out on my upper lip, as I wonder what the implications of this are. I squeeze his hand and hold it tightly.

"I'm starting to fall in love with you, Ginny, and I realize that is my best Christmas present of all. I'm hoping you are starting to love me too." He adjusts himself in his seat while I sit silently, listening to his words. I swallow a huge lump in my throat and wait. "I'll be leaving first thing in the morning. My flight leaves at noon. I'll be sure to contact you over the next few days. You'll hear from me while I'm away. I can't guarantee that I'll call daily, but I'll try."

"I'm overwhelmed," I say quietly. I don't know which is more surprising, Mike moving here or his words of love. My stomach clenches in trepidation and anticipation. Looking up, I say, "I'm feeling hopeful about us too."

He squeezes my hand and leans in for another kiss. It is gentle and somewhat timid like he is hoping he hasn't said too much. I kiss him back with equal reserve.

"I want you to have a wonderful time with your family," I say. "It's such a special time of year. Say hello to them for me, especially your mom."

"I will. My mom will like that. She'll like you," he smiles. I think that I will also like her. He seems touched that I have extended Christmas wishes to her. "My brother's three kids will keep us in chaos. They come to the family home for Christmas, usually with a bunch of friends in tow. There is usually some outdoor skating and hockey going on somewhere. It's fun. My brother's oldest daughter is expecting her first child. My mother is very excited about that."

"It is lovely to expect a baby. There will be lots of joy in your home this year. I can't wait for my house to fill up with all my people," I reply enthusiastically. My eyes light up, and I smile at the thought of it.

He reaches into his glove compartment and pulls out a small box meticulously wrapped in Christmas paper. It must have been wrapped by a professional because I've never known a man to wrap a gift this flawlessly. He places the box into my hand and folds my fingers around it.

"Open this on Christmas morning," he says. "I hope you like it."

"Oh my," I say. I had expected to receive something from Mike, but I hadn't expected it to be a small box. I'm not sure what my expectation was, but a tiny box makes me nervous. In a whisper, I reply, "I will. I have something for you too."

I reach into my purse and hand him the small wrapped box I prepared earlier in the day. The box I am giving him is tiny too. When I was deciding what to get Mike, I had no idea what I could give the man who has everything. I decided that if I were going to invite him into my life wholeheartedly, I would give him a key to my house. I had a unique key cut with a white background and a red maple leaf on it. I have a fleeting thought that the gift inside the box he has just given me is probably worth more than the $4.99 I spent on him. Still, I like to think that my gift is priceless.

Putting the box into his hand and looking at him with a smile, I say, "Promise me you won't open it until Christmas Day."

"I promise," he laughs and quietly adds, "Thank you."

"Thank you, Mike. And thanks again for a lovely evening." I look steadily at him this time, and he meets my gaze. "I guess I had better get into the house. I don't want you to run out of gas in this subzero weather."

I lean toward him and kiss him on his mouth. His lips are hungry and meet mine with a sexual thrill that goes right through me. I squirm at the memory of our encounter earlier in the evening and smile as I kiss him. A rush of warmth floods my body. Aphrodite already has on her hot pants and is hurriedly pulling on her white go-go boots. I shush her as I wrap my arms around his neck and hug him tight.

Reaching for the door handle, I say, "I'd best get in."

"Good night, darling," he says quietly. "Merry Christmas."

Getting out of the car, I turn and tell him, "Merry Christmas to you as well."

I am about to close the car door, but I stop. I lean into the car and tell him, "Mike—I'm looking forward to New Year's Eve more than you know."

I am feeling powerful and confident as I smile at him and close the car door. I walk up the path to my house and unlock the door. He waits until I wave goodbye and let myself in. I stand in the doorway and blow him a kiss. He waves back, and I see the smile on his face. I can't help but wonder what delicacies are in store for me on New Year's Eve. Aphrodite is leaning back and licking her lips in anticipation.

Chapter 9
BFF

Jessie and I are snuggled on the couch. She's on one end, wearing her pink fleece jumpsuit with a blanket on top of her. I would die of heat exhaustion if I wore that. I am on the other end in my pyjama pants and an old waffle-knit sweatshirt. I've tucked my feet under her blanket. It's Saturday night, and we are watching our favourite Christmas movie for about the fiftieth time together. We have watched this movie together at least once every year since we've known each other.

We don't have a traditional day for watching it as we do for the tree decorating party. It repeatedly plays over the Christmas season, making it easy to find a showing that works for us both. Once we discovered that we were both fans, it just became a ritual for us. One year when the girls were children, we wrapped presents together in the wee hours of the morning, and it was playing in the background. We had loads of fun giggling and singing and pretending we were Santa. We had gotten in from a late-night Christmas Festival, poured ourselves glasses of port, and started wrapping gifts. It was a joyful night.

Jessie is such a good singer, and she knows the words to every song. I sing the songs too, but I purposefully sing more quietly so I can hear her over myself. Tonight, she has her hair tied back with one of those full-sized head elastics, and she is squinting at the television. She looks like an angel lying there, absent-mindedly sucking on a peppermint candy cane—one of the few sugary indulgences she allows herself at Christmastime. I watch her out of the corner of my eye because she knows the dialogue too, and I don't think she is aware that she mouths the words as the characters speak. Her toes tap in rhythm to every song. Sometimes, she gets up and acts out a segment. It's hilarious when she collapses in exhaustion at the end. I'm not sure which I enjoy more, her antics or the movie itself.

A commercial comes on the air. Jessie stretches and yawns.

"Hey! Guess who I saw today? Remember Buzzy from high school?" she asks me, sitting up in her spot. "He was checking into the hotel with his family. They are up here for a few days over the holidays. It was such a surprise to see him."

Of course, I remember Buzzy. He was tall and gangly with long brown hair that was straight and flowed down over his shoulders. Since it was the seventies, he looked quite fashionable. We called him Buzzy because he always had the single earphone from his transistor radio plugged into his ear, and the transistor itself tucked into his shirt pocket. He was quirky because he would walk down the halls of school dancing to the beat of a song that only he could hear. He was totally in his private world, but somehow he was too untouchable for kids to pick on.

Radio reception was weak back then, depending on your proximity to the station—the closer you were, the better the reception. About the only station Buzzy could pick up on his transistor was an AM pop station. One time someone asked if they could listen. Buzzy was an amiable guy, and he let the kid put the earphone up to his ear. The story goes that there was so much static the kid could only hear a buzzing sound with a rock song playing faintly in the background. After that, everybody just started calling him Buzzy. He grew up to be a radio disc jockey and has a syndicated show that plays out of Toronto. I listen to it once in a while. Isn't it funny how things go? You never know where your passion will lead you.

"How is he?" I ask. "It's been so long since I've seen him that I don't know if I would recognize him."

"Oh, he looks the same—minus the long hair," she says, shifting in her seat. "He seems well. He had his kids with him—he's got four of them! The youngest looks about thirteen. His wife is gorgeous."

"Isn't that nice," I say carefully. "What was it like running into him?"

"It was fine. We chatted for a while in the lobby and thought we might try to get together for a coffee or a drink tomorrow sometime. I gave him my number so he can text me. I'm not going home until next week, so I'll be around," she replies calmly.

My Jessie can be counted on to put her best face forward. I know that running into Buzzy could not have been easy for her. Some things and some people, we never forget. At one time, Jessie knew Buzzy quite well. She used to go out with his best friend in high school. They hung out together all the time. His best friend's name was John. John was also tall and gangly, but he had more of a football hero kind of look. He was an exceptionally handsome blonde-haired, blue-eyed teenage boy. Jessie was crazy about him.

It was the one time, in all the time that I've known Jessie, that I didn't see her very often or at least not as much I wanted. John asked her if she would go to the Christmas dance with him. It was the year we were in grade twelve. She was all starry-eyed and consumed with happiness in anticipation of the date.

Her mom took her shopping and bought her a new dress for the occasion. It was a deep red colour, almost black or purple in hue. Her skin looked creamy against it, and it suited her complexion perfectly. The dress was floor-length because that was the fashion back then, to wear long dresses to what we called formal dances. It had a flowing A-line skirt with cap sleeves and a fitted princess-cut bodice.

Back then, Jessie's hair was long. It hung in ringlets if she let it dry naturally. Her big sister, Jenny, was in the second year of university and did Jessie's hair that night. It was a peasant-style hairdo with the front pulled to the back and secured with a dark red velvet bow. Long tendrils of curls framed her face on each side. We thought she looked positively ladylike. Her mom said that it was okay if she wore some makeup, so Jenny did that too. She put a bit of powder blue eyeshadow on and a hint of peach coloured blush, finishing the look with clear lip gloss. It was a very seventies look, and to us, Jessie looked absolutely beautiful.

She was so excited I thought she was going to burst. I hadn't known what a crush she had on John. I knew she liked him, but she had crushes on a lot of boys, and she would flirt with anyone who had the time to pay attention to her. For all her flirtatious ways, she hadn't had a boyfriend yet. She had gone on dates with guys to movies or the local bowling alley but had never done anything romantic like this. Being invited to the Christmas dance seemed romantic to us at the time.

I also got ready at Jessie's house that night. Jenny was kind enough to do my hair and makeup as well. The dance started at eight, and we were ready to go by seven. We hadn't thought about John picking me up too. Jessie and I were a twosome and did everything together. It was natural for us to go to a dance together. We weren't sure if John knew that Jessie and I came as a package. Mrs. McPherson had already fed us dinner, so there was nothing to do except wait for him.

We were sitting in the living room waiting when we heard John drive up. He had an orange muscle car with a black racing stripe down the centre. We looked at each other, and Jessie clapped her hands together and tapped her feet excitedly on the floor. She was bursting to run to the door and fling it open, but she contained herself. Her parents would expect nothing less from her.

After John knocked on the door, our eyes met Mrs. McPherson's, and we waited expectantly. She put her finger to her mouth and gestured for Jessie to relax and slow down. She wiped her hands on the front of her dress. Mrs. McPherson was so used to having an apron on all the time I think this was automatic for her. She patted her hair down. I remember thinking that she was probably looking for renegade curls and bobby pins. Doctor McPherson remained seated in his chair, swirling his nightly scotch, while Mrs. McPherson deliberately made her way to the door.

She opened the door with a warm greeting. She had a big smile on her face, and the fact that she loved kids showed in everything she did. She welcomed John into the foyer. By now, Dr. McPherson had made his way to the entrance and was extending his hand in greeting. If John was nervous, he didn't show it. Jessie and I still hadn't moved from the couch. We knew better. When Mrs. McPherson decided that John had been appropriately welcomed, she indicated to Jessie that he had arrived, and this was her cue that she could stand up and greet him also.

I will never forget the look on her face when she saw him. I am notorious for blushing when I feel shy or embarrassed, but at that moment, Jessie was as peachy coloured as she could be. She gushed with enthusiasm. John wore a powder blue tuxedo with a white ruffled shirt and a white bow tie. His shoulder-length hair was parted down the middle and hung straight off his face.

When he presented Jessie with a corsage, she was speechless, which was extraordinary in itself because she's seldom without something to say. Her mother prompted her by suggesting how beautiful it was and how much Jessie loved red roses, asking how he knew it would match Jessie's dress perfectly? What a coincidence. I'm sure Dr. and Mrs. McPherson had a good laugh at our expense once we were on our way, but they were gracious and helpful to us at the time.

There was a pause as Jessie and John looked at each other and then again at the corsage. It was Mrs. McPherson who suggested to John that he put the corsage on Jessie. She helped him get it out of the box and pulled the stick pin out. He awkwardly attached the corsage to the bodice of Jessie's dress, on the left, over her heart, as Mrs. McPherson suggested. He was full of fumbling fingers as all our eyes watched him. John was cautious not to touch Jessie inappropriately. Mrs. McPherson expertly re-pinned the corsage and straightened it for him so seamlessly he didn't notice that she did it.

Mrs. McPherson insisted that we have a photo session in the foyer and on the stairs before she would let us be on our way. When we were done, she got Jessie's coat out of the closet and helped her into it. She did the same for me. We were finally ready to go. Dr. McPherson reminded John of Jessie's curfew as we made our way out the door. I hopped into the front seat beside Jessie, who had tucked into the middle, and we were off.

John and Jessie were inseparable over that Christmas season. I remember being jealous because she barely had time for me. We still talked on the phone every day, but I rarely saw her over the Christmas holiday. I would ask her if she wanted to come over or if she wanted to go skiing or skating, and often the answer was that she and John were going to go to the movies that night, or that she was going over to his house, or that he was coming over to hers. It was the first time since I met her that I felt excluded, and the awful part for me was that I missed her.

I was happy for her that she had a boyfriend. She liked boys intensely, and she had wanted a boyfriend for a long time. I had never had a boyfriend and had only ever been on a handful of dates. Honestly, I was scared about the whole prospect.

I missed our sleepovers the most. We used to sleep over at each other's houses almost every night during the holidays, and it was especially fun at Christmastime. But, that Christmas season, I only slept over once. My nose was significantly out of joint. I'd get the odd invitation to meet the two of them at the local coffee shop along with some other kids or go to the local movie theatre to watch a movie. I would go, and it was fun to see them, but I missed my alone time with her.

Jessie and John seemed downright grown-up when they were together. He would hold the door for her and carry her books. He would pick her up in the morning and drive her to school in his car. They would hold hands in the hall and, now and then, I would see them necking by her locker between classes. That winter session at school, I barely saw her except for on the basketball or volleyball court. I was grateful for sports because that's what always pulled the two of us together. The fun part for me was when our team would travel somewhere after school and take a bus to get to the game. Then it felt like old times because we would share a seat and gossip our hearts out about how in love she was and what a great guy John was. She would tell me everything. Often in too much detail, making me feel embarrassed and babyish.

That spring break, Dr. and Mrs. McPherson took all their girls to Hawaii for a holiday. I was jealous once again because I missed my friend. First, John was taking her away from me, and then her family was too. I wondered if I'd ever see her again or ever get her all to myself. That one-week, spring vacation seemed endless.

It wasn't until track season started in May that I got my Jessie back. I went to track tryouts, fully expecting to see her there. I was stunned when she didn't show up. She was our best track athlete. She was a blue ribbon runner and was one of the best contenders at the school district track meet year after year. I phoned her that afternoon when I got home from school and asked her if she had sprained her ankle or something. Why hadn't she come out to track tryouts?

She told me she just hadn't felt like it. That didn't make sense to me. If there was something Jessie always felt like doing, it was running. It was especially weird considering that we were in grade twelve. Jessie is very competitive, and it wasn't like her not to join the track team. I asked if I could come over after supper, and she agreed.

Up in her bedroom that night, Jessie told me she thought she was pregnant, and she hadn't told anyone except me. I was stunned. She was eighteen and about to graduate high school. Jessie was our valedictorian and was starting university in the fall to be a doctor like her dad. She couldn't be pregnant.

She whispered to me that she had missed two periods and didn't know what to do. She didn't feel very well and was experiencing morning sickness all day. I sure didn't know what to do. This news was way beyond my level of expertise. My instinct was to tell my mom when things went wrong, but I didn't think I could tell my mom this, and I was betting that Jessie was feeling the same way.

With Jessie's dad being a doctor, it would be hard to get a pregnancy test without him finding out. I remember us looking at each other with scared expressions. It didn't seem as though there were very many options. I remember she held her head in her hands, and she cried a quiet, hushed cry. The McPherson household had lots of ears, and crying was another thing that was hard to hide.

I told her that she still had to come out for track tryouts. They were going on all week. Our coach had been asking about her today, and everyone was wondering why she wasn't there. I told her that if she didn't join the team, people would suspect that something was wrong. We worked out the timing of it, and it turned out that by the end of the school year, she would be four, maybe five months pregnant. She wouldn't be showing yet, or at least not very much. Then it would be summer, and that would buy us two months.

It turned out that by July, she had confessed to her mom and dad. She didn't have much choice. She was starting to show, not so much in her tummy, but in her boobs. They were giving her away on a daily basis—getting bigger by the moment it seemed. And rather than the wrath she expected, her parents reacted in a calm and supportive manner.

Her father took her to the hospital for her first prenatal examination. Everything checked out and was as it should be. They estimated that her due date was around the end of October or beginning of November. Her parents suggested that rather than start university in September, she could begin in January instead. I often wondered if that is why she went in for a business degree like me—because I had paved the way, and it was easier. Her parents assured her that all would work out and not to worry. All was well and good until she told John.

Things hadn't cooled down between the two of them, and I suspected he was crazy about her boobs exploding out of her bikini. She and John went for a walk at Kitsilano Beach one evening, and she told him. John was a nice boy, but the word boy is the operative word. He was a boy. Sure, he was eighteen and could have sex—but he wasn't a man. John was good-looking and young and free and smart and immature. And, his girlfriend had just told him that she was pregnant—he was going to become a father.

It wasn't long before Jessie wasn't hearing from him. Just like that,

John ended everything. He stopped calling and taking her out. He didn't drop over for coffee with her and her mom. He broke up with her without actually breaking up with her. He just stopped. Jessie was distraught and more than broken-hearted. When she phoned his house, his mom would tell her he wasn't home and that she would pass on the message that Jessie had called. But, he never called back. Jessie cried a lot that summer, and I was the one who did most of the listening. She put on a happy face for her parents, but it was all she could talk about when we were alone. My heart ached for her.

That fall when university started, and there was no sign of John, I asked our friends about him. Someone said that Buzzy had told him John had decided to go to university back east. I huffed inside because I thought that seemed fitting for a coward like him. When friends asked about Jessie, I told them that she and her parents had gone to Europe for a family vacation, and she was planning to start in January.

There was never any doubt that she would have the baby. The hardest decision for her was whether or not to parent it. After much deliberation with herself, her parents, and her God, she decided that the best thing for herself and the baby would be to make an adoption plan. Her parents were willing to help her raise the baby, but I don't think she could raise the baby of a boy who had abandoned her, regardless of how much she had loved them both. It would have been her constant reminder of the love she had had and lost.

Baby McPherson arrived early in November, and Jessie never saw her baby boy. When the nurse asked if she would like to see her baby and hold him, she shook her head no and answered with eyes full of tears. I remember going to the hospital to see her the day her baby was born. I was excited and concerned and hopeful. I skipped classes that day, so I could go to the hospital to be with her. I was rushing into her room when I stopped dead in my tracks. Chills ran up and down my spine at the sound I heard.

It took me a long moment to comprehend what I was hearing. I finally figured out that it was the quiet voice of Dr. McPherson. I inched closer and peeked through the gap between the door and the door frame. I could see that he was holding Jessie in his arms. She had her head down, and she slumped into her father's body. Her body was wracked with sobs. He was patting her hair and kissing her on her head. In his Scottish brogue, he was saying, "There, there, me bonnie lass. Let it all out. I've got ya in me arms, and I'll hold ya forever. Everything will be fine, me wee lassie. You wait and see. Let it all out and cry 'til there are no more tears."

I felt like a terrible eavesdropper, and I was startled by the eerie sound coming out of Jessie. I had never heard anything like it before. Her devastation created that sound. It was a heartbroken, mournful cry that seemed to come from something other than a human body. I couldn't believe that this sound was coming out of my best friend. Jessie had boundless energy and enthusiasm, and she was so full of life and fun. I had never felt so heartsick and helpless in my life. There was nothing I could do for her. She was in the best place she could be—her da's arms.

I waited outside the door for a long time. Dr. McPherson stopped in the doorway as if to catch his breath when he left Jessie's room. When he saw me, he wiped his eyes and tried to act like he hadn't been crying. He said that Jessie had fallen to sleep and that the rest would do her good. When I suggested that I should go home, he disagreed. Dr. McPherson said that I should go in and be there when she woke up. He said she would want to see me, and that she shouldn't be alone right now. He knew I would be the medicine she needed. I did as I was told and tiptoed into the room to be with her.

Jessie looked small in her bed. It was like the delivery had sucked the life out of her. She had dark circles under her eyes, and her skin was ashen. Her arms looked thin, resting above the sheets, and I could see the bump her tummy made under the covers. I was surprised to see that because I had expected that her belly would be completely flat again once the baby was born. I sat down quietly in the chair by her bed and waited. She slept fitfully and tossed her head with restlessness.

When she woke up, I was there, holding her hand. When she saw me, her eyes filled with tears, and she choked back a sob. I didn't know what else to do, so I stood up and wrapped my arms around her neck and held her. She cried that awful cry. I did what I saw her dad do, and patted her hair and kissed her head. My heart was breaking for my friend. Her situation was so unfair. She was the most worthy girl I knew, and she deserved much better treatment than this. I later learned that John's parents had never called her family to acknowledge the birth of their grandson. We shouldn't have expected anything more from their son.

But, that didn't alleviate her heartache. Her broken heart was real. She had lost her love. He was her first love. And she had thought it was real—a true love—the way only a teenager can believe and feel. For all her flirtatious ways with other boys, she had given John her virginity. She was as naïve as I was about pregnancy. She wasn't a bad girl. She was an uneducated girl, just like I was. For all the bravado of what we thought of as modern times and free love and the birth control pill, things weren't all that progressive for young women.

Jessie had loved him, and she thought that John had loved her. Maybe he had. Perhaps he was just as scared as she was, and didn't know what to do either. Possibly he hadn't told his parents. We don't know what became of him. I imagine it couldn't have been easy for him either, but all that loss had to have been more difficult for Jessie.

She had lost her love, but she had also lost her baby. Jessie had signed the adoption forms releasing her child to the authorities, and she lived with her decision. She said that the file could be open so that if her child ever wanted to find her, he could. To this day, she hasn't heard from him. He would now be closer to forty than thirty. Jessie never speaks of it because I don't think she can. It is buried deep within her, and she keeps it safely tucked away in the depths of her heart. It was a treasured time, and he was a precious boy—her sweet baby. He was all hers to hold in her memory, even though she had never met him. I know that when I see a tall, redheaded man, I look twice to see if it might be him. I can only suppose she does the same.

It was a long time before Jessie got back to being her old self. She was pretty quiet and stayed home most nights, never going to a university dance or a pub night. When I asked her to go with me, there was always an excuse. She was tired, or she had too much homework. But, I knew she just didn't have it in her to go. She had to let her wounds heal. I would often come over to her house for a sleepover, but things weren't the same for a long time. It was well into our second year of university before she started to snap out of it. It was near the end of our second year, right around the time she introduced me to Paul, that she began to perk up. I think she thought that if she wasn't going to be a doctor herself, maybe she could marry one, and Paul seemed like a good prospect.

A lot of young women back then didn't take university very seriously. It wasn't necessarily a means to a career like it is today. Attending university was considered by some, usually our mothers, a way to meet eligible bachelors more than anything. I didn't know it at the time, but those university boys are the cream of the crop, as far as husband prospects go— providers anyway—the way girls were taught to think about husbands back then. I remember hearing someone say that her parents had sent her to university to get her MRS degree. I didn't get it at first, but then it dawned on me what she meant. Jessie didn't fall into that category, but I think she felt like she owed her parents something so colossal, she could never repay them. I'm sure Jessie's parents didn't feel that way, but I think it sent her on a relentless hunt for the perfect husband.

"I guess I don't get to hear any more of the details of your sexual encounter last night," she says hopefully, changing the subject.

She knows I have told her everything I am going to tell her about my sexual adventure. I can't get into the dirty details the same way she can. But, I am unsettled, and I have to tell her the biggest event of the night.

I stretch out, entwining my legs into hers and blurt, "He told me he is moving to Vancouver and that he is falling in love with me."

She bolts upright in her spot and braces herself against the arm of the couch, "Get out of here!" she hollers. If she could have reached me, I would have been on the receiving end of a big whack on the arm.

Getting up from the couch to stoke the fire, I turn to her and say,

"Yes. That's how he ended the night. He gave me a tiny box to open on Christmas Day and said that he is falling in love with me."

Letting out a low whistle and throwing her head back, she exclaims, "Whoa! I wasn't expecting to hear that! I knew he was going to seduce you last night, but love? That's something completely different! How do you feel about that? I just thought it was great that you let him seduce you. I was impressed by that alone!"

She already knows I'm not in love with him. I was completely surprised by his words. I'm not in love with him, so how can he be in love with me? But after last night, I certainly am in lust for him. I didn't know my body could respond like that anymore. It hadn't even bothered me when he touched the loose tummy skin under my belly button. Aphrodite's head is still spinning around in satisfaction. I, too, am happy and relieved that I let myself get sexually entangled. It felt good to let myself go and relax about it.

"I know! I'm not sure if it was the wine or the penthouse suite or what it was exactly, but I was able to let myself be swept away. It was a very romantic night. It felt incredibly good to be held and touched that way," I hug myself and groan with satisfaction, as I smile and whisper. "He was so good."

I am blushing, and Jessie's face is beaming. "That's wonderful!" she cheers. "Yahoo!"

"I know! I'm happy about it too. Let me be clear. Mike didn't exactly say he is moving here, but he told me he is moving his head office to Vancouver, and that's the real reason he is spending the winter here. He told me he hoped that staying in Whistler would allow us to get closer. Then he told me he is falling in love with me."

"Wow!" Jessie's eyes are as big as saucers. "I'm stunned to hear this. It makes sense, though. I couldn't figure out why he was hanging around here all winter. He has managers to run things, so it didn't make sense to me why he's stayed here so long. I wondered if he wanted to get away from the harsh winter back east and enjoy some first-class skiing instead. Wow." She repeated, more to herself than me.

I can almost see the cogs turning in her brain as she ruminates over this new information. With a bright voice, she claps her hands together in delight and suggests, "Let's open the gift Mike gave you!"

There's nothing she likes more than a wrapped present.

"No! I said I wouldn't open it until Christmas Day!" I am aghast.

"Well, who is going to know?" she asks. "Are you going to open it in front of everyone or up in your room all by yourself? Come on! I want to be here when you open it. I can't wait to know what's inside! What does an entrepreneur with everything buy someone he is falling in love with?"

"Do you think we should? I'll tear the paper!"

"Oh, big deal—so what! Who will know except you and me? Rewrap it if you have to and put it under the tree. Come on! No one will know, except us!"

Hesitating, I go to the tree and pick up the box. I had placed it on one of the branches so it wouldn't get lost amongst the heap of gifts that will soon be under the tree. Jessie hops out of her seat and grabs it from me. She dashes back to the couch, holding it in the palm of her hand.

"Come on!" she says, curling her index finger, indicating that I should get over to her. She winks at me and offers the box up toward me. "Open it!"

"Oh, okay—but don't tell anyone I did this!" I take the box from her and start to peel back the tape carefully. I don't want to tear the paper.

"Oh, hurry up!" She has never been patient opening a gift.

The peeled back paper reveals a highly polished, handcrafted wooden box that looks like ebony. I peer inside and find a gold necklace. The pendant is a small sphere, about the size of a gumball. When I look at it carefully, I see that it is Earth. But, there is something different about it. The continents are not as they are now, but as they were millions of years ago. It's Pangaea! I can make out the shapes of the continents the way they fit together like a puzzle, and I see what will become North America. There is a tiny diamond embedded where we might approximately be today. The piece is exquisite and made to design. The little card with it says, "Let me give you the world. Mike."

The symbolism of this gift dumbfounds me. Mike has thought this through very carefully and must have ordered this necklace long ago for it to be ready in time for Christmas. My eyes meet Jessie's.

"It's beautiful," she whispers as if someone else might hear.

I put the chain around my neck and go to the mirror, putting my hand to the bauble and stroking it. I am astonished by its pure beauty and elegance. I can't believe that Mike thought of this.

"It's lovely," I agree quietly.

"What are you going to do now?" she asks sincerely.

"I don't know for sure," I say while continuing to look at myself in the mirror.

"Are you going to take it off and rewrap it?" Jessie asks.

"No. I don't think so. I think I'll wear it."

"Wow," she says quietly. We both sit for a few moments and admire the tree. It is quiet in the neighbourhood, and everyone's Christmas lights are sparkling outside.

"I'm not sure I'll ever take it off," I finally say. My head is down, and my finger is gently caressing the diamond. "I love it."

Jessie leans in toward me. "Are you falling in love with him?" she asks, studying my face.

"I'm not sure," I answer honestly. My eyes start to fill with tears.

It's been many years since I've been in love. I know what it felt like to be in love with Tony. I was young, and it was my first love, which made it all-consuming and passionate and wild. Every moment was bliss. I had my parents to guide me, and my best friend to support me. Because of all that, Tony and I had a great love together.

What isn't to love about Mike? He has every quality that I should want. I am still enjoying the satisfaction of my body's rapture, and do not doubt that he will be a marvellous lover. He can buy me the world, and apparently, he is willing to, according to his card. It is impossible not to consider the kind of life he could give me. But, it would be a very different life from the one I have now.

I have butterflies in my tummy like I have not experienced since Tony.

I'm not sure if they represent excitement or fear or love or all three. I am incredibly interested in Mike. I am pretty sure I could genuinely care about him. Is that love? Maybe it's what love becomes. I don't know yet.

Chapter 10
Two Lovers

It is pitch-black in my room. The phone is ringing incessantly. I bat around in the dark, trying to find it. I finally come in contact with it and knock it to the floor. Swearing under my breath, I manage to find the receiver.

"What!" I demand crossly. It bugs me when Jessie calls so early, especially when it's Sunday. I don't know what she could want to talk about that we didn't already hash to bits last night.

"Wake up on the wrong side of the bed?" a man's voice asks.

I'm startled, and my head is foggy. I'm not sure who it is. For a fleeting moment, I think it is Tony, and my next thought is that I really am going insane.

"Who is this?" I ask abruptly. My mother would have been aghast at my lack of manners.

"It's Mike," he says, laughing.

Sitting up, I rub my eyes and look out the window. There isn't a glimmer of light yet. I wonder what time it is. There is a three hour time difference between here and Toronto, so it must be very early in the morning.

"Oh, Mike! Good morning!" I find my words and quickly apologize.

"No, no—I'm the one who is sorry. I knew I would be waking you up. I apologize for disturbing your beauty sleep, which I might add works perfectly for you."

I like how he effortlessly slips in that compliment. He is smooth, that is for sure. I can't help but smile. Stretching and stifling a yawn, I tell him, "It's nice to hear your voice," I say with sincerity.

"It's nice to hear yours too. I've been missing you," he adds.

"I've been missing you also," I surprise myself with my automatic response. "Thank you for the beautiful Christmas gift."

The words just slipped out before I could stop them! I am silently horrified at myself. Biting my lip, I punch my fist down into the covers of my bed. I hadn't made a plan about whether or not to tell him I had opened his gift. My fingers are rubbing the little ball, and I love how warm and smooth it feels to my touch. I am smiling and hear him laughing in my ear.

"I wondered if you would wait until Christmas Day!" he teases. "I didn't think you would open it early."

"I'm thoroughly embarrassed," I reply. "Ordinarily, I wouldn't have. I would have waited. Jessie was here last night, and she coaxed me into opening it. We're not going to be together on Christmas Day, and she wanted to be the one who was with me when I opened it. I hope you don't mind. It was a childish thing to do."

"I don't mind. It's endearing. I'm glad you like it."

"I love it. It's beautiful. Thank you for such an incredibly thoughtful gift."

"You are very welcome."

"Did you open mine?" I ask.

"No, I haven't opened it yet. It is still tucked away in my suitcase. I won't open it until Christmas morning."

Relieved, I say, "Good. Open it when you are by yourself."

"It will be the first thing I do when I open my eyes on Christmas Day. I will put it by my bedside, so you will be the last thing I think of before I go to sleep, and the first thing I think of when I wake up."

"I hope you like it," I say sheepishly. I know my gift is no match to Mike's, at least monetarily, but I know it's a thoughtful and significant gift. I hadn't put any kind of card or words with it. I assume he will figure it out. I hadn't mentioned love, but the gift itself is a gift of promise. My upper lip is about to burst into a layer of sweat. I push my hair back and wipe my brow as I realize he could take it as the key to my heart!

"I'm sure I'll love it," he says quietly, then adds, "I called early your time because we have a big day here today. My brother and his family will be getting in around noon, and it will be bedlam after that, so I thought I'd better call now because the day will get away on me, and it will be midnight before I know it. We are all going to the opera tomorrow night, and the next few days will be jam-packed. I wanted to be sure to check in with you."

He's going to the opera. I don't know anyone who goes to the opera. I wonder what opera performs at this time of year, and all I can think of is *The Nutcracker*, but that is a ballet, not an opera. I have seen it several times myself. I love it—it is such a feast for the eyes and a lovely Christmas tale. I imagine Mike in his tuxedo. I see myself in a delicate gown, holding onto his arm, entering the opera.

"Are you there?" he asks.

"Oh—yes. Sorry," I reply.

He chuckles, "I thought maybe you had drifted off to sleep."

"Oh no, I was just thinking about the opera," I say. "How lovely for all of you."

"It's a nice evening. It is a tradition for us. We all go every year. A local opera company puts it on, and it's quite good. It's *A Christmas Carol*, my mother's favourite. It is all in keeping with the season and a big night for us all."

"It sounds splendid." My mind wanders, and I giggle to myself as I envision Ebenezer Scrooge singing in falsetto to the Ghost of Christmas Past. I imagine Mike's family all together at the opera. I visualize them dressed in their finery, never mind the fact that I don't know what any of them look like. I'll have to get Mike to show me a picture. I keep imagining his mother to be like the queen, small and hunched over with coiffed grey hair. I'm not sure how old she is—he describes her as elderly. She could be quite spry, like my mother. In my mind's eye, she is dressed in a regal suit while bundled into a magnificent winter coat and matching hat, gloves and sensible dress boots. She would be holding gracefully onto the arm of her favourite son, Mike, as they make their way into the opera house.

"Maybe you'll get to join us one day," he adds.

I snap back to reality at the sound of his voice, and I squirm at the suggestion of his words. My upper lip is now completely wet. I say, rather too quickly, "Maybe I will." Oh my goodness—where did that come from? Shut up! Shut up! Shut up! But, as I try to quiet my inner voice, I am surprised by how much I hope this fantasy will come true.

"Well, my darling, I'm sorry to have woken you so early. I just wanted to say hello and let you know I arrived safely. I hope you can go back to sleep. I'll let you go now, and I'll be in touch in another couple of days."

"Okay. Thanks for calling. Thanks again for the beautiful present."

"You are most welcome. Sweet dreams."

He hangs up, and I lie there in the dark with the receiver in my hand. It is making that buzzing sound that indicates it's been off the hook for too long. The prerecorded operator's voice comes on, telling me to hang up. Looking out the window, I am trying to keep a level head and have clear thoughts. Mike is a wonderful man. I don't ever want to lose sight of that. He's a wonderful man who says he loves me. I roll over, my back to the window, close my eyes, and hug myself back to sleep. A smile spreads across my face as I drift off.

⌒

"How was ice climbing?" I ask Paul, sincerely interested. He's asked me to join him a couple of times, but I've declined his invitation each time. Ice climbing is a demanding sport that I don't quite have the strength for, not to mention the nerve. Being stuck up there on the side of a rock face covered in frozen water is disconcerting beyond what my fear centre can handle, and my brain would never be able to grasp it. It's such an unnatural thing to do, I think I would be holding my breath the entire time, and the fear I would experience is unimaginable.

"It was excellent. The conditions were just right," Paul answers.

"That's super. I'm glad you had a good day."

It turned out that I had a rare day by myself today. After my early morning wake-up call, I managed to sleep until almost ten o'clock. That is unheard of for me, but it sure felt good. It must be the pace of the holiday season catching up with me. I have been tired for the last few days, and I enjoyed the long sleep.

I spent the day puttering. I wrapped some gifts and put them under the tree. I went over the holiday menu and made a list of the few things I still needed to get from the grocer. The store was bustling, and I was glad to have had lots of time. You never know—with all the tourists in town for the holiday season, the grocery stores can run out of the things you want.

I knew Paul had gone ice climbing today and that he wouldn't be coming for dinner tonight, so I enjoyed a light dinner of toast with peanut butter in the early evening, and I was settling down with a cup of tea when he called. It's nice to talk to Paul, and I'm happy to hear his voice. A couple of days have gone by since I last saw him and I have missed him. I pull the blanket over my feet as I curl up on the couch.

"Listen, Gin—I wanted to confirm plans for the twenty-sixth and make sure we are still on for dinner that night."

"Oh, yes, we are! I'm looking forward to it. It will be nice not to have to make dinner for the big crowd. It will be lovely to have you serve me for a change!" I tease him.

"And that's what I'll be doing, don't worry about that!" he replies, laughing. "How does seven o'clock sound? I'll pick you up. We can eat around seven-thirty, maybe eight."

"That sounds perfect. I can't wait," I say with sincerity. Paul rarely has me over to his house, and I can count on one hand the number of times he has made me dinner there. It's a busy time of year for him, and I know that preparing a meal for me will be hard for him to do with everything else he has filling up his day. Feeling somewhat guilty about this, I ask, "Is there anything I can do to help out?"

"No, that's fine. Everything is under control. I've been cooking for days now in my spare time and filling up my freezer with delectable delights to entice you with," he laughs again.

I giggle too and allow myself the treat of being spoiled by him, "Okay then. Dinner at your house on the twenty-sixth it is. It's going to be fun, Paul. Thanks."

I am looking forward to being alone with him in his house. It's not like Paul and I don't get any time alone with each other. But, somehow, this invitation is different. I remember his words about our time together and think this is going to be a special night for just the two of us.

We hang up, and I decide to head off to bed. I crawl under the covers, but I can tell it will be one of those nights. And I'm right. I read my book for what feels like a gazillion hours, yet here I am, looking out the window and still feeling restless. I try not to eat in the evening or have dinner too late because it can disrupt my sleep. I'm not sure what is bothering me tonight—maybe it's just because I slept so long this morning. I used to be a good sleeper, but this is happening more and more to me lately—damn menopause. I roll over and punch my pillow. Pulling the covers up to my chin, I rub my feet together because they are cold. My socks are on the floor by the bed. I reach for them and slip them over my toes without letting any of the cold night air under the covers.

There was a time when Paul would check on me in the night. I could call him any time, and he would come over when I was having a hard time. The months after Tony died were especially bad for me, and I counted on Paul a lot. I don't know if it was because he is a doctor or because he is a man, but I found him more comforting than Jessie. I never wanted to disturb Jessie at night because she works hard at her job, and I wanted her to be successful. Jessie can be overly emotional, and during those dark days, that wasn't helpful to me. Part of me felt that medical personnel, doctors, in particular, are so sleep-deprived that making a house call in the middle of the night wouldn't be a big deal.

Sometimes he would come over, and we would sit in the kitchen and have a cup of tea. Sometimes we talked, and sometimes he let me cry while he didn't say a word. Now and again, he would hold me and rock me. One night he crawled on top of the bedcovers with me, held me in his arms, and spoke quietly to me the way a mother soothes her crying baby. Paul's arms around me in the darkness of the night helped me through. I woke up in the morning, fully dressed with a blanket placed carefully over me, and he was gone.

Both of my girls were quite sick the day before Tony had his accident. They both had chest infections and fever. I was anxious about their condition, so I phoned Tony at his office, but he had gone to an emergency at the hospital. His medical assistant put me through to Paul, and he said he would come over right away.

After examining them, Paul prescribed an antibiotic. It was almost suppertime. I would have to get the prescription filled later. It's strange the things you remember about seemingly insignificant moments in time, but I had a pot of meat sauce simmering on the stove. After we came down from checking on the girls, I went to stir the sauce and broke into tears. I had been operating on almost no sleep from keeping a night vigil in the girls' room. It seemed that when one child fell asleep, the other one woke up, and I had spent most of my last couple of nights rocking them. I was dead on my feet. Paul got up from the kitchen chair he was sitting on and came to me. He wrapped his arms around me, and I let myself go. I couldn't believe the extent of my tears.

He was suggesting that I go lie down when Tony walked in. I was so relieved to see him. I ran to him and threw my arms around his neck. I wiped my eyes and said I was going to try to sleep for a while. Paul said he would go to pick up the prescription. Tony seemed troubled and in a bad mood. As I climbed the stairs to our room, I remember hearing Paul explaining to Tony that he had come over after I called looking for him. Then I just heard men's voices talking as my head hit the pillow, and I fell asleep.

The house was quiet when I woke up, and I could hear Tony's steady breathing beside me. I had fallen asleep fully clothed. I slipped out of bed and went to the girls' room to check on them. Tony had left a note saying that they had had their first dose of antibiotics at eight o'clock. They were both more peaceful than they had been earlier in the day. I snuck back to our bed and woke hours later with a start, disoriented and knowing that I had overslept. That's how the worst day of my life began. That day was misery from beginning to end.

It's a long time ago now. People are right about what they say about time being the best healer. Given enough time, a person will get over the heartache. The love of your family and good friends certainly helps, and I couldn't have gotten through it all without them. But time is what softens the edges. Time is what makes it blurry and on the periphery of your daily life—rather than in the centre. Tony is regularly on my mind at this time of year, and if I let him, he can still weigh heavily on my heart. Paul is undoubtedly the one who has pulled me through the darkest of my days. I will be forever grateful to him, and I will always love him.

Chapter 11
Christmas is ~~Coming~~ Here!

"Will I see you later?" I ask Paul, hopefully. This crazy week has gone by so fast. I've had my shop open late every night this week. Jessie has been working overtime hours, which means we've hardly had time to speak to one another, and I haven't seen or talked to Paul in days. It's a whole week since I last spoke with him. I can't believe it's already Sunday week! My family is due to arrive this afternoon. The big day is just around the corner.

"I'm not sure. I have to play it by ear. If I can't make it for dinner, I'll try to swing by in the evening. I'm looking forward to giving Ronnie a squeeze," he jokes.

My mother is crazy about Paul. The first time she laid eyes on him, she exclaimed something embarrassing about his gorgeous eyes. Saying that to my friend when I was twenty was out of character for her, and I remember wondering if she had been drinking. I had wished the ground would open up and swallow me whole.

"Oh, you two have been nursing your love affair for too long!" I giggle. "Just come on out and declare your love for her! Let it be out in the open!"

He laughs and replies, "I do love her; that's for sure. It will be good to see both of your parents. I'll try to make it over. It depends on how tired I am and how long the day turns out to be."

"Well, there will be lots of food, so if you can't make it in time for dinner, you know you can eat here later if you come by."

My mom and dad are more like parents to Paul than his were. Both his parents are gone now, but he wasn't close to them when they were alive. His father drank himself to death, and Paul did not go to his funeral. He did go home when his mother passed, but he hadn't seen her in a long time. I know he sent her money and made sure she was taken care of, but other than that, he didn't see her. I guess deep hurt lives within you for a long time, and love isn't necessarily enough to find forgiveness or understanding of others' choices. I know she was never his defender, and he felt she betrayed him. She was probably too busy protecting herself to give him the care he needed and deserved.

On the other hand, Paul and my mother are close. They liked each other right from the beginning. Back in the early days, whenever my mom knew that Paul was coming over, she would make something especially good to eat, and it was usually *his* favourite, never mind what the rest of us liked. My mother is one of those women who always looks good. She still takes the time to put herself together, but I am sure that when she knew Paul was coming over, she spruced herself up more carefully. The two of them clicked right from the start. They would laugh and joke with each other, which was different from the way both of them behaved toward me. I have never fully understood that.

Paul dotes on my mom in a way that my brother and I, or even my dad, never do. He brings her flowers that somehow manage to be her favourite, or a book that he heard was the latest rave—little things, just because. He makes sure I look after my mother, and that I'm the dutiful daughter. He knows I talk to her all the time on the phone, but if I haven't given him a recent report on what is going on in Ronnie's life, he is sure to ask. I think he loves her more than Jessie does, and she's known my mom since we were teenagers.

I catch him up on my last few days and tell him what to expect with the whole crew arriving at the house. I will be taking the next few days off work. I have a woman who comes in for me on occasion, and I always plan for her to put in extra hours at Christmastime. I might go in and check on things sometime over the next few days, but my time will mostly be with my family.

Cath called yesterday to tell me she has decided to come up today with my parents and brother. I am silently relieved because I don't like her to drive the highway by herself. I know she will be safe in my brother's hands. She sounded hungover on the phone and tired from the party she had been to the night before. She told me her exams went well and that she is happy to have them over and done. She is enjoying her time with her university friends. I suspect there is someone she is interested in, and I hope to hear more about him once she gets home.

The doorbell rings as a courtesy. I know it's Jessie. I wave to her as she lets herself in.

"Jess just got here, so I should go," I tell Paul. "I hope to see you later."

I turn my attention to my best friend. Whenever she enters a room, a whirlwind follows her, and this morning is no different. She kicks off her boots and shimmies out of her coat, just dropping everything in the foyer. She rushes to me and gives me a big kiss and hug. It is always excellent to see her, even after all these years. She is fresh and fun, and delightful. She looks radiant this morning in her blue jeans and a long-sleeved, white cotton T-shirt.

"Happy Christmas, my darlin' friend!" she squeals, holding onto my shoulders while jumping up and down. "I love this season! I am excited to be going home! Let's have some coffee."

She rushes into the kitchen and makes her way to the cupboard, digging out her favourite cup and one for me. She doesn't get home much because her job takes up most of her time. She sets aside a solid week or more around Christmas to be home with her family. It's especially important to her since her dad died. She and all her sisters make an extra effort for their mom. Jessie's managers take over for her in her absence, and I imagine they too put in a lot of hours during this time. She works the rest of the season, but Christmas is sacred to her.

"What are we having for breakfast?" she asks, looking through the cereal cupboard.

"I had an egg when I got up, so I'm not hungry right now. I'll just have coffee," I say, as I get the coffeepot set up and started.

She selects a cereal for herself and nestles into her chair.

"I'm hungry this morning," she exclaims while taking her first few bites. "Must be all the overeating I've been doing lately." She rubs her tummy as she says it.

"Oh, please," I remark in disgust. Her stomach is as flat as ever. Knowing her, she probably had fish and salad for supper last night—and no dessert. She is diligent and dedicated to her healthy diet. Almost no sugar passes between her lips. I am envious of the resolve she has around avoiding sugary foods. I have to work a lot harder at that than she does.

"Well, my jeans are tighter than usual this morning, but what can I say, I've consumed a lot of cocktails these past few weeks!"

"You look beautiful," I say, pushing my hair off my face. I haven't done anything with myself yet today. I had another sleep-in and haven't been up a terribly long time. I jumped into my sweatpants and a sloppy shirt this morning because I knew I'd be tidying the house and setting out food. I'll have a quick shower after Jessie leaves, hopefully before my family arrives.

"Beauty is in the eye of the beholder, I guess," she says, brushing off my compliment. "Hey, how are things? What's happened with Mike— have you heard from him lately?"

Jessie and I have had brief chats and quick check-ins this week, but we haven't had a good chinwag because we've both been so busy. "Yes. I spoke with him yesterday. He's had a hectic week at work getting things wrapped up before the holidays. He's busy with the Christmas bustle now too. He's running around shopping today and getting organized for the main event."

"Haven't we all! I've been running flat out all week. I'm sure looking forward to having a few days off. Hey—you never did tell me—did you confess to him that you opened his present?" she asks, leaning across the table and whacking me on my arm while taking her last mouthful of cereal and licking her spoon.

"I did. I just blurted it out. I couldn't keep it in," I say, as I touch my new necklace. I still haven't taken it off.

"What did he say?"

"He laughed at me. He said he wondered if I'd be able to wait. I feel like such a child about it."

"Hey, wait a minute—it was me who convinced you to open it. You didn't have that juvenile idea all by yourself! I want some of the credit!" she says, leaning across the table and whacking me again. "Careful what you say. I'll get hurt feelings."

We burst out laughing, looking at one another. It did seem childish opening Mike's present early, but that's what's amusing about it and made it so much fun to do. I lean back on my chair and hold my stomach, tipping back my head and letting out a full belly laugh.

"Oh, it was fun opening it! I haven't felt that sneaky in years!" I continue, wiping tears of laughter from my eyes. "He didn't mind that I opened it. He said he hadn't opened my gift to him yet. He plans to open it Christmas morning when he wakes up before he goes down and joins his family. He said I'd be the first thing he thinks of on Christmas morning."

Jessie whistles and says, "Hubba! Hubba! He's hot for you. Seriously though, he's genuine about all this, isn't he?"

"Yes, I think he is," I reply quietly.

She looks at me carefully and doesn't say anything. She doesn't have to ask the inevitable "and how are you feeling about it all" question. She already knows the answer.

"Well, hang in there," she says. "You'll know how you feel about it as it unfolds. Listen to your gut. It is never wrong."

"I suppose you are right about that," I say. I haven't ever had to depend on my gut for anything like this in my whole life. "That's what people say, anyway."

"What did you get him?" she asks.

I haven't discussed this with her. I am shy to tell her what I gave Mike. It seems like a big step when I think about it in hindsight. Maybe I should have gotten him a sweater.

"I gave him a key to my house," I say quietly, trying to sound nonchalant.

"What? Are you kidding me? I can't believe my ears!" she exclaims. "Have you been holding out on me? Are you more serious about him than you've been letting on?"

"No, I'm not holding out on you. You know everything. I'm just trying to loosen up. I'm trying to open myself up and allow this to happen. I'm tired of being alone, and I'm tired of acting self-protective, and I wanted to give him something special. Also, I had no better ideas. I was stuck on what to get him."

"Well, that's the gift of the century! That sends him a big message."

"I suppose it does. The key doesn't mean that I want Mike to live here or anything like that. I just want him to have the same privileges as you and Paul. I want him to feel welcome in my life. I didn't enclose a note with it. I just put it in a box and wrapped it up. I reckon he'll figure it out."

"That present is going to blow his mind. It's blowing mine!" Jessie says with wide eyes, a look of surprise still on her face. "Does Paul know that's what you gave Mike?"

"No! I haven't told anyone except you."

"Wow. That blows me away. You talk about wanting to take things slowly, but this is a big invitation."

"I know it is. I think I'm ready."

"Well, I hope so because New Year's Eve is just around the corner!" she says while smiling and rubbing her hands together in anticipation. "Speaking of Paul—what's up with him? Is he coming over later?"

"He's going to try to come over so he can visit with his beloved Ronnie," I reply with a giggle. "I swear those two can't get enough of each other. Did I tell you he's invited me to his house for supper on Boxing Day?"

"No," she says in a low voice, looking at me suspiciously. "You never told me that. What's that all about?"

"Well, he says we might not get many chances to be alone together anymore, and he wants to have some alone time with me over the holiday."

"He's invited you over to his house at Christmastime? And he wants to take you away from your company?" she asks.

"Yes, well—I guess there really isn't another time," I reply.

"Hmm," she says quietly, pouring herself a refill of coffee. "I'm not sure what I make of that. You've only ever gone over to Paul's house for dinner a couple of times the whole time you've lived here. It seems weird to me."

"It seems weird to me too, but what can I say. It will be nice to go over to his house and spend the evening with him, even if my mom and dad are here. I'll see them plenty over the holiday season. Which reminds me, what day are we going shopping for my New Year's Eve dress?"

We have a loose plan that I will come down a few days before New Year's, while Jessie is in Vancouver, and we will go shopping. Years ago, the summer after Jessie had her baby, she was feeling down, and it was an insufferably hot day, so we decided to go shopping and get into the air conditioning. We ended up in the designer evening gown section at the most expensive and exclusive store in the city. We tried expensive gown after expensive gown. It's a wonder the shop keepers let us do that. It must have been obvious we weren't going to buy anything. It was then that it made sense to us why movie stars look so lovely in their dresses. We learned that designer gowns have an inner lining with bones built into them that frame your body. Anyone can look good in a dress that costs seven thousand dollars. That was the cost of those dresses back then. I can't imagine how much they cost now.

When we first discussed shopping for my New Year's Eve dress, Jessie had to do some fast talking to convince me that that was the place where we should shop. I guess she remembers those exquisite dresses, too. Jessie said that I'm not allowed to go out on the town with Mike wearing a dress that I bought thirty years ago, or one from a regular dress shop. She said this is an unprecedented event and that I will have to dress impeccably. I suppose she is right. I don't have an occasion to wear a dress very often, and I don't like them all that much, but I see her point. If he is going to take me out for an extraordinary night on the town, I guess I had better look the part. She convinced me that there will be a sale rack and that we will be sure to find something there. I told her that my budget is five hundred dollars. She agreed, but her fingers were probably crossed behind her back as she said so. She also made me promise that I will buy a new pair of shoes to go with my outfit. *And* I had to promise that I will go to the salon and get my hair and makeup done. I think this is a special night for her as much as it is for me.

"How about the twenty-eighth? I have almost two weeks off. I've taken some extra time off this year and don't have to be back at work until January second. That gives us time to keep looking in case we can't find what you need."

"Okay, that sounds good. I'm not sure which day my mom and dad are heading home to Vancouver, but probably the twenty-seventh. Either way, it will work out. Hey, did you meet up with Buzzy the other day?" I ask.

"I did! I had coffee with him. He came up to my office so we could have privacy," she replies. Jessie's office is quite spectacular. It has a bird's-eye view of the ski hill and is more than just a closet with a desk and chair. She has a lounge area complete with a wet bar that makes it more like a living room than an office.

"How'd it go?"

"It was fine. It was tense at first, but as soon as I addressed the elephant in the room and asked him about John, we settled down. I just asked him straight out if he still kept in touch with John or if he ever heard from him. The short answer is that they are not friends anymore and that after John moved back east, he never heard from him again. I guess some folks deal with their demons by cutting off their past." Her head is down, and when she lifts her face, her eyes are brimming with tears. Continuing, she says, "We had a nice visit. He asked about the baby. He wondered if I ever saw him or if I knew anything about him. I said I didn't and that I had never heard from him. He said he was sorry that had happened to me."

Tears spill from her eyes, and she wipes them quickly. She looks away. My heart squeezes with grief for her. I know she has never gotten over placing her child for adoption, not to mention the heartache of losing John. Nothing can beat the intense emotions of young love. I lean across the table and wrap my arms around her. Her body convulses, and she gulps a breath of air in a quiet sob.

"You deserved better than that. You know it," I pat her hair and comfort her as if she is my child, wiping her tears with my thumb. I kiss her cheek and tell her I love her. Changing the subject, I say, "Hey! Let's exchange our gifts!"

This is a ritual for us. I don't know why we bother to exchange still, other than it's a habit. We have this funny thing we do. We buy each other the same gift each year. I know what Jessie is going to get me, and she knows what I am going to get her. The funny part is that it is such an inconsequential gift. I get her a box of her favourite mint chocolates, and she gets me a box of my favourite peanut butter chocolates. The same confectioner even makes these delectable bonbons.

A long time ago, the summer after our first year at university, our parents let us go camping with friends from school. We only went to Alice Lake, not far from home. We took all our supplies and packed some special treats for ourselves. Jessie and I both loved these chocolates, but we only ever had them at Christmastime. We thought they would be great to take on our camping trip, though we felt rebellious doing so. The best part was that we thought we wouldn't have to share them with anyone. Our mothers were stingy with the family Christmas chocolates—they would portion them out with protective care—usually passing the box around once per night and then putting it away. We were only allowed to have one—we could never just have the whole box to ourselves. There was a houseful of guests to share with, but when you are a young person, often you want to be selfish and a glutton.

We set up camp and went for a swim. The boys we were with went back to camp first. We girls stayed out on the dock and sunbathed for a while. When we got back to camp, the boys were sitting around on the camping chairs, drinking beer and eating chips. They were watching us and laughing amongst themselves. We didn't pay them much mind until we went to our cooler and discovered that our boxes of chocolates were gone. We looked at each other, realizing that they must have taken them. We had planned on stowing the chocolates away into our tent and eating them in the night when we wouldn't have to share with the others. It was going to be our secret indulgence.

When we asked for them to hand over the loot, they tried to look innocent, but after a round of laughter, they confessed that they had eaten the chocolates. They pointed to the fire, and we could see the remains of the boxes burning up. Jessie and I were so mad. We would have left right then if we could have, but we had driven up with one of the other girls. That night in our tent, as we talked about how mad we were, we came up with the idea of exchanging our favourite chocolates as Christmas gifts. We knew that if the chocolates were a personal gift, our mothers wouldn't make us share with anyone, and no one else would dare eat them. It's a funny little thing to do, but we like it, and it continues to be part of our time together at Christmas.

I retrieve my gift from under the tree and slide it across the table. Jessie passes mine to me. We always open them at the same time and then guiltily indulge in a couple each. My box is different this year—it feels bulky at the bottom. When I remove the paper, a wad of money falls out. One-hundred-dollar bills are spilling all over the floor! What is going on? We have a pact that the gift is the same from year to year. We never change it up, so what the heck is all this money? I pick up the stash, and count ten one-hundred-dollar bills altogether! Jessie shrugs her shoulders and beams an impish smile at me. She looks very pleased with herself.

"What's all this about?" I ask while fanning the bills in my hands.

"It's something I wanted to give you to pad your spending money for your New Year's Eve outfit. Your five-hundred-dollar budget isn't going to cut it, so I thought I'd help out," she answers.

"Are you kidding me?" I exclaim. "I can't accept this."

"Of course you can—and you will. I'm not taking it back. I'm so excited for you! I want you to look like a princess, and I want to be part of your special night in any way I can. If that means dressing you up like a doll, then I will, and you can't stop me," she announces defiantly.

I push the money across the table toward her. She pushes it back.

"I'm not taking it back," she says, shaking her head. "You have to spend it on your New Year's Eve outfit. And it's your Christmas present, so you have to spend it all and not share it."

She has such a big smile on her face. Her generosity is extraordinary, and I am speechless.

"Come on, think about it—we've exchanged a box of chocolates with one another for almost forty years. The way I look at it, if I had bought you something other than a box of chocolates all those years, I would have spent way more than a thousand dollars. You have to take it. There is no way you are going to find a dress for the amount of money you have budgeted, and you have to get shoes too, so just take it, and I don't want to hear another word about it."

I run the dollar bills through my fingers, counting them again. They are brand-new bills. I guess hundred-dollar bills don't get used all that often, but these are crisp and unused.

"I went to the bank and ordered brand-new bills for you," she says as if reading my mind.

I look up at her and whisper, "Thank you." There's no use arguing with her. She will have her way about this. I have to concede.

"You are welcome," she smiles at me. "We are going to find you a knock-out dress. I just hope we can find one for a measly grand!"

I laugh at the amount of money she has just proposed we spend on a dress, and I put the money on the table beside the chocolates. I get up from my chair and move toward her. Inviting her to hug me, she gets up from her chair and comes into my arms. We embrace for a long moment—how I love this dear friend of mine.

The doorbell rings, and we both jump as if we are a couple of secret lovers caught in an embrace. The clock on the stove says it's eleven-thirty.

It must be my parents.

I look at Jessie and say, "Crap! That must be my mom! Look at me—I haven't even showered yet!"

"You look fabulous in your sweatpants! Don't worry about it!"

"My mother will be horrified when she sees me!" I exclaim, pushing my hair off my face and wishing I had a ponytail tie handy.

We move toward the door, but I pull her sleeve and stop her before leaving the kitchen. She stops and turns to face me.

"What's up?" she asks.

"Jess," I say slowly. "Thank you. Thanks for being the best friend in the entire world."

I am choking up, though I'm elated. This gift is Jessie's way of telling me that I have to open my purse strings for my special night. I know that when we hit the store on the twenty-eighth, we are going to have fun, and remembering how much that bra and panty set cost me, I know I am going to spend way more than I had planned.

Squeezing my hand and smiling her dazzling smile, she says, "You are welcome, my darling friend—right back at you. Come on! Let's not keep them waiting—let's let them in!"

She turns to the door, and together we greet my family and welcome them home for the holidays.

Chapter 12
A Mother's Love

It's interesting how your adult home morphs and slowly becomes the family's home as time passes. There was a time when my parent's home was where we would all congregate. All the holidays and get-togethers celebrating life's special moments took place at their house. We still have some events at my mom's and dad's place—like their birthdays, but somewhere along the line, the torch was passed, and my house became the family home.

It feels good to open up my house to my family and have everyone home. I am happy that they want to come here and let me share my home with them. I guess coming here is a little holiday for everyone. It's a place to get out of the rat race of the city. There is something special about Whistler beyond the mountains and the resort atmosphere. It's a magical place. Maybe it's the crisp mountain air. I don't know what it is, but it's certainly a place we've all come to love.

Years ago, when Christie was small, we would go to Vancouver for the holidays. But, it was hard because we only ever had two days away from home. We would leave on Christmas Eve and drive to Delta to go to the midnight church service with Tony's folks. Tony would try to shut down the office by three in the afternoon so that we could get there on time, but that wasn't always possible. We would have a late dinner at his mom's, open gifts, and go to church. It was everything we could do to try to get to bed no later than two a.m.

The next morning, we would get up early and open presents from Santa and try to be on the road to my parent's house by eleven in the morning. My mom had brunch ready for us. We would exchange gifts, play with toys, have Christmas dinner and flop into bed early. We spent Boxing Day reorganizing our treasures, indulging in leftovers and getting back on the road, so we could arrive home at a reasonable hour for Tony to work the next day. It seemed like more trouble than it was worth, and if we hadn't been as young as we were, we likely wouldn't have been able to keep up the pace.

After Catherine came along, we used that as our excuse to stay home. We invited everyone to come and stay with us. It was a ton of work until I got a routine established and figured out how to organize the meals for all those guests. But, in the long run, it was much better. Tony could even go to work if he had to.

We would move the girls into our room, and my brother would stay in their bedroom—possibly with his latest girlfriend, but more often alone. My mom and dad would stay in the spare room upstairs, which eventually became Christie's room. Tony's mom and dad would take the downstairs guest room, the one I now think of as Jessie's room. It all worked out, and we all had such a good time.

The grandmas were around to share in the cooking and dote over their granddaughters. The grandpas would go off together and entertain one another, often with Tony, my brother and Paul in tow. Sometimes they would go ice skating or to a hockey game at the arena. Sometimes they would go cross-country skiing or just go for a beer in town. It was pretty stereotypical behaviour, but it was what the older men were used to, so we all went along with it. It was miraculous that we all got along. It was so much fun and still is.

My brother and Dad are currently flopped on the couch watching a hockey game, while Christie and Cath are working on a puzzle in the living room. I hear Eddie playing with his cars making *vroom, vroom, vroom,* noises. My mom and I are washing the supper dishes and cleaning up the kitchen. She is at home in my kitchen, and I am grateful for that.

"Tell me about your young man," she says, with a cheeky smile on her lips.

"Oh, Mom! Please!" I laugh as I say it because it feels good in an old familiar sort of way.

My mom is washing the dishes, I am drying them, and she is interrogating me about my love life! If I think about it, I do the same thing with my girls, so the apple doesn't fall very far from the tree. Maybe it's just what mothers do. Regardless, it is delightful to feel like a teenager again, if it's only for a second. She laughs out loud, too, and rests her hands on the sides of the sink. She has rubber gloves on to protect her manicure. I have never known her to wash the dishes with her bare hands.

"Seriously," she says. "I know we've talked on the phone, and you've told me things about Mike here and there, but this is our chance for girl talk. Tell me about him. What's he like? I see you have a new piece of jewellery around your neck. Is that from him?"

My mom is the original eagle eye, and she never misses a beat. She raises her left eyebrow as she inspects my new necklace. My fingers touch the gold ball at my neck, and its warmth comforts me. I chuckle to myself—"girl talk"—my mom is old-fashioned. I love that about her. She keeps one foot grounded in the way things used to be. The good news about that is that it's all the best things from yesteryear—all the propriety. The things that make us behave ourselves and keep us in check.

She looks fabulous but seems to be smaller than when I saw her in November. She looks thinner than usual. I fleetingly hope that she is alright. She still wears her hair in a long bob, and she has her red lipstick on that matches her red fingernails. I wonder how she gets her lipstick refreshed after a meal. I never see her reapply it—it just reappears on her lips as if by magic. I figure she has probably ingested about fifteen pounds of lipstick in her lifetime.

I know there is no wiggling out of this, and I don't really want to anyway, so I tell her more details about Mike and my relationship with him.

"It's serious then," she concludes.

"I suppose it is," I admit sheepishly. I look at the floor and rub at a mark with the toe of my shoe. I haven't told her about our plans for New Year's Eve yet, but I will have to confess before this conversation is over.

"Goodness gracious, Virginia, lift your head and look at me. You are a grown woman. You have nothing to be shy about or ashamed of," she speaks sharply. "I'm not a prude. I have some experience with what goes on between men and women. I'm not just your mother. I am a woman first."

The image of my parents having sex flashes through my mind, and I groan inside. My mother is beautiful, but it's still hard for me to think of her as a sexual being.

"Have you had sex with him yet?" she asks directly.

There's nothing like getting right to the point. I am blushing. It's rushing right up my neck and about to hit my face. My upper lip will soon be glistening. I take off my sweater.

"No," I say quietly.

"Will you? What are you waiting for?" she asks.

There is nothing like the third degree. No one can make me squirm like my mother.

"Mom," I say pleadingly.

"Sit down." She points at the kitchen chairs. The dishes are done, and she has hung the rubber gloves over the edge of the sink to dry. She is filling the kettle for the customary post-supper cup of tea. I do as I am told, and sit at the table and wait. She gets the cookie tin and places nine pieces of shortbread on two plates—four for the girls and four for the men—two each and one for Eddie. She also sets out two teacups and saucers and places one piece of shortbread on each dish. That is for the two of us. My mom is all about portion control. The container is put away so that none of us are tempted to overindulge.

She has only been here a few hours, and she has already taken over and is bossing me around. I secretly love it and hate it at the same time. She pats her hair down and takes off her apron before delivering the cookies to the other room. When she gets back, she sits on the chair across from me and pours the tea. She slides my cup across the table and prepares her own. She has hers with a drop of cream—not milk—cream. She calls it cream tea. To her, it is the way tea should be drunk.

"Don't 'Mom' me," she warns gently. She has a feigned cross look on her face and a slight smile on her lips. I cringe, hoping that I don't look and sound the way she does when she mimics me. Her voice is whiny, and she tips her head from side to side. "Virginia, this conversation is long overdue. I should have talked to you about this many years ago, but you were very unapproachable, and I thought it best to let it be. I knew that one day you would heal and be ready to move on, but young lady, it has taken you a long time!"

I squirm in my seat and worry that I might blush again. I have only just cooled down from the last outburst. I rest my chin on my hands and look at her. I can't get out of this, so I brace myself and let her talk.

"I haven't been a good mother to you around this topic. I let you wait too long. I should have encouraged you years ago to move on. I knew you were stuck. I have done a lot of praying for you, my dear. I so desperately wanted you to be strong that I neglected your happiness, and I let you wallow when I should have guided you in a new direction," she says quietly. She is looking directly into my eyes. Her eyes are bright and kind, full of love and concern.

I am speechless and remain silent.

"Ginny, you've been sad for many years. I worried that you were depressed. I'm not of the generation that deals with depression very directly. We are not like your generation, where you fix everything with a pill. We tend to fix our problems with a martini and a visit to the minister. I didn't know if I should suggest anti-depressant medication because I was never sure if you were depressed. You have been so darned loyal. I haven't understood why you've been so dedicated to a dead man. But, I have had faith in you, and I trusted that you would work this out for yourself.

Darling, in my opinion, you have waited far too long, but I am thrilled to hear that you are finally going to move forward with a love interest!"

She reaches across the table and takes my hand into hers. She pats my hand gently and strokes the skin on the back of it.

"He has asked me on a date for New Year's Eve," I start. "He is planning to take me out on the town in Vancouver. That's going to be the night we …"

I can't say it to my mother. I can't tell her what I am planning to do. It's so piercingly quiet in the room you could hear a pin drop. Neither of us speaks until my mother breaks the silence.

"That's good, dear. It will be good for your soul. I am happy for you."

Good for my soul. I guess I know what she means, but I'd never thought of it that way. It's how sex helps to develop the bond between two people who love each other. That's the soul of it. It's the part that makes your heart joyful and fulfilled, the part that causes you to experience bliss.

Refilling our cups, she puts the teapot down and looks at me, "Can I ask you something personal?"

This conversation is pretty personal already, and I wonder what could be more personal that she needs permission to ask. Meeting her gaze, I nod my head ever so slightly and bite my lower lip. I know I am furrowing my brow.

"Don't frown, my darling—it will give you wrinkles," she reprimands automatically.

I reflexively smooth my face and perk up.

"Ginny, I am happy you have found someone you want to spend time with. I am glad he is someone special to you. But I have to ask you a hard question. Things can be clearer to others than they are to ourselves, and I want to make sure that you haven't missed something here. I want you to think about why you haven't ever pursued a relationship with Paul. He is the man you have spent a lifetime with, and it seems to me that it doesn't get any more special than that. I'm just wondering why you haven't considered him."

The question floors me. Paul. I haven't pursued a relationship with Paul because he is Paul. It never seriously crossed my mind. He is just always there. I never asked for him to be there for me, he just is. Our relationship just is. I know that we love each other. The thought of potentially losing him so I can be with Mike makes me tear up. I know I am lucky to have Paul in my life. Memories of our life together swim in my head. I have visions of us at the lake with the girls when they were small. I see us all skiing together when they were teenagers. I remember the countless Sunday night dinners we have spent together, nights hovering over the homework table, birthday parties—everything. She is right. Paul and I have spent a lifetime together in almost the same way that a husband and wife do. I don't know why I have never considered Paul.

"Darling, I am only saying this to you because I don't want you to make a horrible mistake. I repeat—I am very happy for you, but I am pointing out something I think you haven't considered. Paul loves you, my dear. It is obvious in everything he does. He has loved you for years. I am not sure why you have never noticed."

Feeling panicky and nauseous, I know I am going to burst into flames. I resist the urge to take my shirt off. My mom's eyes are full of concern, and mine are full of tears. I get up from my chair and move to the kitchen sink, where I slide open the window. I billow the neck of my T-shirt, letting much needed fresh air inside, but the coolness doesn't begin to take the edge off my discomfort.

"Come and sit down," my mother encourages. "And close that window. It's freezing out there. I'm sorry. I didn't mean to cause you embarrassment, but I'm concerned that you might be making a mistake, and I would hate to see that happen after all this time. I think we have all waited too long without acting."

"I have been thinking about Paul!" I blurt out too loudly. I can't stifle my words. "He's been heavily on my mind lately! I can't get him out of my head. I even had a dream about him the other night. I am distressed about the possibility of losing him. Jessie says that I probably can't have Mike and Paul too. She says that Mike probably wouldn't go for that.

He and I have fought about it already, and our relationship has barely started! The girls are accepting of Mike, but overall, they are lukewarm toward him and are only accepting him because they want me to be happy. But, they love Paul with all their heart. I'm just miserable about it, Mom, and I don't know what to do! This experience with Mike is foreign and strange and exciting and captivating at the same time. But I don't want to lose my life!"

There. I said it out loud. Actually, I sobbed it. I am almost gasping for breath. I said to my mom what I couldn't say to Jessie. I need my mom's help. I trust her sound advice. My heart is squeezing in my chest, and my stomach is upset. The house is uncharacteristically quiet, and I wonder if everyone is listening.

"That's the curious part, my dear—you probably already know what you need to do, and you are the only one who truly does. Trust yourself, and don't be scared. Search your heart. The answer will be there. Just listen carefully to what it is telling you."

"I'm scared, Mom—I'm so scared." My voice is a whimper, and my eyes search hers pleadingly. I want her to make it all better and decide for me and tell me what to do. Again, she takes my hands in hers and lifts them to her lips. She opens my palm and places a kiss in the centre. She wraps my fingers closed and holds my hands in hers. Her eyes are also filled with tears, but I find comfort in them. Her love circulates through my body as I let her caress my hands. Safe in the security of my mother's love, I know everything will turn out just as it is meant to.

We eat our Christmas dinner on Christmas Eve, so we have been preparing food all day. We usually eat around six o'clock, and then we open presents, then we go to church. We open presents from Santa on Christmas morning, but we open all the other gifts on Christmas Eve. We started doing that a long time ago because it just makes Christmas Day easier. We like to spend Christmas Day on the ski hill and have leftovers for supper on Christmas night.

I glance at the clock and see that it's just about five o'clock. Paul will be here soon, and then we can carve the turkey. We are just about ready, and as per usual, everyone has a job. The girls do the mashed potatoes. My mom sets the table, makes the gravy and deals with the Christmas dainties for dessert. Paul carves the turkey, and Dad is in charge of the champagne. My brother makes the salads, sets the chairs around the table and does all the background work, like putting music on and stoking the fire. Eddie has a job this year too—he set the cutlery, under the watchful eye of my mom. I oversee the whole operation and take care of the vegetable casseroles and turkey. I give the table a final perusal.

My mom sets the most beautiful Christmas dinner table. She packs her porcelain china dishes with her and brings them from home. Her mother gave her the entire set when she and my dad got married, and she still has each original piece. Her china is plain white, and I know that doesn't sound like much, but when she gets everything else in place, her table looks spectacular. She sets the table in layers of white with splashes of gold and a shock of red. The red is something different every year, and this year it is the tiniest poinsettias I have ever seen. She uses a florist in Vancouver, where I assume she specially ordered them. She keeps her house full of fresh flowers regardless of the season. The table napkins are plain white cotton trimmed with gold piping, and as delicate as gossamer. She spent about an hour ironing them and then folding them correctly. They look like white, puffy clouds floating amongst the heaviness of the cutlery and plates and crystal.

My mother is the one who got us into skiing on Christmas Day. She has led what you might think of as a country club sort of life. There are three things my mom likes to do—she likes to play golf and tennis in the summer, and she likes to ski in the winter. I have the most fabulous photo of her on the wall in my living room. It was taken when she was sixteen. She is dressed in her wool ski sweater and wool snow pants, and she is wearing her signature red lipstick. Her hair is piled on top of her head, and she has a muff around her ears. She is leaning up against the side of my grandparent's ski cabin and is holding her skis with her free hand. She has a smile on her face as wide as a barn, and she looks so pretty it almost takes my breath away. When I look at that picture, I get a surge of pride that she's my mother. It's my favourite photograph of her. It's because of her that I learned to ski. She made sure that we took skiing lessons when my brother and I were kids, and by the time we were teenagers, we were both pretty competent on the ski hill.

She comes into the dining room and stands beside me, wiping her hands on a dishcloth. She has been helping the girls with the mashed potatoes.

"What do you think? Did I miss anything?" she asks.

"It looks gorgeous, Mom. I don't know how you do it. If I set the table, it would just look like plates and cutlery and salt and pepper shakers.

Your table looks like a masterpiece."

"Thank you," she says smugly, with satisfaction in her voice. She is such a perfectionist.

"I think you missed a napkin over at that table setting," a deep voice speaks into our ears from behind. We both jump, and before I know it, Paul is lifting my mom into the air and swinging her around. She has the most blissful look on her face as she kisses him hello.

"We didn't hear you come in!" she squeals. "I've been waiting for you to get here. You were supposed to come over last night, you naughty boy. I've missed you!"

I make eye contact with Paul, and I can't help but smile at him. He knows the effect he has on my mother. I roll my eyeballs slightly and greet him with a kiss and a hug.

"I'm sorry I wasn't able to make it over last night. Didn't Ginny tell you I couldn't come?" he asks with a laugh.

"Yes, she did, but that doesn't make up for it. You should have been here. You know I don't like to be kept waiting," she pouts.

"Forgive me?" he begs, and somehow, magically, he pulls out a single red rose from behind his back and offers it to her. It isn't a long-stemmed rose. It's a country rose full of beautiful fragrance. God only knows where he got that at this time of year. He never ceases to amaze me when it comes to spoiling my mother.

She accepts the rose and bats her eyelashes at him. Breathing in its scent, she says, "Paul, it's lovely—you do spoil me!"

"Is someone over here making a pass at my wife?" my dad asks, with a puffed-up chest. He moves toward Paul and extends his hand. They shake hands and exchange a half embrace. "Good to see you, young man. How have you been?"

"I'm all the better for having laid eyes on your beautiful wife," Paul teases.

"Can I pour you a cocktail, old boy?" my dad asks, patting Paul on the back, possibly harder than is necessary. Paul peers over the swinging doors into the kitchen to see what is going on in there.

"Do I have time? How much longer is it before dinner?"

"You have time," I say. "It's Christmas. We make the time."

"What would you like?" Dad asks. "I'll get it for you."

"I'll have a glass of Irish whiskey, please. Neat."

"You've got it. I'll be right back."

My dad heads over to the sideboard to prepare Paul's drink, and we all move into the kitchen.

"It smells incredible in here. My mouth is watering." He lifts the lid to the turkey, which is sitting on the counter by the stove. I automatically smack his hand away as he pulls at a piece of crisp skin. The girls swarm him for kisses as he pokes the skin into his mouth and gives them each a hug.

"Dinner won't be long now. You can carve any time you are ready. Sip your drink, and get yourself settled first. No hurry," I say, rubbing his shoulder and smiling at him.

He looks at me fondly as he accepts his drink from my dad. He takes a sip and leans against the counter. Taking a deep sigh and licking the turkey grease off his fingers, he remarks, "Now that's a drink." He has another sip and works it around his mouth like he is chewing on it.

"The season has been keeping you busy then," my dad states.

"It sure has. I couldn't make it over last night because we had an emergency at the hospital. The ski patrol has been working overtime too." Pushing up his sleeves and sharpening the carving knife, he takes a sideways glance at Christie, who is adding butter to the potatoes and asking her sister if that is the right amount. She catches his eye and nods in agreement.

"That's for sure, Uncle Paul! I worked hard yesterday. Things are hectic!" she shakes her head as she says it. Cath is pouring the cream into the potatoes, and Christie is nodding in agreement that that is enough. Cath turns on the electric mixer to whip the potatoes, and we all have to shout to hear each other.

I take the casseroles out of the oven and place them in the chafing dishes on the sideboard. My mom helps me by putting the serving spoons with the dishes. Paul starts carving the turkey. We elected him for this honour many years ago because he is always the last to arrive, and we joke that he is the closest thing we have to a surgeon. My dad gets the champagne ready. He likes to have an ice bucket beside his spot at the table, allowing him to top up people's glasses with ease. He takes his job seriously.

We take our seats at the table and hold hands. We aren't the most religious people in the world, but we honour the spiritual aspect of Christmas together as a family. It's not just about presents and extravagance for us. There is something profound that draws us together at Christmas, and I like to think that it's baby Jesus. Christmas reminds us of what is essential in life. We bow our heads while my brother recites our dinner prayer.

"Thank you, Jesus, for what we are about to receive. May we be truly grateful for the bounty of this food and the love of this family. Amen."

Eddie's sweet voice rises out of the blue above everyone else's. He is singing a classic Christmas hymn that I'm surprised he knows. My mother sings with him to finish off the verse. I see a tear in her eye and hear a quaver in her voice.

"How did you learn that old song?" she asks, patting Eddie on the hand.

"I leawned it at Sunday school," Eddie tells her.

We all exchange curious looks. This is the first I have heard of Eddie attending Sunday school.

"We thought it was time for Eddie to start his religious education," comments Bradley. "So he would have a better understanding of what Christmas is all about."

There is a chorus of "Amens" around the table. I'm sure my left eyebrow automatically rose when I heard the words "religious education," but who am I to question these things? Everyone seems satisfied with Bradley's explanation, and we don't press for further details. We cross arms to break open our Christmas crackers.

Our Christmas crackers aren't random, and they don't come from the store. Each year on Christmas Day, we draw the name of someone we will buy for next year. That treasure gets put inside their Christmas cracker the following year. We have to have the gift into my Mom's possession by November, and she makes the crackers. She is such a fussbudget that they are, of course, perfect. She makes a paper hat and slips it into the cracker along with specialty chocolate from a store she loves in Vancouver. The *pièce de résistance* is the special trinket that was selected especially for you. Each cracker is marked with our name in gold calligraphy, done in my mother's hand. She took a calligraphy course so she could learn how to do it properly.

With a whoop and a cheer, we pull our crackers and look inside for our surprise. We never know who got it for us, which is half the fun. I unfold my green paper hat and put it on. It has my name inscribed on the front. I pop my chocolate into my mouth and close my eyes in delight. I sink into my chair and let the silky softness melt in my mouth. My taste buds are working overtime. I am hungry! I search inside the cracker for my trinket, and I find a small plastic stethoscope. When I look at it more closely, I figure out that it is a lapel pin. I pick it up and turn it over to make sure that it is what it seems.

"I think I've got Paul's gift," I say, with a puzzled look. "Paul—do you have mine?"

"Nope, I don't think so," he says, wiping his mouth. I see a small bottle of Irish whisky in his hand, and he is returning the lid after taking a sip.

"You got the right gift, Mom." Christie offers. She is wearing a conspiratorial look that I don't understand. Giggling, she squirms in her seat as she catches Paul's eye.

"What are you two up to?" I ask suspiciously. This gift makes no sense to me. I shake my head and put it down, dismissing it.

"You'll have to wait and see," she says slyly. She is about ready to burst, and I am surprised she can contain herself.

We start passing the bowls around the table, and the gluttony begins. We truly have more food choices at Christmas dinner than at any other meal throughout the year. Just taking one spoonful of each dish makes a plateful of food that I am not sure I will be able to finish. We usually do the dishes right after eating, but not at Christmas. After eating our Christmas dinner, we move to the living room and open presents. We tell ourselves it gives our food a chance to digest. Really—we just want to tear into the gifts.

This year Bradley is playing Santa along with Eddie, who is delighted with his new role. They both have Santa hats on, and at four years of age, Eddie is utterly excited about Christmas. Handing the presents around takes longer than usual this year because Eddie has to stop and open each one of his and play with it for a while once he sees what it is. Then the curiosity gets to him, and he has to tear into another one. He chucks our next round to us so he can get back to his.

I look around the room and think about how fortunate we are. Boxes are strewn everywhere, and crumpled paper is piled high. I know my mother has to work hard at restraining herself from gathering up the wrapping paper and folding it carefully to be used again next year. I laugh inside because my father and I never let her get away with doing this. We gather up the paper at the end of the gift-giving and stuff it into a big box, and my dad will burn it in the backyard burning barrel on Boxing Day. It drives my mother—and possibly a few neighbours—crazy, but that is what we do.

The last of the presents have been handed around and opened. Eddie is in a frenzy of delight, playing with his new toys and asking a million questions about Santa and how Santa will know where to find the right chimney to come down to deliver his presents. He is just learning the concept of magic and is seriously concerned about Santa not being able to find him. Bradley and Christie are full of the right fathomable answers. I make a move to start collecting the paper when Christie announces that she has found another gift on the tree.

"Hey, Mom," she says brightly. "There's a card here with your name on it."

"There is?" I ask absently. I can't imagine who would give me a card.

"You had better open it," she says, passing it to me.

The others become quiet, and I am aware of all of their eyes on me. I'm wondering what they all know that I don't know.

"Open it!" she says too loudly.

Taking the card, I move over to the couch and sit down beside my mom. I look around the room and wonder what they are all up to. I take the card out of the envelope and look at it. It is a specialty card that reads, "To Mom at Christmas, from your loving daughter." I open the card and see there is a piece of paper enclosed. I take the time to read the card first, holding the piece of paper in my hand. I sense that Christie wants to grab the card from my grasp and shove the enclosed paper into my face. It's a beautiful card all about the love between a mother and a daughter. I am tearing up because she's never given me a card like this before.

"Mom—hurry and read the letter!" she shouts. She stomps her foot like she used to do when she was a girl. Her feet are bare every chance she gets, even in the middle of winter.

I see that the letter is written on university letterhead and is from the Faculty of Medicine. I am curious, and I can't imagine what sort of gift I would receive from them. I wonder if this letter has something to do with Tony. Possibly it's a memorial in his honour, but I can't imagine why.

The letter begins, "It is with great pleasure that I write this letter to inform you of your acceptance into the Faculty of Medicine." I don't understand what I am reading. I wonder if this is a copy of Tony's acceptance letter into medicine. Has this been resurrected from the family archives? I skim read down to the bottom of the letter, and I don't see Tony's name anywhere. My eyes go to the top of the page, and I check the date. The date was only a few months ago. Re-reading the letter and paying closer attention to the details, I see it has Christie's name, in full, on the next line, indicating that she is accepted into the Faculty of Medicine! It says she begins her studies in January when school resumes after Christmas break. I lift my head and look at the others.

"Remember the stethoscope from your Christmas cracker?" she asks. I nod my head.

"I am accepted into medical school, Mom!" she prompts me.

I am silent.

"I challenged the entry exam and passed," she states with a broad smile. She's lovely with her soft curls and her bright blue eyes.

I let her talk.

"I start in January! Gran and Gramps have offered for Bradley and Eddie and me to live with them until something comes available in family housing. Bradley has a job in Vancouver, and Eddie is signed up for daycare that the faculty offers to its students who are parents."

I am still gawking at her.

"I'm going to become a doctor, Mom!" she squeals. She can't restrain herself anymore as she lets herself jump up and down.

"It appears you have a brilliant young woman for a daughter," Paul pipes up.

Still holding the letter in my hand, I say, "I know ... I know I do."

"The kids can use the top of the house," my mom offers. "There is plenty of room up there for them to have their privacy. Your father and I spend all our time on the main floor these days. It will be wonderful to have some youngsters in the house again."

I look around the room at all the members of my family. They are all standing there with smug, knowing looks on their faces. Well, my mom and dad and Paul are, anyway.

"You all knew about this?" I ask, looking at each one of them.

"I didn't know about it," Cath shakes her head, an astonished look on her face. I vaguely think that her face must reflect how mine looks.

My brother is stretched out in his seat and is laughing at the look on my face.

"You should see yourself right now, Ginny. I wish we had been video-ing this!" he says.

"I don't understand," I say.

"It's just like Christie explained," Paul said. "She came to me several months ago telling me that she thought she would like to be a doctor, and asked me if I could help her. We've been studying together for quite a long time now. Nights when I haven't made it over for dinner, were usually because Christie and I were working together."

"Times, when you hadn't heard from me for a few days, was because I was swamped with work and things to study," she adds.

"I did some digging for her. I phoned an associate of mine at the faculty, a woman Tony and I knew in medical school, to see what she could tell me. I learned that there are two intake periods and two entrance exams. Christie had missed the entry exam for September intake, but we had plenty of time to prepare for the second writing. Last summer, when Christie and Bradley went on holiday, they weren't really on holiday. They were down at your parent's, and Christie was writing the entrance exam. She received the news of her acceptance into the program back in October. It's extraordinary that she's achieved this. She has some pre-med courses to make up, but they are going to let her into the program." Paul explained.

"I can't believe my eyes and my ears!" I exclaim, looking at the letter again. "How did you all keep this to yourselves?"

"Well, we started by not telling everyone," Christie says. She looks at her sister and laughs. "We knew Cath wouldn't be able to keep the secret, and she has only just found out now, along with Uncle James. Gran and Gramps have known for a long time because we asked them if they would help us out with a plan."

She moves toward us and sits on the arm of the couch beside my mother. She puts her hand on my mother's shoulder, and my mom takes her hand in hers and pats it lovingly.

"This is incredible news!" I exclaim. I have never had a more pleasant surprise. My daughter is going to go to medical school! I can hardly believe my ears. My head is swimming. "I hardly know what to say."

I get up from my spot and move toward Christie. My arms are open to her, inviting an embrace. She comes into my arms, and I hug her. I hear myself gasping and realize that I am sobbing tears of joy. Paul's arms wrap around us from behind, and Cath's arms encircle us from one side. I smell my mother's perfume, and I know she is also in on the hug. I wipe my eyes and step back to look at my daughter.

"Aren't you a precious darling," I say to her. "You have always been full of surprises."

"Some of my surprises weren't as good as this one," she says sheepishly. Eddie has his arms wrapped around her leg. She picks him up and kisses him on the cheek.

"Eddie was the best surprise of all," I say, kissing his other cheek and languishing in the gorgeous squishiness of it and the faint smell of cookies. "But, this one takes the cake. I'm blown away and have to re-read this letter."

I sit on the couch and hold my head in my hand. I hear people moving around in the dining room and the kitchen, but the letter has monopolized my attention. I marvel at this amazing turn of events and how life will change dramatically for my daughter and her small family. I'm tremendously happy for her. I look up to see she is still standing in front of me, waiting.

"You've taken my breath away, my sweetheart," I say to her. "I can't wait to talk more about this and hear all your plans."

"Well, we are moving on the twenty-eighth. We have to be out of our place by the thirty-first, and since the twenty-eighth is Friday, we thought we'd take the weekend to move. Then we have time to clean our place before the end of the month. Gran says it's okay to move in anytime it's convenient." She sits down beside me and rubs her hands together as if she is nervous. "Our place is full of boxes, and I was afraid that Eddie would spill the beans. I kept telling him that we were going to wrap them up for Christmas presents! Thank goodness he believed me!"

We laugh as I pat her on the leg.

"This is just amazing," I say. "It's a lot to take in."

"I know," she says, peering at me out of the corner of her eye. "Are you okay?"

"Of course, I'm okay!" I exclaim. "I'm just thoroughly surprised."

"I guess you thought I was going to work on the ski hill for the rest of my life and maybe just have another baby," she says quietly.

I'm not sure if she is putting herself down or if she is chastising me or just describing our world as she sees it.

"I honestly never gave it much thought. It doesn't matter what you do with your life, as long as you are happy," I say quietly back, looking into her beautiful eyes. I see something different when I look at her. For the first time, I see a young woman with goals and aspirations, not just my aimless daughter, who seemed to make nothing but mistakes.

"Why medicine?" I ask her.

"It's something I've been thinking about for a long time, Mom. For as long as I can remember, I've wanted to be a doctor. I just never told anyone. I felt too misguided to be any good at it or taken seriously if I said anything. I thought it would be impossible because of my educational background. Uncle Paul and I were skiing together one day last winter, and I finally got the nerve to ask him about it. That's when the ball started rolling. I'm so glad I asked him. Mom, I'm so excited!" she has her head down and is speaking quietly, but she looks up at me with those piercing blue eyes, and she smiles at me. Tears spill over the rims of her eyes. "You know I remember Dad, and I want to be a doctor just like him."

Her words are heartfelt—powerful, and determined. I love those qualities about this fine daughter of mine, even though that same power and determination have resulted in us locking horns. My throat squeezes and a lump forms there, making it hard to breathe. I take her all in—her smell, her petite strength, her being—she is mine through and through. She is the spitting image of her father, and he is with us at this moment.

"I'm proud of you," I whisper into her ear. Pulling back, I look into her eyes and kiss her. I repeat, "I am *so* proud of you."

"Come on, you two, enough of this kissy-kissy stuff!" My brother interrupts us. "We have to get going to church! It's almost time for the service."

We both wipe our eyes and look at each other.

"My goodness. Is it that time already?" I ask, looking around and patting my hair. "Did you guys clean the kitchen?" Clean-up is complete, and I didn't even notice.

"Dishes are done. Food put away. Ski boots are lined up at the door and ready for the morning," James jokes. "Come on! Let's go! People are waiting. We've got places to go and people to see!

We slip into our boots, grab our coats and hop into my brother's sedan. The others have left already. In a matter of minutes, I am sitting in our church, singing my heart out to my favourite Christmas hymns and listening to the minister tell us the story of Christmas. Surrounded by the people I love most in the world, I hear their voices rising to the rafters, and I appreciate the natural harmony. We are all different, yet all the same. We are a family of hearts beating as one, celebrating the promise of peace on earth and joy to the world. My heart and my body are filled to bursting, and I am rapt with love. A smile spreads across my face, and I am beaming. I sing louder and can hear myself above all the rest.

I am the luckiest woman in the world. I have everything. Leaning back into my seat, I look up at the cathedral ceiling of the church. I have a healthy and prosperous family. My mom and dad have perched themselves a few feet away on the same pew as me, holding hands and singing at the top of their voices. I have a successful business, a beautiful home, the best girlfriend anyone could ask for, a man-friend nestled in beside me, and I have a boyfriend. And, he's not just any boyfriend—he's spectacular. I have everything and then some. I smile up at the pulpit and hug myself.

Chapter 14
Truth

I pull into Paul's driveway and step on the foot pedal to engage the emergency brake. I told Paul not to bother picking me up. It seemed weird. It felt too much like a date. I just said to him that I would drive myself over once I got the family settled. The last two days have been relatively uneventful and quite relaxing. After having some fun skiing with my family yesterday and today, I was on the receiving end of a few curious looks when I said what I was doing tonight. My mom had a smug smile on her face as I hugged her goodbye, and she wished me a good night.

I step carefully out of my old pickup truck. It's a gazillion years old and is probably considered vintage by now. Tony and I bought it from my dad when we moved up here. My dad bought it brand-new in 1965. Considering what my dad did for a living, I don't know why he thought he needed a truck in Vancouver, but it was handy to lug things around and fun to take for a ride. My dad took meticulous care of it, and after all these years, it still doesn't have that many miles on the odometer. It is a classic turquoise colour. I think the locals in town make fun of me because of the vehicle I drive, but I don't care. I've never seen the need for an upgrade, and it's handy to have a truck for work.

We had some fresh snow overnight, and the sun came out this

afternoon, so it might be icy this evening. I don't want to slip. I tread carefully to the house. Paul's outdoor Christmas lights are on, and he has somehow found the time to shovel his driveway. I am amazed by his ability to get it all done. The motion light comes on, illuminating my way. Just as I raise my hand to knock on the door, it opens, and his gleaming smile greets me. He has a cocktail in his hand, I think it's a Manhattan by the look of it, and he passes it to me as he kisses me hello and holds the door.

"I heard your old jalopy," he teases. He drives an SUV, which in my opinion, is not any better than my vehicle, just more modern. I whack him and tell him to shut up. He feigns injury and laughs, saying formally, in a mocking voice, "Allow me to take your coat, madam." I love the twinkle he gets in his eye.

"Of course, fine sir," I reply in my best British accent. Taking a sip, I hold my drink in one hand while he helps me shimmy out of the opposite sleeve, then I shift hands while he holds my coat for me and allows me to escape entirely. I hold my free hand up for him to pull my glove off, then the other one while I continue to balance my drink. He hangs my coat and scarf in the closet.

"It probably would have been easier just to give me my cocktail after I got out of my coat," I comment, kicking off my boots and setting them on the boot tray by the door.

"Ah," he says, shrugging it off. "We orchestrated that like a couple of old pros. Come on in and make yourself comfortable."

"Thanks," I say, taking in my surroundings and settling in on his couch. His place looks lovely. It's been a long time since I've been to his house. He never puts up a Christmas tree—he enjoys mine instead. He says he has no need for two Christmas trees, which makes total sense considering how much time he spends at my place, especially over the holidays. Running my hand over the arm of the sofa, I ask, "Is this new?"

"It is. I got it in the fall. Don't you remember me telling you about it?" he comments. "I ordered it that weekend that I went down to Vancouver in October. They just delivered it a couple of weeks ago."

I grimace and know that I am frowning because I don't remember him telling me about it. I'm especially surprised that we didn't go shopping for it together. I remember what my mom said about getting wrinkles if I frown, and I attempt to straighten out my face.

"Oh," I say sheepishly. I see Paul has also picked up a new area rug. It's modern and fresh over his old fir plank floors. He has also given his walls a fresh coat of paint. I remember that because I helped him with it last summer.

"Don't start thinking that there is something wrong with your memory. It just slipped your mind. You've had a few things going on lately to keep you occupied over and above my new couch," he says soothingly. He knows that I worry about memory loss. Things slip my mind these days, and it concerns me. I used to have such a good memory. He tells me it has more to do with menopause than anything else. I'm not crazy about hearing that either.

"It's nice. I like it," I say, running my hand gently over the fabric. Feeling my stomach growl, I lift my nose and sniff. "Supper smells divine."

"Thank you. It will be ready soon," Paul says as he stretches out on the couch beside me. "How was your day?"

Tucking my feet up underneath me, I survey him. He looks tremendous. He's done something with his hair. I can't decide quite what it is—it's smoother or shinier or something. Maybe he just combed it. I laugh silently to myself. His hair is soft and loose around his face, slightly curly and still dark with hardly a trace of grey. He has on a pair of tailored, dark grey wool slacks that I have never seen before. The black jersey sweater he is wearing hugs his muscles and compliments him in all the right places. He never dresses like this. He lives in his jeans. He even wears them to his office. He is the most casual doctor I've ever known. I squirm in my seat and realize I have taken too long to answer his question. He is looking at me with a smirk on his face. I blush and avert my eyes, quickly taking a sip of my cocktail. I am so busted.

Chuckling, he says, "I also picked up some new clothes when I was in Vancouver. Do you approve?"

I am horrified that I've been caught checking him out, and my face turns beet red. I meet his gaze and try to hide my embarrassment. I nod my approval and say quietly, "Yes. You look very nice."

"Thank you. So do you," he says, admiring my pink sweater. It's a gift from my mother for Christmas. She was pleased to see me wearing it tonight. I will give it to Jessie after Christmas.

"What did you ask me?" I say, changing the subject. I don't know if it is my imagination, but I think his gaze lingered on my breasts. I secretly hope my nipples aren't showing. I try to inadvertently run my hand by my breast to check if I have worn a T-shirt bra.

Sipping his drink and lifting his eyes, one eyebrow raised, he says, "I asked you how your day was."

"Oh," I pause, starting to cool down. I hope my face isn't the same colour as my sweater. I am grateful that I haven't begun to perspire. "My day was wonderful. We all slept in today and had a lazy start. James shovelled my driveway, and Dad burnt the Christmas paper in the backyard burning barrel. He likes doing that. He would probably like to have a bonfire out there. Mom and I snuck away together and got in an hour of cross-country skiing this afternoon. It was glorious with the fresh snow, and it was so pleasant when the sun reappeared."

"Yes, it turned out to be a nice day. Just enough snow to freshen things up."

I nod in agreement and ask how his day was.

"It was fine. It was surprisingly quiet today."

"That's good," I say with a smile. "Paul, I haven't had a chance to thank you properly for what you've done for Christie. I've been thinking about just how lucky I am. Thank you very much."

"You're welcome," he says quietly, looking directly at me. "Christie's a good kid, and she needed a break. I had suspected for a long time now that she wanted something more for herself but didn't know how to make it happen. I told you I'd do anything for you." His eyes search mine. There is a silence between us. I meet his gaze and consider what my mother said to me the other night. I wonder if she is right. Maybe

Paul does love me in a way I haven't recognized.

"You mean for my daughter."

"Yes, that too, but I mean for you." He holds his gaze, and there is no mistaking his meaning. Clearing his throat and getting up from the couch, he moves over to the end table and picks up a wrapped gift. Bringing it back to the couch, he sits down beside me and presents it to me. Placing it on my lap, he says, "I was going to give this to you after supper, but there's no time like the present, so you may as well open it now. I couldn't give it to you the other night. It's too personal."

"What is it?" I ask, very surprised. I can feel myself warming up. I blame it on the alcohol surging through my veins and the fluffy sweater I am wearing. The present is beautifully wrapped with extravagant paper and a delicate bow. The box is heavy and the size of a large book. I look at him questioningly.

He gestures with his chin, and his eyes smile at me. He urges me on, "Open it. It's for you."

He moves over to the fireplace, adjusts the logs and adds another one. Leaning against the wall, he observes me, takes another sip of his drink, and waits. I sit there, running my fingers over the beautiful paper, feeling more uncertain by the minute. I look up at him questioningly.

"I don't understand …" I start.

"You will," he interjects. "Open it. You'll see. It's just a little something."

On the tag, he has written, "To You, From Me." I smile. He isn't a man of many words, but his words mean something. I start to pull the tape off the paper carefully. The paper is pretty, and I don't want to tear it. I'm more like my mother than I thought.

"Get in there," he encourages. "Give it a rip. You don't have to save the paper."

Laughing at myself because he has read my mind, I look up at him and bite my lip. I squeeze my eyes closed and tug at the paper, tearing it down the centre. I hate doing it, but it is fun. When I have finally pulled the paper off, I discover a plain white box. Lifting the lid carefully and peering inside, I find a beautiful photo album.

I lift it out carefully and place it on my lap, running my fingers over the cover. It looks like watered silk. It could have easily been mistaken for a wedding album except it is navy blue, rather than the traditional white. The first page has a picture of me with my two girls sitting on my lap. Christie looks about seven, and Cath is about three. We had this thing we used to do when they were small, where we would kiss each other all over each other's faces. I would say to them, "Kisses are free." We would squeal with laughter because there was usually tickling involved. I remember this picture because it was my birthday. It was the first one after Tony died. The girls were showering me with kisses, and we were all laughing. Our joy is prominent in the photo. Paul has written on a tiny piece of perfectly cut paper, "Kisses are free" and placed it below the picture.

My eyes fill with tears as I lift my head and look at him. I can't believe he remembers this.

"What is this?" I ask.

"Keep going," he nods.

I bring my attention back to the album and leaf through the pages. There is picture after picture of me with my girls, me with Jessie, me with Paul, the bunch of us all together. There are pictures of Christmases past. There are pictures of camping trips, birthdays, days on the ski hill. There are captions throughout, written in Paul's hand on small pieces of paper. He has written what the event was or where we were or something special or funny that was said. It's astonishing. It's a catalogue of events covering almost my whole adult life. Tears drip onto the pages, and I wipe them away quickly. I don't want to stain the beautiful paper.

I look up at him. I am barely able to speak. I choke out, "This is incredible."

His eyes meet mine, and he doesn't say anything. He shifts his weight as he continues to lean against the wall by the fire. He smiles at me. I look back at the album and come to the last page. There is a five by seven picture with Lake Garibaldi in the background. We are all there. Cath is about twelve, and Christie is about sixteen—it was her platinum blonde stage. I've never seen this picture before. It was a hard hike and a gratifying day. We're all flushed, sweaty and dirty, and it shows that we had been working hard. I don't know who took the photo. Everyone is looking at the camera and smiling a big smile—everyone, that is, except Paul. Paul is looking at me. He has his arm around my shoulder and is looking right at me with a great big smile on his face. The look of love on his face is unmistakable, and there is no denying it. The caption on the paper underneath the picture says, "I love you." I look up at him, and I see the same look on his face right now. Why have I not seen this before? Where have I been?

"What's going on, Paul?" I squeak. "I don't understand."

"You don't?" he questions. "I put together a Christmas present for you. I didn't give it to you on Christmas Eve because of its private nature. I thought you might be embarrassed if I gave it to you in front of everyone."

I can't tell if he is teasing me or not.

"You love me? What does that mean? You love me. I love you too, but I don't understand this gift!" I say sharply.

"Yes—I love you," he states plainly. "I've loved you for many years."

My head is down, and I am frozen in my spot. He places his drink on the mantle and kneels on the floor in front of me.

"I wanted to put together an album of our life together—so you could see the love between us—the life we've shared. I hope you like it," he says quietly.

"I'm stunned," I reply quietly, not lifting my head. I run my fingers gently over the picture, trying to take it all in. Part of me wants to throw my arms around his neck and kiss him. He smells good, and I am aware of the warmth of his body beside me. But it's Paul. And I can't move. I'm starting to get hot, and I'm not sure if it's anger boiling up inside me or fear. My mother's words float through my mind. *"Paul loves you, my dear. It is so obvious in everything he does."* I have to be careful. I have to think, but I can't. My heart feels like it is going to pound right out onto the coffee table. I can't look at him.

"Why have you never said anything before now?" I ask shrilly. "Why have you never acted on this?"

"It always felt like the time was never right," he states quietly. He moves to the couch beside me. His head is down, and he is not looking at me.

"What do you mean the time was never right?" I ask. My voice sounds as if it's coming from a distance, but I can tell I am shouting at him. I can't stop myself. "In all these years, there was never the right time?"

"No. There wasn't," Paul says sadly.

"You're such a coward," I accuse. I don't know why I'm reacting this way. This album is the most beautiful gift I have ever received—it's thoughtful, heartwarming and full of love. It is my life. It is my life with Paul. My voice is screaming inside my head as I wipe sweat from my brow and keep my head down.

"Maybe I am. Don't you think I haven't regretted my cowardice? I've wanted to tell you this for years, but I was trying to do the right thing. I never wanted to lose you."

His love is right here. It is palpable, and all I have to do is reach out and grab it. It's filling up the room and suffocating me. His voice sounds desperate, and I feel terrified.

"All this time, you were trying to do the right thing? How ridiculous," I say, slamming the album closed. I'm furious with him and want to slap him.

"Yes, Ginny. I was trying to do the right thing," he states quietly.

I feel sorry for him, sorry for us, and sad for all that lost time. I'm overwhelmingly angry with him, and my instinct is to run. I get up from the couch, but he catches my arm and won't let me go. Turning my body with his grip, he holds me inches from his face. He is looking directly into my eyes.

"Ginny, I was there that night. I heard everything. It's the reason I never said anything to you. I—"

I cut him off, ripping myself away from his grip and yelling in his face, "What are you talking about? You're there every night. What night? What did you hear? I'm so mad at you I could spit."

"Well, don't spit. Calm down, please," Paul says gently. "And listen. I have a story to tell you. It's something I should have told you long ago."

His voice is full of despair. I place the album on the end table and accidentally knock my glass onto the floor. It breaks, and the ice cubes tinkle. Neither of us makes a move to clean it up. I can't get the image of that picture out of my mind, with those three little words underneath. My breathing is shallow and stressed. Sweat trickles down my back and also down my legs behind my knees. My cheeks are hot, and it is all I can do not to cry. I put my head down and turn away from him.

"Do you remember the night before Tony died?" he asks.

It is such a laughable question I can't bring myself to answer.

"Do you remember? Answer me!" he demands. "All these years have gone by without us having this conversation. We are going to have it now."

"Of course, I remember. What about it?" I ask.

"I was there that night. I heard you. I heard everything you said to him that night. You thought you were alone, but you weren't. You also thought you were whispering, but you weren't. It was late. I never left the hospital through all of those terrible days. I don't know if you know that. I couldn't bring myself to leave you. If there was ever a time that you needed me, it was then. I was there lurking in the shadows, even when you didn't know it."

"How admirable of you," I say bitterly.

"Ginny, you need to understand that I heard everything you said to Tony that night. You were curled up on the bed beside him, and you were pledging your life to him. You were sobbing because you felt guilty about some misunderstanding the two of you had had that morning before he left for Vancouver. You were telling him how you would spend your life making it up to him. You were talking about the old times, the good times, the fun our gang of friends had had together. You were promising that he would continue to be the man in your future. You pledged your life to him that night, Gin! It was the saddest thing I have ever heard.

"I know the two of you were dynamite together. No one knows better than me that the two of you had it all. Ginny, I wanted to be that guy—all those years of dating and marriage that you had with *him*—all I ever wanted was for it to be *me*. I wanted to be the one you curled up with at night. I wanted to be the one whose babies you had. I wanted you from the moment I first laid eyes on you.

"Remember that day we first met, and I invited you girls to that year-end dance? It was you I invited to the dance, not Jessie. I had to see you again. That's why I asked you both to meet us so that we could go to the dance together. I hadn't told Tony about my plan. He didn't know I had intentions for you. Jessie was hard to manage that night. I didn't want to be rude to her because I didn't want to put you off. I tried to keep things light. I wanted to get to you so badly that night, but I knew I had to be careful. I couldn't lose you when I had only just met you.

"That was a fun night. Remember the crazy dancing we all did? That big crowd of kids we used to hang out with? I just kept asking you to dance with me, and you kept accepting. I thought things were moving along really well. I had to resist putting my arms around your waist and kissing you. I waited for that last dance to come, so I could wrap you in my arms and feel you close to me. I had to do some fancy sidestepping to head off Jessie before she could corral me. I'll never forget how it felt to have you in my arms for that dance. I was in love right then and there, for the first time in my life."

"What?" I interrupted. "I don't believe—"

"Be quiet. Let me finish. Do you remember? You gave me your phone number when I asked you for it at the end of the dance. That was one number I never 'accidentally' lost," he sighed as he put his head down and ran his hands through his hair. "You were the most beautiful girl I had ever seen."

Neither of us speaks. I hear his breathing, and I think I hear a sniffle. I don't look. My eyes are focused on my lap.

"Ginny—he got to you before I did!" Shaking his head, he turns away from me, and his shoulders shudder as he braces his head in his hands. "I didn't phone you right away because I was busy with year-end exams, and I had a lot of studying. I thought I'd wait a few days before I called so that I could ask you on a proper date.

"Tony shocked the hell out of me when he came home and told me he had run into you on campus. He told me you went for coffee together, and he asked you out on a date. My blood ran cold when he said that you had agreed to go. What was I going to do? Call you and ask you out on a date? Of course not! I hadn't told him about how I was feeling about you. He had no idea. It was too late, and I had missed my opportunity.

"So—yes—in all these years, there never seemed to be a good time to tell you. Why do you think I asked Tony to go into practice with me? Did you ever think about that?" he demands.

"Not really. No," I reply quietly. "I just thought Tony was your best friend and you wanted to work with him."

"You are as much of a fool as I am," he snickers. "I never wanted to lose my bond with you, Gin. I couldn't be your husband, but I could be the best friend you ever had. I have loved every moment of our life together. Your girls—I love your girls as if they are my own. You might think after Tony died that I had my chance. Oh yes, I had my chance at last," he says, pulling at his hair.

"All my waiting was going to reward me with my prize. Do you have any idea how guilty I felt about Tony's death? I never wished that on him! I never wished that on you! I never wanted that for any of us. It killed me to watch your agony. I had to use everything I ever learned about being a doctor to separate myself from my feelings. I never saw anyone as grief-stricken as you. That night when I heard you pledge your undying love to him, it was the end of it for me. I knew that I didn't have a chance. I never once had a chance because you never saw me that way. I was just Paul to you. Good old Paul, who was hanging around like he never had anything better to do."

"Don't say that. I never thought that," I interject defensively.

"Possibly not, but you never thought anything else about me either." He stokes the fire and continues.

"There's something else you don't know—something I've never told

236

anyone. Something else happened on the day of Tony's accident." His knuckles are white, and he is flexing his hands into fists.

"Tony was in a mood the morning of his accident. I knew he had that big meeting in Vancouver and that he should have already been on the road. When he arrived at the office, I called out a greeting, but he didn't answer me. I wasn't sure if he hadn't heard me or if he was ignoring me. I left my office, where I had been dictating some notes, and called out to him again. 'Leave me alone. You sound just like Ginny,' was what he said. It wasn't like him to be foul. I didn't know what he was talking about, so I asked him.

"He said, 'You don't have to run to her every time I'm not available. It's okay for her to deal with things independently without "Uncle Paul" running to her side. I know you love her, but you don't have to go over to my house to be with her all the time.'

"His words hung in the room between us. I felt gut-punched. I went back to my office to let him get on with what he needed to do. He followed me in there and shouted at me to not walk away from him. He was caustic that morning. I told him I thought he wanted some space to get organized and that I'd let him get to it.

"He snickered and said, 'You and Ginny—you're both the same—wanting to organize me. I can organize myself.'

"I gave him a steady look and waited for him to continue. He was standing there in the doorway of the surgery looking at me, and in a hauntingly quiet voice, he said, 'Answer me. You love her, don't you?'

"This had all come out of nowhere. All I had done was say hello to him. 'Of course, I love her. You know I do. I love all of you.' I replied carefully.

'No. It's more than that. You love Ginny.'

"He leaned against the doorframe and looked at me straight on. There was no avoiding him or his accusation.

'You want my wife, you completely unforgivable bastard. You have wanted her for a long time. It's all clear to me now. I don't know how it is that I haven't seen it before this.'

"The image of him is burned into my memory. He shifted his body so that his back was against the door frame. He tipped his head back and put his hand to his forehead, his voice caught, and he was so quiet I could barely hear him.

'I was watching you, you know. I was there at my house last night when you were holding my wife. Oh, I know you saw me eventually. The two of you were so caught up in each other you hadn't heard me come in. You had your arms around her, and when you finally lifted your head and opened your eyes, you could see I was standing there in the doorway of my kitchen. I had been there long enough to see the look on your face when you held her.'

"'I've never crossed the line with Ginny. I don't know where this is coming from or why you are talking about it. Shouldn't you be on your way?' I said to him, admitting nothing.

'Oh, fuck off. I'll be on my way when I'm damned ready. Answer me! You want my wife, don't you?'"

Paul looks at me with pleading eyes. There is a wild quality to them I have never seen before, like a trapped animal with no way to escape. He wants me to understand something that has been long buried. Something I wonder if he completely understands himself. He rubs his eyes roughly, as if trying to focus better, and continues.

"How was I to answer? My best friend had just accused me of wanting to sleep with his wife. There was no good answer to that. He would see through a lie, and I couldn't tell the truth, so I said nothing. The silent air was heavy between us. He lunged toward me and tried to take a swing at me. I grabbed his wrist and held him firmly. There was no way he was going to hit me. I told him he had better be on his way. He backed down. Looking me dead in the eye, he said, 'This conversation is not over.'

"I remember twisting his wrist while holding him back. I met his gaze and said, 'I beg to differ, but it is.'

"I released him from my grip and pushed him away from me. Without saying anything further, he pushed his hair back with his hands, gathered his things and left the building. I heard his tires chirp as he screeched out of the driveway. I sat at my desk with my head in my hands until our assistant arrived for work.

"It was the worst day of my life. I lost my best friend that morning, and I had also lost you. You were the two people I loved most in the world. I couldn't believe what had just happened. Part of me felt a huge relief. My secret was finally out and didn't have a grip on me anymore. I had put myself in this precarious position, and I finally had to make a decision. I could pursue you, or I could leave. I decided to leave, and I would tell him that night. I wouldn't destroy your family. I would sell Tony my half of our practice and relocate. I would eventually get over you."

My eyes are riveted on Paul. My brain feels like it is going to burst out of my skull. A vein is throbbing in my temple. I can't believe what I am hearing. After all these years, all this time, everything we have been through together—he tells me this. Staring at him, I am paralyzed with fear and nausea.

"The next thing I knew, we were all working on him in the ER. The police had called me to let me know about the accident. I wasn't on call that night, but I thought I'd better get to the hospital to help. I arrived just a few minutes before the ambulance. We had all hands on deck, knowing that it was Tony coming in. We ran to the ambulance to help as he was being unloaded. My heart sank as soon as I saw him. It was plain to see that he had sustained a severe head injury and was in bad shape. After we examined him, I knew it would be a miracle if he lived.

"In all honesty, Ginny, I never knew how to tell you after all that. You spent so many years in mourning. You cried for a long time, and all I could do was be there for you. I could just come around every day and help to make things feel normal. I felt sorry for you. I couldn't make your hurt go away. I couldn't replace him. I could only ease the day to day of it all. Here we are today—and here you are—going into the arms of another man, yet again.

"I knew you had met Mike for the odd coffee, and I also knew that nothing much had happened between the two of you. I started this album at the end of last summer. I wanted to put together something special for you this year. I wondered if maybe you were finally ready to move on. I knew you would love a trip down memory lane. I could put together the ultimate Christmas present for you and spell out how incredible our life has been together.

"We've had all those years, Gin—all those years. They mean everything to me. That night, when you announced that Mike was your boyfriend, I was floored. Then you announced that you were going to Vancouver for New Year's Eve with him. I am not going to lose you again, Ginny. I've waited my whole life for you."

He grabs my arm, forcing me to stand and pulls me close, looking at me with those eyes that know everything. Those eyes I was lost in the first time I saw him. He leans into me and kisses my lips. It's a hard and desperate kiss, a kiss full of longing and desire. It sends shock waves up and down my body and electrifies me.

I pull away from him and look into his eyes. I reach back and swing my open hand at him, smacking him sharply on his cheek. The sound reverberates throughout the room. Everything stands still in that moment, and the silence between us is oppressive. All I can hear is my ragged breathing and the sound of blood rushing through my ears.

"You bastard," I say. Somewhere in the recesses of my mind, I know I am acting unfairly toward Paul, but at this moment, I don't care. I am glad my purse is by the door, and I don't have to look for it. I shove my feet into my boots and don't bother to get my coat. I walk out of the house and slam the door. It shudders as I lean against it to catch my breath. Walking slowly and deliberately to my truck, breathing deeply, I set my jaw and swallow the lump in my throat. I start the motor and drive away.

⁓

My hands are shaking as I try to unlock the door of Jessie's condo. It's three tries before I get the key into the keyhole. Cursing under my breath, I let myself into the refuge of Jessie's home. I can't go to mine. I left for Paul's house just over an hour ago. If I go home now, I'd have to come up with an explanation about why the evening ended so quickly.

Jessie's house smells like Jessie—her perfume, her soap—very feminine. I am immediately comforted, and I stand motionless for a moment, trying to find some peace. Kicking off my boots, I drop my keys and bag on the floor. I find the biggest, fuzziest sweater available to cuddle into. It, too, smells like Jessie, and it's like she is wrapping her arms around me, giving me a comforting hug.

I turn up the thermostat, and her gas fireplace immediately springs to life. I'm not confident that I will come across anything to eat or drink, but I hope to find a bottle of wine. Her fridge isn't very full at the best of times, and as predicted, is empty. Rummaging through her cupboards, I find a bottle of red wine. I locate a corkscrew and open the bottle. Jessie only buys wine that has a cork. She thinks wines with screw caps are inferior. I take a long sip and wait for the warmth of the alcohol to course through my veins. I have another long gulp from my glass before I leave my spot in the kitchen.

It's a sanctuary in Jessie's living room. Calm and peaceful colours engulf the room, shades of white with splashes of light blue and grey. Compared to mine, her decor is modern and straightforward in its design. My house is all wood and heavy and full of oversized antique furniture and dark colours. Hers is airy and light.

She has a pure white leather couch and matching love seat, but I elect not to sit there. My favourite chair is in the corner of the room. It's harder to get in and out of these days, but it's just what I want right now. It is a new piece of furniture but is old in its design—it's an aquamarine velvet beanbag chair. She has a turquoise coloured fuzzy throw over it and a couple of fluffy white pillows that, at first glance, could be mistaken for long-haired lapdogs. I sink into the chair, tuck the pillows under my arms and cover myself with the blanket. I take another long pull from my glass, close my eyes and try to relax.

I am stunned by what Paul just told me. Tears well up in my eyes, and I let my emotions go. There is no one here to hear me, and I don't have to explain myself. I am alone in my anguish, and let myself cry with utter abandon. I cry for all the things that have felt unfair—lost love and lost time.

I cry so hard that my nose is completely stuffed, and I can't breathe. I wipe my nose on Jessie's sweater in an attempt to clear my nasal passages. It's probably a very expensive sweater, and I experience a pang of remorse. I still can't breathe. Struggling out from my nest, I make my way to the bathroom, where I find the softest tissues. Blowing my nose relentlessly, I bring the box with me. I won't be able to go home until after midnight to make sure that everyone is in bed. I look a fright. There would be a lot of explaining to do.

I go to the kitchen to retrieve the wine. Jessie keeps bottled water in the fridge, so I grab a couple of those too. I'm a firm believer that water and wine are a good combination. For every glass of wine I consume, I have a glass of water, so I don't get too tipsy or a hangover. My stomach growls, and I realize I'm famished. Tucking a sleeve of stale crackers under my arm, I haul my loot back to my spot in the living room.

Hunkering down into my seat, I pour myself another glass of wine while guzzling a bottle of water. I relax into the buzz of the alcohol. My head is swimming with memories, as I pull the blanket to my chin and nibble a cracker. That photo album is the complete history of my life here in Whistler. It's my life—my life with Paul. My chest squeezes, and I gag on the cracker in my mouth. A fresh onslaught of tears causes my throat to close, and I think I might die for a moment. Then I laugh to myself as I envision whoever finds my dead body. There's me, wrapped in my best friend's sweater smeared with snot, cocooned in her beautiful blue blanket with crackers stuffed into my mouth, a partially consumed bottle of wine, along with bottles of water and used tissues everywhere. What a sight!

I think about what Paul told me tonight. He's right—there is a connection between us—we have chemistry. I remember that night at the dance. We had the last waltz together, and it felt terrific to be wrapped in his muscular arms and pulled close to him. He was so beautiful. I remember wishing that he would bend his head down and kiss me. I knew all the girls were looking at us—and me—with envy. I gave him my number and hoped he would call, but he didn't.

242

A time long ago, after Tony died, the two of us went out one night for dinner to some fancy restaurant. We got all dressed up, which was rare for both of us. I can't remember the reason, but we went out together and had a great time. We drank martinis all night long and ended up taking a cab home. My house was too far away to walk, and we had had far too much to drink to consider driving.

We slid into the back of a cab and giggled all the way home. It felt good to be giddy and reckless and carefree, regardless that it was just for one evening. Something happened that night. We both slipped out of our moulds and left our roles behind for a while. I wasn't a widow and the mother of two little girls, and he wasn't the responsible doctor. We were just a couple out on the town, looking for a good time.

When the cab rolled up to my driveway, there was a moment. Paul was on one side of the taxi, and I was on the other. Our bodies or hands weren't touching, but we were close. We stopped talking and laughing, and it was quiet between us. I remember not wanting to go into the house by myself—I wanted him to come with me. We didn't want the night to end, but Jessie was in the house babysitting, and I couldn't invite him. The night was over, but it shouldn't have been. We should have gone to his house first, but we didn't. Neither of us made a move toward the other. We were as close as two people could be, but there was an invisible wall between us. It was an impenetrable wall built years ago. The magic and potential of that moment passed, and I gathered my things and hauled myself out of the cab. We never talked about it, and it never happened again.

Sure, there have been plenty of kisses, hello and goodbye, and the odd holding of hands and snuggles on the couch when watching a movie. There has been lots of physical affection between us. It is the type of love that sustains many couples. We have that—we just don't have sex. I can't explain it and he probably can't either. It's just the way it is.

He's a gorgeous man. After all these years, he barely has a single grey hair, and his physique is as good as ever. Tall and dark and beautiful, he is a feast for the eyes. Women still turn their heads to look at him when he enters a room. He has a presence, and those ever-knowing eyes are infinitely sexy. I squirm in my spot and stretch my legs out in front of me.

I rub my hand over my crotch and luxuriate in the thought of him. After all this time, is this something we could do? He told me that he loves me. He wants to be with me. After all this time, he is finally telling me that he wants me. Is it something that would work? I rub myself again at the thought of him and roll over onto my side. I think about the dream I had about him and wonder if that means that we could do this. I think about what my mother said. Follow my heart.

Then there's Mike. What about him? Mike is handsome and sexy and rich. He is new and exciting. Mike is the endless possibility of a boundless future—a clean slate with no history. And he loves me. He calls me regularly and says he misses me. He tells me about the details of his day, his family and his holiday season. He is near perfection. I rub my crotch again and think about our sexual encounter the night before he left. I shudder gently at the memory of him. We have sexual chemistry going for us, that's for sure. I sigh in anticipation of New Year's Eve.

Paul has felt guilty all these years. He has felt responsible for Tony's death. How ironic considering that all along *I* have felt responsible for Tony's death. I've thought that if we hadn't argued that morning, then that terrible event wouldn't have happened. He would have come safely home to me that night if only I hadn't been such a shrew that morning. I've felt that his death was my punishment for behaving badly toward him. No wonder Paul and I have both been stuck. No wonder he has felt responsible for me. I have been so blind.

I roll onto my back and rub my eyes. It's after eleven and will soon be safe to go home. My dad has a piece of toast and a cup of coffee while he watches the late-night news, and then he goes to bed. No one ever stays up after him. It's not that I won't be detected when I arrive home. They will all hear me come in because they will all be waiting for me with inquiring minds, but no one will approach me tonight to ask about my evening. I'll be able to sneak up to my bed and hide in my room. It's the onslaught of questions in the morning that I dread.

My dad would never in a million years inquire about my evening. My mom will ask, but she will wait until we are alone. My brother would ask me in front of the entire household, given the opportunity. Cath will not take her eyes off of me and watch my every move until I feel like a suspect in a criminal investigation. Her eyes will burrow into me relentlessly and follow me everywhere until I offer some sort of news.

I pick myself up off the floor and start to tidy my spot. I fluff up the bean bag chair. Jessie doesn't like to have an imprint in it that shows someone has been sitting there. She calls it an ass print. I giggle at her sense of humour and lack of grace. She calls it like it is. I fold the blanket and lay it carefully across the chair and place the pillows where I found them. Sticking the wine into the cupboard and vacuuming up the cracker crumbs, I step back to survey my work. I'll tell her I was here, so she knows, but I want to leave things in the same condition I found them.

I decide to keep her sweater on because it'll be well below zero outside now. Turning everything off, I grab my stuff and head out into the cold. I am clear about only one thing—I have no idea what I am going to do about my life.

Chapter 15
Consequences

My toe is tapping impatiently on the floor of the change room. I am sitting on a plush velvet bench waiting for my shopping attendant to bring me yet another round of dresses. It's like I'm in an episode of some silly reality show. I am not amused and sigh deeply. Jessie made an appointment, so we would be sure to have a successful shopping spree. It was thoughtful of her to do so and excellent foresight because I am distracted and indecisive. If it had been up to me, I would be back at my parent's house by now, resigned to wear my faithful little black dress for New Year's Eve. Jessie is off somewhere, looking at shoes and accessories. It is dangerous to unleash her in a store like this. I dread seeing the cost of what she will bring back.

There is a polite tap at the door. I sit up in my seat, adjust my kimono and tell the attendant to come in. I decline her offer to help me get into the dresses, which is probably giving her stress. I thank her as I close the door behind her. The dresses she is bringing me are stunning but so impractical. I look through what she has brought. Yellow. I don't think so. I quickly dismiss that one and put it to the back. I'd look like a big ostrich in it with all those feathers that adorn it. I may as well wrap myself in a feather boa and call it a day. Green—definitely not—that colour suits Jessie, but not me. Besides, I'd look like a peacock with rhinestones around the neck and down the train. I can't believe I am trying on gowns that have trains. My wedding dress didn't even have a train. This entire expedition feels pointless.

There's a nice red one. I put it to the side. There is a black one that I like, but I don't want to wear black. There is a midnight blue one that catches my eye, and I decide to give it a try. One is a floral that reminds me of Hawaii. One is a black and white sequined number that is more like something you'd wear in Las Vegas. The attendant doesn't get me at all. She brought me a gold lamé mermaid-style dress that is entirely over the top, and a beige ball gown, which is altogether too bridal. I shake my head in disgust—all rejects.

I let my kimono slip to the floor and take the red dress out of its bag. The lovely part about trying on fancy dresses is that each one is stored in a see-through plastic bag to keep it clean and safe from damage. The dress is wool—it will be too hot. I slip it over my head and try to straighten it out. It zips up the side enabling me to do it myself—it's sophisticated looking and stylish, yet not over the top. I'll put it in the "maybe" rack. I'm afraid to look at the tag to see how much it costs. I told the attendant I wanted sale items, but I don't believe that all these dresses are on sale.

"How are you doing, ma'am?" beckons the attendant's cheerful voice. "Can I help you in any way?"

I don't like to be called ma'am. I feel old when I hear that, and I don't like feeling old. I should be used to it by now because I am old. I remember the first time someone called me ma'am, I just about gagged. I was walking down a street in the village with my two girls in tow, and this young guy in ski gear came rushing up behind me. He said, "Excuse me, ma'am, I believe you dropped this." It was a diaper from the diaper bag I had slung over my shoulder. Somehow it had fallen out, and I remember wondering what else had dropped out of the bag. Taking it from him, I thanked him. I could see he was only about eighteen, maybe twenty. I was in my early thirties and was far too young to feel like a ma'am, but I could see how I looked like one to him. I remember feeling humiliated, and I couldn't think of a good reason to feel that way. Was it because of the diaper? Was it because I was older than him, yet I found him attractive? Or was it just the use of the word ma'am?

"I'm fine, thanks," I comment through the door.

"Please let me know if I can help you," she prompts.

If my sales assistant has read my mood, she is probably hoping that I'm not in here taking a pair of scissors to these beautiful gowns. I don't answer her and return to my work. I'm annoyed that trying to find a dress for New Year's Eve feels like work. The black one is nice, but probably too sparkly for my liking. I step into it carefully and straighten myself out in it. I don't bother to do up the zipper—it's not my style—end of story. I jam it back onto the hanger and move on to the next dress.

"Can I come in?" It's Jessie tapping on the door.

I unlock the door and open it a crack. She slips in and assesses my look. I'm in my panties and down-to-basics bra—proper foundation garments for trying on beautiful gowns—a bra that means business along with panties that are high in the waist and long in the leg. She lets out a low whistle and says, "You'll have to put on more than that."

"Shut up," I say to her, while I take the blue dress out of the bag.

The attendant takes this opportunity to step into the dressing room as well.

"Shall I take this dress, ma'am?" she questions as she points to the black one. She has a judgmental look on her face as she tucks the dress back into its bag.

"Yes, please," I say with a nod. Gesturing toward the other rejects, I say, "And please take those as well."

"Certainly, ma'am," she replies crisply. She gathers the gowns up in her arms and makes her way out of the room, being careful not to step on any of the garment bags.

"How are you doing?" Jessie asks, lightly closing the door. "Do you have any candidates yet?"

"Mostly rejects," I say, gesturing my head toward the red dress, "One good one, but I think it'll be too warm."

"It's also too plain. You're not going to the movies, you know."

"Shut up," I tell her again.

She ignores my grumpy mood and shows me what she has found. Growing up in a household of girls, she doesn't get frazzled by being told to shut up. A little hair pulling might upset her, but not a simple "shut up."

"Check out these shoes! Aren't they pretty?" she squeals. They are gorgeous, despite the fact that they are silver. I have never had a pair of silver shoes in my whole life.

"They are silver," I manage to say.

"Silver is the new beige! Seriously, silver is a neutral colour that goes with everything," she is as sincere as can be as she removes the shoes from their box. I see the name of the designer and cringe because they are going to cost a fortune. "Look at them! Aren't they stunning?"

They are stilettos with a crystal-encrusted satin band that swoops across the toe and tucks in around the back of the foot. They are glamorous yet understated.

"Try them on!" she urges, shoving them in my direction.

"Okay! Okay!" I say irritably. "Help me get into this blue dress first."

This dress is slim-fitting and has a long zipper up the back. Jessie kneels by my feet and holds it by the bodice, opening it wide so I can put my foot through. Sitting down, I'm careful to put both my feet in the hole before I dare stand up. We check that the dress is draped safely around me and that I'm not stepping on it anywhere as I stand. She pulls the dress up over my body and moves around to my back to start zipping. The zipper starts at my bottom and goes all the way up to my neck. She pulls and zips, tucks and zips, and finally, she is done. We both turn to look in the mirror at the same time.

This is the one. It is lovely. The fabric drapes over my body in such a way that I actually look curvaceous. It is formfitting, but somehow not tight. It doesn't stick to me—it flows over me. It has a shallow scoop neck and three-quarter-length sleeves. The necklace that Mike gave me sits perfectly in place and twinkles at me as if it's winking. The colour flatters my skin and eyes. The dress has a small train that dusts the floor, with a splash of crystals embedded along the edge. Almost regretfully, I know the shoes are going to coordinate perfectly.

Jessie breaks the silence first by letting out a gasp. "You look stunning," she says earnestly. "Try the shoes on, quick!"

She bends over to slip one of the shoes onto my foot. She adjusts it for me at the back. I brace myself against the wall while she helps me get into the other one, and we both stand back again to look in the mirror. I can't believe my eyes. This dress is the prettiest thing I've ever worn. It's even more beautiful than my wedding gown. It fits me like a glove. I can't believe how perfect it is, and I'm thrilled by its elegance. I wiggle my hips to make the dress move, and it effortlessly swishes around me. I have to admit I am almost as excited as Jessie, who is jumping up and down, clapping her hands.

I sit down and put my feet up, getting a good look at the shoes. They are incredible. I marvel at the ingenuity of master shoe designers. There is no doubt that these are expensive shoes—they scream class and style. I can't believe it, but I love them.

Again, Jessie is the first to speak. Her cheeks are flushed that beautiful pink colour that they go when she is excited, and she says dramatically to me, "Oh! You look beautiful. I wish I could be with you to see the look on Mike's face when he lays his eyes on you! And, by the way, you are going to need help with that zipper—if you know what I mean—I'll come and help you get ready!"

I grunt and don't answer her.

She sits down on the floor of the dressing room and crosses her legs. She looks at me with a mystified expression.

"Are you going to tell me what you are so pissy about, or are you going to make me guess?"

I look at her blankly. I want the illusion my new shoes and dress have created to stay with me a few moments longer before my bubble bursts, and I come crashing down. I honestly don't know where to start.

"Well?" she insists. "What's going on? You are insufferably bitchy! And trust me—from everyone else's perspective, you have nothing to be bitchy about!"

What is she saying? Who is this "everyone else" anyway? Are people talking about me? I can see Jessie and her sisters sitting around the kitchen table at the McPherson house, gossiping about me over their morning cup of coffee. I roll my eyeballs in exasperation, knowing Jessie hates that.

"Don't roll your eyeballs at me!" she reprimands crossly. "You have been insufferable. I don't get it. You have the most incredible date coming up, and you are acting like it is some big hardship. Do you have any idea how many women would line up outside his door for a date like this? I have a good mind to take those shoes off your feet and return them to the shoe department. You don't deserve them!"

I protectively pull into myself and murmur, "No. Not the shoes." I tuck my feet under the skirt of my dress, so the shoes are out of sight.

"Are you going to tell me?" she pushes.

"I'll tell you, but I can't tell you here. Get me out of this dress and let's go for a drink," I suggest. "I could use some food. It must be almost dinnertime."

Checking her phone for the time, she tells me it is almost 4:30. We have been at this for nearly four hours. No wonder I am tired of it.

"Okay. I'll get the attendant to help you out of that dream dress, and we'll get out of here."

She leaves the room, and before I know it, my dress is boxed up and delivered to my parent's house. Miraculously, it doesn't need alterations. My heart races when the total comes to well over two thousand dollars, but I try to tell myself that it is just money and that it will be well worth it.

Settling into our seats in the back of a noisy bar downtown, I know it is time to unload my burden. If there is anyone I can talk to, it is this angel. So far, I've managed to dodge the true confessions bullet with my family. Miraculously, my mother hasn't questioned me. It must be driving her crazy. The day before we left for Vancouver, I thought she was going to grab me and lock me into the bathroom with her so we could have some time together, but fortunately, I've not been caught alone with her. Cath has been partying with her friends and seems to have forgotten about the event. As per my prediction, my dad hasn't bothered me about it at all. He would never ask me a question about my personal life. I had a dodgy moment with my brother, James, the morning after I visited Paul's house.

He happened to catch me in the kitchen alone and started interrogating me about my night. I kept giving him evasive answers and not making eye contact. Finally, he said that he saw my truck at Jessie's around nine o'clock and asked why that would be. James is a lawyer, and I thought he was going to launch into the third degree on me, so I gave him the death stare and nothing but a closed-lip response. He got the message and left me alone after that.

Taking a sip of my cocktail, I look across the table at Jessie, who is patiently waiting for me to begin. She knows when to wait for me to open up. She raises one eyebrow at me and continues to wait for me to speak.

"Paul told me he loves me," I finally blurt out.

Jessie says nothing and continues to wait.

"Did you hear me?" I ask. "Paul told me he loves me!"

"So?" she states. "What's new about that?"

"Excuse me? How about everything!" I say sharply. I can't believe she doesn't see this as a big deal. How could she be so laissez-faire about what I said? "Everything is new about it! He told me he *loves* me!"

Taking a bite of the celery garnish from her Caesar cocktail, she says, "Well, you had better come up with something more earth-shattering than that to cause this mood because that seems like old news to me."

I can't believe her reaction.

"Jessie," I begin. "He had me over to his house for dinner the other night. That alone is unusual. When I got there, he was all dressed up in some fancy pants that he had purchased. He combed his hair, and he had on a lovely sweater. He smelled good too."

"Okay. Go on. So Mr. Casual can get dressed up. Big deal. There must be more to the story than that," she sounds almost bored.

"Jessie!" I don't understand why she isn't putting two and two together. Maybe she is, but in her usual insufferable style, she is trying to drag all the dirty details out of me. "We were having a drink when he handed me a Christmas gift. He said it was too personal to give to me on Christmas Eve, with everyone there, so he decided to wait until he had me over."

"This is starting to sound more interesting. What was it?"

"It was the most lovely photo album. It's gorgeous and filled with beautiful moments from my life, told in pictures. Each picture is a special memory either with my girls or you or Paul or all of us. Each one had a caption meticulously written underneath it."

Popping some peanuts into her mouth, she says, "That sounds pretty crafty. Since when is Paul into scrapbooking?"

Ignoring her comment, I say, "The last photo in the book is a picture I've never seen before. It's one of all of us at Garibaldi Lake. Remember that big hike the bunch of us went on that time with the hiking club? It was that day. Everyone in the picture is looking at the camera and smiling, except Paul. He is looking at me. The caption says, 'I love you,' and the look of love on his face is unmistakable."

Jessie frowns. She also practices not furrowing her brow because she doesn't want lines, but I guess she can't help it right now. "I don't get it," she says. "You mean the honourable Dr. Tate has finally made a move on you?"

"What's that supposed to mean?" I ask.

"Oh, come on! Ginny—he's loved you for years! I thought you knew that. You two have had the most annoying relationship I've ever seen."

"Are you kidding me?" I ask.

"No! I am not kidding you! I was wondering if the two of you would ever figure it out or if Paul would ever have the guts to do something about it other than coming over and washing your dishes."

We sit silently for a moment while we both ruminate over the information on the table. I gulp down the liquid at the bottom of my glass and order another drink.

"Jessie," I finally say. "What are you talking about?"

She sees the concern in my face and hears the uncertainty in my voice. The expression on her face softens as she decides to take a gentler approach.

"Ginny," she says. "You and Paul are the closest thing to being a couple that two people can be. You've been together for years, and don't try to kid me that you don't know there is sexual energy between the two of you. There always has been, right back to when we first met him. I wondered why Tony put up with it, but then I thought maybe he didn't see it. Honestly, for years I've been puzzled by the relationship the two of you have."

I wasn't expecting to hear that. Paul and I have sexual energy that is obvious to other people? Really? Where have I been? Why don't I know that? I remain quiet and let her continue.

"I've been wondering for years why you two haven't gotten together. I thought for sure after Tony died that you would both finally do something about it."

Those words hang between us. I take a sip of my drink and swallow the lump in my throat. My eyes begin to well up. I decide to tell Jessie the rest.

"Tony and Paul fought about me the day of Tony's accident. Tony accused Paul of wanting to sleep with me. Paul confessed to me the other night. He has felt responsible for Tony's death all these years."

Both of her eyebrows shoot up in surprise at hearing these words. She munches on the rest of her celery stick and sits back in her seat, looking at me. For once, she is speechless.

"Keep going," she finally says.

"There's not much more to tell. Tony accused Paul that morning of wanting to be with me—you know—in a sexual way. Paul just kept silent and admitted nothing. He told me he decided that day to sell his part of the business to Tony and move away. He said he would have eventually gotten over me."

Leaning toward me, Jessie takes another handful of peanuts. Popping one into her mouth, she looks at me hard and steady. She whispers, "Continue."

"He said that he is not going to lose me again to another man."

Jessie's eyebrows both jump up again, and this time they stay in place, making her eyes look wide with surprise and wrinkling her forehead even more.

"Okay. Now I don't get it. You just spent over two thousand dollars on a luxury gown for a New Year's Eve party with Mike. Does that mean that you rejected Paul?"

"I haven't cancelled New Year's Eve, if that's what you mean," I hang my head low and look down. "Jessie, I slapped him!"

"You slapped Paul!" she says, with newfound surprise.

"Yes. He told me all those things, and then he tried to kiss me, and I hauled off and whacked him a good one right across his face. I stormed out, and that's the last that I saw of him. He has called the house, but I've refused his calls. He didn't come over to my place before I came down to Vancouver. I haven't seen him since."

"Why did you slap him?"

"I don't know! It's just how I reacted. All that information came at me, and I was so surprised, and he looked so good, and he smelled so good, and I felt so mad at him for not doing anything about it sooner!" I put my head down again and look at the floor. "Jessie—all that precious time has gone by, and he didn't do anything about it!"

She sits quietly for a moment, assessing me, "Well, neither did you. Why was it Paul's responsibility?"

She reaches across the table and squeezes my hand. I raise my head to look at her, and my eyes fill with tears.

"You're right. I didn't."

"Do you know why not?" she asks.

Biting my lip, I shake my head and tear splashes onto the table. I wipe my eyes.

"You've been pretty unapproachable all these years, you know," Jessie offers. "Think about it. Other than the odd coffee date that I've pushed you into, you haven't gone out with the same fellow twice until last summer. That's not normal."

"I didn't want to," I say defensively.

"Is it that you didn't want to or that you didn't need to?" she asks, her eyebrows are up again, questioningly.

She is right. She has just stated what, deep down, I have known in my heart. I had everything I needed. I had Jessie, and I had Paul, and I had my girls every day of my life. I didn't need anything more. Have they enabled me all these years? My mom said I was stuck and that she should have encouraged me to move on. Have I been my own worst enemy all this time?

"I can't believe you slapped Paul," Jessie says, almost to herself. Her head is down, and she is munching on peanuts. She asks, "What are you going to do about all this?"

"Well, I just spent a fortune on a designer gown. The side of me that's angry is going on that date and following through with my plan—even if it is irrational."

"You are going to make him pay by sleeping with another man? You can't be serious. Are you going to contact Paul? You should, you know."

"I can't talk to him. I don't know what to say."

"You'll think of something. Don't needlessly hurt yourself and him. Remember, he loves you, and he has for a long time. And you love him. Above all—even if you don't want him romantically—he is your lifelong friend, and deserves for you to call him."

"I can't."

"Ginny, I never thought I'd say something like this to you, but you are better than that. Call him," she says sternly. It is a command, not a request.

Jessie is as severe as I've ever seen her. I cast my eyes away and reach for my purse so I can pay my bill. My stomach is cramping at the thought of talking to Paul. As Jessie and I get into a cab to make our way over to the west side, I realize I have forgotten to eat. That must be why my stomach is upset. It probably doesn't have anything to do with Paul.

Chapter 16
Cinderella, Who's Your Fella?

I check the clock by the bed and see that it's a little past seven. I've been sitting here on the edge of the bed, unable to move, for what feels like ages. I've been watching the time tick by and replaying the last few minutes over in my mind.

Mike will be here at seven-thirty. He is staying upstairs in the penthouse as he had planned, but he reserved this executive suite to allow me my privacy. He thought I would be more at ease with this arrangement, rather than staying in his guest bedroom. He was right. He said he wants everything to be perfect. Until the last few minutes, it has been.

He sent a car around to my mom's house at one o'clock, so I could be at the hotel by one-thirty for early check-in. I took my time getting ready. Relaxing, I luxuriated in the bath and then had a short nap before Jessie came over. We knew that I would need some help getting into my dress, and we had some fun fussing over me. It felt reminiscent of my wedding day. Jessie was poking at my hair and helping me with my makeup that day too. It felt good to have her here with me. I had my hair done earlier in the day by my mom's hairdresser, but Jessie did my makeup. She wanted to make sure I had dramatic smoky eyes for this special occasion. I think she just wanted to be here with me to share this experience.

Just before she left, she asked me if I had called Paul. I said I hadn't. Jessie and I have never fought the whole time we've known one another, but she is genuinely cross with me now. Her face got dark and stormy, and she was having a hard time picking just the right words. I think she wanted to lace into me like she might have done if I was her sister. Standing in the doorway of my hotel room, she shoved her arms into her coat and briskly did up the zipper.

"Do you know what you are doing?" she asked me sharply, stomping her feet at the same time. I was surprised to see that her eyes had tears in them.

I held her gaze and tried not to tear up myself. I don't know for sure if I know what I am doing, so I didn't answer.

"Ginny! He is your best friend! Well—other than me. Imagine how he is feeling. If something significant like this happened between the two of us, I would be devastated if you didn't call me or refused to take my calls when I reached out to you. I can't believe you haven't called him. Quit being such a baby and do the right thing!" Her voice was both imploring and chastising.

I felt a chill between my legs. It's a feeling I get when I am scared or startled by something. It's a muscle reaction that feels like my vagina is snapping shut. My eyes filled with tears, and I dabbed the corners with a tissue. I couldn't risk smeared eye makeup at the eleventh hour. I'd never be able to repair it properly, and it sounded like Jessie would likely not do it for me.

"I don't know if I can forgive you if you don't phone him," she said darkly. It wasn't a threat. "I don't understand your behaviour."

I could see myself standing in the middle of the room, dressed to the nines, waiting for the date of a lifetime to begin. But, I felt small and insignificant. A tremor of fear moved through my body and clutched my core. I felt completely alone for the first time in my life.

I knew she was right, and I was wrong. I felt childish and foolish.

I looked at her and said quietly, "Okay. I'll call him."

"It's the right thing to do, and you know it." She was fierce in her response.

"I'll call him. I promise," I said to her. I walked toward her and took her hand. As I squeezed it, I felt a lump form in my throat and a wave of nausea flood my stomach. At that moment, I thought I would die without her friendship. I would have nothing without her. I hate that she is mad at me. I need to make it right, both for her sake and Paul's.

"Well, hurry up. You don't have much time," she said, wiping her eyes and looking at the clock. It was a quarter to seven. With her head down, Jessie let go of my hand and reached for the doorknob. We didn't hug and giggle about what a dreamy night I'm going to have. She didn't wish me Happy New Year. Stepping through the doorway, she stopped and looked back at me. She said, "Don't make the biggest mistake of your life, Ginny."

She closed the door behind her and was gone.

Don't make the biggest mistake of my life? Going on a New Year's Eve date with Mike is the biggest mistake of my life! Or is not phoning Paul the biggest mistake of my life? There is no doubt that my date tonight is going to be grand. The consummation of my love affair with Mike will be a turning point in my life. I will be free from the past.

So here I sit, staring at the clock. I know I have to call Paul, but I don't know when. Do I call him right now? Mike will be here in less than half an hour, and I can't afford to get upset. He arrived yesterday from Toronto. I'm excited to see him, but I am nervous. I've spent the last several days getting myself into the right mindset for this night. I haven't wanted anything to upset the apple cart. I have to stay in the zone. My mind wanders to the last time he and I were together, and I get a promising rush of warmth between my legs. I've spent a lot of energy convincing myself that I will follow through with this plan. I am not going to let myself back out. It will be good for me to move on. I'm going to do it, damn it!

I bite my lip and put my beautifully manicured finger into my mouth. I am about to bite down on my fingernail when I reach for the phone and dial Paul's number.

His phone rings once.

It rings twice.

Then three times.

His phone rings a fourth time, and I am about to hang up.

On the fifth ring, I hear his voice, deep and soothing.

"Hello?" he says loudly. He is out of breath like he has rushed to the phone. I hear people's voices and music playing in the background. Who is there? He never told me anything about having people over on New Year's Eve! I hear a woman laughing.

"Hello?" I hear him say again. "Is someone there?"

Paul doesn't have guests over to his house. It sounds like a cocktail party going on! I envision him wearing his perfectly tailored slacks with his perfectly combed hair. My mouth is opening and closing, but I can't find the words. The party noise in the background has completely thrown me. It's everything except what I expected. I'm stunned and silent, with no plan in place.

"Ginny? Is that you?" he asks. I hear the woman in the background laugh again.

Oh no. I've been found out! Fear vibrates down my arm, and my hand shakes violently. I can't speak. Panic rushes through me, and I put the phone receiver down and disconnect the call without saying a word to him. Nausea overcomes me when I remember that I am the only person in the world who does not have caller ID. He will know it was me because the hotel number will have shown on his phone. I moan and put my head in my hands.

I jump out of my skin when my phone rings. I stare at it, unable to move. It rings six times before it stops. I can't take my eyes off of it. The red button flashes, indicating that I have a message. I continue to stare at the phone and try to swallow. With a trembling hand, I reach out and pick up the receiver. I press the button to pick up the message and hear Mike's voice. He is calling to tell me he will be five minutes late. Five minutes late! Five minutes. I look at the clock on the wall and see that it is seven-twenty. I have fifteen minutes to compose myself. I hang up the phone and sit numbly on the edge of my seat.

I close my eyes and breathe. I breathe to the bottom of my torso—filling my gut with air as much as possible with this dress on. I breathe out slowly, working hard to ground myself. I open my eyes and remain still on the couch. I wiggle my fingertips. I wiggle my toes. It appears I can still move. I'm not paralyzed like I momentarily wondered. I make my way to the bathroom and sit down on the toilet. It's a lot of dress, and I'm careful to hold the entire skirt up from the floor. I certainly don't want to catch the train on the heel of my shoe.

I have another moment of fear as I imagine Mike undressing me and seeing me in these ghastly underpants. I guess at that point, he won't care if he sees me in a pair of bloomers, and I'm likely not the only woman he has ever seen that way. I giggle hysterically to myself at the absurdity of my thoughts and question if I am borderline psychotic.

Moving to the sink, I wash my hands, being careful not to splash on my dress. I'm infinitely relieved when I see my eye makeup is still in place. It's worth buying waterproof mascara and eyeliner—it works. My lips are perfect. Jessie was diligent about outlining them with lip liner and filling them in with long-lasting lipstick. I glance at the clock, which is embedded into the mirror amongst a spray of crystals. It's seven twenty-eight. I have seven minutes.

I use a blotting tissue on my nose and forehead. The anxiety I have been experiencing has wreaked havoc with my face. It must have happened when I burst into flames after I hung up on Paul. I am such an effing idiot. I have got to get a grip. I refresh my makeup back to a powdery finish and brace myself on the countertop. I look into my own eyes and concentrate, taking three more deep breaths.

As I'm walking down the hall, I hear a knocking on the door. This is it—it's showtime. I steady myself before opening the door and present Mike with what I hope is a dazzling smile. His eyes light up when he sees me, and he takes me into his arms.

Kissing me on my mouth, he says, "Hello, gorgeous!"

He takes a step back so he can admire me. His eyes are appreciative, as he looks me over from top to bottom and then back up again. His eyes rest on my mouth. He embraces me once again, pulls me close and kisses me deeply, his tongue a hot, searching probe. He has his hand on the back of my head, and he pulls my hair a little bit. I have a fleeting vision of a caveman dragging his woman into a cave to have his way with her. Mike is hungry for more. I hope that my hair is firmly secured and can take this kind of treatment. He buries his face in my neck, and takes a deep breath, nuzzling my ear with his clean-shaven cheek.

"That's more like it," he whispers as if to himself. Stepping back, he takes me in again and says, "You are a vision. Spin around for me and show me the view."

Doing as requested, I twirl around in my spot and giggle, feeling like a schoolgirl getting picked up for prom.

"What a beautiful gown," he comments sincerely. Taking my hands in his, he says, "You look ravishing. What a beautiful woman you are. I've missed you. It's good to see you."

"Thank you," I say timidly. I am thrilled that I am not wearing my thirty-year-old little black dress. "I've missed you too. You look fantastic. I love your tuxedo."

He has taken his topcoat off and tossed it onto the couch. I can't imagine who the designer is, but I am sure his tuxedo will be seen on the red carpet this year and that it cost more money than I have ever spent on anything, except possibly my house. His suit has clean lines and fits him perfectly. He has a white bow tie against his crisply pressed pleated tuxedo shirt. His tie is not the sort that clips on—it's a hand-tied one. I'm impressed that Mike has tied it himself. His cummerbund is also white, and his shoes are blinding, they are so shiny. I giggle to myself at the vision of him in his underwear with those funny looking sock suspenders that hold a man's dress socks up.

"What are you giggling about?" he asks playfully, pulling me into his arms again.

"Oh, nothing—I'm just elated to see you," I say honestly.

He looks incredibly handsome—I can hardly believe my eyes. His hair usually falls naturally, as if it has no hair product, but tonight he has it slicked back. He looks like a movie star. He kisses me again, and I let him. It is good to be in his arms. I take a deep breath and try to relax into his embrace.

"You smell good," he says into my ear. "I could eat you right up."

My vagina twitches at the erotic suggestion. His kisses are hot and wet.

Pulling away, he stops kissing me and says, "We'd better not get ahead of ourselves. We can't have dessert before we have the main course."

Why can't we have dessert before the main course? I've literally always wanted to do that, but in this case, it would take a lot of tension out of the evening ahead of us if we had sex first. His eyes flicker as he moves into the room and looks around.

"What do you think of your suite? Does it meet with your satisfaction?" he asks.

"It's perfect. Thank you so much for this. I appreciate being given the time and space to get into my comfort zone."

"Good," he says sincerely. "That's good. I want you to be comfortable. And ready."

"I am," I reply with what I hope sounds like sincerity. My confidence is building. "Shall we have a drink? I could call room service."

"No, we had better get on our way," he answers. "Cocktails begin at eight o'clock, and I don't want to be late."

"Very well," I agree amicably. "Let's go then."

I go into my bedroom and retrieve my mother's mink stole. I was flattered when she offered it. My father bought it for her years ago, back when it was fashionable to own and wear such an item. She's probably had it in storage for fifty years. I thought it was likely that I would be safe wearing it tonight. I don't believe that I'll have red paint sloshed onto me on New Year's Eve in Vancouver—at least I hope not. It is the only thing in my, or my mother's wardrobe that can remotely keep up with my dress. Placing it carefully over my arm, I know I look very elegant.

The telephone rings, and I freeze. It can only be one person. I can't answer it. I don't know what to do. If I pick it up, Mike will know everything. Yet he will think it's weird if I don't answer it. I decide to bluff. I start to blush. Averting my eyes, I think I must look suspicious.

"That'll be Jessie. She's excited about our evening. She is probably just checking in for one more bit of gossip while the night is still young," I hope he buys that. My body is beginning to heat up.

"Go ahead and answer it if you like," he suggests.

"No, that's okay. I'll speak to her tomorrow. Let's just get going," I offer, praying for it to stop ringing.

Mike drapes the stole across my shoulders, helping me tuck into the armholes. The red message light blinks as I reach for my clutch and take his arm. My stomach clinches, and I attempt to silence a tremor of fear as we make our way through the building. It seems everyone knows him, at least the people who work in the hotel. They acknowledge us as we pass, holding doors, tipping their hats, greeting us with happy smiles. I get a sense of what it must feel like to be a celebrity. Mike has a limousine waiting for us, and the valet cheerfully wishes us a Happy New Year as he closes the door of the limo.

I hope my surprise is not all over my face when we pull up to the fanciest restaurant in town. It's one of Vancouver's heritage buildings, and it is right in the heart of downtown. It's where Vancouver's elite go to see and be seen. I have never been here. My dad scoffs at the place, saying that his private club is good enough for him. I know my awe is evident when I catch Mike's eye, and he appears thoroughly entertained. Averting my eyes, I know I am blushing. I'm such a country bumpkin. I pray to God that I don't break into a sweat.

The driver opens the car door and assists me as I get out. Mike comes out the same door, shakes the driver's hand, and wishes him a Happy New Year. The driver pulls the car forward and parks in a spot nearest to the entrance, marked reserved. That limo will not be going off to assist other clients. He is ours for the night. It occurs to me that Mike probably has him on retainer. What a different world from mine. We make our way up the grand entryway and are greeted once again with happy smiles and well wishes.

"Good evening, sir. It's nice to see you again. We've been expecting you," the doorman says, as he cheerfully acknowledges our presence. He tips his hat to me and says, "Ms. Parker."

Ms. Parker! I'm surprised to hear him greet me by name. I wasn't expecting that. Feeling important in the presence of this incredible man beside me, it's like *I* am the movie star with all this attention and luxury.

"Felicity will show you to your table, sir."

The maître d' nods toward the impressive woman I assume to be Felicity, and we follow her. I'm immediately impressed by her perfectly coiffed hair, her manicured and polished presence. Her dress looks as if it is as dear as mine. It is long and black and flowing. She is not carrying menus. She is formal and composed as she makes small talk with Mike. Two young men await our arrival, and on cue, they pull out our dining chairs. I am ready for the festivities to unfold once my stole is removed, my body is comfortable in its seat, and I have a champagne cocktail in my hand. I must look flabbergasted because Mike is laughing at me.

"What?" I ask, trying my darnedest to be coquettish.

"You," he laughs. "You don't do a good job of hiding your thoughts."

"I'm astonished, that's all," I say in my defence.

"I can tell," he says, looking around. We are in a small room all to ourselves. It has beaded curtains that hang in the doorway, but I see it also has a wood panel door that slides closed for complete privacy. I wonder how many women have been privately attended to in this room by Mike and other men before him.

"Do you like it?"

"Of course, I like it. What's not to like? It's incredible. I've never been here before," I admit.

"In that case—welcome! I hope it's the first of many enjoyable visits."

There is something about the way he said the word *welcome*. I catch his eye and see that he must be the proprietor of this establishment. That would explain this private room, the parking spot, the preferential treatment and why everyone knows him. As our eyes meet, he raises his eyebrows and nods his head slightly, confirming my guess. I had never thought about Mike owning other restaurants. I knew he had the chain, but I hadn't thought that he might own separate businesses.

"I liked it, so I decided to buy it," he states nonchalantly, as if this beautiful restaurant, complete with wood panelling, crystal chandeliers, stained glass windows and original art deco design, were a shirt on sale at a flea market. Shrugging, he continues, "It's my favourite pet. Well, next to you, that is."

I smile at him and swallow as he looks at me fondly. This restaurant would have cost millions. I remember when it was sold. It was a big deal because it had been a family-run business for years, and it was all over the news when a group of investors approached them and made them an offer they couldn't refuse. Was Mike the group of investors? Can one person be a group? I have so much more to learn about him.

The restaurant is roaring with life. The privacy of our alcove gives us a bird's-eye view into the main dining area. The room is enormous. It must hold at least one hundred people. The decorations are perfect—white and gold are splashed everywhere, with fairy lights encircled by organza. The central wooden dance floor is polished to a high shine. The opulence is dramatic and profound, reminding me of the *Titanic*. I sincerely hope this evening will have a better ending than that.

Mike holds his glass in the air and makes a gesture toward mine. "To us," he says, looking directly at me. "Happy New Year to you, my darling."

His eyes hold mine and look at me steadily. Our glasses touch and I take a sip of my champagne. I know I am in for an exquisite night.

"We made it in time for cocktail hour," flashing him a smile, but sounding trite and meaningless. It's all I can think of to say.

From my vantage point, a massive clock on the wall tells me it is eight-thirty. I wonder what Paul is doing. It is over an hour since I called. That had to have been him ringing me back. I squirm as I think about the message light flashing, and I regret not picking up the phone.

"Yes," he says, taking another sip of his champagne. "Indeed."

A waiter in a black tuxedo and white gloves enters the room. He sets before me a small, gold-rimmed blue plate. On it are three bits of melba, loaded with black caviar. I am under no illusion that this is anything other than the finest Russian caviar. The melba I am used to comes from a box in the supermarket's cracker section, but this melba is handmade. It's authentic in its shape and texture, and I'm betting it tastes better than what I'm familiar with.

I take a bite and feel the tiny eggs pop inside my mouth. I like the sensation of the hard cracker combined with the delicate spawn. While taking a sip of my champagne, I wonder who the woman is, whose voice I heard in the background at Paul's. I didn't recognize the laugh. I thought I knew all of Paul's friends. I absent-mindedly pop a second melba into my mouth. I'm dismayed by my level of curiosity.

Mike is telling me a story of something that happened with his family on Christmas Day. I smile and nod, hopefully in just the right places. His mother sounds darling. A lot of people call me darling—my mother, Paul, Jessie and Mike too. It's a lovely pet name. I used to be called "my girl" or "baby" by Tony. Never having had another love interest, I've never been referred to by any other endearment.

There is something in the way Mike says "my darling" that bothers me. "Happy New Year to you, my darling." Rolling it over in my mind, I'm trying to decide if I like it. Is it my imagination, or did he say it like he owns me, emphasizing the "my" more than the "darling"? Will I be just another possession to him? He said I was his favourite pet, after this restaurant. Did he say "after this restaurant" or "as well as this restaurant"? I suppose it doesn't make much difference, but what does he mean? Am I a pet to him? Do I want to be compared to a restaurant or an animal?

I can't imagine what he sees in me. Why does he want to be with me, anyway? Am I a challenge to him, or does he see me as a push-over? Something he wants to conquer? Or does he truly love me? He says he is falling in love. Is it as hard for him as it is for me? Touching my necklace, I roll it between my fingers while considering his thoughtfulness and attentiveness. He did call me almost every day when he was away. But, he doesn't captivate me as Tony did. Is it okay to not be engrossed by your love interest?

Watching me touch my necklace, he says, "Tell me what your favourite Christmas gift was this year."

Bringing my thoughts back to the table, I wonder if I've missed any of the conversation. I hope there hasn't been a lull. My face lights up as I think about Christie. I tell Mike all the details about the surprise that I received from her. I tell him about the plastic stethoscope that was inside my Christmas cracker. I know my face is beaming with pride and excitement. She and Bradley and Eddie moved into my parent's house on the weekend, but they are back in Whistler tonight enjoying New Year's Eve with their friends.

"She wouldn't have been able to do it without Paul's help. I'm beyond grateful to him," I blurt out at the end. I feel dewy retelling this story. I know I am gushing with joy. Thinking of my daughter and the future she will have because of her efforts and those of my friend makes me very happy.

"I see," Mike responds. "He's very good to all of you."

"Yes," I say, somewhat embarrassed. I shouldn't have mentioned Paul. "Yes, he has been a good friend to me for a long time."

"Yes," Mike says quietly.

Panic strikes me! Should I have said that my favourite present was the gold necklace I am wearing? I love it, but it's not my favourite gift. Was he fishing for compliments? My mind flashes to the gorgeous photo album I left on the coffee table at Paul's. I can't tell Mike about that! A fine bead of sweat is starting to form on my upper lip. I take my napkin and hope that I am discreet in dabbing it away. I pop the third bit of caviar into my mouth as a distraction.

"There's a lot of love between the two of you," Mike continues.

I am silent, and I avoid his eyes. I can't look at him. I should be able to look at him! I can't look at him because if I do, he'll know. I won't be able to hide my feelings. He'll see that I shouldn't be here with him and that I shouldn't be doing this.

"Ginny, look at me," he says gently.

I keep my head down and shake my head no.

"Ginny," he repeats, "look at me."

I can't lift my head. My eyes fill with tears.

Stop! Stop! *Stop!*

I hear him get up from his chair. His gleaming shoes appear in my sight as he kneels in front of me and takes my chin in his hand, raising my head. His beautiful face is centimetres away from my own. Tears spill over the rims of my eyes. He is looking at me with deep concern, and it is evident that he cares.

"That was him on the phone, wasn't it? It's all you can think about."

I nod my affirmation. Mike's eyes are brimming with tears too, and that pulse of fear rushes through my vaginal area once again.

"Go to him, darling," he says. "Go to him. Sadly for me, it's obvious you don't want to be here."

There he goes calling me "darling" again. This time it sounds different. Unable to turn my head, I cast my eyes to the floor and bite my lip. I am ashamed of myself. I shouldn't have played a part in this charade, but I wanted to make this work. I tried to move on and start a new life, but I know I can't. Not with Mike. Tremendous relief pulses through me as I throw my arms around Mike's neck, and sob into his ear. He knows. He knows something that I haven't been able to admit to myself. He knows, and he is letting me go.

I remember that moment in the back of the taxi with Paul all those years ago—the moment that was a crossroads for us—and a missed opportunity. If we had acted at that moment, we might have become a couple long before now. With certainty, I know that if I don't make a move this moment, I'll never get another chance with him.

My mother is right. She is always right. I never wanted to let myself think about my life with Paul. I like things the way they are, and I have never wanted to complicate matters. What I know for sure is that I don't want to lose him. I love him.

"I wondered if perhaps you were the only person who didn't see it," Mike says plainly.

Through my tears, I see the waiter come to the door with a tray in his hands. His eyes take in the scene before him, and he steps aside discretely. Over his shoulder, I see the hands on the clock ticking away the seconds. The time is nine-thirty. Composing myself, I look into Mike's lovely eyes. They are full of kindness and empathy. He understands. Or at least he is trying to.

"Mike, I'm sorry!" My eyes are searching his desperately. What more can I say? I know he is right. I know I have to go. "I never meant to hurt you. Please believe me."

"I do believe you, Ginny," he says quietly. "You can't have a life without Paul. He is too much a part of you. You have too much history together, and I can't compete with that. It's true what they say. Money can't buy happiness—just fantastic restaurants."

It was kind of him to attempt a joke. It eases the moment and helps us both to relax. Taking his face in my hands, I kiss his mouth one final time. He is the sweetest thing. He has helped me beyond what I can put into words. He has made me a woman again and taught me that I already have everything I will ever need. For that, I am grateful.

I reach my hands to the chain around my neck and undo the clasp. I look at it one last time, then carefully place it in the palm of Mike's hand. I close his fingers around it and kiss his fingertips. I pretend not to see the tears in his eyes.

I look at the clock, and he reads my mind.

"Take my car," he offers. He knows I have to get to Paul. "You'll never get there in time for midnight otherwise. You'll never catch a cab tonight, and I don't imagine you want to go to your parent's house to get your truck."

I giggle at the picture that pops into my mind. Me, running to my parent's place to pick up my truck, and without explanation, hopping into it in my extravagant gown to blast my way home in the middle of the night. It's like a bride running away with another man on her wedding day.

"Seriously—take it. My driver will get you there safe and sound. I can get myself back to my room easily enough. I can't be the one to stand in the way of true love."

I stand up and straighten myself out, my dress falling in a perfect cascade around me. My exquisite shoes poke out beneath the folds of my gown, and I am a fairy tale princess making my way to my love. I have to go! The clock is ticking. Like magic, I am snuggled into the back seat of Mike's limousine heading north to Whistler.

I watch the lights twinkle on the Lion's Gate Bridge as we make our way to the North Shore. My eyes close and I thank God for the blessings He has bestowed upon me. I pray that I am not too late. As the car passes the section of the highway where my beloved Tony was lost to me, I send him my love, and I know that I am not.

Chapter 17
Ready or Not, Here I Come

Paul's house is dark as the limousine pulls into the driveway. His Christmas lights aren't on, and there are no lights on inside the house. For a panicky moment, I fear that maybe he isn't home. Pulling my mother's stole tightly around my shoulders, I grab my clutch and tuck it under my arm. I thank the driver and wish that I had a couple of those one-hundred-dollar bills in my purse to tip him. I don't, so I can't. I apologize and tell him he can go. I know I can get in, and I will be safe from the cold of the night. The driver wishes me a Happy New Year as I close the door and make my way to the house.

I knock tentatively at first. There is no sound of movement inside. The car continues to idle in the driveway. I knock again and still hear no response from inside. The next time I knock, I pound on the door and call out Paul's name. This time I hear the sound of footsteps making their way to the door—my heart races with anticipation. I can hardly wait to see him. Doing up his jeans and pushing his hand through his hair, he opens the door. He greets me, bare-chested.

"What the—?" he questions. "Ginny?"

"Yes! It's me!"

He is disoriented, the way someone is when they have been

sound asleep.

"What's going on?" he asks. Taking me by the arm, he pulls me into the house and closes the door behind me. "What time is it? What are you doing here? Look at you!"

He peeks through the glass at the top of the door. Mike's limousine is pulling out of the driveway.

Turning to me, he says, "Ginny?"

Repeating myself, I confirm for him, "Yes! It's me!"

I want him to snap out of his stupor and throw his arms around me. He needs to hurry and wake up!

"Paul! It's me! Ginny! I'm here! Wake up and hug me! It's almost midnight!"

He wraps his arms around me and gives me the hug of my life, lifting me off the ground and swinging me around. Putting me down and rubbing his eyes, he looks at me again and smiles.

"I thought I was dreaming," he says.

"You're not dreaming. I'm here," the words come rolling out of me. "Paul, I've been such a fool. I'm so sorry. I'm sorry for slapping you. I'm sorry for not taking your calls. I was at a loss, and I had to figure things out. I'm sorry, and I hope you will forgive me. Paul—please tell me that it's not too late. The gift you gave me the other day is the most beautiful gift I've ever received. *You* are the best gift I could ever ask for. Paul, I love you with all my heart, and I hope that you still love me."

That feeling of fear rushes between my legs for the third time tonight, as I realize that Paul may not be alone. I pray with every ounce of my being that the woman whose laughter I heard is not lying warm in his bed, listening.

"Ginny."

"Paul, I love you. I *love* you! I love you so much I can hardly stand it. Please tell me that you forgive me. Please tell me that you love me back."

"Ginny. I will always love you. I've loved you from the moment I first laid eyes on you. I told you that. Nothing has changed for me. A silly slap can't change something like that."

My heart feels like it is going to spring right out of my chest. I jump for joy and feel like I am channelling Jessie. Flinging my arms around Paul's neck, I kiss him hard on his mouth as he pulls me close and wraps his arms around me tightly.

"I'm going to do something I should have done the first night I met you," he says as he bends his head toward me and searches for my lips. This time they are gentle. This time they probe mine with a loving softness like none other. He kisses me in a way he has never kissed me before. He kisses me the way he should have through all the years of our life together. His tongue flicks into my mouth and searches for mine.

My knees weaken, and he strengthens his grip around my waist, cinching me up and pulling me closer to him. I can feel his erection through the folds of my dress. The tingling rush throughout my body is exquisite. I throw my head back in ecstasy, and he starts to explore my neck with his lips.

"Oh, yes," I hear myself say.

He nuzzles my neck gently with soft kisses. He nibbles my ear. He whispers with hot breath, "I love you, Ginny."

I think I am going to die of pleasure. Paul's lips return to mine, and he kisses me more. Picking me up and carrying me into his bedroom, he lays me down on his bed, kissing me all the while. His fingers find the zipper of my dress and ease it open, pushing the bodice off my shoulders. I am braless, and he moans upon discovering my nakedness. His lips clamp onto my nipple, sending my body into bucking convulsions, and I call out with ultimate satisfaction. Hungry for more, he hurriedly works to pull my dress over my head.

"Your breasts are as beautiful as I've always imagined they would be," he says and returns to his task.

I am soaked and writhing under his touch. I am more than ready for him.

"Make love to me," I beg.

"Oh, I'll make love to you, my darling, all in good time."

There it is again. This time "my darling" sounds perfect—right and natural. This time, hearing those words doesn't leave me feeling hollow, and wondering if he meant it.

He swiftly removes my panties, and I'm not concerned that they are the size of a house. He never takes his eyes from mine—those eyes with that knowing look. That look that made me squirm the first time I saw him, and I've spent a lifetime wondering about. He is about to show me.

I'm splayed on his bed, naked, desperate with anticipation for him. I caress him and feel the warmth of his chest with my hands. Kissing his skin, I rub my face on his chest hair, breathing him in. He lays me back on his bed and kisses my belly. Planting his tongue into my belly button, he licks me as his hand touches my vulva, making me squirm and cry out with pleasure. He runs his fingers along the length of my labia and moans when he discovers how wet I am. Slipping his finger inside my vagina, I buck into his hand, and I come instantly when he puts his thumb onto my clitoris.

"That's it, Gin," his voice resonates in my ear. It's almost a whisper. He vigorously grinds his hand into me, moving his finger in and out. "That's it. Come for me. Ohh—I've wanted to hear that sound all my life. Go ahead and scream for me."

When my orgasm subsides, he moves his mouth to my mound. He opens his mouth and takes me all in. All I can feel is heat and wetness and his pulsating lips. His tongue circles my clitoris, teasing me until I think I might lose consciousness. My hands grip the sheets, and I hope I don't tear them. He places his swirling tongue directly on my clitoris, while simultaneously slipping a finger into my vagina once again. Hollering in gratification, I move into him and writhe under his touch.

He moves away from me, and I greedily grab for him, clutching at him, desperate that he not leave me. I open my eyes to see him standing at the end of the bed, removing his jeans. His eyes are on fire as his pants drop to the floor. His magnificent physique magnifies his glorious erection. His pubic hair is black and thick, and his penis is pulsing with life. Taking hold of my ankles, he pulls me to the edge of the bed, parting my legs. Slowly and deliberately, he places his penis at the opening of my vagina.

"Don't tease me. I can't take it anymore. Make love to me," I beg.

Wordlessly, he runs the head of his penis along the length of me, languishing in my heat and wetness. His eyes are intent on mine. He places the head into the opening of my vagina and holds it there. I pulsate all around him, pleading for more. Obligingly, he slowly pushes his penis into me and keeps himself right up against me. His eyes are on mine, and he says, "Ginny, I love you. I have always loved you. I will always love you."

"I love you too. I love you with all my heart."

He pushes into me, and we move in unison. I tip my head back and thrust into him as hard as I can. I have forgotten how good this feels. He plunges into me repeatedly, moving in close and holding us there, almost stopping. Then with unceasing effort, he pumps me with short quick strokes. He pounds into a long hard rhythm that fills my world and takes my breath away. I am lost to him and totally his. He moves in me relentlessly until I can stand it no longer, over and over, in and out. My body revels in desire and wildly bucks him back as he makes love to me. He lasts through my orgasm and continues his unremitting pursuit. I am ecstatic with bliss and release. I continue to push into him as hard as I can. I come again, and his body tightens. He throws his head back, moves forward and bites into my shoulder in one final thrust as he fills me.

Epilogue

I am basking in the sun, naked on a rock in Cyprus. I stretch out and adjust my towel underneath me. My swollen nipples are blazing beacons of delight, shining skyward. I have to be careful they don't get sunburned. I can't believe how many times I have made love in the last few months. Aphrodite is smiling down on me approvingly—no longer does she have to tap dance on my shoulder. I get it now in more ways than one.

Paul is looking like Adonis as he makes his way out of the clear blue water. The sun shines on his glistening body, and droplets of water create a tiny rainbow as he shakes his hair. Or is that a halo? I giggle to myself because it definitely is not! He is a devil between the sheets.

It's been a whirlwind of events since New Year's Eve. We spent the first few days of the new year celebrating our newfound status. I stayed at Paul's house, and we made love about a thousand times. We caused a stir because people couldn't find me and I hadn't called anyone. I wasn't home to answer my phone and Paul wasn't picking up his line. It seems irresponsible to have done that, but we were just too busy to talk to anyone.

Once we came up for air, we called everyone and passed along our news. Jessie was the happiest of all, although my mom has taken the credit for making this happen. Paul moved into my house a few days later and proposed to me on Valentine's Day. We were married in my parent's living room on the first day of spring—representative of our new life together. We enjoyed a weekend honeymoon with family and friends. Now here we are a couple of months later, in the Mediterranean, indulging in a three week holiday, something neither of us has ever done.

The first time we got together with the girls after we broke the news, I wasn't sure they were ever going to let go of Paul's neck, or stop kissing him. They were both jumping for joy! He is the closest thing they have had to a father, and their love for him runs deep. Cath is holding down the fort at home after completing her year at university. She has already started her summer job. Christie is settled into her medical program and will be moving into family housing in September. I've never seen her so happy. Her joy brings relief to my heart. Mom and Dad will miss them all when they move out.

The warmth and hot sun beating down on my body make me hornier than ever. I think it has the same effect on Paul because he can't get enough of me! As he approaches me on my rock, he takes my hand and leads me back to our private cabana. I know what he's after. I steal a glance at my wedding ring, twinkling in the sunshine. Two large diamonds twisted together in friendship—one for him and one for me, nestled inside a traditional gold band. I've never been this happy in my life and didn't know that I could be. I am amazed by the joie de vivre that has taken over my world. All I had to do was let it.

How absolutely lovely!